MW00603991

BY HISHAM MATAR

In the Country of Men

Anatomy of a Disappearance

The Return

A Month in Siena

My Friends

My Friends

My Friends

A Novel

Hisham Matar

RANDOM HOUSE

NEW YORK

My Friends is a work of fiction. Names, characters, places, and incidents are the products of the author's imagination or are used fictitiously. Any resemblance to actual events, locales, or persons, living or dead, is entirely coincidental.

Copyright © 2024 by Hisham Matar

All rights reserved.

Published in the United States by Random House, an imprint and division of Penguin Random House LLC, New York.

RANDOM HOUSE and the HOUSE colophon are registered trademarks of Penguin Random House LLC.

Published in the United Kingdom by Viking, an imprint of Penguin General, part of the Penguin Random House group of companies, and in Canada by Hamish Hamilton Canada, an imprint of Penguin Random House Canada.

Library of Congress Cataloging-in-Publication Data
Names: Matar, Hisham, author.
Title: My friends: a novel / Hisham Matar.
Description: First edition. | New York: Random House, 2024.
Identifiers: LCCN 2023018544 (print) | LCCN 2023018545 (ebook) |
ISBN 9780812994841 (hardcover) | ISBN 9780812994858 (ebook)
Subjects: LCGFT: Novels.
Classification: LCC PR6113.A87 M9 2024 (print) | LCC PR6113.A87 (ebook) |
DDC 823/.92—dc23/eng/20230622
LC record available at https://lccn.loc.gov/2023018544
LC ebook record available at https://lccn.loc.gov/2023018545

Printed in the United States of America on acid-free paper

randomhousebooks.com

9 8 7 6 5 4 3 2

First U.S. Edition

Book design by Caroline Cunningham

To my late friend and publisher Susan Kamil,

who believed in this book well before a word of it was written

and whose memory helped me to write it.

My Friends

1

IT IS, OF COURSE, impossible to be certain of what is contained in anyone's chest, least of all one's own or those we know well, perhaps especially those we know best, but, as I stand here on the upper level of King's Cross Station, from where I can monitor my old friend Hosam Zowa walking across the concourse, I feel I am seeing right into him, perceiving him more accurately than ever before, as though all along, during the two decades that we have known one another, our friendship has been a study and now, ironically, just after we have bid one another farewell, his portrait is finally coming into view. And perhaps this is the natural way of things, that when a friendship comes to an inexplicable end or wanes or simply dissolves into nothing, the change we experience at that moment seems inevitable, a destiny that was all along approaching, like someone walking toward us from a great distance, recognizable only when it is too late to turn away. No one has ever been a nearer neighbor to my heart. I am convinced, as I watch him go to his train for Paris, that city where the two of us first met so long ago and in the most unlikely way, that he is carrying, right where the rib cages meet, an invisible burden, one, I believe, I can discern from this distance.

When he still lived here in London, hardly a week would pass without us taking a walk, either through the park or along the river. We sometimes got into a debate, usually concerning an obscure literary question, arguments that, perhaps like all arguments, concealed deeper disagreements. I would sometimes, to my regret, for the gesture has always displeased me, tap my forefinger on his chest and let my palm rest there for a fleeting moment, as though to keep whatever it was that I believed I had placed there stable, and I would once again take note of the distinct pattern of his ribs, the strange way his bones protruded, as if in constant expectation of an attack.

He does not know that I am still here. He thinks I have left, rushed off to the dinner engagement I told him I was already late for. I am not sure why I lied.

"Who are you eating with?" he asked.

"No one you know," I replied.

He looked at me then as if we had already parted ways and the present was the past, I standing at the shore and he on board the ship sailing into the future.

That burden in the chest, I can see, has rolled his shoulders back a little, causing his hips to fall forward so as to compensate and stop him falling, at the slightest push, face-first. And yet he does look, from this distance, like a man possessed by action, moving forward, determined to enter his new life.

These past years since 2011, since the Libyan Revolution and all that had followed it—the countless failures and missed opportunities, the kidnappings and assassinations, the civil war, entire neighborhoods flattened, the rule of militias—changed Hosam. Evidence of this was in his posture but also in his features: the soft tremble in the hands, perceptible each time he brought a cigarette to his mouth, the doubt around the eyes, the cautious climate in them, and a face like a landscape liable to bad weather.

Soon after the start of the revolution, he returned home and, perhaps naturally, a distance opened between us. On the rare occasions he visited London, we were easy in one another's company but less full-hearted somehow. I am sure he too noticed the shift. Sometimes he stayed with me, sleeping on the sofa in my studio flat, sharing the same room, where we could speak in the dark till one of us fell asleep. Most of the time, though, he got a room at a small hotel in Paddington. We would meet there, and the neighborhood, arranged around the train station, which fills the surrounding streets with a transitory air, made us both feel like visitors and accentuated the sense that our friendship had become a replica of what it had once been when he lived here and we shared the city the way honest laborers share tools. But now when he spoke, he often looked away, giving the impression that he was thinking aloud or involved in a conversation with himself. And when I was telling him a story, I would notice myself leaning forward slightly and catch an almost querulous tone in my voice, as though I were trying to convince him of an unlikely proposition. No one is more capable of falsities nor as requiring of them than those who wish never to part ways.

2

YESTERDAY EVENING HOSAM ARRIVED from Benghazi. We sat up talking till dawn. He slept on the sofa and did not wake up till early afternoon. We had to leave immediately for St. Pancras Station, where he was to take the train for Paris, to spend two nights there and then fly to San Francisco. London was the place where he had lived. "I must see you," the text he sent from Benghazi read, "before I go to the ever, ever after." Paris was where, twenty-one years ago, when he was just young enough to sustain the fantasy of self-invention, he had lived for an interlude. "I want to see it one last time." He said this yesterday, just as we entered my flat.

I had gone to collect him from the airport, and the whole way home, on the tube from Heathrow to Shepherd's Bush, he spoke in English of little else apart from his new life in America. He did not say anything about the last five years he had spent in Libya, when that was all I hoped to hear about.

"It's mad. I'm as surprised as you are. I mean, to plan to live indefinitely in a country I've never been to before, in a house I've never seen, one my father bought on a whim during a work trip when he was young, long before I was born. And now I'm intending to bring up my child there, in America." After a little pause, during which the train bulleted through the tunnel, he said, "Poor man," referring to his late father.

As the stations passed and the doors opened and closed and passengers left and new ones got on, he told me what he had told me before about how his father had fallen for Northern California.

"He planned to go there every summer, only to then be barred from travel altogether and for the rest of his life."

Here he laughed and I felt obliged to join in.

A young family were now sitting across the aisle from us. The man was black and handsome, with a mild defiant look in his eyes. The woman was white and blond, speaking in near whispers to her son beside her. The boy looked about nine years old, with a ball of curly hair that doubled his head in size and held the light in shades of brown and gold. His mother would occasionally pass her fingers through it. He stood facing us, the boy, with a hand on each parent's knee. He swayed a little as the train moved. There was something slightly performative about them. They knew that they were a beautiful family. The three of them let their eyes rest on us and seemed to be tuning in to what Hosam was saying. He often had this effect on people.

"Can you imagine," he went on, "a house bought on impulse, only to live the rest of your life unable to see it? Even in the hardest of times he refused to rent it. Until Point Reyes"—that was the nearby town—"became allegorical, a byword for the lost and the impossible, my family's Atlantis."

We rose aboveground and the carriage was filled with light. The beautiful family glanced at the view that passed outside the window behind us.

Having shipped all his belongings to California, Hosam was traveling lightly. I recognized the old bag. Small, blue, and battered. It was the same one he had used when he moved back from Paris, and later when he would go with Claire, his girlfriend, to swim in the River Dart in Devon, as they both liked to do from time to time. Seeing the familiar object made me long for those old days when Hosam lived in

London and for a good while in the flat beneath me, which occupied the entire ground floor of the mid-terraced house, with an uncared-for garden in the back. My bedroom was directly above their sitting room, and many nights I fell asleep to the soft murmurings of his and Claire's voices.

Things had happened naturally. Hosam had returned to London and the flat below was available. He hesitated at first and I knew not to push. The low rent sealed it. A little while later, Claire moved in. She was Irish, gentle, clever, and with a hard edge that made it clear that you did not have to worry about her, that the last thing she wanted was your concern. I remember once we were waiting for her at a café and she was late. Hosam kept checking his phone. I asked if he was worried. He looked genuinely baffled. "Worried?" he said. "I never worry about Claire." They had met at Trinity College Dublin, where Hosam was reading English and Claire History. She liked to remind us that she too was an exile here.

"But I tell you," Hosam went on, more privately now, leaning closer but continuing to speak in English, "these past few weeks, as we have been packing and arranging for the move, my old man, God have mercy on his soul, has been on my mind. I know it sounds crazy, but I'm convinced he knew this moment would come, that his black sheep—the son who, as he had told my mother, was destined either to achieve great things or else to be a complete failure—might one day turn his back on everything and go to America, the country from where people never return."

We reached our station and, walking to the address where he had once lived, he remarked on some of the changes that had taken place since the last time he had visited: the old bakery that had been taken over by a supermarket, the attempted improvements to Shepherd's Bush Green—that large triangle of grass that has always been surrounded on all sides by traffic.

He fell quiet when we arrived at the familiar street, with a row of houses on either side. I was quick with the keys, have always been, and in all the years that I have lived here I have not locked myself out nor lost my keys or wallet once. There were the unchanged common parts, with the post scattered on the faded carpet, the lights that went out before you reached the top landing.

"But Paris," he suddenly said, as we were climbing up the stairs, "that is pure nostalgia."

He left his suitcase in the kitchen and went directly to the bathroom, leaving the door wide open. He soaped his hands and face, continuing to speak of his plans, how he wanted to walk all the familiar streets, revisit the Jardin sauvage Saint-Vincent, where he had once taken me. And, as the evening progressed, a new expression came over his face. Sitting in my kitchen, with his small bag beside him, he appeared as if he were not only sitting beside his belongings but to one side of his heart, enduring the distances between Libya and America, between his former life and the future. Perhaps now that he was in London, at the in-between place, and had heard himself tell me of his plans and no doubt sensed my lack of enthusiasm, the true nature of what he was embarking on suddenly felt exposed: the fantasy that he could go to America as though it were another planet and none of the old ghosts would be able to follow him. It was obvious that this tour of his former two cities was in part motivated by regret for the passing of the life he had once enjoyed before everything changed, before the Libyan wind that tossed us north returned to sweep its children home.

"We are in a tide," he had said back in the passionate days of the Arab Spring, when he was trying to convince me to return to Benghazi with him, "in it and of it. As foolish to think we are free of history as it would be of gravity."

3

I HARDLY SLEPT LAST night. Hosam woke up late, downed his coffee, and we left the flat with the place unmade, as if we might return at any moment and resume our sleep.

We got the 94 bus to Marble Arch and from there changed on to the 30. We sat on the upper deck, he by the window looking out and I watching him. I thought of all the lines he had crossed since he last lived here. After more than three decades of absence he had finally returned home to see his family. He had fallen in love with his cousin Malak, who, he had told me in an email, "appeared as my destiny." He had joined the revolution and found himself carrying a gun, taking part in several key battles, until he reached Sirte, the dictator's hometown. There he and a group of fellow weary fighters took part in the most consequential confrontation with the regime's forces. After an airstrike, they had tracked down the highest prize: Muammar Qaddafi, the Colonel himself, or, as Hosam referred to him in the email he sent me a few hours later, at 2 A.M. his time, "the kernel of our grief," hiding in a pipe in the sand. "He was unsteady," Hosam went on to describe, "like an old frail uncle. And wasn't he that to us, less a politician and more a mad relative?"

I read the email the moment it arrived, at about 3 A.M. my time. In those days, sleep often eluded me. I pictured him in his borrowed room in a house in Misrata, the phone lighting up his face blue. Misrata, 150 miles northwest of Sirte, was where, he informed me, he and the others dragged the corpse of the dictator.

A few days later, when Hosam was back with his family in Benghazi, he texted:

Remember Phaethon?

He was obsessed with proving that his father truly was his father. "Th' astonisht youth, where-e'er his eyes cou'd turn, / Beheld the universe around him burn . . . / Then Libya first, of all her moisture drain'd, / Became a barren waste, a wild of sand."

According to Ovid, our country burned because of a quarrel between a father and a son.

In these past months of endless fighting, of sleepless nights, always on the move, I often found myself thinking of this story.

Only to then find him, our maddened father, hiding in a drainage pipe in that same wild of sand.

It was not long after this that Hosam married Malak. The couple had a child. He worked for the new Ministry of Culture and, when everything crumbled and the various groups contesting power began to point guns at one another, he retreated from public life, and one day, five years after his return to Libya, he and Malak decided to emigrate with Angelica, their four-year-old daughter, to America.

4

"LANDED IN SAN FRANCISCO and I'm already in love," Malak had texted Hosam last night, as he and I were about to eat supper. He read the rest of the text to me and then added, more to himself, looking down at the phone, "It's noon there. Wonder what they'll have for lunch?"

In three days from now, he will be reunited with them, and they will make the two-hour drive north to Point Reyes. Everything has been set in motion.

"I have never been to America," he reminded me when we were on the bus. "But these past weeks I have been seeing it in my mind. Northern California. Cypress trees I know. But what does a redwood smell like?"

A little while later, as the bus turned on to Marylebone Road, he asked, "Do you think it's a good idea? America—I mean, to live there?"

I wanted to say nothing, to come across as neutral, partly out of kindness and partly out of revenge for the times he would tell me what I ought to do, how I ought to live "a fuller and more active life," as he had once put it, and return to Libya.

"It's a good place to bring up a child," I finally said, even though I had no idea whether America was a good place for children, or even what such a place might conceivably be like, the components and attributes that would constitute it. "Especially California," I continued. "'The Sunshine State.'"

He laughed. "For goodness' sake," he said, "don't go to Florida thinking you'd find me there. You will visit, won't you? I mean, I know you have a thing about flying."

I have only been on an airplane once in my life, from Benghazi to London, and that was back in September 1983. In 2011, shortly after the 17 February Revolution, when I considered returning home, I planned to do so by land. Hosam said he would join me. "To step on the old earth at the same exact moment." It would have taken three days and involved several trains and a ferry to Sicily, another to Malta, and from there a hovercraft, which would have reached Tripoli in only a couple of hours. I had pictured it all and saw the old coast drawing in, the wind filling our ears, making it difficult to hear anything either one of us said.

"That's right," I said. "The Sunshine State is Florida. I would love to visit you in California."

He seemed to believe me. "Who knows," he said, trying to sound encouraged, "you might even love it so much you would want to stay. A one-way ticket. We would be neighbors again. And Angelica can have her uncle beside her."

I saw myself stepping on to the plane with sleeping pills in my pocket.

We arrived at St. Pancras Station with time to spare. I suggested we go sit in the café on the mezzanine of King's Cross Station instead. "Less frantic," I told him. The real reason was that I wanted to be surrounded by commuters, people heading out for the weekend or returning home, as they seemed more settled and their joys more modest. On my regular visits to the British Library next door, I would come here before heading home, to this same café, to let my eyes rest awhile on the undramatic spectacle, which made it all the more startling when someone ran to embrace another person, or wiped away tears as they headed to their train.

We ordered our coffees and sat not facing one another but to one side of the small round table, like old men watching the world go by, or else expecting Mustafa, the third in our triangle, to miraculously turn up and join us. But Mustafa was back in Libya and was unlikely ever to leave it. My two closest friends have gone in opposite directions: Mustafa back into the past and Hosam out toward the future.

I suspected that Hosam too, with his small suitcase beside him, felt a little detained, eager to leave this moment behind and set off on his journey. We drank our espressos and embraced, possibly, I thought, for the very last time.

We had met in 1995, when he was thirty-five and I twenty-nine, and, even though we have known each other for twenty-one years, it surprised me when I heard him whisper, "My only true friend," speaking the words rapidly and with deep feeling, as though it were a reluctant admission, as if at that moment and against the common laws of discourse speech had preceded thought and he was, very much like I was, comprehending those words for the very first time and, perhaps, also like I was, noticing the at once joyous and sorrowful wake they left behind, not only because they had arrived at the point of our farewell, but also because of how they made even more regrettable that illusive character of our friendship, one marked by great affection and loyalty but also absence and suspicion, by a powerful and natural connection and yet an unfathomable silence that had always seemed, even when we were side by side, not altogether bridgeable. I do not doubt that I have been equally responsible for this gap, but nonetheless I continue to accuse him in the privacy of my thoughts, believing that a part of him had chosen to remain aloof. I could perceive his remoteness even in the most boisterous of times. But now those words were the final verdict.

Then, just before he walked off, he said, "Stay here," meaning, I suppose, that I should not walk with him. But the way he spoke those two words echoed the time when he had returned to Libya and I had refused to accompany him, unwilling or unable to go back home, "Reluctant Khaled," as he and Mustafa took to calling me during the wild passions of those days of the revolution, when my only two Libyan friends turned into men of action.

"Stay here," he said again, and this time it sounded even more like a solicitation of a vow; as though what he was really saying was: promise you will always be here.

And here I am, still at King's Cross, watching him walk across the busy concourse with that air of indifference, as though if he were to collide with another individual, he might simply pass straight through them.

Go after him, I tell myself.

I remain in my spot, inside this coat and this minute, as time folds all around me. The entire age of our friendship is contained in this instant.

London, the city I have been trying to make home for the past three decades, thinks in certainties. It enjoys classifications. Here the line separating road from pavement, one individual from another, pretends to be as definite as a scientific fact. Even the shadows are allotted their places, and London is a city of shadows, a city made for shadows, for people like me who can be here a lifetime yet remain as invisible as ghosts. I see its light and stone, its shut fists and loitering lawns, its hungry mouths and acres of unutterable secrets, a muscle tightening all around me. I am watching my old friend, the distance growing between us, from within its grip.

Go, run after him.

Or run directly to the ticket desk and surprise him on the train.

Or keep to a different carriage, and a few hours after the train pulls into Paris call him and say you caught the next train and arrange to meet at the old café on the corner of Carr de l'Odéon, where you spent several afternoons and evenings, twenty-one years ago when you first met, getting to know each other. Part ways at the place where it had all started.

But I remain where I am, with my window closing and my solitude drawing nearer like a building looming large. It presses its cold stone against my back. Hosam is now a speck in a forest of heads. Perhaps if I follow, I will be free. Or lost and unmoored. It takes a great deal of practice to learn how to live.

Go, I hear the command, and this time I run. I am already at the staircase, jumping three steps at a time, startling those around me, passengers going and coming from places that will remain open to them. I weave through the crowd and I am surprised by how quickly I manage to cross the distance. There he is, his innocent back so close that, if I were to reach out, I could lay my hand on his shoulder. I let the gap grow a little, following him out of the station. He stops, waits for the lights so as to cross the road to St. Pancras. If he turns around now, how would I explain myself? But when did I ever feel the need to explain myself to him? Anyway, he seems already gone, already elsewhere, entranced by the plans he has made for himself, "To finally commit to the particulars," as he put it last night as we ate in my kitchen, sitting at the small table by the window overlooking what once was his garden and those of the neighbors. I encouraged him with a smile and smiled more easily when he showed me a picture on his phone of his daughter. Noor—but he calls her Angelica. She looked small and formidable, not so much that the world was hers but that she, by some magical confluence, had become the world. He laughed and embraced me.

"Why Angelica?" I asked without thinking.

"And why not?" he said, blushing with pride.

"Why not indeed," I said.

The lights change and I follow him into St. Pancras. When he reaches the check-in desk, I hover at a good distance. He goes through the barrier and, just before he disappears around the corner, he looks back. He does not appear to see me, continues on his way. Or perhaps he did see me and the blankness in his eyes is the blankness we all carry deep within us toward those we love.

I go to stand by the live Departure boards. His train might be delayed or even canceled. After several announcements, calling passengers to board, the good minute goes. I picture him stepping on to the train, the doors closing behind him, and the heavy carriages rolling out.

5

I LEAVE ST. PANCRAS and set off westward on the Euston Road. It is six in the evening on the 18th of November 2016, and the late-autumn sun has already set. The twilight is glazing the sky a deep blue. The streets are brighter and more animated, making it seem as if light does not come from the heavens but rises upward in earthly rays, now fading pink into the clouds. It is Friday. The pavement is full of pedestrians, their heads forming a dark and shifting river. Traffic is thick and filling the air with a sad metallic odor. The easy scent of fallen leaves is still perceptible in the background. I decide to walk. Maybe the five- or six-mile journey home will tire me enough to sleep.

Suddenly I am glad Hosam has left. There are comforting illusions to being alone. I could have just arrived, having stepped off a train for the very first time, a visitor, a man on a "city break," as the tourism industry calls it, or starting anew, entering streets that are dead clean of memory.

Back in March 1980, many years before I met Hosam Zowa or even knew that he was a real person, I had heard of him from the BBC Arabic World Service, and listened, utterly spellbound at our kitchen table in Benghazi, to a short story he had written. What made the event even more powerful was that it was read in the voice of the legendary broadcaster and journalist Mohammed Mustafa Ramadan, a native of our city and the star presenter at the BBC. I was fourteen, and the four of us—my parents, my thirteen-year-old sister, Souad, and I—had just finished lunch and were still sitting around the kitchen table eating oranges. They were in season and the room was filled with their perfume. The peel, which Mother removed in one continuous swirl, lay coiled on the table. The radio whispered in the background, tuned, as it was permanently, to the BBC Arabic World Service. Big Ben chimed darkly. Like many people in the Arab World and former colonies then, I heard London well before I ever saw it. I pictured its famous clock tower standing at its very center, with the entire city, its buildings, squares, and streets, arranged in a perambulatory fashion around it.

"Huna London." This is London, Mohammed Mustafa Ramadan said, the words that always followed the chimes and opened the news hour.

Recognizing his voice, Mother went to turn up the volume. We thought of Mohammed Mustafa Ramadan as our very own, and agreed that his voice was made sweeter by the slight Benghazi inflection. Yet my parents could not, even within the small and familiar social structure of our city, locate his family, making his unusual name, made up of three first names, seem even more enigmatic. This lent weight to Father's claim that it was a nom de plume that the outspoken journalist had adopted in order to evade detection. But, notwithstanding the prominent position he held at the BBC, which irritated the dictatorship, and his weekly column in *Al Arab* newspaper, where he regularly exposed the oppressive practices of the Libyan and other Arab regimes, what Mohammed Mustafa Ramadan was about to do next had never been done before or since on the BBC and remains, particularly in view of the tragic events that followed, his most defiant act. It was certainly the point in time after which nothing was the same again, not for him and, although I did not know it then, not for me either.

When I look back, trying as I am to locate my first encounter with

Hosam, my mind returns to that fateful afternoon in my family's kitchen in Benghazi—in the house that no longer exists, each one of its ancient bricks now reduced to rubble, but that I can still picture clearly in my mind, entering it as though a real place—where, together with my family, I listened to a story that I was never again able to unhear, and that, I can see today, had set my life toward the present moment.

"My colleagues and I," began Mohammed Mustafa Ramadan, "have decided, if you would indulge us, kind and gentle listener, to do something that has never been done before."

Father turned up the radio even louder and, although we were all listening attentively, asked us to please keep quiet, which made Mother laugh and made him repeat himself.

"We have decided that before reading the news in the usual manner, we will share with you a short story. Yes, a piece of literary fiction. We understand that this is highly unusual. However, we are guided by the opinion that at times a work of the imagination is more pertinent than facts."

Here, whether for dramatic effect or because someone was trying to change his mind, Mohammed Mustafa Ramadan paused for maybe four or five seconds, which felt like an eternity.

"The author," he continued, "is a young Libyan student at Trinity College Dublin, the venerable Irish university where Oscar Wilde and Samuel Beckett studied." He then spoke the name slowly, carefully, as though its letters were made of broken glass: "Hosam Zowa."

Here there was another pause.

"Never heard of him," Mother said. She asked Father if he had and he shook his head.

"For the benefit of full disclosure," Mohammed Mustafa Ramadan continued, "Mr. Zowa is not only my compatriot but a friend too. I'm honored to call him that. But I assure you, dear listener, that I am not prejudiced by my association. The story was published today, in a newspaper that will remain nameless; one, I'm confident, you are familiar with."

"*Al Arab*," Mother said, guessing the name of the newspaper.

Father blinked slowly to say, I know.

"It's edited and printed here in London," Mohammed Mustafa Ramadan said.

"See?" Mother said.

"But, because of its free and open attitude, it is banned in nearly every Arab country. Such is the state of our present, the lamentable present."

The word "present," repeated twice, hovered for a moment above us.

Mohammed Mustafa Ramadan announced the title of the story, "The Given and the Taken," and began to read. My father stared into space, utterly focused. Souad occasionally lifted her eyes from the table to look in my direction or at Mother or Father. Mother kept her eyes on me.

Before putting on his socks, the man lay down on his back in the middle of the room and tried to remember where he was meant to be. A cat paced around his body. He felt the moist tip of its nose touch the big toe of his left foot. It began to lick it. It was not an unpleasant sensation. He could feel its rapid breath when the animal started, tenderly, almost affectionately, nibbling on the soft skin. The refinement of modern life, he thought, as he considered how the comforts of cotton socks, shoes and slippers had made a delicacy of his feet. But then the cat bit into him, puncturing the skin. The sting was sharp and precise and yet began to recede the moment the cat licked the blood clean. It paused for a moment and then it purred and rested and purred some more. He felt an unexpected satisfaction at its pleasure. He thought that he too ought to close his eyes a little. When he woke up, there was still the clocklike rhythm of the cat's breathing beside his foot. It licked the sore spot again, then turned to its own paw, bathing it with licks and using its teeth to scrub and nibble it clean. It stood by listlessly, facing his foot, before it dug its teeth once again into his toe and snatched off a piece of flesh. He looked up and its eyes showed no outrage, no remorse, but stared right back at him. He laid his head down. The pain was unbearable and tremendous and yet, the man thought, "unbearable" was not the right word. If anything, it was surprisingly bearable. He remained stretched on the floor of his room while the cat worked diligently and calmly. Every time it licked and comforted the wound, it pried away another piece of flesh, until it finished the toe. It moved on to the next one.

The strange thing was that, as the cat ate, the man began to see, as vividly as a film running in front of him, the history of his toes, from their life in the womb to the present day, their adventures and misadventures, which were his own, but rendered in mockingly heroic proportions, so that, as he was being eaten, he felt he was also being mourned, albeit sarcastically. This grotesque spectacle of his life became more hypnotic the more the cat continued its diabolical scheme. It worked with unquestionable determination. It ate its way up the man's legs and arms as he continued to watch and marvel at the life story of his limbs, the memories lost and now caught all at once as though in a net, an elaborate retelling of a modest life. Although the cat's appetite seemed bottomless, particularly for a creature of its size, it did not rush or hurry to satisfy it, and this confidence was, it turned out in the end, its boldest weapon. Now the man was nothing but head and torso. His head, which, he concluded, was the only thing he truly could not do without, remained perfectly intact. The cat approached slowly, pausing by his left ear, as if about to tell him something of grave importance. Instead, he heard his own voice.

Up to this point in the story, Mohammed Mustafa Ramadan read soberly, in the dispassionate tone of a news reporter, but now a shallow quiver, like a feather trapped in a tunnel, entered his throat. He paused and repeated the last line, "Instead, he heard his own voice." It did not work; he did not manage to rid himself of the emotion.

He opened his mouth and said, "No." The word filled the room. It sounded astonishingly clear. He knew he was not speaking for himself alone. The cat lifted its head and departed, leaving the man to finally resume his life.

The story was so brief that it could not have taken Mohammed Mustafa Ramadan much more than a minute to read. I was not sure what to make of it. I felt infected by it. For the days and weeks that followed, I tried to push it out of my mind, but it remained always there, in the depths, rising at the most unexpected moments: when I was waiting for the school bus in the dark at that undecided hour when the day had begun but dawn was still to break, or when it was my turn to mop the courtyard, which lay in the middle of the house like an open secret, naked to the sky but unexposed to any of the neighbors, so that you could take your clothes off and no one would ever know. I found myself thinking about Hosam Zowa's depiction of a defeat that was also a victory. At such moments, I was unable to ignore the story's claustrophobic atmosphere, manifested so horribly in the man's inexplicable lack of objection—which is rendered all the more upsetting by how effective his protest proves to be when it eventually comes. The story entered my dreams, where I sometimes saw myself as the limbless figure, in constant need of looking after. What I remember most from those dreams was the savage sense of my own helplessness. This, together with what happened to Mohammed Mustafa Ramadan shortly after he read the story, frightened me. I became, in silent and private ways, powerfully aware of the fragility of all that I treasured: my family, my very sense of myself, the future I allowed myself to expect.

6

THE MYSTERY THAT SURROUNDED the identity of Hosam Zowa excited my parents and particularly my father. He was a historian, part of the first generation to go to university after independence, which is to say, given the restrictions the Italian occupation placed on Libyans, he was among the first in the country to get a higher education. He went on to earn a PhD from Cairo University.

When I was growing up, he had to me the reliable air of one who believes in time, in the human initiative to measure it, but also in its supremacy over human affairs; that everyone, their deeds and character, will not only yield to time but be revealed by it, that the true nature of things is concealed and the function of the days is to strip away the layers.

After 1969, the year Qaddafi assumed power, my father quietly turned down academic posts and lucrative positions on state-sponsored committees and disappeared into a job that suited neither his talents nor his ambition: he became a general history teacher in a middling school in a low-income neighborhood of Benghazi. Eventually, he was promoted to headmaster. He accepted only because refusing would have raised suspicion. I remember hearing him once tell

Mother about some protracted conflict among the teachers that he was attempting to resolve, then pausing for a second before resigning himself to the verdict that "It is almost always best to leave things be. Most problems have a habit of resolving themselves." This was also the advice he gave my sister, Souad, and me on more than one occasion. It was out of the question that we would enroll in his school in case that exposed him to accusations of preferential treatment. But, notwithstanding all his carefulness, from time to time a cloud of vague paranoia would descend on him, and he would become convinced that someone somewhere was plotting to discredit him.

He was obsessed with the political history of the Arab World, with a focus on the rise of nationalism, what he liked to describe as "the colonizers' parting gift." He conducted his research in the dark, in his spare time, never publishing a word of it. This policy turned his vocation into a hobby and a refuge. The walls of his study at home were lined with books from floor to ceiling on subjects such as the Ottoman Empire, the Italian invasion of Libya, the British Mandate for Palestine. Stacks, arranged in columns on the floor, rose precariously like one of those ancient towered cities of Yemen.

I saw my father back then as a man living in the belief that the world does not require him. I sometimes accused him not so much of a lack of courage but worse: a lack of faith. More than three years after we listened together to Hosam Zowa's short story, I went to study in Britain and carried with me this corrupted shadow, as all false impressions are, that I had painted of my father. I brought it with me when I arrived in front of the Libyan Embassy in St. James's Square, in the heart of London, to take part in my first ever political demonstration. There, I told myself, now you know that you are not him. And, even a few minutes later, when the bullets sounded and mayhem descended, I thought of my father, the man who still believed that it is "almost always best to leave things be," as the placid, silent, and colorless backdrop against which my life must be animated.

But, before all that, and following the radio broadcast, Father began to look into the identity of the mysterious author, and this was how the first things I learned about Hosam Zowa were brought to me by my father.

"The Zowas are a well-known family," Father told us. "Sidi Rajab Zowa worked for King Idris. He was His Majesty's personal adviser, nicknamed 'The Radar,' on account of his intuitive abilities. It was said that there was no thought that Idris had that was not first anticipated by Sidi Rajab. He perfectly understood the old man's political reluctance, his self-effacing manner, his preference for quiet resolutions. Like the fate of our doomed King, the Zowas suffered when Qaddafi came to power. Their assets were frozen. They were barred from travel. But they had a son who got away just in time," Father said. "He was at school in England when the order came and so he remained there. Perhaps he is the author."

We tried to imagine him not being able to return home. I remember my mother gazing into the middle distance and saying, to no one in particular, "A nightmare." And then we pictured him going to Ireland for university.

One afternoon a couple of days later, Father said he had some special news to tell us. "I found where the Zowas live and you won't believe it. Not only are they in downtown Benghazi but on a corner of the street parallel to ours."

I remember the thrill we all felt. Immediately after lunch, without telling anyone, I went to find the house. My steps slowed as I approached it. It was that hour in the afternoon when the heat begins to wane, rising into the blue open sky, leaving the air beneath distinctly lighter. The windows on the second floor stood wide open. I could see the occasional shadow move across the white ceiling, the light bouncing off an object, and caught faint sounds of cutlery, the footsteps of hard shoes on tiles, the voices of women. It was, to my boyish mind, strange to think that such a peculiar story should arise from the imagination of someone who had grown up in such an ordinary home.

Years later, when Hosam returned, this was where he came to, where he would live and from where he would visit my parents, with whom he quickly became close, filling some of the emptiness I left them with.

But, whereas back then I was looking to the future, even if vaguely and abstractly, my father was far more concerned with the past. The more he discovered about the Zowas, the more interested he became.

"A curious family," he declared, a week or so into his inquiry. "At once honorable and roguish, a house condemned and claimed by all warring sides. The Zowas are like Libya itself, in a way. Hard to know who they are backing or what they really are."

Our afternoons continued to be spent sitting around the kitchen table. That story, which, from what I could tell, had nothing to do with the past, had cast us into our country's history. Father brought volumes to read to us from. We often remained there until it was suppertime, with none of us complaining. We learned that when Italy invaded Libya in 1911, the Zowas were among the first to join the resistance and fought gallantly for fifteen years, until, without offering an explanation, they attended the parade to welcome Benito Mussolini on his first visit, in 1926.

"The Italian sat on his horse," Father said, "as local tribesmen marched in a procession, flashing their swords in the sun and performing, with the absurdity that every act of mimicry must carry, the Fascist salute, which," Father added, "in their dark hands looked ironic, as though poking fun at the conquering Emperor. What's more," he went on, "Mussolini's stallion, a small and tightly wound Arabian, wouldn't keep still. Every few seconds, it struck its hoofs and swung its tail from side to side, causing the 'little Italian,' as Libyans liked to refer to Mussolini, to be nudged this way and that. The Zowas refused to join the procession or even to dismount. They sat on their dark horses, muscular and gleaming, which, in contrast with Mussolini's, stood as still as rocks. They observed the entire spectacle as though it were meant for them and the invading Italian had come all the way to Libya to entertain them. Mussolini's face," Father told us, "upturned and with that signature expression of contempt that one historian had described as 'oddly coquettish,' was baffled and intrigued. In the buildup to his visit, Mussolini had been told of the Zowas, of their effective campaigns against his army, of their bravery but also of their willingness to switch sides. A meeting was arranged. One of Mussolini's aides documented it in his autobiography. 'These men belong to an ancient tribe,' he wrote. 'They did not salute Il Duce. They were still and silent, waiting for us to make the first move. It cannot be denied that I detected in these savage men an untamed nobility.' Then the Italian officer noted that after the meeting ended, 'a smell, which initially was sharp, remained long after they left, mellowing and turning delightfully fragrant. It was a local variety of musk, we were told. The following day Il Duce was brought a bottle, but the difference between that perfume and what the Zowas wore was like the sad gap between the first flowering of jasmine and days later when the scent, having spent itself, turns oversweet and heavy with decrepitude.'"

Father was very satisfied with this, and we all complimented him on having found the quote.

"The translation is mine, but it is pretty much accurate," he said.

"Bravo," my mother told him, looking proud and amused.

The Zowas proved to be useful collaborators, delivering such devastatingly accurate intelligence that in 1931, five years after they met with Benito Mussolini, Omar al Mukhtar, the leader of the Libyan resistance, the man they had been loyal to up till then, was captured and publicly hanged. Mussolini rewarded the Zowas handsomely. They became supremely rich and started to weave their coat of arms in gold thread into the hems of their caps. Father found a picture of it printed in one of the books from his library. It showed an olive tree with a crescent moon and three stars dotted above it.

"That's terrible," Souad said.

"Traitors," Mother declared.

"And this wasn't the full extent of it," Father said. "Ten years later, seeing how the British were doing in the war, the Zowas turned again, 'the way sunflowers follow the sun,' as one of our more lyrical historians put it, this time aligning themselves with al Senussis, claiming the etymological root of their family name to be zawya, the educational and welfare centers al Senussis had established and maintained since the nineteenth century, from Tobruk to Lagos. What's more," Father said, "their timing was impeccable, because, in 1951, the patriarch of al Senussis became monarch of the United Kingdom of Libya."

"They have no principles," Mother declared and folded her arms.

Father smiled, as though we were all his students and he expected such a reaction. "On each occasion—" he attempted to resume but Mother interrupted.

"Men who can be bought," she said.

Here something had to happen. Someone had to make tea or invent a reason for the silence—the silence we all needed—to continue a little longer. Mother pulled out a cigarette. Father lit it for her and then lit one for himself. I went to fetch an ashtray.

"But each time," Father said, addressing Mother more particularly now, "their maneuver had been so perfectly timed that it made it difficult to claim that they were motivated by opportunism alone. They joined the Italians when the Libyan resistance was still strong, and then joined al Senussis when it wasn't certain that Italy and its ally Germany would lose the war."

"Traitors," she said again.

"Perhaps. They kept their silence and never volunteered a justification."

"So what?" she told him.

"They never felt obliged to explain themselves or the blood of the opposing factions that they helped to spill."

"That makes it worse."

"Perhaps," he told her again. "But that, as history testifies, is an effective strategy, for their actions come to resemble a pattern that is guided less by ideology, less by temperament or ethics, less by principles—"

"They obviously have none," she said.

"And more by a natural order, one as self-assured and free of self-justification as a gust of wind taking part in a storm."

"How can you say that?" she told him. "Stop trying to sound poetic. Put it plainly. They have blood on their hands. Should be strung up."

With reddened cheeks, Father smiled in that way he did when he was about to divert the conversation. "Children," he said, "your mother is a radical. A very beautiful radical, but a radical nonetheless." He tickled her and she laughed but in the wrong way.

King Idris selected Hosam's father, The Radar, to accompany his nephew and heir to the throne, Crown Prince Hasan, on the first al Senussis state visit to the United States, in 1962.

"They landed in Washington," Father told us, opening the atlas on a map of the United States. "Then," he said, marking the route with his index finger, "they flew all the way to Colorado. From there, they went to San Francisco, where they visited the University of California at Berkeley."

That, I later learned, was when the cabin near Point Reyes was purchased. Recently, during one of the long Sunday afternoons I now spend in the British Library, I came upon a photograph deep inside a book that was not even about my country but the unlikely subject of higher education in postcolonial Africa, which showed the young Sidi Rajab Zowa suited, wearing trendy sunglasses, walking beside Prince Hasan, who was elegantly dressed in Libyan clothes and hat, down Euclid Avenue in Berkeley. I took a photo of it with my phone and zoomed in till Hosam's father's face filled the entire screen. Only the bony structure reminded me of him. I sent it to Hosam in Benghazi and he texted back immediately.

"Amazing," he said. "Where did you find this?"

Then several hours later he wrote: "It's the face that gets me. The optimistic assumption in it that he would take his new wife and the children they were yet to have and spend holidays there."

A little while later he texted again. "Astonishing how most people take it for granted that they will have children and that they will spend many summers with them?"

7

THERE ARE MOMENTS, MOMENTS like this, when an abstract longing overcomes me, one made all the more violent by its lack of fixed
purpose. The trick time plays is to lull us into the belief that everything lasts forever, and, although nothing does, we continue inside
that dream. And, as in a dream, the shape of my days bears no relation
to what I had, somehow and without knowing it, allowed myself to
expect.

I continue down the Euston Road as though I have just arrived
and my thirty-two years lived here could be collected in the palm of
a hand. There is still time. I could return and spend the rest of my
days beneath the same sky under which I was born. Maybe I would
then forget everything that had happened, or not think so much
about it. Or maybe I would turn into one of those returnees I recall
from childhood, men who had lived other lives elsewhere and who
persist, even years after their return, to give in to reminiscing, recounting, when the mood takes them, half-recollected stories and
anecdotes to amuse their audience, who, in turn, are sometimes entertained and at other times obliged to tolerate their long stories

with the wary patience of those who know they must not abruptly wake a sleepwalker.

Mohammed Mustafa Ramadan came to London the year I was born, in 1966, to work for the BBC. One English newspaper described him as "passionately pamphleteering against his country's government." I have often pictured him, as he walked these same streets I am walking now, as someone, like me, moving forward while looking back, liable at any moment to crash into something. He would have believed, as indeed I did when I first arrived, that he was safe behind the armor of exile. But it turned out that at the very moment that my family and I were listening to him read "The Given and the Taken," and in the following weeks, as my father entertained us with stories about the Zowas, the present was marching on and about to collide with the BBC journalist, the man who, when he spoke on the radio, seemed to be speaking to you alone.

The Libyan government was one of the pioneers of what came to be called "The Killing of the Word," the diabolical campaign that several Arab regimes embarked on in the 1970s. It was accelerated in the 1980s and continues to be occasionally practiced today and therefore cannot be said to have ended. Its main purpose was to get rid of, often in spectacular ways, outspoken journalists: shooting them in the middle of the street, or while eating lunch in a busy restaurant; or abducting them to torture and murder them, leaving their disfigured bodies as a warning to anyone who dared to criticize those who ruled over us. The details of such attacks did indeed cling to the memory. They stained the mind with blood. Arab journalists, editors, and publishers began to flee. Most went to London. Eventually, an entire people's press was transplanted abroad, until the overwhelming majority of Arab newspapers and magazines then were written, edited, and printed in London. Poets and novelists followed. And, despite the fact that a few were assassinated here, the city remained the center of exiled Arab intelligentsia until well into the 1990s. It cannot be said that they prospered here. If anything, they withered, grew old and tired. London was, in a way, where Arab writers came to die.

Back when I was fourteen, living in Benghazi, with no intention of leaving home, the thought of ending up living in London for the rest of my life would have never crossed my mind. I had the vague impression, partly inspired by the chimes of Big Ben, that the English capital was a melancholy place and that this gathering of Arab writers there, which included authors my parents held in high regard, such as the Sudanese novelist Tayeb Salih, the Syrian poet Nizar Qabbani, and the Lebanese journalist Salim el Lozi, took place at night, long after the sun had set. I imagined that London was perched at the edge of a terrifying precipice, a precarious place but one that afforded an expansive view, making it seem at times to my boyish mind that these Arab exiles were driven away less by fear and more by courage.

Years later, on mentioning this to Hosam, he thought it was exactly that sort of courage that was the problem. "For a writer, exile is prison," he said, "a severing from the source, and so, courageous or not, he dies in front of our eyes." Then Hosam's own eyes turned mischievous and he said, "Fuck exile," which sounded good, like the crack of a whip, and so he said it again and laughed. We both did. And, from then on, "Fuck exile" became a refrain, our private platitude, added as if a blessing: "Enjoy your meal and fuck exile," "Good night and fuck exile," "Safe travels and fuck exile."

A few weeks after Mohammed Mustafa Ramadan read Hosam's short story, his lush and warm voice paused in the middle of the evening news. "The London-based journalist and publisher Salim el Lozi, ignoring advice not to return to his native Lebanon, flew to Beirut to attend his mother's funeral. He has not been seen since."

My parents knew of Salim el Lozi. They had read and admired his novel *The Émigrés*. And for the next few days they followed the story closely. Whether out of carelessness, or numbed by the shock, or deliberately wanting Souad and me to be exposed to the sort of world we were inheriting, they did not think to shield us from the horrific facts that began to emerge.

Salim el Lozi was kidnapped from the airport the moment his flight landed. "Ten days later," Mohammed Mustafa Ramadan told us in a broadcast the following week, "his body was found on the outskirts of Beirut. Evidence showed that he was tortured."

This, we were soon to learn, was an understatement. The author's right arm had been broken in several places. The hand at the end of it, his writing hand, had been amputated and skinned. For days afterward, I would look at my own hand, trying to imagine the veins and tissues and bones unmasked. A careful silence fell on our house. I found el Lozi's novel on Father's shelf. I took it to my room and began reading.

"I did not want a story," the book begins, "certainly not a murder, least of all the death of someone I almost knew. I was a newspaperman from Beirut on holiday in Europe and I wanted peace, which for me meant beaches (the smarter ones), restaurants (the best), and most of all girls (quite a lot of girls). I had a couple of weeks away from investigating the tangle of other people's lives and politics. The idea was to live my own life for once."

I continued reading, feeling a peculiar effortlessness in doing so. The sentences, which were now disembodied from the man who had written them, seemed suspended, so light on their feet that I hardly noticed my progress through the pages. I had the sense that the book I was holding, a dead man's book, did not yet know of the sad news. I looked at the author's portrait on the back cover. The healthy smiling round face belonged to a man, very much like the narrator of the novel, who had no qualms about seeking out his pleasure. A few pages in, there was this line, which I felt the need to read over and over again until it lodged itself in my memory: "Yet writers were never their own masters, and I knew that one day I needed to write something . . . which would finally tell the rest of the human race what my muddled, belligerent, unstable, peace-loving, and fractious part of it was really like, particularly in exile; exile being a thermometer of our times."

Over the next few days, as I lived inside *The Émigrés,* we continued, the four of us, to follow the story of the mutilation and murder of its author, which both the BBC and the Libyan state media, each driven by an opposite motive, diligently reported.

8

I CONTINUE DOWN THE Euston Road and reach the four caryatids, strong women carrying on their heads the roof of the porch that leads into the crypt of the St. Pancras New Church, maidens from the ancient Greek town of Karyai, followers of Artemis, each with a kink in her hip. In one hand they are clutching an extinguished torch, in the other an empty jug. They are guardians of the dead. I stand beneath them. Their large eyes, as smooth as eggshells, stare down blankly at me.

I must keep moving. To live is to act.

I continue down the Euston Road and turn north, taking the back roads till I reach Regent's Park. I walk along its southern edge. The air here does not move but is cool and wide and expanding. Out of nowhere a blackbird calls, its repeated clicks forming a single line that stops just as abruptly as it started. Otherwise, it is quiet. I step on a twig and it snaps, the sound hanging in the air for a second. Fuck exile, I think, and hear myself laugh. The trees, shy giants, are perfectly still and loom large in the dark interior of the park. I can easily climb over the fence but I dare not. The twilight has dissolved entirely now. The clouds have scattered, making of the black sky an

abyss. I am frightened of these waves. Tonight the night is not a fragment of day, not a chapter of time, but an indefinite territory. "Why
does night fall?" The old question returns to me now. It used to strike
me with such practical force when I was a little boy and the arrangement of things was in question. I asked it in order to prolong the day
a little longer, sensing the futility even as I repeated it, watching my
mother's face, which, depending on her mood, was distracted,
amused, or mildly irritated. And, although the question stopped, the
mystery has persisted. It still comes to me when I wake in the middle
of the night, when it is at once too early and too late, and I stare
blindly into the dark, which seems as vast and bottomless as history. I
am convinced then that, even though I am covered in a blanket, I am
absolutely bare, that the night had, without my knowing how or to
what end, stripped me naked. Turn, curl up to hide the fact, to retreat
into that sweet half-death of sleep, hoping the light will come. And
even today, at the age of fifty, half a century old, that question emerges,
renewing the suspicion that night, even when a city such as London
slows down, besides maintaining the natural cycle, has its own secret
purpose.

I turn the corner that hugs the park and catch the bronze glimmer
of the dome nestled in among the trees, the column of its sandy
minaret rising up beside it. On the 11th of April 1980, shortly after
the severed body of Salim el Lozi was found on the outskirts of Beirut, Mohammed Mustafa Ramadan left work early and walked along
this very same pavement, I imagine, to attend Friday prayer at the
Central Mosque by Regent's Park. He had planned to meet his wife,
Nadia, and two-year-old daughter, Hanan, by the entrance. Mohammed was forty years old and by this time had been living in London
for fourteen years. Perhaps he still imagined himself one day returning home, or perhaps he had silently resigned himself to a life lived
eternally abroad. He carried copies of the day's *Al Arab* newspaper
to distribute for free at the end of the prayer. The paper contained
his latest column, in which he likened the Libyan dictatorship to an
occupying force, comparable to the Italian Fascists who had once

ruled over Libya. As he approached, he found two men lingering nervously beside the gate in painfully tight jeans. They looked about half his age. He did not know this, but their names were Najib Jasmi and Bin Hasan el Masri. They had recently arrived separately from Tripoli. Jasmi, as I later learned from Hosam—who had become obsessed with these details—rented a flat in Princess Court in Queensway and el Masri one in Cornwall Gardens in South Kensington. Neither man knew or had ever met Mohammed Mustafa Ramadan. It is not even clear if they ever listened to him on the radio. They had a photograph and the address of his place of work. A couple of days after arriving at Heathrow, they had taken it upon themselves to wait all day across the road from the BBC's Broadcasting House in Portland Place. When they spotted their man leaving the building, the thrill was like that of an inside joke, casting a secretive glow of superiority. Mohammed Mustafa Ramadan was completely oblivious to all this. When he arrived at the mosque, he spotted the two men. How young and nervous and out of place they seemed. Nadia too had noticed them. They made her uneasy. She whispered something in his ear and he nodded a little impatiently, the way he perhaps did when she would ask him not to forget to carry out a certain chore. He lifted their daughter into his arms and kissed her. There was no time. They had to go in and carry out their ablutions. They quickly agreed where to meet after prayer. Nadia took Hanan from him and carried her across the courtyard and into the women's section. Mohammed watched them till they vanished. He paused for a moment, perhaps considering his options, and entered the mosque. He went down the stairs to the washrooms. He might have wondered if there was a back door, a way out that might exit on to the park, from where he could easily disappear. He was sure Nadia would later agree that the precaution, although surely needless, was nonetheless prudent. To make up for keeping her waiting, he might have then taken her out to the cinema, stopping for a pizza on the way, and later ice cream as they walked home. But come, he would have told himself, rolling up his sleeves, your mind is running away with you. No one dies before their time. And, anyway, they wouldn't dare. Not here. Not in London. He dried his face, climbed up the stairs slowly, and found them at the top landing, looking nervous, pretending not to be waiting. He caught a look of fear in their faces, and that comforted him somehow. He remembered his father, during the tensed moments before the slaughter on Eid, reminding him, as was his habit, of the source of the ritual. Testing Abraham, God had conferred on His prophet a macabre vision, one ordering Abraham to slaughter in sacrifice his own son. The father proves himself willing to kill his own child and the son willing to die in order that his father can prove his obedience to God. But, just as Abraham is about to slice his boy's throat, God rewards him by putting a stop to the action and instead offers father and son His contentedness in the form of a lamb. He remembered the look of fear and foreboding in his father's eyes every time he told the story, which always made him hold his tongue and not ask his father the question that was uppermost in his mind: why would God want to reward absolute obedience, regardless of the consequences, when He had bestowed on us reason, granting us not only the ability but the responsibility to arrive at our own decisions? His old man, he now decided, must too have been frightened by the tale. Then he thought, how small the two men were. Their bodies were small but also their will. It is difficult to kill a man, he told himself. Far more difficult than one suspects. And that is a hopeful fact: that life is on the side of life. Then he thought of his father again—or so I imagine.

I am now at the mosque. I walk across its large white courtyard, which glows grayly in the night. I find the doors open. I go down the same staircase. I wash. I climb up, take off my shoes, and enter the large carpeted hall, its ceiling lifting above me. Perhaps, when Mohammed Mustafa Ramadan walked in here that afternoon, he placed the copies of *Al Arab* newspaper that he had been carrying right in front of him, so that every time he knelt to place his forehead on the

ground, repeating three times, "How perfect is my Lord, the Su-
preme," he saw them and breathed in that dear and familiar smell of
freshly printed newspapers. It evoked lunch breaks and lazy afternoons, moments stolen during the commute and open, slow Sun-
days. That smell was also the wish that once a thing is printed it can
never be erased, that time can come and go but a documented fact
means the world cannot continue to pretend that nothing happened.
And he might have recognized then, more clearly than ever before
and with lucid conviction, that this was the extravagant hope that
resided at the very center of his life, what animated and enlivened it.
And this would have come with a sense of gratitude, understanding,
perhaps for the first time, that he was among the lucky ones whose
life and days and minutes had been lived purposefully. I imagine he
positioned himself at the rear lines, so that, as soon as prayer was
over and he had bidden peace and farewell to both angels, the one
residing on his left shoulder, which tallies up his sins, and the other
on his right, which records the good deeds, he could slip away, leaving behind the newspapers. He would find Nadia and Hanan and,
quickly hailing a cab, disappear into London, the city of infinite
streets. But then maybe the futility of such a plan was already seep-
ing into him. It would take ages for Nadia and Hanan to appear. And
the moment he thought of them a sad and proud feeling rose in him.
He would not run. He would walk unperturbed. He found his shoes.
They had lost the warmth of his feet, but the soft leather was a comfort. The bodies crowding around him. Men with perfumed necks,
perfumed for prayer. The sky finally above him. His eyes adjusting to
the brightness. The hopeful comfort of leisure, the weekend finally
opening up before him. All that senseless anxiety. Nothing but the
exhaustion of an overworked mind. He breathed in the air. Considered going back to fetch the newspapers. He pictured them spread
into a fan shape across the carpet, trampled by passing feet. He decided against it. Words will find their way, he thought.

The first of the tiny loud explosions. The guns, it was later discovered, were small enough to fit inside a jeans pocket. Then the second.

Everyone, all the scented bodies around him, retreated, scattering outward, expanding like a ripple or the speeded-up bloom of a rose. And right there, at the center, was the body of the man with the distinctive voice, the broadcaster who made you feel that he was speaking to you and to you alone.

9

THE NEWS OF MOHAMMED Mustafa Ramadan's death was announced triumphantly by a woman newsreader on Libyan state television: "A stray dog has met his just end."

We turned on the radio and heard a man, in a tired and withdrawn voice, corroborate the terrible news.

My mother cried, Souad cried, and I did too behind a closed door in the bathroom. My father hardly spoke a word for the following few days.

Then it slowly came. We, the same four people who had admired Mohammed Mustafa Ramadan and shed tears for him, began, while still enduring our grief, not so much to justify his murder but to find reasons for it, to try, in the absence of any justice, to make sense of the senseless act, and gradually, like a rising tide, we diverted some of the blame on to the dead man's shoulders.

"He should've been smarter," Mother declared.

Souad tried to object. "How can you say that?"

"Well," Mother told her, "he wasn't a naive child. He knew what he was doing."

A strange power came over my mother here. She seemed entirely convinced by her words. In a sudden transformation, she dispelled the meek and sad air that had accompanied her over the preceding days.

"Are you saying he deserved it?" I asked.

"No," she said, and looked a little exhausted at having to explain herself. She lit a cigarette, turned her chair slightly toward Father, and brushed with the back of her hand a perfectly clean spot on her lap. She exhaled a fabulous cloud of smoke. She bunched up the fabric of her dress, revealing two strong knees, which struck me then as not belonging to her but to a younger woman.

"Of course he didn't deserve it," she finally said. "But—"

"No, he didn't deserve it," Father said in a gentle but strangely loaded voice. "What your mother means is that he might have been able to avoid it." He paused before adding, more to her, "But who can say?"

"Well," she told him, "you don't go to the lion and tell him he's no good to his face."

It did not matter that none of us, not even Mother, was convinced. Our minds were already imagining how the deceased could have been more careful, kept a lower profile, held his opinions close to his chest, walked quietly beside the wall, found ways to be content. And, over the next few days, this other, timid version of the journalist and radio presenter began to take shape in my fourteen-year-old mind. I congratulated him on surviving, on being more responsible, on being a better husband and father. But this version of Mohammed Mustafa Ramadan was less vivid somehow, less easy to understand or to trust. He read out the news on the radio without the passionate inflections, none of that proud determination, that independent and somewhat lavish enthusiasm that hit the airwaves right after the English presenter solemnly announced, "This is London calling. This wavelength now carries our morning transmission in Arabic," early in the morning, as I dressed for school, when the sky outside was still black, and the formidable yet intimate voice of the Libyan would offer his greeting, declaring that the day had begun. That feature, I imagined, would not exist in the man who would have survived. Nor, more consequentially for me, would he have defied convention and the rules of the BBC and read "The Given and the Taken," the short story that cast a long shadow across my life, by an unknown Libyan author who was his friend and who would, fifteen years later, become mine, a man, as I would later learn, disapproved of by the Libyan regime, and whose protagonist speaks the one word that none of us could have spoken then, and which, read by Mohammed Mustafa Ramadan, was momentarily given back to us: "No."

10

IN THOSE DAYS, MY father subscribed to several international literary and academic journals. They crossed borders and seas before the postman deposited them into our letter box. We often teased Father.

"Oh, look," Souad would say, "the *Journal of Modern African Studies* has just arrived from Cambridge."

"That's nothing," Mother would put in. "I have here, and all the way from Chicago, the *Journal of Near Eastern Studies*."

In the months after the reading of Hosam Zowa's short story, and the horrific assassinations of Salim el Lozi and Mohammed Mustafa Ramadan, and from within the palpable disquiet that these events left in our house, I began to leaf through these colorless publications, nursing a hope that I might somehow come upon a clue, a piece of valuable information, that might nudge my life—to where or what end I did not know.

In *World Literature Written in English,* a journal with a declared interest in "postcolonial writing," I came upon an essay titled "The Consequences of Meaning in the Infidelities of Translation," written by Professor Henry Walbrook, whose one-line biography stated that he taught English with a focus on postcolonial literature at the University of Edinburgh. I struggled through it with my basic English, having to look up so many words that the dictionary did not leave my side. Professor Walbrook wrote of "the systematic lack of correspondence between intention and expression," that "Translation, any act of translation—from one language to another, from a feeling to its expression—inevitably changes the sense. Even a faithful interpretation," he claimed, "loses a measure of meaning, sheds it, very much as when a cliff is corroded by rough weather. This," he went on to say, "inserts, whether involuntarily or not, new implications."

I remained at our kitchen table, within that afternoon silence when my parents and sister napped, slowly translating Walbrook's essay, feeling frustrated at my inability to fully understand it or understand why, instead of being worried about the loss, the author seemed fascinated by it, making the case that "Even though it is right to see such inaccuracies as instances of loss or corruption, we might also welcome them for their unmanaged expression. In other words, as well as being bad, there was something good and, indeed, hopeful about the event, for, if nothing else, it proves that whatever we touch is altered; that no matter how weak, unimportant, poor, restricted or unfree our lives might appear to be, it is impossible for us to pass through the earth without leaving a mark."

Nearly three years later I applied to study English at the University of Edinburgh. I was accepted and, amazingly, given my parents' refusal to find an influential relation who might help my application along, I secured a government scholarship.

Bidding me farewell at the airport, my father held me not in his usual easy embrace but in one more constricted.

"Don't be lured in," he said, the words emanating from his very core.

"I won't," I said, assuming he meant the usual temptations that might lure a teenager.

He held my hand tightly, squeezing it harder than he had ever done before. The force frightened me. It made it seem as though I were in danger of falling. The pupils of his eyes turned small and dark and slowly, in a barely audible tone, he said, "Don't. Be. Lured. In."

Long after the plane took off, sitting in my seat, wrapped in the jacket he had given me, I kept wondering what he meant by those words. It was my first time flying, the first time crossing the border of my country, and so my father's words, the perturbed expression on his face, like a grove rustled by a gust of wind, are connected in my mind with leaving home. And even though I kept trying to convince myself that he only meant to warn me off youthful excesses, I knew it was something else. I thought back on how, on the days leading up to my departure, Mother's and Souad's sadness seemed more than the occasion merited. When I said this to Souad, she responded, "You just don't get it, do you?" and looked at me as if I were a stranger.

I did not get it and I continued to not get it for a long time. I misunderstood their concern. It was caused not only by fear and longing but by something that should have been blatantly obvious—which is that if you were to leave Libya back then in 1983, there would be few reasons why you would want to return.

11

BY THE TIME I arrived in Edinburgh I was free of all concern. I was gripped by the newness of things, the unfamiliar architecture and faces, the way the people and the clouds moved. I got to the house where I would be staying and, after the formalities with the landlady, I walked into my bedsit and closed the door behind me. The room— a single bed, a small desk beneath the window, a wardrobe big enough for one person's belongings—was a place I had all along anticipated. Although it was in a foreign city, the room was uncannily recognizable, as if I were already in the future and this was a memory. I unpacked.

A knock came on the door and an affable Libyan student from my scholarship group introduced himself. "Saad, from Zuwara," he said, and immediately asked whether I had ever been to his small coastal city in the far northwest of the country.

"Sadly not," I said, and, following his example, introduced myself as "Khaled, from Benghazi."

"Oh, yes, I've been there," he said. "Well, you have certainly missed out. Zuwara is a major capital of the world, ranked up there along with London, Paris, and New York." He laughed delightedly at his own joke.

He sat on the edge of my bed. I leaned on the desk and, for want of something to say, I asked him what his interests were.

"Interests?" he said. "What a strange question. I have completely liberated myself of those. My chief motive, dear Khaled, is to enjoy myself, spend a few years abroad, as far away from Zuwara as possible."

I laughed. He watched me and then laughed too.

"You see," he said, "I have resigned myself to the fact that I live in a world of unreasonable men and the only reasonable thing to do in this situation is, best we can, avoid their schemes."

"What an excellent idea," I said.

"Avoid their schemes and have fun, which is why," he said, "you must come with me this minute to meet the others."

I grabbed my jacket and followed him, thinking everyone else in our group would be as easygoing as Saad. Instead, they were, almost without exception, exactly the opposite, dull and cheerless, their demeanor stamped with that wary suspicion that infects some of my male compatriots when they leave home. What baffled me was that Saad had nothing but praise for each of them.

Sensing my lack of enthusiasm, he said, "I've saved best for last. Mustafa al Touny. You will see. You two will get on. For I can tell, my dear Khaled, I can already tell what kind of a person you are."

I followed him through several corridors until we reached the canteen. There, leaning with his shoulder against a column, looking as lavishly bored as an abandoned building, was Mustafa. He seemed lost down some personal reflection or regret. I remember thinking, he had given something up to get here, for, as well as looking disused, he also seemed to have been misused. His closely cropped hair—which was against the fashion of the time—his clean-shaven face, and slight physique made him seem cautious and self-contained. Perhaps he is already missing home, I thought, or had left something there unresolved. When he saw us approach, he looked straight through us. Even after he took hold of my hand and we repeated the usual meaningless platitudes, I could not tell whether he had actually heard me at all. I detected his Benghazi accent, and a slight working-class inflection. But it was not until I gave him my full name—Khaled Abd al Hady—that Mustafa seemed to arrive back from wherever he had been. Did I know Ustath Kamal Abd al Hady, he asked, the headmaster?

"He's my father," I said.

He embraced me.

Saad let out a laugh. "Didn't I tell you?" he said, nudging my shoulder. "I told him you'd get on," he told Mustafa.

"I spent the last two years at his father's school," Mustafa told him. "His father is an excellent man. An excellent teacher." Then he looked at me and said, "And can be very funny," and laughed.

Back then the state sent scholarship students abroad in small bunches, each bound together with one or two "Wires," students whose job it was to spy on the others. Another name we had for the "Wires" was the "Writers," as they came not so much to study but to produce reports on the rest of us. The effectiveness of the system lay precisely in its vagueness. You remained on guard and in need of exoneration because you never could be absolutely certain what might land you in trouble and destroy the miraculous piece of good fortune of studying abroad. Another equally small minority were the "Readers," students who had come to actually study. In our group, Mustafa and I were the only "Readers," which was why Saad thought we would get on. The rest, that happy majority to which Saad belonged, had come to do nothing, which was the least controversial of the three activities and, therefore, required no justification.

"You pity us poor creatures," Mustafa told him after we had all come to know each other a little, "afflicted by that rare condition that compels an individual to go to a bookshelf, pick up a book, and

read it from start to finish for no reason other than the sheer pleasure of it."

But even back then I sensed that Mustafa and I read differently.
He entered books with pointed implements. It mattered to him
whether he agreed with the author or if he believed them to be of
sound character. He consulted their politics, their opinions on various
topics, and experienced a passionate keenness, which showed itself in
his eyes every time he believed he had determined their ethical standing. What was curious is that, regardless of the verdict, whether con-
demning or exonerating, this process inspired in him the same
response, an enthusiastic and excited relief, and it seemed only then
that he could close the book and forget all about it.

I wrote home every week. The letters I received, no doubt like
the ones I sent, were opened on the way. No effort was made to
conceal the fact. The envelopes were torn and then resealed with
transparent adhesive tape that ran unsteadily, folded on to itself in
places, and sometimes arrived unstuck. The actual pages of the letter would often be crumpled, or displaying the crescent moon of a
coffee cup, no doubt as proof of witness. And it worked, because, as
I read, I wondered what that anonymous third party had made of
every sentence and, when it came time to reply, I never could altogether vanquish him from my mind. I felt myself to be if not writing
for him, then leaving things out for him. This changed the tone of
our letters, and must have been, in part at least, the purpose of the
policy. Our exchanges, in the company of a suspicious authority, became self-conscious, wary of mentioning personal details or express-
ing easy intimacies. I no longer wrote, for example, "Kisses" at the
end of my letters. It unsettled me most deeply when, on one occasion, my mother, whom I had never heard say anything positive
about the regime, exalted the virtues of the dictator, giving him
three whole sentences. I did not write for two weeks after that. She
never did it again.

But before this, in Father's first innocent letter, which he wrote in reply to my informing him of the happy coincidence of meeting his former student Mustafa al Touny, he wrote, "Yes, I knew he was applying. I wrote him a reference. Very pleased he got a place. He is a good lad. I was always happy to lend him books. His only fault is a quick temper. I tried to teach him not to judge too quickly, that some books, like some people, are shy."

12

DURING THOSE EARLY MONTHS at Edinburgh, I felt a new excitement, a practical optimism, and I entered each day believing it was mine. I was not only learning the ways of a new life but felt myself to be engaged in an experiment in living, one that posed no risks, because I believed that at any moment I could press the "reset" button and return home. That time remains the happiest of my life.

I got on with Saad and the other Libyans in our group, including the "Writers," but, apart from Mustafa, the only other person I thought of as a friend was Rana, a Lebanese architecture student. I never introduced them. I liked the fact that I could keep these friendships separate. It allowed me to express different sides of my character, to retell the same anecdote, altering its details, or to change opinion about a particular subject and feel no obligation to explain myself. Mustafa, although he never said it, disliked that I kept Rana to myself. I suspected, even though I could not then understand why, he secretly objected to my friendship with her, to my friendship with anyone who was not him. Rana, on the other hand, preferred this policy. She did not introduce me to her friends either—all of whom looked intimidatingly cool and sophisticated—and, when once we agreed how much we liked this arrangement, she said that it gave us "free rein to gossip." I had never trusted anyone so easily or so completely. I believe I was the same to her. We watched foreign films in her flat, where she lived alone. She enjoyed my cooking and I liked to cook for her. We sometimes went to the Edinburgh Filmhouse, and, even if we loved the film, we enjoyed our criticism even more, walking out of the cinema laughing at our own pretentiousness. I liked laughing at myself with her. Was I falling in love? What would have become of us if I had remained in Edinburgh? Several times in her flat, or later when she collected me from Westminster Hospital and gave me a place to hide in Notting Hill, or later still when it was my turn and I went to be beside her in Paris as she convalesced, throughout all the years we have known each other, I saw the line marked between us and at times considered crossing it. Even tonight, as I walk this circuitous route home from St. Pancras to Shepherd's Bush, I wonder what would have happened if I had.

As though by magic, three years from when I read his essay on translation, I found myself sitting in a large lecture hall listening to Professor Walbrook. I had never before met someone whose work I had read. At one point, when he looked up, scanning his students, and for a fraction of a second his eyes fell on me, I believed, against all logic, that he recognized me. He looked younger than I had imagined, perhaps in his mid-thirties. His introductory remarks were nervous, but then, when he began his lecture, which was on Tennyson's *In Memoriam A. H. H.*, "Possibly the greatest poem ever written about friendship," as he put it, all that disappeared and a natural passion and ease came over him. When he told us that the poem was in response to the premature death of the poet's most intimate friend, Arthur Henry Hallam, who had died at the age of twenty-two, Walbrook momentarily looked up at us, perhaps to remind himself that we were not far off that age.

"Tennyson's 133-canto elegy," he said, "stretched over a decade and a half."

Are God and Nature then at strife,
That Nature lends such evil dreams?
So careful of the type she seems,
So careless of the single life . . .

"An artist encounters an untranslatable experience and it causes in him such violent wonder and disquiet that he must try, with what will he can, to overcome the gulf, to attempt to reconcile 'God' and 'Nature' with 'the single life.' Here we have two untranslatable experiences. The first is the friendship, which, like all friendships, one cannot fully describe to anyone else. The second is grief, which again, like all forms of grief, is horrible exactly for how uncommunicable it is."

I walked out of that first lecture exhilarated. I remember how anxiously my heart raced in my chest when, a couple of months later, in November, just as the new winter was gathering its troops, I approached him at the end of class and asked whether he would like to meet over coffee.

He smiled and said, "Here we don't drink coffee," but that he would gladly meet me on Friday evening at the nearby pub.

That whole week I lived in anticipation. When I reached the door, I stood outside in the cold air for a moment, listening to the warm rumble of the interior, watching the obscured shapes through the frosted glass. Inside, the air was milky with smoke. I found him standing at the bar. We spoke and he seemed, in this setting, less of an analyzing academic and more of an accepting and openly curious presence. I had to ask a few times before he would tell me anything about himself. Eventually, he gave in.

"I'm from London," he said. "Lived with my grandmother. The two of us rattling around in a big empty house. Except, it wasn't that big. I couldn't wait to get away, of course."

I blushed. I was not used to people speaking that way about their own family.

"She was wonderful. Very kind. It was just that being brought up by your gran—it opens your eyes too soon to decrepitude," he said, and laughed.

He did not say anything about his parents, and I wondered whether the candid way in which he talked about his grandmother was partly intended to deflect from that subject.

"What does the name Walbrook mean?" I asked. I used to ask such questions back then.

"Not sure," he said. "It might not mean anything at all."

"But all names do," I said.

"I suppose they must," he said.

"It's the name of a hill in London. I looked it up."

This need to prove to the natives, even those as exceptionally learned as Walbrook, that I knew as much about their culture, or could know as much about it, would become a bad habit. Even today I sometimes wonder, had I not been so keen to impress and blend in, what else might I have learned when I was young?

"Walbrook is one of the oldest settlements in London," I continued. "You could say, it's London's original name."

"Is that right?" he said, not hugely interested. After a little pause, he said, "Tell me about your life back in Libya. I'm afraid I know very little about your country."

"I grew up in the same Ottoman house where I was born, in Benghazi, right in the heart of the old downtown, very close to the seafront. The house belonged to my paternal grandfather and to his father before him. Each, including my father, was born there."

"What does your father do?"

"He's a teacher. Although what he really is, is a historian, a secret historian. Couldn't do it professionally because of the politics." I could feel the ground giving way, a well opening up beneath me. "I once read in his papers—I did not mean to pry but I walked into his study to fetch a book and found the handwritten pages on his desk and once I started reading I couldn't stop—a critique of dictatorship, arguing why totalitarianism is, in the end, unsustainable."

There, I said it. I knew that I might have ended my father, just like that, snapped his neck in two. Walbrook watched my face. He seemed to understand. But where did he stand? I remembered my father trying to persuade me that even among Italy's Fascists there were those who indulged in literature, clever people who were capable of acts of kindness. "The world," I remembered him saying, "is a complicated place." Father had looked at me then with concern in his eyes, doubtful whether he should have said anything at all, or perhaps doubtful if I would be able to find my way in such a world.

"Did you attend your father's school?" Walbrook asked.

"No," I said. "He worried too much that he might be accused of giving us, my sister and me, preferential treatment." And then, I do not know why I said this, I added, "My father worries a lot."

"I'm sure he has good cause," Professor Walbrook said, and then after a brief silence asked, "Would you tell me more about the house?"

I was delighted by his interest. I dived into a description of its layout. I asked the bartender for a napkin. Walbrook, with an amused smile, opened his small pocket notebook and handed me his pen. I drew the box of the courtyard, even dotted in the position of the grapevine in the corner, and showed him how the house was arranged around it. I then described the view from the rooftop. "On a clear day," I said, "you can see all the way to Crete." That was not true, but the lie seemed to happen ahead of me, without my full consent. This too was to become a habit. It is far too tempting, when you are away from home, to make stuff up.

"You miss it," he said. It was not a question.

"I'm not sure if I miss it or if I'm just enjoying telling you about it," I said, and before he could speak I added, "It was there that I came across your essay 'The Consequences of Meaning in the Infidelities of Translation.'"

He chuckled. "Poor you," he said. "How on earth did you do that?"

But it was clear that he was flattered, which for some reason made me choose not to tell him that he was the reason why I applied to Edinburgh in the first place. After we parted, I wished I had. I also wished I had told him about the Libyan short story that was read on BBC radio in place of the news: not only because he probably would have found that interesting, but also because in my mind he and Hosam Zowa were, in a profound yet elusive way, connected. Walking home in the dark that evening, with the streetlamps burning weakly, the night air as piercingly cold as a hard fact, I became convinced, in ways that were too vague and mysterious for me to grasp then, that it was Hosam Zowa's story, read in the voice of the soon to be assassinated Mohammed Mustafa Ramadan, that had led me to Professor Walbrook's meditation on the infidelities of translation—on what is lost and gained through the retelling of even the simplest story, the fear of being misunderstood, and the inevitability of it—and that this was what had brought me to Edinburgh.

13

I LEAVE THE MOSQUE and turn back toward the city, toward the
bright lights of Soho, the landing and the falling place, where I spent
that first night I came to London, intending only to be here a day and
then return to Scotland, only to remain for what is now thirty-two
years.

Seven months into my life in Edinburgh, I received yet another
opened letter from my mother. In those days, she and I used to exchange weekly postcards or letters. She was writing to tell me about
an exciting rumor stirring in Benghazi.

"The mysterious author of that frightening short story about the
monstrous cat is finally coming out with a book. It will be published
under the same title: *The Given and the Taken*. Do look for it and
when you read it let us know your opinion." She then ended her letter, as she often did, with the words, "I wrap you in my remembrance."
But now, thinking of the intruder between us, the sentiment made me
embarrassed.

It turned out Mustafa had once met my mother briefly when she
drove by to collect my father. "He insisted on introducing us," Mustafa said proudly. I informed him of the news and he, having missed

the broadcast, was even keener than I was to find the book. He telephoned all the Arabic bookshops in London and one in Manchester, where he had a maternal uncle. None had it or knew of it.

It was shortly after that when we heard that the authorities had rounded up a number of students from the University of Tripoli and Benghazi's Garyounis University, the school Mustafa and I most probably would have gone to if we had not been so lucky, and thrown them in jail. There were claims that several were tortured and some killed. It made me terribly anxious. I tried my best to ignore it. Mustafa, though, was visibly distraught. He said he had not been able to sleep since hearing the news.

"You know how people exaggerate," I told him. "I'm sure it's not all that bad."

He looked at me and said nothing.

The following morning, he came knocking at my door. He walked in before I could answer. I was still in bed. He pulled over the chair and sat beside me. He stood up again and went to the door, listened for a moment, and flung it wide open.

"What's going on?" I said.

"Are you sure no one else is here?" he whispered.

"Why? What happened?"

He shut the door and sat down again, like a doctor visiting his patient. He smelled of cigarettes and sweat. I remember thinking, whatever it is, keep calm and don't get involved. The thought brought back my father's words at the airport.

"A demonstration will take place tomorrow," he whispered, "in front of the embassy in London. I checked train times and the bus schedule. Nothing will get us there in time. We have to go today to make it. Pretty much right now. Spend the night there. I found a hotel."

He then looked at me and how many times have I thought back to how his eyes seemed at that moment: nervous, uncertain, seeking reassurance.

"It'd be fun, wouldn't it, to go to London?" he said.

14

WE TOOK THE BUS and arrived in London that evening. As we plunged deeper into the city, its lights gathering all around us, I could sense my blood moving through me like a thing trapped, pulsing in my neck, my ankles, tapping at the fingertips. I kept licking my lips to cool them. My heart, captured by a powerful premonition, knocked violently.

Mustafa said he had booked a twin room at a hotel in Soho's Wardour Street. "From there St. James's Square, where the embassy is located, is a ten-minute walk." He seemed pleased with the arrangement, but evaded the question when I asked him how he had found the hotel.

We got off the bus at Haymarket just after 9 P.M., ate at a McDonald's on Shaftesbury Avenue, and then went to find the hotel. I asked him again, as the receptionist was writing down our details, how he had come to know of this hotel.

"I have my sources," he said, amused by the mystery.

When I insisted, he accused me of being distrustful. Finally, he told me that it was Saad who had recommended it. I was furious, too furious to say anything, and it was not until a few minutes later when we were inside the room that I spoke.

"Now that Saad knows, everyone knows."

"I didn't tell him what we were coming to do," he said. "People come to London for all sorts of reasons."

"Don't be naive," I said.

"They know fuck all, believe me," he said.

And all this was said in whispers, as though we were already convinced that we were being watched. We smoked continuously. It was obvious that Mustafa too had misgivings. Like a soldier, he needed to summon the passion of his cause. He spoke of the students back home and how they were violently treated, adding new details here and there to deepen the outrage. As he spoke, I felt my body sink deeper, becoming ever denser and more helpless.

"We owe it to them," he said. After a short pause he lifted his head and asked, "Don't we?"

I lit another cigarette and we sat in silence, breathing. I listened to the faint sound of the air enter and leave him and caught myself tuning the rhythm of my breathing to his. His leg rocked and only stopped when I stood up.

"Let's go," I told him.

We ran down the stairs, walked the streets, stopped at an off-license, and bought half a liter of vodka. We passed it between us.

He struck my forearm suddenly and said, "Oh, God, we forgot the balaclavas."

"What balaclavas?" I asked.

"Because we are Swiss and demonstrating in front of our embassy represents no danger," he said sarcastically.

He quickened his pace. It was eleven at night. We went into an all-night newsagent. The man behind the counter was amused by the question and asked where we were from. Mustafa lied and told him Tunisia, burying the vodka in his back pocket.

"As-salamu alaykum, brothers," the man said, and told us that he was from Pakistan. "Are you going to rob a bank, brothers?" he said, and laughed alone. We should try one of the sex-toy shops, he said, they might have them there. When Mustafa asked if those would be open at this time, the man said, "Brother, people here need sex toys twenty-four hours a day. It's an emergency service." Now we were all laughing.

We found one such shop and giggled up and down its aisles. And, just when we were beginning to suspect the Pakistani had played a prank on us, we found two black polyester balaclavas.

"May God bless the Pakistani," Mustafa said as we left.

"Amen," I said, and we both had another swig of vodka, the alcohol watering our eyes.

Perhaps it was that, or the comedy, or the relief we felt at being able to attend the demonstration with our identities concealed—that we would be both there and not there at the same time—that made me feel supremely confident. Mustafa sensed this and seemed vindicated by it. He put his arm around me, and we turned down a narrow cobblestoned street.

"Not now," he said, "not ever, will we cease to be friends."

We embraced, slapped one another on the back, and the echoes of those strikes sounded metallic against the old houses of Meard Street. I remember the name because, as we embraced, my eyes wandered up the neatly laid black bricks, separated only by a thin white line of mortar, and I thought, how beautiful they were and made a mental note of the street name. That day and the morning after, those precious hours before everything changed, I was oddly convinced that I must try to remember every detail. And here I am back on Meard Street, looking up at those same bricks.

"Now tell me, Mr. Khaled," he said, as we continued weaving through the back streets of Soho, "son of the great headmaster, Khaled, the reader of *Wuthering Heights* and Ivan Turgenev, Khaled, the man who believes that if only people would read more the world would be a better place, my dear and beloved friend, have you ever been to a strip club?"

We giggled and pushed each other about.

Then in a loud booming voice he announced in English, "Ladies and gentlemen, Khaled, the proud son of Benghazi, is about to descend into the underworld. Have mercy on him, angels." I tried to cover his mouth.

A few turns and we were standing, hovering like nervous spies, opposite a bright red neon sign that read GIRLS GIRLS GIRLS. When I was young in Benghazi and would go to the high rocks with the boys, there was always one who would, without ceremony, dive first. None of us then had a choice but to follow. Mustafa, without saying a word, plunged down the narrow stairs. I went after him, with barely a step between us. A man who looked sleepy and bored ushered each of us into a tiny cubical that was the size of a telephone box. I did not know what I was supposed to do next. The man thumped his fist against the door, shouted, "50p, in the slot," and walked away muttering to himself. I pushed in the coin and a tiny window opened on to a naked woman spread on a circular bed covered in bloodred satin. The bed was on a platform that turned slowly. A bright spotlight made the woman's skin look unnaturally white. When my grandfather died and my father washed the corpse and I asked him later what it was like, the only thing he said was how shockingly pale the old man had become. The woman was talking to someone else, another woman resting in the shadows, and, as the bed turned, she turned her head in the opposite direction, and I thought of water spinning down the drain.

"And what did he tell you?" she said. "The bloody cheek."

All the while her hands were doing something between her legs. When the bed had come all the way around and she was finally facing me, I saw that she had a dark brown birthmark, the size of a chestnut, on her left jaw, and that her fingers were holding her vagina wide open, in the bureaucratic manner in which you might show your passport at a border. It looked like a monstrous creature yawning. I was eighteen, and this was the first time that I had ever seen a woman naked.

Without a warning the lid fell like a guillotine. I walked out and thanked the man. He did not respond. I then heard Mustafa laughing right behind me.

"What the fuck are you thanking him for?" he said.

We returned to the same McDonald's on Shaftesbury Avenue and ate ice cream. We climbed back to our room and lay each in his bed, smoking until we fell asleep.

15

THAT NIGHT I HAD disjointed dreams. Dreams of waiting. Standing in a long line by an unfriendly border. Killing time before the bakery opens. And then I am in the courtyard of my father's school, shuffling along in an endless queue that turns upon itself to fit inside the limited space, tightening with each coil like a spring in a clock. It is impossible to determine whether I am nearing the front or still at the rear. Only when I reach the head of the line do I realize the purpose of all this. An inoculation jab delivered by a nurse in white who is the same woman in the strip club. I recognize her from the birthmark. She and I are now sitting face-to-face. I cannot take my eyes off the chestnut on her left jaw. It is oddly beautiful; the skin there is velvet and tender. I think about how to compliment her on it, but then, instead of an injection, she takes out a gun, places the muzzle, still hot from the previous patient, not on my arm but against my chest.

I woke up and Mustafa was not in the room. I washed my face and stood by the window, watching the street below. A fruit seller had set up his stall and was turning the apples so their stems all faced upward. Men and women walked in different directions, dressed for the workday, which was to them, as it was still to me, a day like any other, open,

familiar, a variant of all the other days that had come before and those
yet to follow, exciting exactly for its familiarity, for being both new and
predictable, uncharted and known.

I had no idea then that I would come to know this part of town so
well, that I would spend countless evenings with the author of that
enigmatic short story, drinking at his favorite bar, the French House
on Dean Street, where, in Hosam's first year in London, he had met
the great painter Francis Bacon. This made Hosam, although he was
only six years older, seem to belong to another time, that, as well as
being the Libyan who had written one of the best collections of short
stories I had ever read, he was also mythically connected to London
and particularly to Soho. He told his own history of it, stories that
were no less fascinating for being dubious. He claimed, for example,
that Karl Marx, who, it is well established, had lived at 30 Dean Street,
had another secret life on the parallel Frith Street, where he kept a
mistress, and that a great many of the long days that the German phi-
losopher had allegedly spent sweating it out at the Reading Room in
Bloomsbury, composing his lasting theories, were, in fact, spent in
that other house. When I asked Hosam for his source, he replied, "A
professor at Trinity told me."

"Yes, but have you seen it written anywhere?"

"No, but some things have the truth in them; I mean, it makes perfect sense, doesn't it, that a man so preoccupied with finding an alternative way to organize society and economics should himself have had
an alternative life? Besides, it pleases me. I like imagining him shut-
tling back and forth between the two lives. And, anyway, doesn't his
prose hint at this? I don't mean that it's duplicitous necessarily, but
that it endlessly sidesteps one thing so as to reach for another . . ."

Having not read Marx, I had no clue what he meant. But I did read
Joseph Conrad and did so closely. So it interested me more when
once, as we were walking down Beak Street, he said, "Have I shown
you this yet?" and shot down a narrow alleyway barely wide enough
for a man to lie down. It had the unsuitable name of Kingly Street.

"It's here," he said, and crossed to the other side. "No, here, yes, this is it, where one night, very late in the hour, Joseph Conrad, believing himself to be pursued by a Russian spy, took out his pocket-knife and hid, waiting. As soon as his pursuer appeared, Conrad sneaked up behind him and slit his throat."

The story was so far-fetched that it did not deserve any attention, but what I remember most was the strange excitement that came over Hosam then.

"It was probably why," he went on to say, "soon after this, Conrad, despite all the friends he had in London and his burning literary ambition, moved to the country, where he could look out of his window and be able to see from afar if an enemy were approaching."

A key turned in the door of the hotel room, and Mustafa walked in carrying cups of coffee and egg sandwiches. We ate standing, then drank the coffee and smoked a cigarette at the window. We tried on the balaclavas in front of the mirror. Even I would not be able to tell that this was me. I tucked the mask in the back pocket of my jeans, leaving half of it dangling out. Mustafa did the same. That was how we stepped out.

We crossed Shaftesbury Avenue without waiting for the lights to turn. Drivers blew their horns and we laughed. We greeted complete strangers: "Good morning to you, sir. And good morning to you, madam." We did not care that most of them ignored us. We were about to embark on something important. The April sky, blue and unblemished and brilliant, attested to this. I was grateful for Mustafa and grateful to him for having convinced me to come. I looked at him walking beside me and saw a man who knew what he wanted. And I so much wanted to be a man who knew what he wanted.

I thought of telling him the dream I had had last night. Mustafa had a thing for dreams and liked to try to interpret them. "When I'm old and everything is done," he once told me in Edinburgh, "I want to speak only about three things: ideas, food, and dreams."

With every step the world made way, opening the path in front of us, and yet the street—the lampposts and cars and buses and shop-fronts, the faces of passersby, the beauty of some of the women and the finality of some of the men—made the day seem to retain a reluctant warning: that all the days from here on will be contingent on this one, that this, more than any other day, was the beginning of the future. And so, beside an implicit sense of foreboding, I felt a raw hope too, a violent optimism that anything was possible. It excited and frightened me.

Tonight, as I walk through the same Soho streets, I wish something had tripped me. I continue to believe that if only I had interrupted our momentum, stopped at a café or paused at a street corner, closed my eyes at the sun or told Mustafa my dream, relayed it to him in all its detail, we might have been spared what was to come.

I wander into Chinatown. This was where Mustafa and I found ourselves that morning.

"After the demo," he said, looking at the activity all around us, "let's come here."

"But our bus leaves at three," I reminded him.

"Fuck that," he said. "Let's stay another night, celebrate."

"Great idea," I said, and we both let out a laugh, a short and cautious laugh. "I have never had Chinese food," I said.

"Neither have I," he said.

"Well, that's dinner sorted, then," I said. "And let's not stay long at the demonstration."

"No, no. A couple of minutes, do our duty and get the hell out of there."

"Exactly," I said, and we both laughed again, but this time with deliberateness, to drown out whatever it was that our earlier laugh had revealed.

Suddenly we were in Leicester Square. All these places we had heard of. We stopped and looked about us, excited by the lights, the rising activity, a waking monster stretching its limbs. But we were late and had to keep moving. We talked quickly about our plans for the afternoon, the evening, the night, the next day, and did so with a note of daring in our voices. We asked for directions to St. James's Square, but after a few turns we were still not there. The next time we asked we were told that it was in the opposite direction. I became hopeful. Maybe we would never find it, or would get there after the fact. I imagined us years later recounting how we had had the right intentions but, because of our poor knowledge of the city, had lost our way. And I imagined myself describing our younger selves as brave and saying the words "Innocence has a perilous heart," and there and then I decided, no, better say "naivety": "Naivety has a perilous heart." But now we were back at Haymarket, by the same spot where the bus had dropped us off the night before. We turned into Charles II Street and crossed Regent Street Saint James's. From there we could see the tall trees in the middle of St. James's Square. Tonight, as I enter the square from the same direction, the same treetops are trembling against the dark sky. But on that day they appeared perfectly still, eerily so, as though their branches had never moved nor were made for moving. We could hear the chants echoing against the stone buildings. Mustafa stopped, faced me, and, like a pair of anxious robbers, we donned our balaclavas.

16

THE DEMONSTRATION WAS LARGER than I had anticipated. It appeared as solid and insurmountable as a brick wall.

"See, didn't I tell you?" Mustafa said with a quiver in his voice, referring to the fact that everyone taking part was masked.

Several journalists were already present, with television cameras assembled and pointed at the crowd. Why are they here, I wondered? After all, Libya is a small country. Who cares about a bunch of students demonstrating in front of its London embassy?

Mustafa grabbed hold of my arm and pulled me along. I remember thinking, he needs to calm down, I must tell him to calm down. One of the masked protesters began walking toward us. There was something confrontational about the way he moved, as if expecting a fight.

"It's excellent, brothers," he shouted above the noise, "that you are here."

"It's our duty," Mustafa replied, thickening his Benghazi accent.

But the man remained there, his eyes on me now.

"Yes," I said. "Our duty."

He shook our hands with great force and led us to a stack of placards on the pavement. We selected our slogans and pushed our way into the crowd. There was little resistance, and we soon found ourselves standing against the barriers. Strange, I thought, that we both should feel the need to prove our commitment, given that no one could tell who we were and therefore no one could blame us for turning up late or accuse us of half-heartedness. Our names were protected. Yet I do not think I have ever before or since felt such solidarity. The distinctions between those of us in the crowd fell away. I remember wanting to live more like this.

A few police officers mingled in the wide gap between us and the embassy building. One of them was a woman. I remember being surprised by how young she looked. Nearly as young as we are, I thought.

We chanted our slogans in Arabic, fragmented and at such a low volume that, I imagined, our English witnesses might think we were engaged in some collective lament.

I looked about me and Mustafa was not there. He had drifted three or four rows back, gazing up at the surrounding buildings. I called to him and I heard the panic in my voice. He swam through the thick grove of figures and came right behind me. For a moment I was not sure it was actually him. Whether to anchor himself or to reassure me, he placed his hand on my shoulder. We should leave, I thought, and thought it for the first time on his behalf. His hand moved to the middle of my upper back, right in between the shoulder blades. I remembered what he told me of his father's dark moods. How as a boy, crouched in his hiding place, he would listen to his old man searching for him with an urgent breath.

The windows of the embassy were shut and the early spring green treetops in the square and the blueness of the sky reflected inexactly against the uneven glass. Walbrook had explained this to me: that in the old days glass was not set but rolled out in sheets, which resulted in the imperfect surface. Three men stood a couple of steps behind the first-floor window. They looked interchangeable and, dressed in dark colors, their forms appeared like cutouts. They were laughing. But then it was clear that they were not laughing at all but arguing and doing so violently. Several others around me took notice. Someone said, not too loudly, "Fuck them," and that inspired a brief and gloomy confidence. We began to stir, coiling within our own mass. Mustafa took his hand off my back and wrapped it tightly around my arm, just above the elbow, and began to steer me through the restless crowd. When I looked back at him, his eyes were unrecognizable. Bodies pressed against me from all sides. They smelled familiar. Their mothers too, I assumed, had placed small bottles of orange blossom and frankincense in their suitcases. Like me they also disliked the old-fashioned scents and never used them. But, also like me, out of love and longing for their mothers, they had buried the perfumes deep in among their clothes in the wardrobe, where slowly their scent permeated the garments and the air around them.

The three men were now standing immediately behind the windowpane, egging one another on. Whatever it was that they were discussing had turned into a dare. They faced us. One of them tried to open the sash window, but it would not budge. Another had a go and the lower panel came up unwillingly in starts and stood open. They leaned out and shouted but could not be heard. One of them then disappeared and returned carrying something black and bulky. It was only after he had pointed it in our direction that I realized what it was.

"They won't dare," Mustafa said, shaking my arm. Then he shouted at the top of his voice to all those around us, "Hold your places!"

The ridiculousness of that phrase was like a stone falling into my mind. My thoughts rippled and my knees began to tremble. Mustafa shook my arm again and I could not tell whether he wanted us to leave or if he was telling me to go forward.

"Hold your places!" he shouted again, but this time his voice sounded like a stretched wire about to snap.

I wanted to shut myself in. I was a house that had been left wide open. I thought of falling to the floor and, if he would not let go, pulling Mustafa with me, crawling through the forest of legs, not minding the shame in it. I blamed him because he was the only barrier, the only one who would know the face behind the mask. I pulled him close and shouted right into his ear, "I'm done with this shit," but then, before he could respond, I could hear my own voice scream, louder than I ever thought possible, the name of our country, over and over. Mustafa let go of my arm and joined in. The others did too, and, with that collective spirit, which is as mysterious as the motion of a school of fish or a murmuration of starlings, we became a harmonious mass, fervent and perfectly in rhythm.

We divided "Libya" into its three syllables, chanted in rapid staccato. The name was one part black and the other white, one solid and the other air. We added a small and nearly inaudible *a* at the beginning and a further exhaling *ah* at the end. This way the word expired just before it was renewed again: *a-Lee-be-ah, a-Lee-be-ah* . . . The name grew brighter and freer the more we called it. But, even as the chant shook my body, I wondered if, to the assembled police and journalists, what we were saying did not sound like "Libya" at all but rather the English word "alibi." And perhaps we had deliberately merged the two words because at that moment we understood, more vividly than ever before, that each and every one of us lived a life that was in desperate need of validation.

We went on and on, and now Mustafa, mouth wide open and eyes shut, looked even less recognizable. I could not be sure that the man behind the mask was the person I knew, the same one I had walked here with just moments before, making plans for the evening. It is impossible to trust someone whose face you cannot see, even someone you know well, perhaps especially someone you know well. And it must be easier to cause harm this way, that if one wanted to hurt someone, to wound them or end their life, the less one knew about their face, the better. Faces complicate things. Suddenly the balaclavas seemed to expose us to greater danger. We should take them off. We should take them off and run.

It was clear for all to see now that the black object the men in the window had been wrestling with was a machine gun. They lifted it up and screamed at us. The air was crisp and visibility so good that, even though we were kept by the police barriers some sixty feet away from the embassy front door, I could see the bulging veins around the men's necks as they shouted, leaning over the windowsill. But it was no use: there was no way they could match our volume. Two of them began struggling with the gun. The third watched, then grabbed it off them. All I could think now was, no way, not here, not in London, not in front of all these people. I stood captured by my own disbelief, incapable of moving.

The bullets sounded. Even then I thought, surely, they are just trying to scare us, firing into the sky. Except the sound itself—a series of tears like the wind ripping sails—did not seem all that impressive. What did impress me was the sensation. It literally pressed into me and then ran through me with unremitting force, unquestionable, until it reached the very center of my brain and halted there for a moment before turning back and scorching outward, pushing with it everything that I was, everything that I did not even know I was, to the outer limits. I was now empty and standing, my life reduced to a single unbroken line of a swirl locked inside a child's glass marble. And there it rolled out, that marble, rolled out of me, taking everything with it.

17

I MUST HAVE BEEN out for only a few seconds, because when I opened my eyes it was still pandemonium. I lifted myself off the tarmac. The embassy window was now empty. They had gone to reload, I thought. People were running in all directions. Those who remained were on the ground. I saw Mustafa among them, a few feet away. He was clutching his stomach with both hands. A liquid as dark as date syrup seeped through his pale fingers. I could not believe it. What I was seeing was a sleight of hand. I watched him without moving and without being moved. One of the policemen was yelling desperately. Lying beside him in a dark bundle was that young policewoman. Just then I remembered hearing her body hit the ground. The thud it made was a tree felled in a thicket, a child falling out of bed. I looked once more at Mustafa and then, without knowing where to go, I began walking.

A half-forgotten memory emerged, the excitement of being at a loose end in a city: Benghazi, Edinburgh. I had felt it that morning too, when I woke up alone in the hotel, and for a moment wondered if Mustafa had gone to the demonstration without me. And just as quickly it receded far into the horizon, a child who had swum too far out into the depths. My body was cold. A brutal heat burned inside my chest. It was cut open and the pain was rising. Behind me the sky was as clear as before. The trees were unmoving, as though distancing themselves from what had happened. It's just a scratch, I told myself, and kept walking, putting one leg in front of the other, until I reached the small side street that goes north out of the square. Like throwing a blanket on a fire, the cacophony dampened. I thought of Henry— Professor Walbrook—and thought of him for the very first time by his first name, remembering what he had told me in the pub when I asked him about London: "Notwithstanding its swagger, it's a shy city, fashioned by and for interpreters, too fond of distinctions and barriers, where, between one street and the next, the entire world can be remade."

There was a drain in the gutter, the size of a letter, with slim metal grilles running in lines. I sat on the pavement beside it. I let my eyes drift down into the hole and imagined the long and desolate network of tunnels stretching from here throughout the entire city, a secret map, which, when it rains, murmurs its hushed life. It was not a scratch. I saw my blood gather in a black pool. It frightened and embarrassed me, as if I had suddenly peed myself. The wound in my chest was a little above my stomach, to the right. A horror to see how darkly and thickly the blood was drenching my shirt. I was being eaten up from within. I could hardly sit upright. The street was still empty. I tried to look elsewhere, at the building opposite. My eyes settled on a large window on the first floor. The glass had been recently cleaned. Then, just when I thought the room was vacant, I spotted a man inside, leaning against the window frame and looking directly at me. He appeared to have been standing there all along, observing me from behind the glass. And even when our eyes met, he did not move. His face expressed nothing, neither outrage nor sympathy. Then a hand was on my shoulder. His strong knees were all that I could see of the man squatting beside me. They pressed against the dark blue wool of his trousers.

"You all right, son?" he asked.

I began to cry and immediately stopped as the pain in my lungs was unbearable. I fell forward. From behind he placed his arms beneath my armpits and propped me up. I heard him breathe with the effort.

"You all right, son," he said, but this time it was not a question.

"The fire," I whispered, and it was all I could say.

I could see that my blood had soiled his sleeve.

"The ambulances are on their way," the man said, speaking softly beside my left ear. "Any minute now, son."

It was partly because he called me "son" that, for a confused moment, I was made to believe that through the mysterious fellowship of man something of my father had come to me in this man. I came close to crying again.

Others began to fill the side street. Wounded demonstrators lay on the tarmac, their moans wavering like the pleas of the doubtful. Members of the police and plain-clothed people rushed about. The man behind me leaned back and my head rested on his chest. In the window of the quiet building across the way the man was still there, looking down at the scene. I could hear a helicopter overhead. It was very difficult to breathe. What was worse, I felt no desire to do so. Breathing now seemed to require a kind of faith.

"Any time now," the man said again, as though comforting a child. "Shall I pull off the balaclava, lad?"

I shook my head and he did not ask again.

A paramedic appeared and together with the man behind me lifted me on to a stretcher. I could see now that my double, the man who had been propping me up all this time, was a policeman. For a moment, he leaned over, bringing his face right in front of mine. It is a most peculiar face, I thought, the most peculiar that I have ever seen. It had no distinctive features. I could not be sure that I would have been able to identify it if I had bumped into him in the street. Yet it resembled every other face, including my own. This, even though I could see that he bore no resemblance to me. I saw my mother too and my father and Souad in it. I saw Rana, Mustafa, Professor Walbrook, and, although I was yet to meet him, I was certain that Hosam

Zowa was somewhere in it also. I saw the man who sold newspapers and sweets outside my old school in Benghazi. I saw my childhood friends. And then I saw other faces I did not know. Some of them ugly and grotesque. And then it came, the one face that dominated my childhood, the face of the Leader, the face that demanded to be all the faces.

"Can I take this off now?" the policeman said, meaning the balaclava.

I shook my head again and whispered, "Please, no."

I could still hear the blades of the helicopter. I still retained a hope that I would pass undetected, be able to finish my degree and return home. No one would ever know. People would speak about this day and I would pretend I knew almost nothing about it. "Really? But how could you have missed it? It was all over the news," they would say and I would tell them that I was too busy studying, that doing a degree in a language that is not your own is bloody hard, especially literature, where, naturally, the chief focus of the subject is language and each language is its own river, with its own source and ecology and tides. I would tell them all this and repeat that it really is bloody hard work, because you have to find the spirit of another culture inside you and to do that a part of you has to die.

They placed me inside the ambulance and the policeman climbed in. "Your name, son?" he asked. "And your next of kin here in the UK?"

"Don't have one," I said, and then gave him the first name that came to mind: "Rana Lamesse. Architecture student. University of Edinburgh."

"Lamesse, how is that spelled?" he said, and then almost immediately added, "Never mind."

The paramedic, without asking, pulled off my balaclava. The policeman looked at him and then looked at me. His eyes remained on my face for a couple of seconds before he stepped off the ambulance. Before the doors were shut, I heard him say, "Good luck, son."

It was only once we had set off and the siren began blaring that I noticed I was not alone. There was another person lying on a stretcher beside me. He appeared to be talking to himself. He sounded far away and then so unbearably close and loud. I went up on my elbows and saw that it was Mustafa. Did they know that we had come together? How would they have known that?

"You have to keep still," the paramedic shouted irritably.

"I know him," I whispered.

"You must not speak. You have been shot in the chest," he announced right above my head.

He too was young and probably frightened, but his loud and agitated voice unhinged Mustafa, who began to scream a variety of disconnected insults in Arabic: "Bare-faced fuckers, thugs, hoodlums . . ." When he stopped to catch his breath, his voice broke and he cried and spoke softly as if talking to himself, saying, "Show me your face, my mother, come find me, I kiss your feet."

Tears veiled my eyes. I realized then that behind all the things that I had been thinking and feeling, not only since the shooting but since the day I was born, was the ready name of my mother. I saw the outline of her hand again, her cheek, the delicate and strong conclusion of her neck, where the collarbone comes in. I swore I could smell her perfume. She was there in the ambulance beside me. I looked about and the paramedic fixed my shoulders down. "Please, sir," he repeated. The pain spread from inside my chest to every part of my body. It established its terrible authority until it was both behind and ahead of me, rising in both directions, as I tried to catch my breath in between the waves.

We arrived and I was pushed, headfirst and at great speed, down a series of long corridors. Countless figures lined the sides and they peered down at me with relentless eyes. Then I was alone, at a dead end. A man appeared. He looked too young to be a doctor. All I had on was an open jacket, a loose shirt, and a T-shirt beneath it, but he struggled to undo my clothes. He returned with a large pair of scissors with a bright yellow handle and, with pale and trembling hands, began to cut through the fabric, all the while repeating the word "Sorry" as he progressed slowly upward. The hard coldness of the steel occasionally touched my skin, but otherwise he did a good job. When our eyes met, he looked frightened. I watched his face as he took in my wounds. I will never forget what took place next. Out of everything that happened that day this is the one detail I cannot bear thinking about. Bent over me, his shaking hand holding the X of the open scissors above my chest, the young doctor turned his head in the opposite direction and began to yell at the top of his voice, "Here." He called that word over and over again.

18

I HAVE NOT IN all the years since the shooting returned to St. James's Square. You can live a lifetime in a city avoiding places. I have attended none of the annual commemorations. On the odd occasion that I am in a cab and there is a possibility that the driver might choose to cut through here, I ask them to avoid it. But tonight, thirty-two years later, and as Hosam's train is now probably in the tunnel beneath the sea, I find myself here willingly. Here are the same trees, taller still. And here is the spot where I stood, the place where I was cut down. Strange that I cannot remember what the placard I had selected from the pile had read. FREE THE STUDENTS, DOWN WITH THE TYRANT, FREEDOM OR DEATH: those, I remember, were some of the options on offer. A vast distance exists between a protester and his slogan; the entire history of politics exists in that gap. Soon after we had pushed our way to the front, I put mine down against the crowd-control barrier and left it there, feeling no need to explain myself. Mustafa then did the same. That detail strikes me today. I believe if I had told him then that I was leaving he would have followed me, turned the corner; we would have pulled off our balaclavas and agreed that we had done our bit.

When I woke up from the operation, I could not feel my limbs. I had no idea where I was or how I had got there. I slowly remembered one Libyan government official screaming into my ear, "You think you're a man? Then let me see you take off that mask." I became convinced that the windowless room where I was, austere and humming with mechanical sounds, was deep inside a prison in Tripoli. I had passed out under interrogation, which gave them no option but to stop and wait till I recovered. I believed I was guilty, but could not remember of what, and this horrified me, because I wanted so much to be able to confess. They will be back, I thought, and was as sure of this as of the most elemental principles of life. But what was that life now; where did it go? It certainly did not belong to me. As soon as I am well enough to stand up again, I reminded myself, the questions will resume. I thought and thought and thought, digging in the desert for water, for something to give them, a drop of evidence that might then turn into a trickle. And it was this that returned to me the image of my own blood trickling down the drain. I began to emerge, a lone bubble rising to the surface from a shipwreck.

A doctor walked in and said, "Hello, Fred. I'm glad you are up. How are you feeling?" He told me that I had been struck by two bullets. "A narrow distance from the heart. You are a very lucky young man, Fred," he said.

I wanted to tell him that my name was not Fred and therefore everything he had just told me must have been intended for another man. But I could not speak. It was not so much what he said but the way he smiled that caused tears to pool in my eyes.

Beside him now stood a nurse. She was beautiful, so very beautiful that it seemed a made-up fact, an actress brought in to play the part. When the doctor left, she remained there a moment longer. There was a question I wanted to ask her. It was very important, but I could not locate it. It came to me only when she left. It concerned our ideas about bullets, that in films they are often portrayed as gifts, badges of honor. The hero or villain receives a shot and time stops. We watch him clutch the wound, twist on the ground or fall dramatically from a great height through a window, off a balcony or a bridge and down into a passing river. His entire life had been lived toward this climax, this concluding splash. And then things move on, don't they, I wanted to tell the beautiful nurse, life continues, doesn't it, very much the same as it was before. The tears emerged again and this time ran down. I wanted to ask the nurse what had happened to the young policewoman, the one who lay on her side on the tarmac as if stolen from her sleep.

19

I WAS NOW FRED. We were all given fictitious names and told to go only by them, that we ought never to reveal our true identities and that this was for our own safety. To help us remember, the police chose short, monosyllabic names.

The nurse's real surname was Clement. Her first name was Rachel. As the days passed and my mind regained its balance, she became less striking and yet more attractive for it. Her cheeks, lips, and ears turned a deeper pink whenever she was tired or rushed off her feet. When she smiled, most of the action took place in her eyes. At certain times, thinking me asleep, she would gently tuck in my bedsheet like a skilled cook filleting a fish.

I was the last to be moved to the ward designated for our recuperation. The moment I appeared, Mustafa and the other patients clapped, but the applause started weakly and soon after faded away. A policeman always sat guard inside the door, sometimes reading a newspaper, at other times staring down the long room or looking up at the windows that ran in a row above our heads. When his shift ended and his colleague would come to replace him, the two would exchange a few sentences in whispers.

Mine was the bed closest to where the policemen sat, at the start of the ward, and neighboring me on the other side was Mustafa, except now he was Tom.

My few belongings were wrapped in a transparent plastic bag and left on the nightstand. It contained my wallet, the small pocket radio Father had given me, and a copy of the *London Review of Books*, which I had optimistically purchased on our circuitous route to St. James's Square the morning of the demonstration. Only one corner of my brown leather wallet was stained. Strangely, apart from a few brutal wrinkles, the pages of the *LRB* had come through unscathed. And the radio that had come with me all the way from home worked perfectly; the battery light came on strong and constant.

"I made sure they put you here beside me," Mustafa said in Arabic.

One of the nurses approached and, smiling, told me, "Your friend here wouldn't stop inquiring about you. Sometimes every hour. Nearly drove us mad."

"It's been eleven long days," Mustafa told her, as though disappointed in the hospital's performance. When he saw my face, he said, "Didn't you know?"

And the truth was that I didn't; I had no idea it had been that long. I had assumed I was kept in intensive care for four or maybe five days at most.

Neither of us knew the other six Libyans in the ward. They did not seem familiar with one another either. There was a wariness among us to start with.

Mustafa and I exchanged notes on our injuries. He received a bullet in the stomach and it passed straight through him with little damage. He looked remarkably well and was in high spirits. I wondered if he had anticipated something like this all along, and, now that it had come and gone, he was relieved and a little optimistic that God or destiny or fate or whatever it is that decides such things had spared him. His whole manner was animated by that acidic vigor some people feel at having survived a calamity. The distance between how he was now and the last time I had seen him in the ambulance was vast and it disturbed me.

"You were going crazy in the ambulance," I told him.

"How do you know?" he said, and looked at me with genuine confusion in his eyes.

I told him I was there. He said that was not important now. He wanted instead to tell me about all that he had found out.

"After the shooting, there was a siege inside the embassy. It lasted ten days. Can you believe it? And then, under diplomatic immunity, Thatcher allowed everyone, including the bastards who shot us, to leave the country."

"I suppose that makes sense," I said, having no energy for indignation. I took note of the amused looks of the nurses as they saw us chatting.

"Diplomatic immunity my arse," he whispered. "Iron Lady my dick." He moved to sit on the edge of my bed. "Twelve people were shot." And before I could say anything he said, "Yes! You have to know the facts before you can speak. Eleven Libyans, all students, but none—not one, can you believe it?—died. Proof God was watching over us. You and I had it worst; the rest all got light wounds: a scrape or bullet in the leg or arm—nothing serious. Some were released on the same day. Your injuries, my friend, were the most critical."

"Who was the twelfth?" I asked. "You said twelve people were shot."

"Has no one told you?" he asked excitedly. "Yvonne Fletcher was her name, a policewoman, only twenty-five years old. It's God's will," he said, placing a hand on the mattress beside me. "God have mercy on her. Fallen in our battle. Completely innocent."

"What are you saying?" I asked.

"She died a few hours later. A martyr to our cause."

After a brief silence he said, "That easily could have been you or me."

The words "fallen," "battle," "innocent," "martyr," "fate," "you," "me" all tumbled over one another.

I had my own words, blades packed in the mouth, capable of cutting my tongue wide open. I feared speaking them and feared not speaking them, and I knew that, like all things of consequence, they could not be postponed or stored away for later use. If I missed my opportunity now, I thought, I would have to carry those words unspoken forever. Sounds in the dark.

Here Mustafa surrendered a little. There was a new softness in his eyes. Perhaps he was thinking about Edinburgh and could see that I was too. Those in our scholarship group, particularly the Wires, must have put two and two together. I imagined them speaking about it late into the night, hotly speculating, enlivened by a mixture of fury and fascination, perhaps privately relieved, in the way those who fear running out of things to say at social gatherings are when driving slowly past a car crash, that they had personally known two of the injured. They would be happy to supply details that, in retrospect, predicted the event: our keenness on reading, that we were on the side of books, were always seen walking around with them, clutching them under an arm, that even on weekends we were seen in cafés reading and would never go out at night without a slim volume dug deep, like a weapon, in a jacket pocket. They would say we were fearful of reality. And, as everyone knows, too much reading can disturb the balance of a healthy mind, lead it astray, and so on. I imagined Saad: although he would feel obliged to participate in such condemnatory discussions, he would keep his contributions to a minimum. I was certain he did not let on that Mustafa had asked him for a hotel recommendation, as that would have cast suspicion on him too.

"It's been in the news every day," Mustafa said. "New details emerging all the time. The moment we were shot, Qaddafi ordered troops to surround the British Embassy, threatened to hold British citizens in Libya hostage if all the embassy staff here weren't allowed to leave the country unquestioned. The Thatcher government buckled. I have been stewing ever since, thinking exactly what you are thinking now, that as soon as we are up on our feet, we'll be sent home."

Mustafa's ability to read my mind seemed as uncanny as it did inevitable. I must draw a distinction between us, I told myself, make it harder for him to read me.

"But, don't worry, no one will touch us. Two representatives from Amnesty International, a man and a woman, came by and I inquired on your behalf too. They told me that we both have a solid case for political asylum. Almost guaranteed, they said."

I closed my eyes.

"You get some rest," he said, and returned to his bed.

20

MY PARENTS WOULD HAVE definitely heard the news, watched it on television. Did they spot me by my clothes? They would be frantic with worry. I had, up to then, written them a postcard every week. "We made a rule," my mother had written in one of her letters, "that no one could read them unless the three of us were sitting bunched together. This way no one could claim to have been the first or the last." My mother has an intuitive heart. One day I fell down the stairs at school and cut my lower lip. There was a lot of blood and I fainted. When I came to, she was there. No one had called her. This ability came at a cost. It meant she was almost constantly worried. I heard Uncle Osama, her younger brother, tell her once, "You must loosen the strings a little," and her replying, "I can't," and saying it with such finality but also a hint of regret. She could, for no reason other than her instinct or sixth sense, make the expensive call to the university, demanding that I call her back.

I asked Nurse Clement for some paper and envelopes. I tried to start a letter home. Every time my mind went blank. A little while later, Nurse Clement returned.

"Better hurry or you'll miss the post," she said.

The letter would carry a London postmark. How to explain that? I switched to writing a brief note to Rana:

Dear Rana,

I'm at Westminster Hospital in London, but I'm fine. Will need to be here a little longer. Not sure how long. Maybe another week or two or three. Please tell no one. Except maybe Prof. Walbrook, but only if he asks. And if he does and you do, please make sure he knows not to tell anyone else.

I miss you

Khaled

I sealed the envelope and tried not to breathe. I saw my stitches, woven in Xs, running in an uninterrupted wavering line from just below the right nipple, all the way around the side, and stopping a few inches before the spine. I could feel them drawing tighter, like a creaking hemp rope stretched to the limit. I tried to breathe as shallowly as I could and waited. When it passed, that other, less fathomable pain resumed its dominance: a cold fog ballooning inside the lung. Today a lesser version of it returns if I'm not dressed properly in chilly weather. Nurse Clement was busy at the other end of the room. I had another go.

Dearest Mother, Father, and Souad,

London is beautiful. The sky is now cloudy, but a little while ago it was as blue as home. I came with a friend. A short holiday. Maybe a day or two more. We visited the museums and tonight will eat in Chinatown.

Wish you were here.

With all my love,

Khaled

I rewrote it, taking out the line "Wish you were here" in case it expressed too much need.

As soon as the letters were posted, I regretted writing them. It was late afternoon, and the obscured light came softly through the large window above my head. The policeman sat a few feet away from me and behind him were the closed doors of the ward. What lay on the other side, I wondered? Who knew that we were here? A list of our real names must have been drawn up. It must exist somewhere. Who had access to it? Do the Libyan authorities know I'm here?

I turned on the radio, placing the speaker against my ear. Go back to the present, focus on the broadcaster's voice, stay there, collect all that you are and anchor it there. But everything she said slipped away. Until I heard her say a name: "Hosam Zowa."

"Our late colleague," she went on, "Mohammed Mustafa Ramadan, was an early admirer. Mr. Zowa's much anticipated first book is published today. To mark the occasion, we thought to replay to you a rare recording from the BBC archive. Mohammed Mustafa Ramadan reading Mr. Zowa's work not on this program but, believe it or not, in place of the news. It caused quite a stir. Such a thing had never happened before or since: a literary work read in place of the news. It was recorded live just over four years ago. A month later, our beloved colleague was brutally assassinated. Although it was never proved, it's believed that he was killed on the orders of the Libyan government, which is currently under the spotlight owing to the extraordinary events that occurred a couple of weeks ago in London, where a gunman fired from within the Libyan Embassy, wounding eleven demonstrators and WPC Yvonne Fletcher, the twenty-five-year-old policewoman who sustained lethal injuries and later died in hospital. The title of the story, which is now the name of the collection, is 'The Given and the Taken.'"

Even though I knew that Mustafa had missed it the first time around and had always regretted the fact, I pressed the radio more tightly against my ear so no sound could escape. Mohammed Mustafa Ramadan's voice sounded different, younger than I remembered it. I listened as the protagonist was again slowly devoured by the cat. When the presenter returned, her voice seemed moved and disturbed by the story.

"And now," she said, "we can speak to the author himself."

I waved to Mustafa and he came and sat beside me, on the edge of the bed. I turned the radio up and held it in the air between us.

"Mr. Zowa," the presenter said, her voice brightening.

"Zowa? Hosam Zowa?" Mustafa said, and the excitement in his voice made me regret not having called him over earlier.

"How are you, sir?" the presenter said.

There was a little lag before we heard him speak.

"Yes," he said, in a tone that was distant, as if he had been interrupted mid-thought.

The reporter was taken aback. She, having just complimented his work, had obviously expected more than just that one word, or at least expected it to be spoken with a little warmth.

"We have been greatly anticipating your book, ever since our friend and colleague, your compatriot, the late Mohammed Mustafa Ramadan, had introduced us to it. And now your book is published at a pertinent moment, soon after the violent events of St. James's Square, where eleven people were injured and a policewoman lost her life. We are very eager to hear from you about this horrific incident. You do live in London, don't you, Mr. Zowa?"

"Yes," he said again, but this time it was barely audible. Was he talking to someone else?

"And I believe you and Mohammed knew one another. Weren't you friends?"

We waited. He is about to start, I was certain, with a remembrance of his friend, the man who was the voice of our youth. He would refer to his brutal murder at the hands of the Qaddafi regime, and then say something about the peaceful demonstration and the indiscriminate shooting that took place "under the world's eye," as one reporter put it, by order of that same regime. He would then mention Yvonne Fletcher. Her police photograph had appeared in several newspapers, printed in color: she is more laughing than smiling, eyes shy and lively, a face expecting nothing bad to happen. She was by now most probably buried somewhere in this country, near where her parents live, I imagined. I wanted him to collect all our grief, from the beginning of the dictatorship in 1969 to the present, and hold it there for the world to see. I wanted the silence to be broken, the silence that surrounded not only the deaths and imprisonments and disappearances but also the minor acts of cruelty and humiliation, perceptible, from as far back as I could remember, in everything and everyone around me— the architecture, the very tarmac, a loaf of bread, the voices of the singers and the poets—particularly the poets. I never did know how to be released from it and wanted this writer to do it for me. What none of us could have expected then, in April 1984, as I lay on my back in a guarded ward in Westminster Hospital, holding up the radio, waiting for Hosam Zowa to speak, with Mustafa sitting beside me, leaning so close that I could smell him, that anxious scent that had overtaken our bodies during those days, as though we were already old men, was that the fifteen-year reign of the dictator on whose orders Mohammed Mustafa Ramadan was killed and we were shot would stretch out for another twenty-seven years and end only in 2011, in a drama in which the man sitting beside me and the silent one on the radio would both play crucial parts.

"Hello?" the BBC presenter said. "Mr. Zowa, are you there?"

And that was how the interview ended. The reason given was "A technical fault."

"Coward," Mustafa said, in a venomous and unequivocal tone.

"A sudden reluctance, is all," I said, but it was not what I thought. I did not know what I thought. All I knew was that I hated that word "coward" and hated Mustafa for using it.

"What a chance he had," he said. "We are lying here like corpses and he has a microphone to the world."

"The point is," I said, "the book is out."

21

I WROTE DOWN THE book's title and the author's name in Arabic and asked Nurse Clement if she could get it for me from the Lebanese bookshop on Westbourne Grove. "But only if you happen to be in the area," I told her.

"That's near where I go swimming," she said. "I'll get it over the weekend."

I gave her the money for it. I then asked if she had ever had Chinese food. She said she had.

"What is it like?" I asked.

"It's all right," she said. "Why do you ask?"

"Just curious. Never had it before. What are your favorite dishes?"

"Well, let's see," she said. "Sweet-and-sour chicken. I also like that crispy seaweed thing they do." She smiled with her eyes again. "Soon you'll get to try it for yourself."

I asked her about my old clothes. She went and spoke to the policeman guarding the door that day and he came over and stood tall beside my bed. He informed me that our clothes were with forensics and that each item would be returned to us in due course.

"Please tell them to throw mine away," I said.

"I can't do that, sir," he said.

The following Monday, Nurse Clement turned up with two copies of *The Given and the Taken*.

"This way," she said, handing them to me, "you and Tom can read at the same time."

Mustafa blew her a kiss and said, "You are not only the best nurse on the planet but the most generous too."

The cover had a black-and-white photograph of an interior. And only after a few seconds did I notice that the shadow moving out of the frame was that of a cat. Mustafa read out loud to me while I followed. The deeper we got into the book, the less commentary he offered. And when my lungs got stronger, I began to contribute to these readings.

I had a go at translating the title story for Nurse Clement. The following day she said she had read it on the tube and it disturbed her.

"Reads well, though," she then said. "You should do more."

I tried and, as I did, the sentences began to resemble little rooms or nooks carved into the white surface of the page. Good places in which to vanish. Time passed quickly, and there were moments, fleeting but sweet, when I forgot where I was. I thought, when I return to my life—for I still had that hope then—I will have a go at translating the entire book.

Another Friday came and I wrote to my parents again. I was going to mention the book but did not. I told them I had returned to London for the weekend. "Made a good friend. His name is Fred. A student at the university. His parents live in London. His mother took us out for Chinese food again. This time I had sweet-and-sour chicken and a plate of crispy seaweed. Both strange and delicious. I spent the whole dinner telling them about you and describing our beautiful house and our sea. Fred said he can't wait to visit. Tomorrow we'll go to the theater."

I imagined my parents' replies gathering up at my bedsit in Edinburgh. I imagined their contents. What if something had happened to them: my father arrested simply for being my father, or my sister falling and breaking a tooth, Mother slipping in the shower? My brief and happy letters from London would then seem careless and unfeeling. But I also knew I could not tell them what had happened. It was too dangerous for all of us.

I tried very hard not to think about them and spent most of my time reading and rereading *The Given and the Taken*. All its twelve stories, in one way or another, concerned characters who were unmoored and who, like the man eaten by the cat, were at once innocent and implicated in their fate. Today I am less drawn to such writing. It seems too driven by allegory, too keen on a philosophical generality. These days all I want is to be with what is specific. I sensed this even back then, but Hosam's voice pierced through me with fierce tenderness. It had a natural and unforced independence. It was never on the side of power. And so, although I did not completely trust its logic, I trusted its temperament.

In my next letter to my parents and sister, I told them about *The Given and the Taken*. "It's beside me as I write," I reported, and described some of the other stories in the book. I told them of my new interest in translation. It felt good to write something true. I then returned to my pretending: I was back in London, I said, spending another weekend at Fred's house. I listed made-up impressions of the city. I remember telling them about the River Thames, which I had yet to see, describing it inaccurately as being small enough to swim across.

Rana's reply arrived four days after I had posted my letter. I hid it in Hosam's book until I could find a quiet moment. Very early the following morning, the sun poured in and the white ward hummed with the light of the new day. Mustafa and the others were still asleep. I quietly tore open the envelope. How I loved the gentle curls and motion of Rana's handwriting. It hinted at the carefree and uncompromised pace of one not fearing interruption, confident that she would be able to state her case.

My dear Khaled,

You really do know how to worry a girl. I saw you on the evening news and the room spun around me. There you were at the edge of the frame, moving like a sleepwalker. I called every hospital in London. None would confirm. You Libyans! At least we keep it at home, while you go about shooting one another in foreign cities. But, seriously, one minute you tell me, Rana, let's cure ourselves of our countries ("cure": that was the word you used), then the next thing I know you are laying your life on the line for yours. Is that what you thought you were doing? When do you leave hospital? I'll pick you up. My parents keep a flat in Notting Hill Gate. It's always empty. This way you can focus on getting well. You are crazy and can't be trusted with your life, but I'm grateful, Khaled, so very grateful. Write soon and accept the invitation or else I will turn up with the most garish bunch of flowers and embarrass you.

Rana

P.S. Maybe best not to come here. "The Libyan Students of Edinburgh" issued a statement denouncing the demonstrators as "traitors."

22

THE FOLLOWING WEEK, VISITS were allowed. One of the first to come was a middle-aged Libyan whom no one among us recognized. We were told by the police that he had clearance. None of us knew what that meant exactly. He wore an elegant suit and tie. His gray hair was combed back and his black mustache was neatly trimmed. His cheeks shone with aftershave, and a faint smell of lilies followed him around the room. He kept his sunglasses on. They were yellow-tinted and made his eyes seem sadder than perhaps they were. He was accompanied by an aide who remained a couple of steps behind and never uttered a word. His boss went from bed to bed, speaking in soft tones. When he reached Mustafa and me, he stood between our beds and introduced himself. The name was vaguely familiar.

"I hear your injuries were particularly severe," he said.

I told him in detail what had happened and, as I did so, I realized I was describing the events out loud for the first time. He listened and, when I finished, he kept his eyes on me.

"You remind me of someone," he said.

He was now standing so close that if I were to whisper my real name no one else would hear it except him; him and maybe Mustafa, who had his eyes on me, and perhaps also the aide, who stood waiting at the foot of my bed. I opened my mouth but nothing came out. The man sat gently on the edge of my bed. I felt no hesitation now, no hesitation whatsoever. I spoke my full name.

"You are the headmaster's son," he whispered, and, although it was not a question, I nodded. "How lucky you are," he said, "and how lucky he is."

Mustafa stood up suddenly. The man's aide was about to intervene when the man waved him away.

"How do you know his father?" Mustafa whispered, suspicion clearly audible in his voice, then his eyes settled on the shoulder of the man's handsome jacket.

"I knew your dad," the man said to me, "at university. We haven't seen each other for years, but I remember his excellent manners and excellent mind. A talented historian. Would you please," he said, and lowered his voice even more, "but only when you are face-to-face, which you will be soon, God willing, tell him I say hello and be sure to remind him of my fond admiration, which now extends to his brave son." Then he asked us both, "Is there anything you need?"

"Is there anything we need?" Mustafa repeated sarcastically. "Well, let's see, I would like my life back."

There was a short silence before the man bid us farewell, and many times since I have thought back on the strange expression that came over his face then. He looked defiant and yet strangely uncertain. Oddly, particularly given the fact that I was the wounded one, I felt worried for him.

He had a word with the nurses, and then, on his way out, he stopped and said, "Young man, it was good to meet you. It all makes sense now," meaning, I supposed, why I had seemed familiar to him. Several of the others took note of the friendly exchange, and, from then on, they, including Mustafa, would refer to our visitor as Fred's friend.

"Nice suit," Mustafa said. "Definitely Italian."

And that was all he would say about him until, a few days later, packages arrived, wrapped in white tissue paper, which brought to mind shrouds. They were delivered by the man's aide, who, again without speaking a word, placed a package at the foot of each bed with great care and left.

A pair of jeans, trainers, some T-shirts, boxer shorts, socks, and a jacket, together with one thousand pounds in ten-pound notes, for each of the wounded. How did I feel? Grateful and ashamed. Receiving charity is like having the air sucked out of you.

"Wonder what your friend will ask in return?" Mustafa said.

23

ABOUT A MONTH HAD passed now since the shooting, and, although the doctors said I was making a good recovery, they wanted to keep me a few more days to monitor my right lung, which had lost 20 percent of its mass owing to the damage caused by the bullets. I waited. I read the news every day. Now the papers were almost entirely clean of the story of the shooting. The author Hosam Zowa had vanished too. He gave no more interviews and no photographs of him appeared anywhere. Speculation over his identity took the place of any proper discussion of his work. The others in the ward, with little interest in books and only a vague curiosity about *The Given and the Taken*, were fascinated by its author and began to collect gossip about him. They called friends or asked them in person when they visited, and gradually, like weeds strangling a jasmine, tall tales encircled the topic. I tried to volunteer some of the information my father had uncovered about the Zowa family, but it seemed, even to Mustafa, too tangential and uninteresting compared to the rumors.

One declared that the author was a political prisoner who had written his entire book on cigarette paper, managing to fit only one or two sentences on each leaf. This, according to Mustafa, was not impossible. "Hadn't that Egyptian novelist Sonallah Ibrahim done the same? It would certainly explain the gaunt prose," he said, "which isn't natural to us Arabs. For, let's face it, we have many faults, but misery isn't one of them."

Another story claimed that the author of what some now were calling the most important work of Arabic fiction since Tayeb Salih's *Season of Migration to the North* was a Libyan Catholic convert living in a monastery in a suburb of Lisbon.

"This is so unlikely," Mustafa admitted, "that it may just be true. It would also make sense of that story in which an agnostic becomes obsessed with a medieval painting of the Virgin and Child."

That story, titled "The Heretic," ends with the man tearing open the painting to enter it, and the words "I'm here."

Another piece of gossip claimed that Hosam Zowa was the nom de plume of a housewife from Derna, deep in the Green Mountain, that fertile upland region in the northeast of the country where my mother's family are from and, as Father had informed us, the Zowas too.

"That would make sense of the vivid renditions of that landscape in some of the stories, the description of the mountains and vegetation, the way the sea reaches in between the rocks," I told Mustafa.

And, finally, there was the accurate account, which, as it happened, attracted the least interest, that the author was the son of Sidi Rajab Zowa, once adviser to King Idris and confidant to His Royal Majesty's heir, Prince Hassan.

A couple of days later, Mustafa came to me gripped with excitement.

"Just got news," he said. "The author's father went on television, denounced his son, and praised Qaddafi."

"You mean, a rumor," I said.

"No, news. It's almost definite," he said.

The genius of rumors is that they can coexist with the truth, so that it became possible, during those days as I lay captured inside my fate and inside the book, to think of Hosam Zowa as a political prisoner, a recluse Catholic convert, a woman writing in secret, and the exiled son of one of the most prominent families whose father had just come out in support of the dictatorship. A vague and abstract aspect of this conflated portrait remained with me for eleven years, until Hosam and I came face-to-face, and even then a shadow of uncertainty lingered for a while between us.

24

AFTER SIX WEEKS IN hospital, it was finally decided that Mustafa and I were fit enough to be discharged. Suddenly the question of what to do next became inescapable. We discussed yet again the possibility of returning to Edinburgh and came to the same conclusion. He had a maternal uncle in Manchester.

"I told him I'm bringing a friend," he said.

"Thanks, but I'm going to stay here. Rana offered me her family's place."

"They live in London?"

"No; they just have a place here."

"You'll be there alone, then?"

"Yes," I said. "I think so."

He waited till the afternoon before putting the question: "Do you think your friend would mind if I stayed with you?"

"I'd rather not ask," I said.

I wanted to be alone, to live unwitnessed and without having to think about anyone else.

The following day Rana was waiting outside. I pretended to still be packing so as to let Mustafa go ahead of me. He carefully wrote down his uncle's address and telephone number on a piece of paper.

"Don't lose it."

"As soon as I settle in, I'll ring," I said.

We embraced in the gap between our beds.

"I'll wait for you to call me," he said.

He then said goodbye to those still convalescing. He had become popular with them during this time. They all, apart from me, had by now revealed their real names to one another. They exchanged numbers and promises to remain in touch. Mustafa shook hands with the nurses and then returned to me.

"I'll wait for you to call," he said again.

He left, turning one last time to look at me.

A few minutes later, confident that he was gone, I began to feel nervous. I was now without my friend and in a city where I knew no one and where I had been shot. I thought of following him to Manchester. Then I saw our life there with his uncle and aunt, being obliged to meet their guests and each time retell the story of what happened. News that I was among the wounded would then surely travel like wildfire. Mustafa, I trusted. He would never speak. And suddenly I felt excited. I was about to cross a line, to leave one life and enter another.

Nurse Clement kissed me on the cheeks, which I did not expect.

"You take good care now," she said with emotion, and repeated her instruction about how often I should dress the wounds.

25

I FOUND RANA READING *Vogue* in the waiting area, looking cool in her dark sunglasses, white T-shirt, dark jeans, and chestnut leather Chelsea boots. She was in her own world and I wondered how I could now ever be in my own world. She smiled and began walking easily toward me. Seeing us, you might have thought we had simply bumped into one another.

"It's lovely out," she said, threading her arm through mine, her delicate right shoulder behind my left, what was now my good side.

We walked out and a small but ardent part of me, a stone in the skull, wanted to keep turning to look over my shoulder. I resisted and, when I could not, I pretended to be only curious about where we were, gazing back at a building, saying nonsense like "What an interesting area" or "I haven't been outside for so long it is lovely to just look at things."

She knew her way around, weaving us through Pimlico, until suddenly we were on the King's Road. The month was May and it was the height of an exceptional spring, strong and verdant. Open roses hung heavily, dangling off their bushes and over the pavements. Trees were full with leaves and whispered every time the breeze took them. Chestnut trees were in full bloom.

"Let's have lunch," Rana said happily. "I know just the place."

And there it was: a small French restaurant on the corner of a side street.

"Shall we sit outside?" she said, and immediately asked the waiter for one of the tables on the pavement.

I was convinced I was being watched and it took all my might to ignore it, to act as one who was at ease. I went to the toilet and when I saw my face in the mirror it frightened me. It was all mine and yet unrecognizable. Then, as though in a disturbed pool, my features settled into their old arrangement and the horror subsided.

After lunch, we took the bus to Notting Hill Gate. I remember her being full of stories, all in one way or another in praise of London: how she did this here, that there, and how, out of all the cities in the world, this was the one that suited her best.

I could not understand then how one could think that way. It all seemed odd and careless. Odd because I grew up taking it for granted that the city where I was born was the city where I would be buried. I had a passion for Benghazi. I loved her in a private and desperately incomplete way, where hatred or disappointment or longing came in sometimes to fill the gaps. And careless because it seemed that such a love was to be guarded, that it was a life's work.

Rana did not remove her shades as she spoke. I did not know it then, but all this going on about London was the result of nerves. Her friend, shot and his life upended, had no one but her. She then told me about Professor Walbrook, how he had surprised her.

"Turned up at my flat without warning. I still don't know how he found my address. Asking after you."

"What did you tell him?" I asked.

"The truth," she said.

Shame—yes, shame, that's what it was—cold, imprecise, and as endless as a moonless sea. Then I saw it in my mind's eye, felt the tug too, as the rope snapped and the anchor was lost to the depths.

"I followed your instructions," she said. "Told him not to tell anyone. He then looked at me and I knew I did not need to tell him that. He asked if I'd be seeing you and before I could answer he said, 'If you do, please give him this?'" She was already digging in her pocket. "He folded it several times, like old ladies back home do prayers. See what I mean?" she said, handing me a note the size of a postage stamp. "Strange man," she said, and tried to laugh.

I unfolded it and it lay gridded with creases. I immediately recognized the faint blue paper of his notebook, the same notebook in which he would write out for me the name of a book, a painting, a film, or a piece of music. Rana looked away.

Khaled,

I think it was our old friend Jean Rhys who wrote, "There must be the dark background to show up the bright colors."

My personal number on the reverse. Please use it.

Fond regards,

Henry

I remembered his telling me how he admired the way the Caribbean novelist had written about London, "extracting a sad and bitter song from her exile." But I took the quoted line less as consolation and more as a sort of advocacy for the vast metropolis that was now outside my bus window. And perhaps, as he stood outside Rana's door, Walbrook had guessed the consequences, quickly thought ahead, and decided on what was needed.

26

THE FLAT WAS ON the top floor of a converted house. It was arranged across a single room. The bed was at one end and the kitchen at the other, with a sofa and a coffee table between them. It had a wall with slanted windows that ran from knee height to the ceiling and looked out on to the quiet backs and rooftops of the neighboring houses. The bricks there were gray and black, making the green, wherever it appeared, look luminous. There were framed photographs of buildings on the opposite wall.

"Bauhaus," Rana said. "My father is a disciple."

I thought of what she had said on the bus about London being her favorite city, and a world in which one could choose where to live and what architectural style to follow, in which little was native or in which all that was native was transplantable. There was also a large map, dated 1835, showing the muscular snaking motion of the Thames, with London spread on its north and south banks. Rana was watching me watch it. I must inquire about her, I thought. How had these past weeks been for her? She took off her sunglasses and finally I could see her eyes.

"What day is it?" I asked, and it was like someone had pressed the "play" button. We started moving.

"Tuesday," she said, going to the kitchen. She poured two glasses of water. "I have to be off. I might miss my train otherwise. Will be back Friday." She looked toward the sofa. "Maybe spend the weekend?"

"I'd love that," I said.

"But now you settle in."

We said goodbye, and I waited until she reached the bottom floor and I heard the main door open and close. I bolted the flat shut and put on the door chain. I then dragged over the sofa and placed it against the door. I now could see that Rana had bought provisions: fresh milk and bread, two types of cheese, tomatoes, and olives. I pictured her making the five-hour train journey from Edinburgh that morning, preparing the flat, and then going to collect me from hospital. Now she was making the long trip back and it was well past four already. She wouldn't be home much before eleven. I tried to calculate how much she had paid for lunch. She had asked for the bill when I was in the toilet.

Out of the windows the sunlight was orange and fading. I took a shower, stood in front of the mirror. Two burnt eyes peered out blindly at me. They were at the bottom-right side of my chest. And from there the crisscrossing stitches marched around my side and to my back. I cleaned it as best as I could, hearing Nurse Clement's instructions in my head. I was frightened both by the possibility of causing harm and the temptation to do so, to plug my fingers into the new skin, to dig and tear out the ghost of the event. I would not need to press very hard to puncture those two holes, to blind the blind eyes. I dressed it and it was good to have it all covered up in white bandages. I put my clothes on. But I did not go out and did not go out for two days more. When I did, I looked over my shoulder at every turn.

Days passed. It is difficult to keep quiet if you have nothing to do. My mind blundered on. I tried to take note of the cycle of the light. Even when it was cloudy, at the end of the day the sun often burst through and filled the horizon. Unlike back home, here the sun set in slow motion. Long after it was gone, its glow remained in among the clouds. When night fell completely, the windows turned to mirrors. A mercy, I remember thinking, that we are made to tire at the end of each day.

27

NO ONE APART FROM Rana and possibly Walbrook, if she told him, knew where I was. And yet every time I heard the main house door open and close, and the sound of feet climbing the stairs, my heart beat wildly. The phone hardly ever rang and, when it did, I ignored it, unless it rang and stopped and rang again, which was Rana's signal. She called to say she could not come for the weekend after all. "Too much work." I was more relieved than disappointed.

Friday came and went and I did not write home. Writing to them from here seemed impossible somehow. Each day I walked in a different direction. In the evening I went to a pub, and hardly ever to the same one twice. The plan was always not to speak to anyone, but eventually I would feel the alcohol swim in my veins and I would find myself talking to a complete stranger. They wanted to know where I was from. That was the abiding question. And it was in their eyes before they asked it, often from the very first instant, and it remained there regardless of the answer I gave. Perhaps they could tell that I was lying. I was sometimes Tunisian, Brazilian, Maltese. I was sometimes a student, a visitor on holiday. I drank way too much. And would disappear without saying goodbye, pretending to be going to the toilet and then escaping through a side door or, if that was not possible, walking out in plain sight. All this made the mornings hellish. The drinking and all those fairy tales I invented, which caused me to talk endlessly, worsened the pain in my chest.

I came upon the local public library and discovered that I could enter without needing to show any ID. No one asked me anything. As I did not have proof of address, I could not get a borrower's card and therefore could read the books only at the library. This made me more adventurous, reading different authors without feeling the need to commit to them. I would remain there most of the day. I searched in different sections—history, literature, the classics—and sometimes even chose blindly. I would close my eyes and walk along one aisle with the tips of my fingers tracing the spines. Wherever I stopped, that book was my fate for at least an hour.

And this was how, under a good lamp in a corner, I tested things out. I read Seneca and felt myself to be truly in his company, as if he were a magnificent uncle chatting away beside me. His insights were so natural, so readily available, like found objects he had picked up along the way and was now taking out, one by one, and showing to me. Some stopped me cold, such as when he wrote, "No one can wear a mask for very long; for true nature will soon reassert itself." It was because of him that I read Sophocles. I found Oedipus riveting because it is a story of a man who unwittingly destroys his past.

Then one evening, tipsy and daring, feeling myself ready for a fight, to hold a specific object in my two hands and feel it snap, I walked home calling my name, Khaled, out loud, over and over in the night, hearing it ricochet against the houses, pronounced perfectly, and yet not seeming mine at all. I climbed up to the flat, emptied my pockets, and found the note from Walbrook. Before I had time to think, I dialed his number.

"Hello," he said.

"It's Khaled," I said after a long pause and then fell completely silent. I had nothing more to say, but also the question entered like a bullet into my head: what if the line is bugged?

He waited patiently. Clearly in his world it was normal to call and say nothing. I pressed the receiver harder against my ear, and the silence grew vast and more hollow.

"Summers when I was a child," he finally said, "my parents used to rent a cottage in a fishing village on the western Cornish coast. A remote place, windy and wild. All night the fishermen would be out in their small blinking boats. I believed that as long as I kept watch from my bedroom window upstairs, they wouldn't disappear. One of them knew my parents, would come for supper some evenings before setting off. There was something exotic about him, a man visiting from somewhere foreign and faraway. One day he didn't return from sea. Later, when I lost my parents and moved in with my gran, I would see his face in dreams. Then that stopped altogether. I nearly forgot about him until now."

"What happened to your parents?"

"They were killed in a car crash. Unbearable—I remember feeling that it was unbearable, and feeling as though the knowledge of their death was being forced through every pore in my body."

He said this in a steady and unhurried voice, confident of my attention, and I somehow knew he had never said it like this to anyone before.

"How old were you?" I asked.

"Eleven."

"That's terrible," I said.

"Yes," he said. "Terrible, but it was bearable. Even that."

Then he asked a question that in hindsight was ingenious. He did not ask what I needed or what he could do for me. None of those terrible questions. Instead, he said, "Do you know what you need right now?"

At first, I thought he meant it rhetorically, as if in preparation for telling me what he thought I needed. But, no, it was not that at all. And in the space that opened, the things I needed appeared lucidly. Although I could not yet voice them, I saw them flicker momentarily on the horizon.

"You'll know," he said after a few seconds passed. "Will you call again?"

"Yes," I said.

"Will you really?" he said.

"Yes," I said.

"Good," he said. "Very good." And then immediately asked, "Are you good at memorizing?"

"Yes," I said, and chose not to tell him that I knew pages and pages of the Holy Quran by heart.

"Then make sure you memorize my number," he said. "Do it now. Have you done it?" And then he tested me.

28

RANA CAME THE FOLLOWING Friday. She did not seem all that happy. I took her to the cinema and afterward cooked her dinner, but she hardly ate. I had washed the sheets and prepared the bed for her, but she insisted on sleeping on the sofa. There was a hardness in her insistence. The next day was a Saturday, but she wanted to head back to Edinburgh nonetheless.

"I need to catch up on work. Clean my place," she said, looking at her hands.

The black eyeliner she often wore now accentuated the timidity in her eyes, made them look a little bewildered. I would go with her, I thought, wash her floor.

"What are you going to do?" she said.

I did not know why I was surprised by the question.

"I mean," she went on, "you can't go back to Edinburgh and you can't return home. Or can you?"

I had no answer.

"Did you call your parents?" she asked.

"No," I said.

"Don't you think you should? I think you should."

As soon as she left, I became terribly anxious. I tidied up. I took out the money left from the thousand pounds the visitor at the hospital had given me. I was wearing the clothes he had given me. They were now the only clothes I had. And his money the only money I had access to. I counted it on the kitchen worktop. I had spent fifty pounds or so. I had enough for a plane ticket plus gifts. You must bring gifts.

I took a shower and by the time I was done I had decided to return to Benghazi. I will deny everything, I will tell them I was naive, I will apologize, swear allegiance if I have to. And let the others think what they will. After all, what does it matter what people think? All that matters is one's sanity. Besides, nothing is changed by slogans. The truest opinions are never uttered. Most people live their entire lives with what they truly believe buried deep in their chests. Life will eventually return to normal. How mad I was even to contemplate remaining here. The temporary side effects from the shock of being shot. Return to where your ancestors were born and buried. Do not exaggerate the consequences of your actions. Who cares about a bunch of stupid students taking part in a demonstration in a foreign country? I stuffed all the money in my pocket and left.

The streets of London—its traffic and pedestrians and architecture and trees and sky—all seemed made up, like a film set. I decided I would brave flying again and went along Queensway looking for the cheapest airplane ticket. Every time I spoke, I could hear in my voice a new intolerance. I sounded adamant and impatient, the foreignness of my accent even more pronounced. And that voice continued arguing in my head as I left each travel agent.

"Isn't it more radical," it asked, "a truer love, to remain in your native land, in contact with the soil?

"What better political commitment is there than remaining?

"And when was being 'radical' your thing anyway?

"But what is this money in your pocket, then, the money you just counted, the money with which you will pay for your way home, and buy presents for your parents and sister? Isn't it blood money, money literally for your blood?"

"Of course not; it's compensation."

"Compensation for what? What have you been compensated for? Your dedication to freedom, to showing how we are a people who resist tyranny, as your benefactor, the mysterious man in the yellow shades and Italian suit, who claimed to have once been your father's friend, told you and the others? And what of him, the one you trusted without good reason, handing him your full name and, in case there was any doubt, confirming that you were your father's son? For all you know he was sent by the regime to collect names."

The silence that followed, which was not in my head as much as in my hands, an object too delicate to let go of, brought me to a complete halt. All I could see now were the faces of my mother, my father, and Souad, all gazing silently at me. I did not know what to tell them. I had no idea where I was or which way to go. I stood at a street corner and could not even muster the will to pretend to be lost or waiting for someone.

I returned to the flat and could hear the telephone ringing as I climbed up. It stopped just as I entered and a few seconds later started again.

"Just arrived," Rana said. "It's raining here. In comparison London is summer. Sorry I couldn't stay longer. Sorry for my mood. Just have a lot on."

I listened to the echoes of Edinburgh's Waverley Train Station behind her. I should have gone back with her, denied everything, resumed classes, caught up on assignments.

"I hope you know how grateful I am," I finally said. "I mean, the flat, this time here, your kindness. Even if I tried . . ."

My voice gave way, as in those landslides you see in the news, filmed from a great height, when after a relentless rainfall everything shifts—houses, roads, lampposts, trees—a crack in the air, and the land pulls apart. I covered my mouth.

"Hello? Are you all right?" Rana repeated, then stopped, and a couple of seconds later she started speaking softly, not asking questions, not expecting a response. My ears were underwater and her

voice a helicopter above. I could hear its blades slice the air in a furious loop. I could make out only the occasional word, something about
time and the future, about how one has the responsibility to act as
one's own custodian. I remember her using that word, "custodian."
And how no one ever tells us this and yet it is the most essential thing
to know about life, and so on. Now her voice was close and tender and
wild with concern and grief and longing and I tried to stay with it. I
understood then that she too missed the way things were, when we
were equals, friends who could take it for granted that the other person is fine and that the days will be fine, fellow travelers sharing the
same carriage, confident about arriving on time and with little drama.
She said something about Benghazi.

"You have called them, haven't you? Your family. You rang them,
told them you're all right?" After a little silence she said, "I'm sorry
but I must go. Running out of coins. I'll be back on the weekend. Take
care of yourself. Call Benghazi, but please dial the operator and ask to
place a reverse-charge call or else my parents will kill me. Call them
now."

Anything is better than nothing. Life is unbearable otherwise. I
remembered Walbrook's question, concerning the things that I
needed, and my mind drew a blank. I could not retrieve what had
momentarily emerged when he first asked it. There was a fire in my
lungs. You must never cry. For you, crying is not an option. That is
one thing that is certain.

29

I CALLED THE OPERATOR. She read back to me our home number, that familiar number that, still today, even after the house has been razed to the ground, I carry in my head. Together we listened to the faraway ringtone start and stop. My father answered. His voice was astonishingly beautiful. I remember being surprised by it, by how broad and hospitable it was, the shade of a well-rooted tree. Given the chance, I thought, I would confide to it all my secrets, spread myself like a rug beneath it. I imagined him at the desk in his study, the book he was reading now upturned on the wood to save the page, the window behind him framing the grapevine in the courtyard, and the last of the light leaking out of the sky and seeming, as it often did at this hour, to sit like a mist or a layer of dust on all that it touched.

"Good afternoon, sir," the English woman told him. "This is the operator calling from England."

"Yes?" he said, sounding concerned. "Good afternoon, madam."

"I have a reverse-charge call for you," she said with a hint of a smile, no doubt because, I thought, she was amused by his calling her madam, or else wanting, on my behalf, to assure him that his concern was most probably unwarranted. "It's from Khaled." She pronounced my name as though she were saying "Call Ed." "Will you accept the charges?"

"Yes," he said, "of course, and thank you, madam."

"Caller, please go ahead," the operator said.

The instant she hung up, the static vanished and my father drew near, as if we were standing side by side, with our shoulders touching, as when I joined him for Friday prayer at the local mosque. He called out my name perfectly, and in that way he used to do when, walking back home in the evening along the seafront, I would sometimes get distracted and fall behind. He always waited, watching me as I hurried after him, and I would notice an endearing amusement in his expression as I caught up. But this time I did not respond. I had fallen too far behind, been thrust into a different direction altogether, cast out at sea, and now that sea stood between us. There was also the high probability, which I was confident Father too suspected, that there was a third party listening in, that although the English operator had left us, the work of her Libyan counterpart, who had an entirely different purpose, had just begun. But what worried me even more was that if I opened my mouth I might once again come undone. I then heard a whisper and realized that it was my father praying.

"Dear Lord, guide our path, clarify our minds, pacify our temper."

I understood then what he suspected: that to help make a further example of us, the authorities would have made sure to run the news clip over and over on state television, the way highlights from a national football victory are replayed to raise morale. Father, Mother, and Souad would have seen it several times and, like Rana, might have recognized me from the jacket that Father had got me as a going-away gift. I felt my love for him gather itself up—as heavy and solid as a stone—in my chest. The talented historian who managed to remain independent, part of that silent army that exists in every country, made up of individuals who had come to the conclusion that they live among unreasonable compatriots and therefore must, like grownups in a playground, endure the chaos until the bell rings, resigned to the fact that this may come long after they are gone. I could detect in his steady breath that old and resilient patience, strong even in the face of what he now knew: that his elder child, his only son, who carried his name to pass it on, "Khaled the reader, Khaled the reasonable boy with an even temperament and a gift for weighing things up," as I heard him tell others more than once, "my son with the bright future," had been foolish enough to believe he could hide behind a mask, was among those shot in front of the Libyan Embassy in London on the 17th of April 1984, and was therefore forever a marked man. Opportunities that had once been available to me—qualifying for a scholarship, getting a respectable job, securing a bank loan, and, most crucially, being able to live as a free man—were now uncertain.

I wanted to ask if he still believed I had a bright future. But, in the gap, I saw rise my pride, my dark ardor, and I thought, I refuse to regret my actions. And just then he said, to God or to me or to himself or even for the benefit of our eavesdropper, in case his heart might be moved by the love of a father to his son, "I'm thankful, I'm truly thankful."

"Never forget," he used to tell me, "that the first poem ever written was from a father to a son. Adam's elegy for Abel, which was also an elegy for Cain, who, having killed his brother, must wander the earth. And therefore, according to the history of love and poetry, the love of a father for his son is greater than all kinds of love, greater than that of Layla and Majnun, and greater even than the greatest of all loves, that of a mother for her child. But if you tell your mother, I will kill you."

My father's interest in the history of the first poem came from his favorite poet, Abu al Ala al Ma'arri, and *The Epistle of Forgiveness*, in which "three hundred years before Dante," my father liked to remind me, al Ma'arri's poet-protagonist descends into the underworld but also rises to the heavens, where he questions the first man, Adam, on his alleged poem. But what, in these moods, my father liked to leave out was that al Ma'arri's hero speaks to Eve as well and discovers that she too had written a poem. He learns that, whereas Adam's was an elegy, and therefore concerned with the past, Eve's was about the future, her hopes and fears for her family's prospects in their eternal exile on earth. After I finished packing and he sat on my suitcase so it would zip shut, and I heard his heavy breathing turn inward, he rushed off and returned with his old copy of *The Epistle of Forgiveness,* which he had had since he was a student, and he insisted we open the suitcase again. When I protested, he said, "There's always room for one more book."

That volume was now in Edinburgh. It had in the margins his scribbled notes, the sentences he had underlined, the folded corners where he had paused, which allowed me to read along with him, two pairs of eyes at once. It was the most precious object I possessed.

He broke the silence with that old and familiar question that, I assume, for a parent is never redundant or unreasonable.

"Are you eating?"

I heard myself laugh. "Yes," I said.

He laughed too, and sounded just as relieved as I was.

"And how is your health?"

"Good," I said.

"You are telling the truth?" he said.

"I swear it on Grandfather's grave," I said, which I knew would settle the matter.

"Excellent," he said. "And do you have friends? I mean, real friends."

"I think so," I said. "How can you tell?"

"Simple," he said. "Do they give you pleasure and do you trust them?" Here his voice faltered a little, perhaps sensing the impossibility of his task—to look after me from across the distance. I thought of the man with the yellow shades, who had once been his friend. I could imagine him fulfilling those two conditions. "Whatever you do," he then said, "don't go looking for a father. No matter the distance, I'm here. Not even the seas."

I did not know what to say.

"I know you understand me," he said.

I nodded even though he could not see me.

"All you need is one or two good friends, that's all. And work, study, and be patient."

"I'm sorry," I finally said.

"What for?" he said, no doubt, I thought, to protect us both. "You have nothing to be sorry for, my boy. You have gone to learn and that is the noblest reason for travel."

"I know," I said, adhering to his strategy. "I know."

"The question"—he spoke as if referring to a conversation we'd already had—"arguably the most important question of all—is how to escape the demands of unreasonable men."

"I know," I said, wishing he would stop.

"Listen, find the open spaces. I know you understand me."

A silence followed. Perhaps he too was replaying in his mind what he had just told me, calculating all the ways it could be interpreted by our silent companion. My mouth was full of questions: how is the clementine tree he and I planted in the courtyard; when last did he swim in the sea; what was he reading just now; what are people there saying about *The Given and the Taken;* is it true that Sidi Rajab Zowa delivered a statement on television; and what did he say and how did he appear?

"Your mother. Souad too—"

"How have they been?"

"Very well."

"And you, how are you, Father?"

"Excellent. That is one thing you never have to worry about," he said. "Let me get them."

I could hear his leather shoes click against the terra-cotta tiles, then the door squeak horribly. That was on my list of things to do for him before leaving: oil the hinges. First thing when I return. Now I was alone with the listening man. At first, I thought I had imagined it, but then he cleared his throat again. I knew what he would say if he were to speak. He would say, "Think you're a man," spoken ambigu-ously, not as a question, and somewhat lazily, as though our eaves-dropper was lying on his back, spread out on a carpet in the middle of a room, as he listened to our call. I heard the hinges again and then Mother and Souad approach. Your last chance to hang up. You can blame it on the line. But then my mother's voice.

"Tell me everything," she said. "How you are? And how come you didn't write the last few weeks? Speak up; let me hear you."

"Yes, I'm well, Mother," I said, and caught the panic in my words. I pretended to be coughing and said, in the clearest, most confident voice I could muster, "Very well. Just busy with coursework. And you?"

"Head to toe? You promise?" And then quickly telling Father, "Don't laugh. And," she said, "are you eating? Your father won't stop laughing at me."

It was then that I knew they had no idea that I had been at the demonstration. They believe that I am in Edinburgh, I thought, and that all is well. This made me momentarily feel that all was, in fact, well. I laughed.

"Now you are both laughing at me," Mother said, which caused Father to laugh even louder.

"He asked me the same question," I said.

"I don't care if he asked you already; I want to know for myself."

And this was when I knew what to say, what I could speak about that would present no danger and be a comfort to her.

"Listen," I said, "I need your help."

"Help with what? What's wrong?"

"It's a very serious question," I said.

"God have mercy," she said.

"When it comes to Libyan tagine, I mean the classic one from the Green Mountain, I know you use potatoes, onions, tomatoes, and lamb, chicken, or fish—right?"

I heard her breath stutter. Then Father was saying something beside her. Souad too.

"Mother, are you listening?"

"Yes, yes."

"So all that is clear," I continued, "but what I'm uncertain about is whether you use garlic?"

"What?" she said.

"Garlic, Mother, do you use garlic in tagine?"

"Of course you do," she said.

"Well, then, that explains it. I made it the other day for a friend and it was a terrible failure."

"Khaled, habibi," she said, "tell me exactly what you did and I will tell you where you went wrong."

30

INITIALLY, I WAS CHEERED up by the phone call, but then my old fears began to creep in. Were my parents only pretending that all was as it had been? They did not ask about Fred or his family. They did not inquire about my studies either. They seemed careful not to ask any questions concerning my life here. Nor did Souad—who, in the few seconds that we spoke, before Father took the receiver from her, sounded as cautious as a lock. What was most unsettling was that each one of us knew our part and played it well. The only authentic things we shared were our love and our fear. As I sat on the sofa in the borrowed flat in Notting Hill, a place that, although it was not mine, was the only place I had, my love and fear were the only things I truly possessed. I held on to them, for they seemed then to be as real as material objects. I was eighteen and in desperate need of someone to instruct me. Independence, which I had up to then held in very high regard, indeed revered it, was now to me a curse, the devil himself. It is dependence that a sane mind should seek; to depend on others and be in turn dependable.

I went over the call in my mind so many times that I hardly slept. I became delirious with confusion. There was no way that I could discern whether my family suspected anything or not. In either circumstance, their behavior made sense. If they believed I had anything to do with the demonstration, they could have not mentioned it, as that would have confirmed the fact to the authorities. On the other hand, if my parents believed that I was still back in Edinburgh, they would not want to ask too many questions, particularly not about my extracurricular activities, in case such details would excite the disapproval of our listener, have us labeled "bourgeois reactionaries," as those who liked the theater and high culture sometimes were.

And then there was the other possibility: that the authorities knew that I was at the demonstration, had got hold of the list of the wounded, perhaps from someone working at the hospital, in return for some money or a brand-new car. I saw that man—who had deliberately cleared his throat in the silence when my father left to fetch Mother and Souad, and did it twice so as to leave no doubt as to who was boss—leading the charge of government officials, turning up at our door, knocking furiously, taking my father for questioning. I saw Souad's and my mother's faces and heard the silence of their worried evening. In this scenario, I thought, my parents' and sister's performances on the phone would have been scripted by the authorities. I wondered if what my father said, about how I never have to worry about him, had something to do with this. But then he would not have laughed so naturally. Unless the state had given him assurances that no one would lay a finger on me, asked him to continue to encourage me to come home once my studies were finished, and therefore his laughter would have had to do with that happy ambition. "This will always be his country," they would have told him, and "All kids make mistakes."

No, I then decided; they would have been smarter than that. If the government knew that I was at the demonstration, they would not have communicated it to my family. They would have wanted them to remain in the dark. From the regime's point of view, I surmised, walking hurriedly to the library in the morning as though I had an important appointment to keep, there would be no benefit in my parents knowing that I was one of the St. James's Square demonstrators. They would want them to expect my return and to remain eager for it. My family, I imagined the authorities concluding, were the bait.

Never call again, I told myself. That is another thing that is now no longer an option. Another thing that is certain. Do not cry and do not call home. At least not for the foreseeable future. And I quickly decided, not because I could see that far ahead, but rather because I could just about muster the ambition, that I would give it three months. In the meantime, write only occasionally. Not too frequently. But not too infrequently either. In three weeks, then four, five, seven. Wean them off. And do not include your address. Not yet. Everything not yet.

Breathing continued to be difficult. I did not leave the flat for a few days. Then Rana called.

"Did you ring them?" she wanted to know. "And how did it go? Wonderful. Didn't I tell you? I'm so glad. You sound much better. I was thinking," she then said. "Don't you want your things? I can collect them and bring them with me on Friday?"

I thought of her visiting my bedsit, speaking to the landlady. I could not remember how I had left the room, if I had tidied up, folded my clothes, made the bed.

"All you'll need to do is call to let them know that I'll be passing by," she said.

"But what if someone sees you?" I said.

"So what?" she said.

"They might follow you?" I said.

"Let them try," she said, and let out a short nervous laugh.

Over the next couple of days, my lungs worsened. Climbing the stairs, I had to stop several times to catch my breath. I woke up in the middle of the night to the sound of a door squeaking and realized it was me wheezing. I called the hospital and they said I should come in. I met with the same doctor who had, with trembling hands, cut open my clothes. He blushed a little when we shook hands. I do not remember his name, but I can still see his face, open and honest, a face that would find it difficult to refuse a request. I think it was this, from within the mayhem of that day, that made him appear younger than he was. He said he was pleased to see me looking so well.

"We have been wondering where to send you your medical report," he said.

I wrote down the address.

He inspected the stitches, apologizing a couple of times for his cold fingers, and then asked how I liked living in Notting Hill. He took a piece of cotton wool and some alcohol and began to rub away the sticky marks the bandages had left.

"It's healed nicely," he said. "You won't need to dress it any longer." He then listened to my chest, explaining, with long pauses, and in a way that made me feel that I was a novel case, that they'd had to remove the top part of my right lung. "But eventually—the body is extraordinary—your breathing will normalize. In the meantime, however, you will need patience."

Perhaps it was being back in the same hospital, or maybe it was the doctor's face and the memory of him screaming, "Here," over and over, or perhaps it was that single word, "patience," that unfastened the gate. I was overcome. I was not crying, but I was not not crying either. I lowered my head and the tears fell. The good doctor put a hand on my left shoulder, my good shoulder. How oddly weightless his hand felt, I thought, and how good of him to just wait there in silence. He then left the room. I put my shirt back on. He came back with a small paper cup half filled with very cold water.

"I want to go home," I told him. "To my country."

His eyes remained on me. This man, I thought, who had helped save my life once, might be able to do it again.

"I wonder if it would be possible . . ." I said. "I mean, I wonder if the report could be changed, put a different reason for the surgery, a tumor, for example, or some sort of accident."

Now his eyes had a shadow of that fear I had seen in them the first time we met. He excused himself and was gone a long while. When he returned, he had with him the older surgeon who had operated on me and who was, I was certain, better at saying no.

"We are very sympathetic," he started. "We really want to help. But, even if we were to put ethical concerns aside, any doctor would be able to tell the cause of the injury. But my colleague said you were having trouble breathing. Describe to me the feeling exactly."

There are moments when the veil momentarily falls and things are revealed for what they are. In that instant, your feet touch the ground, you feel bound to reality, to objects and facts and the present.

"There's something there. I can feel it," I said, and, before much time could pass, I added, "I don't want to dwell on it," and got up.

They gave me an inhaler, some pills, and told me to come back if I did not notice an improvement. "Please try not to exert yourself," the younger one said.

I wanted to ask him in particular if he was sure they had not missed part of a bullet, a fragment, a speck of dust. After all, everything in this world leaves a trace. But, instead, I thanked them and shook their hands.

31

WHEN RANA ARRIVED THAT Friday, I was already feeling better, well enough to carry my old suitcase up the stairs.

"Your landlady was confused," she said. "Two policemen came by and questioned her. 'I don't like trouble,' she said. I told her you were in no trouble but had 'family issues' and she didn't ask any more questions. On the way out I bumped into one of your housemates, or at least he said he was. He startled me. Asked after you and when I didn't respond he said to tell you that Saad sends his best wishes."

That weekend Rana was light and easy and seemed happy to be with me. At certain moments, it was nearly like before. She agreed to take the bed and I slept on the sofa. She stayed till Sunday and was not all that pleased to be returning. I took her to the station, and on the bus I told her that I was making plans to move out, that I was going to get a job and start paying for my own accommodation. "I have no idea how to do all this," I confessed, "but I will somehow."

"You will," she said, and sounded like she might have meant it. She rested her head on my shoulder. "You certainly will," she said, and I was sure that she really meant it.

"Then you will come as my guest," I said.

"I already have," she said.

I returned directly to the flat, intending to open the suitcase, but it remained in the corner of the room for three days before I unpacked it. Rana had placed my mother's bottle of musk in one of my shirt pockets. I took it out and thought to tighten it, which caused the top to snap. I placed it on the bathroom shelf and the perfume quickly filled the place. Rana had carefully folded every item of clothing, fitting them into one half of the suitcase and, in the other half, packed all my books neatly into a puzzle, with hardly a gap in between. There was Father's *The Epistle of Forgiveness* in its maroon leather cover and the other books I had brought with me from home: Badr Shakir al Sayyab's *Rain Song; The Travels of Ibn Battuta*, which was there in my childhood and came with me through my teenage years; the *Strange Case of Dr. Jekyll and Mr. Hyde*, because, besides my parents and the *Oxford English Dictionary*, my other English teacher was Robert Louis Stevenson, the ease of his sentences, which have the honest and vital momentum of nature; the four volumes that make up the novel *Leg over Leg* by Ahmad Faris al Shidyaq, which I was told by my parents stood behind all other Arabic fiction and which, on account of some of its outrageous and scandalous details, ever since its publication in 1855, had rarely appeared complete. My father secured this uncensored copy. And the two volumes I bought from a second-hand bookshop in Edinburgh: the poems of Sylvia Plath and Waguih Ghali's only novel, *Beer in the Snooker Club*, which I was yet to read because I had bought it only a few days before Mustafa and I took the bus to London, and which, perhaps for that same reason, still remains unread today. All in all, my library was made up of ten volumes. I placed them side by side in a row along one of the low windowsills.

When I finished unpacking and believed I had entirely emptied the suitcase, I found that Rana had placed my post in the inner pocket. Seven envelopes from Mother, Libyan stamps, her familiar handwriting carefully stating my name and Edinburgh address, which was no longer my address, in both Arabic and English. I read them all and could detect no change in tone, no sudden concern. A thousand and one things could befall us and the people we love the most would have no hint of it. Which is why we must remain close to them, within an arm's length. When I wrote to them next, I said I had moved into temporary accommodation. "Some friends and I are looking to share an apartment. Cheaper and this way we can do our own cooking. Don't write until I send you the new address."

32

A COUPLE OF DAYS later, the medical report arrived in the post. I cast a quick glance at it and placed it back in the envelope. The following morning, another letter came. It looked official and the postman asked me to sign as proof of receipt. It contained a letter from New Scotland Yard, advising me to appear at their offices in Victoria at my "earliest convenience." It frightened me. I could not understand how they knew my address.

I walked to Victoria unable to erase the tremor in my knees. I was met by two men in dark gray suits. They thanked me for coming and led me into a windowless room that had nothing but a desk and three chairs. The walls were totally bare. The desk was naked except for a large bulging brown envelope. They asked how I was keeping. And, even though their sympathy seemed genuine, I expected their expression to change at any moment.

The slightly older one introduced himself and said that he was in charge of the case. He wore a blue tie diagonally striped with thin red lines. I wanted to ask what he meant by "the case."

"You may be wondering why we've asked you to come in," the younger one said, who wore a plain blue tie.

"It's really only to check that everything is fine," the older one said.

A strange moment came when they asked me to take off my top to show them the wounds. It was now summer and all I had on was a shirt. They stood up and gathered so close around me that I could feel their temperature on my skin. They turned slowly, examining the scars from where the bullets entered, going all the way around my side and to my back, to where they exited. I assumed their interest was bureaucratic, perhaps checking the location of the injuries against the forensic report so as to map out where every person had stood that day. But that alone could not have explained their manner.

"Isn't it healing nicely," the man in charge said to his deputy, as if my body were a matter of public interest.

"Yes," I said, pretending that they knew nothing about me. "I was recently at the hospital and the doctors were pleased."

Something about their silence here confirmed that they knew that I had been to the hospital. That must be where they got my address. Or perhaps they had known it all along. They asked me to put my shirt back on and have a seat.

"Would you like some tea or coffee?"

"No, thank you."

"So, Khaled," the younger man said, turning briefly to his superior, "how are things these days?"

"Are you worried about anything?" his boss added.

"Noticed anything unusual since you left hospital, anything untoward?"

"What do you mean, untoward?" I asked.

They looked at one another, and then the one with the more senior rank said, "It would be prudent to keep a watchful eye."

"In case you are followed," the other clarified.

"In which event," the older one added, touching his tie, "there are things you can do."

"We are here to help."

"For example, if you suspect you are being followed, change direction, pretend you've suddenly remembered something. If the pursuer persists, go into the first police station or telephone box and call either one of us."

They placed their cards on the desk in front of me.

"Make sure," the older one said, "that you speak to no one else but us. We are in charge of this case."

"Why do you keep calling it a 'case'?" I asked.

"Well, what occurred was extraordinary," he said, speaking now as though I were much younger than I was. "Deeply regrettable. We are very sorry for what happened to you."

"One of our own died," the other said.

"Yes, I saw her," I said.

"Deeply regrettable," his superior said again. "Our job now is to make sure that everyone involved that day feels safe and protected."

The silence that followed made none of us easy. I thought of Mustafa, and for the first time missed him terribly. Was he too called in for a meeting like this?

"We will expedite your asylum," the older man said. "We don't advise that you return home for the time being."

Then, after another silence, the younger one asked, "What will you do now, Khaled?"

"I don't know," I said. "Maybe go home or take a walk . . ." I realized then that he meant something else altogether.

They could see that I noted the misunderstanding, but neither asked the question again. They handed me the large brown envelope that had been on the desk.

"Your jacket," the older one said.

"We no longer need it," the younger one explained.

As I came to leave, the older one said, "Remember now, keep your eyes open."

They both seemed satisfied. Two people who believed that they had done their job well.

Out on the street I made several quick turns and then ran to the flat. I looked for Mustafa's number but could not find it. I drew the blinds and tore open the envelope. The jacket came out in one crusted lump and was as tiny as a child's garment. My blood had turned black and was giving off a rusty smell. They had not washed it. This fact—as unreasonable as it was to expect forensics to have dry-cleaned my jacket before returning it—upset me very much. I stuffed it back in the envelope and did something that I occasionally regret. I walked to Hyde Park, found a rubbish bin in a spot where no one could see me, and threw it away. I walked off feeling an emptiness well up inside me. It seemed, for all the emptiness that it was, a presence. It made me want to run away, dive deeper into myself, into that cold desolation, to the very bottom of it, out of whatever it is that attracts us to pain, which tempts us, when we know that a complaining tooth should be left alone, to bite on it.

33

As unnerving as the Scotland Yard meeting was, a weak sense of reassurance did begin to permeate the days that followed. I never went out now without their cards in my wallet. But I rarely looked over my shoulder. Occasionally I would hear platitudes from my childhood repeat in my head: what will happen will happen; no one dies before their time.

I became accustomed to the sounds of the house and the routines of the couple downstairs. They set off to work early in the morning, talking quickly and banging the main door shut behind them. I would catch his aftershave and her perfume in the hallway as I left. They returned less noisily in the evening. I was determined to avoid them, but one Saturday I bumped into them just as they were coming in. After that I did not mind seeing them again, and even hoped I would, enjoying the easy manner of saying hello to people I hardly knew.

The postman came twice, early in the morning and again in the afternoon, pushing the mail through the letter box. The couple subscribed to *The World of Interiors* and *The Economist*. I found copies of both magazines at the library and leafed through them.

By now I had about £700 left. I drew up a budget and worked out that I could live on £35 a week, or £140 a month. This meant I could survive for five months. But I could not stay here for five months.

A few days later the postman delivered a letter and asked me to sign as proof of receipt. I brought it upstairs and did not open it till the afternoon. It contained my asylum papers.

I telephoned Henry. This time I did most of the talking. I did not tell him about my meeting with Scotland Yard. I did not tell him that I spent most days in the library because it quieted my nerves to be lost in a book. I did not say that I had begun to read more systematically, that I would select an author and make my way through their entire work. I did not say anything about the mania of my progress. Nor that there were moments, fleeting and abstract but as vivid as existence, when everything I was and everything that had happened vanished, and I found myself lost inside an imaginary life. Nor did I say that when the library closed, instead of drinking, I walked the city until my legs grew tired. At certain turns I would sense a strange affection on the part of the city—except it was not affection exactly but a correspondence—that as I moved within it, it too moved within me. I felt protected by my anonymity but even more by London, its maze-like streets turning upon one another as though designed for the purpose of keeping secrets. I did not say that during these nocturnal walks I sometimes had to push away the suspicion that I was sinking, drowning irredeemably, and that it felt like death, and all the faces around me seemed to belong to persons who had long ago ceased to exist. At such moments, London was the hereafter. They helped my lungs, these walks, made me sleep better, and, even though the violent dreams continued, they were infiltrated by the day's reading. The grief and confusion and bewilderment and fear seemed no longer mine alone. I saw meadows too. I saw my sea and my parents. The familiar light. And when the morning came, I was undone again, I was cloven in the middle, coming apart. I was not a man but a set of components that each day needed to be reassembled.

I said none of this to Henry. Instead, I told him that I had been reading Jean Rhys.

"What did you make of it?" he asked.

"I copied out some lines. Would you like to hear them?"

"Yes," he said.

"'Still, there were moments when she realized that her existence, though delightful, was haphazard.'"

He did not say anything.

"'The moment comes when even the softest person doesn't care a damn any more and that's a precious moment.'"

"I like that one," he said.

"Me too," I said.

I wanted to tell him that she made me feel sad but not alone and reading her I did not so terribly mind being sad and alone. I wanted to say that I liked those poems by Robert Browning set in Rome only because his descriptions of the light reminded me of home. I then told him I copied out "Parliament Hill Fields" by Sylvia Plath and had been reading it every night before going to sleep to memorize it. I hoped he might ask me to recite it, but he did not. I told him that the local public library had Tayeb Salih's books in Arabic, which was like finding an old friend in the middle of London. He said he wished he could read *Season of Migration to the North* in Arabic. Even though I had yet to read the English translation, I told him that it was an entirely different book in Arabic and far more powerful. I asked him if he knew of a Zimbabwean writer by the name of Dambudzo Marechera. He did not.

"Neither did I," I said. "I picked it up because the photograph of the author intrigued me."

"What was it about it that intrigued you?" he asked.

"I don't know," I said. "He looked cool, too pissed off to write a book."

He laughed.

"Like a man willing to burn himself rather than give an inch."

"Yes," he said ponderingly.

"I admire that, you see," I said.

"Yes," he said again, but not so much in agreement as recognition, as if he had already suspected that I felt this way.

A silence stretched out and into it I said, "I have just received my asylum papers."

"That's excellent news," he said.

"Why?" I said.

He was a little surprised by the question. "Well, because you can work and study. You can live here for as long as you like."

I could not speak for a few seconds after that.

"I have been thinking about your question," I finally said. "The one about the things I need."

"Oh, yes?" he said.

"Three things," I said.

"Very well," he said, and I pictured him reaching for a pen. "In order of priority, please."

"Money."

"Yes."

"A place to live. And an education."

He did not pause but plunged straight into the details. Told me that I would not be able to get a job without having proof of address and therefore that had to be put first. He asked how much money I had, and made a "financial plan" for me there and then.

"You don't have enough to pay both rent and a month's deposit. I will lend you the deposit. You will require a reference too, I suspect. Happy to write one, pretend I was your landlord, a harmless lie. As soon as that's settled, you must begin looking for employment. Something you can secure quickly, a job at a café or a restaurant or, better still, a bookshop, where you would probably get discounts."

I was eighteen, had never worked before, had never lived alone or been in charge of my affairs.

"What if I don't find work, or find it in time, or find it and then lose it? What if I can't pay you back?"

"The entire history of humanity is reliant on people earning their keep," he said. "Let that be a comfort to you. And worst-case scenario you can have the spare room. But you won't need it. You're clever, hardworking. Soon you'll be up on your feet. If I were a gambling man, I'd put a handsome lot on you."

As I listened to him, courage scaled the walls and smuggled itself in.

With each day life seemed a little more possible. I called Henry at every step. He helped me to fill out forms, write a CV, and, when I finally found a flat that I liked and could afford, I ran immediately to the nearest telephone box and dialed his number, told him all about it, and asked if he knew the neighborhood.

"I have always liked Shepherd's Bush," he said. "The market, people from all over the world."

"It's not far from where I'm staying now," I told him, "and I read that, at one point, Robert Louis Stevenson lived here."

"Well," he said, laughing, "then that settles it."

34

THINGS MOVED QUICKLY. IN less than a month I was in my own flat. I unpacked the day I arrived, but, as I did not have any furniture apart from a mattress on the floor and a small breakfast table in the kitchen, I neatly stacked my books and clothes around the perimeter of the empty room. The floorboards were bare and had the occasional narrow gap running in between. In the quiet evening hours, I could sometimes make out a word of what the couple downstairs were saying. The kitchen was small and bright and had a large window. It was the top-floor flat in a small house that was at the end of a long terrace, and so I had a view of the back gardens running in a long row, each fenced off from the other. Occasionally a tree reached upward and marked the distance. The agent was keen to point out that it was rare to have such a long view. The back windows of the houses on either side stood blankly during the day but lit up at night, each a different shade of white and yellow. Someone would sometimes walk past or stand like me, looking out. I did not know then that I would get to know this view so intimately, that I would watch these trees turn and grow for a third of a century.

I had clearly lost the piece of paper on which Mustafa had written down his number. I thought of calling home and seeing if my father could contact his family and get me Mustafa's maternal uncle's number in Manchester. Then I imagined Mother asking why I had not sent them my new address yet. I continued writing them brief postcards from time to time, pretending to be visiting London again. "I write you from here because this is only when I have time. University is very busy." I would then get on a bus and go to a different side of town so that the postmark would not show the area where I lived.

Walbrook wrote me a fictitious reference in which he claimed I had done work for him, assisting with research, and that he had found me "superbly motivated, reliable, and trustworthy." I found a job as a sales assistant at a clothing shop on the King's Road. It was less than half an hour away by bus and I was reasonably good at the job, which had a sales commission attached. As soon as I paid Henry back, I reduced my working schedule to three and a half days a week. I used the rest of the time to read, visit museums, and continue my walks. I discovered that I could sneak into plays and concerts. I would put on a shirt, go into the bar during the interval, making sure I had a book in my pocket. When the bell rang for the third time, I marched up with the others, pretending to be immersed in the book I was reading. And, as people generally dislike interrupting a man reading, I would sleepwalk into the theater. Once inside, I would stand lingering, mesmerized by the book in hand, facing the page determinedly, until, just as everyone had taken their seats and the lights had gone down, I would look up, feigning a slight surprise, and, with the gently embarrassed smile of the elderly, descend into the nearest empty chair. I saw the second half of many things this way. In plays I felt like an intruder, that everyone sitting beside me, their faces lit by the stage, knew more than I could about the story. This was not the case with chamber music, as the second half of a performance was of one or several complete pieces. No preparation was required. And, because I could not choose what to listen to and what to avoid, this clandestine operation earned me a broad musical education.

Rana was busy with end-of-year coursework, but managed to visit a couple of times. She was wonderfully cheerful about the new place and insisted we go to Shepherd's Bush Market to buy me curtains. She chose the fabric, discussed the trimming and all the other details with the man. I made her Libyan tagine one Sunday and this time she liked it. She worried less about me and that relieved our friendship of its overcoat of concern. I could tell that she too enjoyed the lightness. I tried to sneak her into a show. She found it thrilling and outrageous. She looked as guilty as a child, which, inevitably, got us caught. I took her to the places I had newly discovered in the city. We had Italian coffee in Soho and spent afternoons in secondhand bookshops on the Charing Cross Road, she searching the art and architecture sections and I browsing the literature shelves. We would then find a café and show one another our new acquisitions.

When her parents visited, they invited me out for dinner at a French restaurant near Bayswater. Because of the Lebanese Civil War, the family had moved to Jordan, where Rana's father had set up a successful architectural practice. I was somehow sure Rana had not told them about the shooting. I admired them, but they also baffled me. They seemed to be tuned to a different human scale: they were pleasant and confident people who knew how to move in the world and were not going to let any bad news get in their way. The father made a point of saying how he could not wait for Rana to graduate and join his firm. The mother reminded him that Rana was free to do whatever she pleased.

"I know, I know," he said, "but I think it will please her enormously to work for her dad." His laugh was wonderful and infectious. He then asked me, as if it were part of the same conversation, "How is Libya these days?"

I had no idea what he meant.

"Is it a good place to do business? What's the political situation like? Is your guy, Mr. Qaddafi, really as crazy as everyone says? Clearly," he said, and laughed, turning to his wife, "clearly shooting at people from inside your own embassy is nuts, but what is he really like?"

I could think of nothing to say.

"To be from countries such as ours," Rana told him, "is to continually feel obliged to explain them."

"Yes," her father agreed, "but even we the Lebanese don't do such things."

35

IN AUGUST I WAS issued with a blue travel document that allowed entry into Europe without a visa. Rana wanted me to join her and her friend Seham, a Palestinian who was also studying architecture at Edinburgh, on a trip to the Costa Brava, where Seham's parents had a house by the sea. Hugh and Lucy, friends of Seham and Rana, were also going to come. I immediately decided against it, but, fearing I would disappoint Rana, I said I would think about it.

"What is there to think about?" she said. "Listen, I know you hate flying. We will be driving—it'll be such fun—all the way through France." Every other day she called to persuade me. "Tell me what's worrying you?" she would say, and every time she neither judged nor dismissed my concerns. "Hugh and Lucy are good people. And you and Seham are my closest friends. It's time you two met properly. And the sun—oh my God, Khaled, the sun—will be good for our souls. Say yes."

The manager at work agreed to give me two weeks of unpaid leave. I asked the bank for an overdraft and they approved a small one. Rana and her friends drove from Edinburgh to Shepherd's Bush to collect me and parked outside, blowing the horn. The car, an old green Ford

Estate, belonged to Hugh and Lucy, a Scottish couple who had met at university but were already planning to get married. I had not been with so many people and in such a small space in a long while. At one point, as we crossed the Channel on the ferry, we all stood on deck with the wind in our faces. To avoid the tolls, we took back roads through the entire length of France. We all, except Seham, who did not know how to drive, shared the driving, stopping only to refuel or to get coffee and sandwiches. When I was not driving, I sat in the back next to Seham, who insisted on taking the middle seat.

"Least I can do," she said, "given how useless I'm proving to be on this trip."

In the beginning, both she and I did our best to take up as little room as possible, but eventually our bodies relaxed and our temperatures met as our arms and waists and thighs pressed against one another. From the few words we exchanged, and much more from the silences, I was convinced that she knew what had happened to me, that Rana had told her and perhaps even shared with her the fears and concerns she did not share with me. And something about this, I suspected, was behind her initial physical carefulness, that, together with basic decorum, made her mindful of the wounded body that sat beside her.

We passed fields of sunflowers; we crossed rows and rows of northern trees that were still unfamiliar to me—maples, yews, and oaks. We needled through sleepy French villages. We listened to Bob Dylan and Joni Mitchell and I was surprised when everyone admitted that they too had, on more than one occasion, cried listening to Joni Mitchell songs. We talked about what exactly it was about those songs that moved us and I liked the silence that followed.

A confederacy had formed between Seham and me. Now every time she spoke, I felt she was shaping her words for my ears. And whenever I said anything, I thought about how she might receive it, believing that she would understand my meaning better than anyone else. Something about her made me desperately miss my sister, Souad.

The further south we went, the brighter the land turned. We were now among familiar trees—cypresses, pines, figs, olives, and almonds. When night fell, their perfume turned pungent and unrestrained, as though nature were involved in its own nocturnal confession. I rolled down the window and breathed it all in. Seham noticed.

"Smells like home," she said. "Exactly," I said.

Libya and Palestine share the Mediterranean. Everyone but Hugh, who was driving, was asleep. Seham and I turned to speaking in Arabic, whispering it softly. I asked her about her parents. She said that, like Rana's, they too lived in Jordan and got the place in Spain because it reminded them of home. At one point, long after we stopped talking, with the world outside the window black and fragrant, we held hands.

We reached the French–Spanish border by dawn. We had been driving for nearly fifteen hours. We were tired and excited by the prospect of Spain and the Mediterranean Sea, which I could just about smell in the distance, familiar and endless. There was a double checkpoint, a French and then a Spanish one. The French immigration officer would not let me through. He could not understand how I had entered the country without a visa. I pointed out that my UK travel document clearly states that I did not require one.

"That does not apply to you," he said adamantly. "It does not apply to Libyans, Palestinians, or Syrians."

Hugh, Lucy, and Seham tried to reason with him. Rana, on the other hand, was too busy laughing. This annoyed the officer.

"What's funny?" he demanded.

"You won't allow us out of France because you say we shouldn't be in France," Rana told him.

"Precisely," the man said.

Hugh and Lucy spoke French, and that made the man soften a little. Eventually he said he would allow me through but on one condition: that we head directly for the French Embassy in Madrid and apply for a visa today.

"And, in any case," he said, "you will not be allowed into France on the way back without a visa."

We set off, and, after the initial relief, everyone became offended on my behalf. It flattered me at first, but then their outrage turned into questions: Should we go to Madrid now or later? Was the man a racist or was he just overly bureaucratic? Had this ever happened before? And why did I have a travel document and not a proper passport? I answered each question vaguely, trying all the while to seem relaxed and indifferent. Hugh pressed me on Madrid, offered to drive me there.

"Don't worry," I said. "I'll take the train once we are settled. Anyway," I lied, "I have a cousin there and it would be good to see him. Maybe stay a couple of days." And, to avoid any further questions, I made up some story about this fictitious cousin. "He's a musicologist," I told them. "Works on the links between Arabic maqamat and Andalusian music. Plays half a dozen instruments. Very funny guy. Always manages to make me laugh. A good reason to go to Madrid."

Lucy wanted to know what maqamat were and I said that they were musical scales.

"Well, not exactly," Seham said. "They are melodic structures in classical Arabic music."

And how come she knew so much about it, Rana asked?

"I studied music as a child," Seham told her. "But you knew this," she said, and then told us about how she loves music and, for that moment, we all forgot about Madrid.

When we fell silent, Rana told Seham, "Good thing the Frenchman couldn't tell from your Jordanian passport that you're Palestinian."

"Or that your mother is Syrian," Seham told her, and we all laughed.

36

THE SEA WAS BEAUTIFUL and unchanged, and its beauty was part of its fidelity. It was just as I remembered it, and this made it seem as if I too were being remembered by it. By day it was a well of light. It held the rays, obscuring them, a motif turning upon itself, vanishing here, advancing there, dying, continuously dying. Come night, the water turned thick and heavy and black. I entered and it made way. In the deep I sensed that what lurked beneath was alive with intent. You have to be vigilant, I told myself, because perhaps the point is that there is no point: that the sea, its bright and its dark, is not concerned with human yearning. And that people get shot or do not get shot, fishermen drown or do not drown, according to the same logic of nature's insouciance.

The cove the house looked out on could have been plucked from the Libyan coast east of Benghazi, in my mother's country, the Green Mountain, where we often went for day trips, where you swim out and look back at the land rising green and yellow. I told this to Rana when we were alone in the water.

"Just imagine," I said, "that this is the same water."

"Why imagine?" she said. "It is the same. Only without the compli-
cations."

We laughed.

"If this were Libya," I said, "men would be ogling."

"And not only men," she said.

In the brief silence that followed, as we bobbed in the water, facing
the cliff, the rock rising steeply and the pines clinging to it, their
trunks black and their canopies dark green and curling thirstily upward toward the light, she surprised me and went back to the day she
picked me up from Westminster Hospital. Perhaps it was the sea or
seeing me happy that made her admit that she had been worried, that
she had only pretended to be brave, that the whole way to London
she could not stop looking over her shoulder, changing carriages, and
that when the train pulled into King's Cross she took several detours.
She did this every time she visited, she said. And when she had gone
to get my things from the bedsit, she had had a stomachache the
whole night before. She laughed, or tried to, as she said this. She descended and emerged with her head tilted back, her hair combed by
the water, and her face glazed and dripping. There was something
else she wanted to say.

Looking into the distance, she asked, "What did it feel like? To be
shot."

"I don't know," I said, trying to fasten my eyes on the pines, and
saw a thick rope snapping, the shadow of an anchor sinking into the
deep. No, I thought; do not tell her that. "To be honest," I said instead, "I think I was lucky. The bullets saved me from a worse fate."

Droplets clung to her eyelashes. She had a tender but unconvinced
expression.

"I really believe that," I went on, and I felt the heat of some invisible and insincere passion, something like hope or despair or ma-
levolent pride. What I was certain of was that I had betrayed
someone—myself, my friend, or possibly both—and that this fact was
inescapable, hovering between us in the water.

I had my T-shirt on in the water. I kept it on all the while I swam or sunbathed. I made up an excuse to the others that my skin was sensitive to the sun. Once, when I was in the next room and they did not know I could hear, I caught Hugh and Lucy ask Rana about the T-shirt. There was too long a pause before she spoke. "It's his skin, you see. Very sensitive." And I thought, what a bad liar she is, because the silence that followed gave her away, made her sound unconvinced. Perhaps she too shared the objection. Now that she and I were alone in the water, she said, "Why not take it off, the T-shirt?"

I did and tossed it as far away as I could, toward the deep, where the horizon stretched without interruption. She laughed wonderfully and I thought, I hope my T-shirt won't be washed to land.

We swam back and she said, softly as though we could be heard, "If anyone asks, tell them you were in a car accident when you were a child."

"Good idea," I said, but, as we emerged from the water and her eyes lingered on my chest, a faint hint of disgust brushed across her face. I returned quickly to the house and found myself a fresh T-shirt and never removed it again on the beach.

37

ONE EVENING, WHEN THE sun was low, the five of us sat around a small table outside a bar in the square of a nearby medieval village high up on a hill. Our table was covered with glasses and small plates of food. People walked and milled about. There was the fading blue above and the mustard stone of the surrounding buildings. Every fifteen minutes the old clock tower clanked and the small birds, black as ink, splattered into the sky, only to return and have the same trick played on them again. My stern command gave way. The hands clutched around my life eased a little. An open feeling washed over me and left me daring, with nearly no care in the world. I talked and talked, told stories, amused my friends and made them laugh. I caught a look in Rana's eyes that I remembered from the old days in Edinburgh, the time before the time, except now there was a little pride in it too, as well as a hint of relief. "Tell them the story about . . ." she kept saying, and each time I did.

Night fell and the stars appeared. We remained in the cool summer air, drinking and eating, our hands falling on one another's shoulders. The waiter placed a candle on our table, and the flame lit our faces and flickered inside the glass. Then suddenly the tremendous bang of a gunshot. A second later I realized that it was only the throttle of an engine groaning uphill in one of the neighboring streets. But it was too late. I was already a few feet away, frozen in place. I could see Seham, her hand against her cheek, eyes wide open. Rana was the only one who was no longer sitting. There she was, right beside me, her hand on my arm and my arm was shaking. She led me away. We walked in circles through the quiet back lanes until the panic passed. I do not remember us saying anything. When we returned to the others, there was baffled concern on their faces, an uncomfortable silence, and I suspected, in the time Rana and I were away, Seham felt she had had no option but to tell Lucy and Hugh. I would not have minded if she had. We ordered more drinks, remained a little longer, but talked less and talked softly.

Walking along the winding lanes back to the car, Seham and I fell a little behind the others. She brought her shoulder close to mine.

"Are you all right?" she said.

"Yes," I said. "It's a perfect evening."

I continued looking ahead, feeling her eyes on me, hoping she would not ask any more questions. The street curved and, for the few seconds that the others were out of sight, she held my hand.

Later that night, we sat by the edge of the black water, listening to the timid waves. She and I were alone, entirely alone. She asked what place I loved most. It surprised me what came to mind: Derna, my mother's hometown, and I thought of telling her about it, the smell of herbs as we would drive into the hills, the waterfall that comes out of nowhere, the sea always behind you. Instead, I said, "I don't know," and asked her the same question. She said it was this place where we were sitting. "This exact spot." I kissed her and she kissed me back. We kissed long and I felt everything that I was fall and return, fall and return. I did not know that joy could be so painful. That night I could hardly sleep from it. You can have any life you want, I told myself. Any place could be your favorite place too.

But in the morning, when she came toward me, all present and vivid, I did not lend myself. She was shocked, offended, looked as though she had been slapped. I did not know how to backtrack, make myself available again, and it was like a door closing inside me.

A couple of days before we were due to head back, the group began to fret again about my visa. I finally told them of my plan: that I had no intention of going to Madrid, that I did not like embassies, and that I was enjoying myself too much to want to leave the sea.

"We will return together as originally planned," I told them, "but take the main motorway. I'll pay the toll and I'll drive. Now that we are all brown, I will stand out less. If it doesn't work, you carry on and I'll head to Madrid."

None of them disagreed, but none agreed either.

When we approached the border, everyone fell silent. In the rear-view mirror, I caught Seham whispering to herself. The officer waved us through and, when we were a hundred feet in, we exploded in loud cheers.

38

EVERY SO OFTEN I would get a postcard from Henry, usually of a painting by Rembrandt or Titian or El Greco. He would report on a visit to the Scottish National Gallery or the theater, include a line or two about the weather in Edinburgh. Then he rang and asked if I had applied to university yet. He recommended Birkbeck College.

"You can fit it in around work, as the lectures are in the evenings."

"But doesn't that mean it's not very good, then?" I asked.

"Don't be a snob," he said. "This country is already full of them."

I promised I would look into it.

He then said, "I will be in London this coming weekend. Are you free for a quick visit? Saturday afternoon? I want to see where Robert Louis Stevenson lived."

I got some falafel from the Sudanese man in the market. When he commented on my cheerful mood, I told him an old friend was visiting from home. "In that case," he said, "these are on me," and no matter how hard I tried he refused to take my money. I tidied the place and made a pot of tea. It was now August and I had not seen him since April when I was a student in Edinburgh. The prospect of his arrival, of him being in my flat, a figure from the past standing in this newly made life, made me happy and anxious. He shook my hand warmly. He moved around the flat with ease, as though the place belonged to someone he had known all his life. He opened the kitchen cupboards, was impressed by my Italian coffeepot.

"Do you really know how to use that?" he asked.

I remembered that first time I had nervously asked him if we could meet for coffee.

He asked whether the curtains had come with the flat.

"No, I got them made," I said. "Rana helped me."

He smiled. Although he did not say it, it was clear that as well as relief he also felt pride.

"By the way," he said, and stopped. "A man telephoned. Said he used to be my student. Claimed to be a close friend of yours." He took out his notebook. "Mustafa al Touny. I vaguely remembered the name. I told him I did not feel I could give out your contact details without your permission. He was rather upset by this."

"I'm sorry," I said, and confirmed that the man was indeed my friend and that we had been in hospital together.

"Thank God for that," he said.

It was only then that I realized that, as well as being concerned for me, my former professor and now friend or confidant or guardian— I was not sure how he saw it—was also worried for his own safety, that he might be pursued or pressured to reveal my whereabouts.

"You know," I decided to lie, "the Libyan state has forgotten the whole thing. I know for a fact that some of those who were shot have returned home and no one even questioned them. And," I continued, "I don't think I told you, but I was contacted by Scotland Yard. Yes, and they confirmed that I have nothing, absolutely nothing, to worry about."

"Is that so?" he said.

I did not think that he was entirely convinced, but I decided best to leave it there. Instead, I asked, "What are you reading these days?"

39

OUR FORTNIGHT IN THE Costa Brava receded. I missed the sea. I missed Seham even more, missed her terribly, and whenever I thought of her for some reason that brought up my family and I would see their faces emerge and do so more clearly than they had for a while. I had seen pictures of Seham's parents in the Spanish house. I imagined them sitting around a table with my parents, talking the evening away. I even heard what they might have said. She had a brother who was also younger. I saw him and Souad becoming friends, wandering off into the courtyard. I then saw those photos of Seham's family along with ones of mine, framed and resting on the same quiet bookshelf. I asked Rana for her number. I called and one of Seham's flatmates answered. She went to fetch her and I could hear her say, "I don't know. Difficult name."

"Hello, Seham, this is Khaled, Rana's friend, we went to Spain together."

"I know who you are," she said, and laughed. "Or, wait, I still can't place you. More information, please."

When she came to London a month later, we met. I got dressed up. Her eyes lingered for a second on my ironed white shirt. She had limited time, she said, and wanted to see as much of the city as possible. There was a show at the Hayward Gallery, but, when we got there, we found the place closed for repairs. We stood and looked out at the river. I felt the need to apologize. Instead I suggested we go to the National Gallery. On the way there I asked about her family. She took the question for what it was, an attempt to fill the silence. But then when she asked about my life in London and whether I was happy, she sounded sincere and I had no idea what to say. I made things up, told her that I loved it here and that I had many interesting friends. She said she was glad and looked at me with slight hesitation, as though undecided whether she could trust me. I wished so much then that I could make her trust me. I wished I could tell her what was on my mind, to ask her, for example, if she believed it was possible to live a happy life away from home, without one's family, if she knew of anyone who had done it.

It turns out it is possible to live without one's family. All one has to do is to endure each day and gradually, minute by minute, brick by brick, time builds a wall.

After that initial call months ago, I stayed true to my vow not to telephone home. But then it was Eid and I was full of longing. The smell of melted honey and butter, coffee, tea, and oranges, the early-morning voices of my parents in the kitchen, money under the pillow, new clothes, sweets in the pockets. I telephoned and my father picked up. He sounded hurt. "I just don't understand," he said. "And to worry your mother so?"

"I'm sorry, so very sorry," I said. "It's just relentless here. I barely have time for anything."

"But it was summer. You were meant to come home for the summer."

"Yes, but I had written to say that I decided to stay and work," I said. "Did you not get my postcard?"

"Fine, but you could have still come home for a few days."

"Together with other students we have started to translate *The Epistle of Forgiveness*," I told him. "We are working from the book

you gave me. It's a scandal, Father, but no one here knows of it."
When he did not respond, I said, "Please be happy for me."

"I am," he said. "But not to call or come home the whole summer."

"I'm doing very well here. I just got distracted. The world took
me." I began to cry. I cried and apologized again.

He asked me to please stop, that it was not that serious a matter.
And, when I did, he said, "It wasn't just your silence, you see. I just
couldn't stop thinking about you. Is everything all right?"

"It is," I said. "It is. It's just the distance. I miss you all so much."

"Remember you are there to achieve something. Tell me," he then
said, "what is your overall opinion of Edinburgh?"

"What do you mean?" I asked.

"You have been there now a year, twelve whole months, and it
sounds like it's going very well. No small feat to be translating *The
Epistle*. Has your English really become that good? And is the city
truly as beautiful as some books claim?"

Perhaps they did not see me in the news footage. After all, Rana
said I was all the way to the far edge of the frame, a speck in a sea of
chaos.

It was at once important and impossible to know what my father
knew and what he did not know about what had befallen me. Were we
speaking in code, or as honestly as those morning conversations when
sometimes he and I woke up before Mother and Souad, and would sit
side by side speaking softly?

After that I called every month or two and always with some fic-
tional piece of good news.

40

MUSTAFA AND I HAD not spoken since we parted at the hospital, which was nearly five months ago now. The silence was all my doing, as, at least up to when I lost it, I'd had his number in Manchester and he'd had no way of contacting me. But the number he had given to Henry was a London number. I dialed it and Mustafa picked up after the first ring.

"For fuck's sake," he said. "I've been in London two weeks already and every day I ring my uncle to see if there's a message from you. You bastard. Worried me sick. What are you doing right now? I mean, this minute."

An hour later, we were at Café Cyrano on Holland Park Avenue. He seemed different. His enthusiasm had waned and something like impatience or boredom had set in.

"I know you blame me," he said anxiously.

This was what I had feared. He knows me better than I know myself, I thought, and resented him for it.

"I don't," I said.

"You do," he said.

"Perhaps a little," I said, "but it's unfair. You didn't force me. No one did."

"Yes, but if it weren't for me you wouldn't have been there and if you hadn't been there you wouldn't be in this situation."

"Don't flatter yourself," I said.

But he did not smile. He held his hands tightly together, shaking a little.

"It really hit me," he said, "when I got to my uncle's. The bullet just keeps running through me." He straightened his back, called to the waiter, and impatiently ordered two more beers.

What I wish I could have told him then is that at that moment I believed no one in the entire world knew me better than he did. That with him I did not have to pretend. I did not have to shield myself from his concern or bewilderment. I did not have to translate. And violence demands translation. I will never have the words to explain what it is like to be shot, to lose the ability to return home or to give up on everything I expected my life to be, or why it felt as though I had died that day in St. James's Square and, through some grotesque accident, been reborn into the hapless shoes of an eighteen-year-old castaway, stranded in a foreign city where he knew no one and could be little use to himself, that all he could just about manage was to march through each day, from beginning to end, and then do it again. I did not know how to say such things then, I still do not, and the inarticulacy filled my mouth. This, I now know, is what is meant by grief, a word that sounds like something stolen, picked out of your pocket when you least expect it. It takes a long time to learn the meaning of a word, particularly a word like that, or perhaps all words, even ones as simple as "you" or "me." But that day, sitting opposite Mustafa, I felt I had no need for words, no need to translate or sum up or exchange an experience for a set of sentences. I loved him for it and I loved him not only because he and I were united by a common fate, but because he appeared then to be a truer version of what a man is, proof that our loss was actually a gain, and everyone else—Hugh,

Lucy, Henry, Seham, and even Rana, all those I worked with at the shop, the waiter who had just brought us our beers, the other customers in the café, and those walking outside, up and down Holland Park Avenue—was somehow innocent, underdeveloped, yet to attain the full sense of what it is to be a human being in a world where people were willing to crush one another. And, just like that, the poisonous notion that Mustafa and I somehow belonged to a superior minority coursed through me. We drank a toast to each other's good health.

"How the hell do you look so good?" he said. "Tanned and rosy-cheeked. Did you get married or something?"

I told him about the Costa Brava, the incident at the border, the sea and how much it reminded me of home.

"Fair enough," he said in English. I was not sure what he meant by that.

"We'll have to go there together one day," I said, more to fend off any possible resentment.

"Now's not the time for holidays," he said, and told me that soon after arriving at his uncle's he took the train to Edinburgh. Seeing how surprised I was, he said, "Fuck them; I'm not afraid? Anyway, I did it for both of us, to leave things tidy. It's the least I could do after all the trouble I got you in. First thing, I went to Saad, to find out what he knew and what he had told the others about us.

"'You went to London to see a Rolling Stones concert,' he'd said, smiling. 'You do like the Rolling Stones, don't you? But be careful. They suspect you; you and Khaled.'

"I bought a carton of Marlboros and went straight to Razzaq's room."

Razzaq was the older and more formidable one of the Wires.

"He looked surprised to see me. But also seemed to have expected it. He let me in, locked the door, and put the key in his trouser pocket. I caught that.

"'A gift from our holiday,' I said, and gave him the cigarettes.

"What a waste of money that was. He took it and said nothing. Don't let him rattle you, I thought, and proceeded with my plan. I pretended to be pleased about what happened at the embassy. 'A few stray dogs got what they deserve,' I told him.

"He looked at me and said nothing.

"I thought, I had walked into this room with my own two feet. That must count for something. After all, I had always got on well with him.

"'Our country has many enemies,' he finally said.

"'Absolutely,' I said, and praised the Leader. 'He's so far ahead that none of his enemies has a chance.'

"He offered me a cigarette. We smoked in silence."

Mustafa lit a cigarette and looked at me in the same way I imagined Razzaq had looked at him.

"I don't know how to say this," he said. "Maybe you won't understand, but I envied Razzaq at that moment. Not his character, certainly not his politics or ethics. I envied his safety. The luxury of it.

"Then he asked, 'Where is your friend, what's his name?'

"The bastard. He knows your name very well. He just wanted me to say it.

"'Khaled,' I told him. 'We both went to a Rolling Stones gig, you know, just for a change of scene.'

"'The Rolling Stones,' he said. 'Mick Jagger. "Under My Thumb,"'" Mustafa said, and laughed. "The bastard. Then I told him that someone suggested we see a place called Cornwall, 'All the way in the southwest of the country,' I said. 'So remote that the news hardly reaches there. We heard of what happened only a couple of days ago when we returned. To be honest,' I said, and told him that this was the reason I had come to see him, 'Khaled and I don't like our degree. We've been unhappy with it for some time: the endless reading, the boring teachers.

"'Literature is for girls,' he said.

"'We want to ask to change universities.'

"'That is above my station,' he said, and went on about how the trouble with the world was that people didn't know their place. 'Ever since Victory Day,' he said, which is what the regime is now calling the shooting, 'all scholarship fees and stipends are on hold until students confirm their position and hand over any information that may help the investigation, anything you saw or heard, no matter how trivial. This before anything else is now the priority. We must secure our country. In your and your friend's case, your long and unexplained disappearance gave me no option but to recommend you both to attend in person.'"

Mustafa said this quickly and looked at me as though he too was unsure what that meant.

"'Attend in person'?" I asked.

"It's obvious," he said. "We will have to go back and beg for forgiveness."

I held my head.

"Well, at least now we know," he said.

I could not find my words and he was too nervous to keep quiet. I was furious that he had spoken on my behalf. But, even as I thought of telling him, I felt the futility of it.

"On the way back to Manchester," he said, "I remembered my father's youngest brother, Uncle Hamed. He lived with us. The first to introduce me to books. Liked Kafka and Dostoevsky and Hemingway. Was exactly the opposite of my father. I loved him. He was a leading member of the independent students' union. I was only nine then. Government thugs came to our house, turned the place upside down, emptied every drawer, and took him away. My maternal uncle in Manchester is convinced the same thing would happen if I went back. I ignored him and called home anyway. But when my father heard my voice, he hung up." Some hidden feeling spread over Mustafa's face and darkened it. "Unlike you," he said, "I never felt close to my parents. My father is hard and difficult. The best I could hope for from him was not to notice me, to leave me alone. Mum is fine but weak, a slave to him. When he couldn't find a towel nearby, he dried his hands on her dress. When he fucked off to work, she sat for a moment in the kitchen, doing nothing. Once, when the house was empty, I went into their room, opening all the drawers. Don't know why. Just wanted to see everything. I liked the one with her silk scarves, the way she delicately rolled each around her hand before putting it away. Made them look like bunched-up roses. Now I keep seeing them unfurled and scattered all over the floor."

Large tears welled up in Mustafa's eyes. He covered his face with his hands and wiped it with such force that it whitened his skin, like weather passing over rocks.

"Did you call yours?" he asked.

I began to tell him about the conversation I had had with my father, but he kept nodding and saying, "I know, I know. This matches up with the accounts I heard from the others. The authorities have not informed the families, which means either they don't know we were involved or they want us to believe that so we'll return and fall into their hands."

"What do you think we should do?" I heard myself ask.

"Did Scotland Yard contact you?" he asked. "Yes, me too," he said. "They feel bad because they screwed up. They apparently had intelligence and ignored it. Or that's the word anyhow."

"Where did you hear this?"

"There are many Libyans in Manchester," he said. "I heard it from some there."

After a short silence, I asked the same question again: "What do you think we should do? I want to go home." Hearing myself say that sent a tremor through me.

"None of those who were with us in hospital went back. I can confirm that."

The word "confirm" had a strange effect on me. Like a stone in the hand.

"What do you think we should do?" I asked again.

We both fell silent. There was no answer, which is why one of us had to say something.

"We should definitely stay put," he said. "Besides, the country is a miserable shithole. Now that we are here, let's make something of

ourselves. Time will solve everything. In a few years no one will remember. In a few years Qaddafi and all his Razzaqs will be history."

I walked home with that stone in my hand. I saw the doctor's ear,
the shape of it, as he told me I would not be able to hide the cause of
my injury. I pictured Mustafa's mother's scarves and saw instead my
mother's. You are the custodian of the well-being of those scarves, I
told myself. I clenched my fists tighter. I hunched my back. Become
smaller, diminish your scale, absent yourself, be as invisible as a ghost.
You are now a danger to those you love the most.

41

THE FOLLOWING MORNING I took the bus to Shoreditch in east London. I tried to rent a PO box but the man said that I would still need to give him a street address. I went into a telephone box to call Walbrook. He did not answer. I paged through the telephone book, randomly selected an address in Edinburgh. Now I had a PO box, a place to which my mother's letters could be sent and where I could collect them. I went into a café and wrote home, giving them the new address. I informed them that I had changed universities, that I had fallen in love with London, and that this new program was much better than the one at Edinburgh. "Besides, I'm learning so much here. And not only from my classes. The museums and the libraries are themselves an education. I'm so excited."

At the weekend I invited Mustafa over for supper. That morning I went to the butcher, got a shoulder of lamb, marinated it in the way my father had shown me in lemon, garlic, and tomato. I could hear his voice as I did it. "More salt than you'd think, and don't forget the black pepper, my boy, a couple of bay leaves, some stalks of fresh thyme, then wrap the whole thing tightly in silver foil so none of the moisture escapes." I put it in the oven for five hours on a low heat and resisted any temptation to open the door and check it. By the time Mustafa arrived, he could smell the roast from downstairs. I had some vodka but he said that would not do and ran out to the shops. I made salad, mashed the potatoes, spread a bedsheet on the floorboards in the middle of the main room, and set our plates and glasses there. Apart from the mattress in the corner, with my books and a lamp beside it, the place was still bare. He returned breathless with a bottle of Spanish red wine. We ate and all the meat vanished and I felt glad that he enjoyed it. He smoked and we drank the rest of the wine. He looked about the place somewhat disapprovingly. I asked him what his flat was like.

"Massive," he said. "Borrowed money from my uncle and rented a three-bedroom apartment." Then he said, with a hint of admonishment, "How could you live in such a small place?"

"I quite like small places," I said. "I can't bear the idea of an unused room. It saddens me."

"This saddens me," he said, and then asked, "What are your plans? What are you going to do with yourself?"

"I'm thinking of going back to school," I said.

"Really?" he said. "I'm done with that. Money is more important. I mean, if you have to choose. And we have to choose. I'm training to be an estate agent. Profitable and easy work. All you do is show people around. But listen," he said, "if you're planning on being an intellectual, move in with me. You won't have to pay rent. And there's furniture for fuck's sake."

He laughed and I did too, but it took months before he would give up on that idea.

Mother's reply arrived the following week. "I am not and will never be used to your absence," she wrote. "But London, how exciting. We know you're busy, but when you can please write back to tell us all about the new university, and your life in London. Where are you living? Are you still friends with Fred and Mustafa? Do you have enough money?"

42

DURING THOSE EARLY MONTHS in London, Mustafa, like a hopeful fisherman, cast his net wide. He pulled many friends into his orbit. But then, on inspecting his catch, he would quickly grow skeptical and begin discarding the undesired ones. Eventually, only a handful remained and they too withered, and by the time he reached the shore and returned to Libya, only I was left. And because one friend is never enough, I too had to be let go of in some fashion. None of this is dramatic, of course, nor is it unusual. Many people are frustrated by their friends. Some, like Mustafa, believe friendship, or the kind of friendship we had, one sanctified by blood, should be, like romantic love, monogamous. This made him perpetually overrun with jealousy. My friendship with Rana, for example, and later with Hosam— particularly that with Hosam—never sat easily with him. Indeed, it made him suffer. Similarly, and in the opposite direction, whenever he wanted to express his passion for our friendship, he would say that we were different from others, that we had walked through fire together, and that there was nothing he would not do for me, take another bullet if he had to, and that no matter how many friends I made, no one would ever understand me as he did. And when he came down from such heights, he would digress into a lavish critique of one of his friends, gossiping with delight. Friendship to Mustafa was a question of competing allegiances. Obviously, or at least to a certain extent, this must be true for me too, or else why would I have felt flattered by such declarations? But this habit made him wary of others and made him, I can see now from this distance, progressively suspicious of humankind. And perhaps all this had proved useful in preparing him for the unlikely path he was to take when, more than a quarter of a century after we were shot in St. James's Square, he returned to Libya and carried arms in the February 2011 Revolution, rising to become one of its militia leaders, a fact that tonight, during my nocturnal walk home, where every step forward conjures up more vividly the past, I find even more deeply unnerving.

But, before this, and during those early days in London, Mustafa's social appetite was optimistic. It became nearly impossible to see him alone. At one point, he fell in with a set of four brothers. They were originally from Benghazi. Rich and glamorous and wild. We had heard of the family. Their father appeared in one of the televised interrogations the state conducted in the early 1980s and broadcast repeatedly during those years. I was not allowed to watch them, but, whenever my parents were out, I would turn on the television and stand right in front of it. I still recall the fascination and horror I felt. The suspect usually sat in the corner of a windowless gray room, looking captured and guilty and lost. All sense had collapsed, and they were now in a world where the rules were unknown.

I had a morbid fear of madness as a child. I feared it the way I feared the dark. I once heard someone on the radio define madness as a state in which nothing is reliable. They had said it mid-sentence, as though it were a well-established fact. One of my teachers described it as the loss of command over one's mind. I remember wondering then what was meant by the word "command" here? If one needed to be willfully in command of one's mind, who was in charge in the first place? The whole subject concerned me and made any occurrence of nonsense—a nightmare, or when I woke up not knowing where I was, or when at a funeral an adult broke down—at once compelling and absolutely terrifying. But none were more so than those snatched viewings of the televised interrogations, when the house was empty behind me and I kept my finger on the switch in case I heard my parents return, the volume so low that I could hear my own breathing above it, mesmerized by the sterile stage set, the macabre atmosphere, the questions asked, and the hard and impatient voices of the faceless individuals who asked them. They, like me, stood behind the camera. Once the accused, an elderly man dressed in a cream suit—a trade unionist, if I remember correctly—was sweating profusely. He continued answering the questions as best he could, when a tiny speck appeared over his groin. I assumed it was a drop fallen from his drenched brow, but then it began to widen and grew until it took on the shape of a cloud.

The father of Mustafa's friends was lucky, spent only two years in prison, and afterward was allowed to travel abroad. He now lived in Cairo and would visit his sons in London from time to time. They had a house in Kensington. I went there with Mustafa a few times. On one occasion I saw the father there. He was sitting in the television room, dressed in a white jellabiya, leaning forward with his elbows on his knees, smoking a cigarette, concentrating entirely on the football match. He shook hands with us without taking his eyes off the screen.

The four brothers had all attended schools in Britain, expensive boarding schools, where every so often they were either suspended or expelled for bad behavior. Being with them, there was always the sense of danger, of something about to go wrong. But they were also capable of great charm and generosity. They dressed well, appreciated fine food, and would take Mustafa and me to restaurants and nightclubs we never could have afforded. They attracted a wide variety of people, city boys and a few shady characters dealing in precious stones and stolen art. Once in their house one of their friends took out a gun and it was passed around the room as though a trophy. My heart raced as it approached. I turned it in my hands for what, I hoped, passed for genuine interest. It was always like this whenever I was there: instinct told me not to attract any attention. Most of the time we hung out in their house, listening to the latest records, drinking whiskey. The brothers liked to cook and would compete and interfere with one another's dishes. At certain moments they appeared like a seething clump of reptiles trapped in the same pit. I often enjoyed myself, but I went mainly because I was worried about Mustafa. I then realized that, although he often insisted that I join him, he too felt the need to keep a guarding eye on me.

One aimless afternoon, one of the brothers, the youngest, came over and shoved himself right beside me on the sofa.

"Adventurous?" he whispered. "Feeling adventurous?"

I had no idea what he meant. He then opened his hand and right in the center of his palm was a bright yellow pill. Mustafa flew across the room in a flash and with ferocious force snatched up the boy by the arm.

"If I ever see you do that again," he told him, his nose right over the boy's face, which, although surprised, had an oddly amused expression, as if he had a happy memory of being treated like this, "I said, if I ever see you do that again, I'll rip your arm off, do you hear?"

The repetition softened the threat. The older brother pushed them apart, filled their glasses, and insisted that they drink to each other's health.

"Poet," he then said to me—they had names for one another and took to calling me that—"whenever you're around your friend is not himself."

Mustafa did not reply.

"A little prim and proper. But when you're gone, the devil in him comes out."

We stayed longer than we should have that evening. Every time I started to go, Mustafa asked me to wait just another ten minutes. I thought he was keen to leave things on good terms with the brothers, but the longer we stayed the darker his mood became. At one point, he began crying. It must be the alcohol, I thought. The brothers gathered around him, insisting he tell them what the matter was, but all

Mustafa did was to hold his hands together until the blood drained out of them. He screamed the most terrible cry. I shall never forget it. He screamed it over and over, carrying it with him as he stormed out. I stopped them from following him, reassuring them that I would take good care of him. I tried to keep up. Eventually, he slowed down and we walked across Hyde Park together without saying much at all. Night had fallen, and it was cool and quiet in among the trees.

"Are you all right?" I asked, and he nodded. "I don't understand those people," I said.

"No, neither do I," he said, and I remember how relieved I was to finally hear his voice.

"I mean, I don't get what they want, what drives them, why they all remain in that house and don't leave, go into the world?"

"Because they are brothers," he said. "And brothers are competitive. And competition is a distraction."

I wondered if he felt that way about me. And then I thought he must feel that way toward his own brother, Ali, who, although younger, had had to assume the responsibilities of his elder sibling, the first in the family to go to university, but who, after winning a scholarship to a university in Great Britain, had gone and squandered the opportunity.

We shook hands at Lancaster Gate. He went north and I turned west.

A couple of weeks later we were back in Kensington again. No one mentioned anything about what had happened. The two middle brothers were engaged in an argument. Something about money. At one point they stood up and ran into one another like rams. Locked in that fierce embrace, they kicked and punched one another with passionate fury. The youngest and the eldest tried to break them up and failed. There was something casual about their effort. I found the whole scene deeply disturbing. I went to try to break them up, but Mustafa pulled me back and said, softly, "Time to leave." He walked out and after a few seconds I followed him. I remember thinking, it is possible to just walk away: one could actually do that, it is an option.

We strolled across the park again. I do not remember what we said precisely, but I vaguely recollect my going on about how strange and disturbing it was to see brothers come to blows. Mustafa hardly said a word. He listened and had the silence of one who knows that he must be gentle with the innocent.

43

A SHORT WHILE AFTER Henry stopped urging me to continue with my education, I asked him if he could write me a reference. I applied to Birkbeck and did so half-heartedly. I went to the interview in that spirit, but something changed when the head of the department led me into her office. Its booklined walls reminded me of my father. Books everywhere smell the same. She sat down in a chair facing me and held in her hand a crisp white sheet of paper. One of her colleagues, a young man with an angular and somewhat austere face, came in and sat next to her. He looked at me carefully, with a hint of goodwill in his eyes.

"Why do you want to study English Literature?" the woman asked.

"I have always liked literature," I said. "English literature." I could hear how unconvincing I must have sounded.

"Professor Walbrook thinks very highly of you," the man said, and at this the woman looked at me with a new softness in her eyes.

I wanted to run out of the room, but then she said, "I'll read this to you." She looked down at the sheet of paper in her hand. I thought, it could be anything: a letter from New Scotland Yard or even from the

Libyan Embassy, urging them not to offer me a place. "And then we want to hear your thoughts."

What a lark! What a plunge! For so it had always seemed to her, when, with a little squeak of the hinges, which she could hear now, she had burst open the French windows and plunged at Bourton into the open air. How fresh, how calm, stiller than this of course, the air was in the early morning; like the flap of a wave; the kiss of a wave; chill and sharp and yet (for a girl of eighteen as she then was) solemn, feeling as she did, standing there at the open window, that something awful was about to happen . . .

The professor's face remained for a second longer on the page before she said, almost to herself, "I think I will stop there. Do you recognize the passage?"

I could not possibly tell her what was going through my mind, that only the year before, also at the age of eighteen, I had been looking not out of but up at an open window and feeling that something awful was about to happen.

The man, who had kept his eyes on me the whole while, asked, "Where do you think the passage is from?"

"I don't know," I said.

"Really?" the woman asked, genuinely surprised.

I thought, well, she is either pretending or I am done for.

The man looked at her and then turned to me again. "What does it make you think of?" he said.

"I'm not sure I understand," I said.

"How does it make you feel?" the woman said.

"Good," I said. "It makes me feel good."

"Why?" she asked. "After all, something awful is about to happen."

"Yes," I said, "but it's the morning air that you think about. And it's beautiful; I mean, the writing."

"And you don't recognize who the writer is?" she asked again.

"No," I said.

"It's from *Mrs. Dalloway,*" she said. "Have you not read Virginia Woolf?"

"No," I said.

"Tell us what you have read," the man said. "Some of the books you like."

I told them about Seneca and Rhys and sensed a strange silence descend when I mentioned Hosam Zowa's *The Given and the Taken,* a book only available in Arabic. My confidence here grew, as I felt I had an advantage over them. I described listening to the story on the BBC Arabic World Service, how it was the first time that a work of fiction had been read in the place of the news. They found this interesting. Gathering momentum, I told them about Abu al Ala al Ma'arri.

"Three hundred years before Dante," I said, "he wrote *The Epistle of Forgiveness,* in which a poet descends to the underworld. Have you really never heard of it?"

44

MY ASYLUM STATUS ALLOWED me to apply for a grant to cover my fees. I started at Birkbeck in October 1985, eighteen months after the shooting. I was excited, and the only people I truly wanted to share the news with were my parents and Souad.

I called and Mother answered. I quickly apologized for the silence.

"It's hard here," I said. "Much harder than I expected, much harder than you can ever imagine. The studies, the pace. No time to look up. But I have some wonderful news. Incredible news. But," I reminded her, "we have to stick to our rule. I have to tell you all at once."

She called out to Father and then to Souad. She asked Souad to fetch her father and come. And then she called out to Father again. In her voice, and particularly when she spoke my father's name, Kamal, there was, right beside the excitement she felt, a quiet panic. I knew then that what she was busy anticipating was less the good news I was about to tell them and more a future in which her son would continue to be kept from her by the demands of a life abroad, a life which, as he had just informed her, was much harder than she could ever imagine.

"He has good news," she told them. "I hope it's good."

I saw them gathering around the telephone, their ears beside the receiver. "Speak, delight our ears," Father said, and when I started, he said, "Louder!"

Standing in my studio flat in Shepherd's Bush, living alone and not in a house with others, I shouted at the top of my voice, "I got a commendation. Best essay of the year."

They will know I'm lying. My mother gave out a long zaghroota. Souad followed and I was amazed because my younger sister had always tried and never before managed it. Now her ululations sounded even stronger and more sonorous than Mother's. I imagined the engagements and weddings they had attended since I left home, my beautiful sister without her elder brother to drive her to and from the women's parties.

"Wait," Father said. "I want the full story. Before anything else, you never told us which university you are now at and whether you are still studying the same subject."

"Yes, English Literature at University College London," I said.

"Oh, well, that's a great school," Father said, proud of his son and a little proud too of his own knowledge of British universities.

"You know it?" Mother asked him.

"Who doesn't know UCL?" he told her.

Souad thought it was cool that I was now living in London.

"Tell us about the commendation," Mother said.

"Well," I said, and now they all shouted, "Louder!"

"It's given by an external committee. Made up of academics from around the country. Among them was Professor Henry Walbrook. Do you remember him, Father?"

"Do I remember him?" he said, taking the receiver. "Indeed I do. He's the reason you went there. You have to send it to us so I can frame it."

"But it was only verbal," I said.

"These things," he explained with the indisputable command of a headmaster, "are always documented, my boy. Ask Professor Wal-brook."

"I will," I said.

"I want a copy in the post."

It would take nearly a year before he stopped asking for it.

45

RANA AND SEHAM PLANNED a reunion, and together with Hugh and Lucy we all met at a pizzeria in Soho. I had suggested the place, and, when we took our seats at the round table, they were impressed by the old grand room with the painted ceiling. I was glad to see them. I felt at ease and a little proud too that they were in what was now my city. But, as the evening wore on and I watched and listened to them converse about their unchanged lives in Edinburgh, which, naturally, were changing but in expected ways—their amused surprise, for example, about how so-and-so had gone to spend their gap year in Peru in order to find themselves, or the other person who was now interning in a famous architectural practice—all their impressions and ideas struck me as either feigned or irrelevant. My contributions dwindled to nothing. I sat back and silently disagreed with nearly every opinion stated, even those that I agreed with. When we walked out into the night air, I wanted to run. Instead I agreed that, yes, definitely, we must do this again and walked them to the tube station. Rana looked surprised when I came to say goodbye. Her stop, Notting Hill Gate, was on the way to Shepherd's Bush and she had banked on our taking the train together. I said I needed to walk in order to think about a paper that was due in a couple of days. We embraced and I went off feeling relieved and regretful.

Schoolwork was demanding. I began to see less and less of Mustafa. I needed all the time I had. I read *Mrs. Dalloway*. I read Richardson's *Clarissa*. I read the Brontës and Dickens. I read Trollope, George Eliot, Thackeray, and Gaskell. I read earnestly and chronologically, from Chaucer to the Elizabethans to Graham Greene. I had some good teachers. I took things too seriously. I was silently horrified, for example, when in the first week a lecturer took us to the college bar and said casually, with a brimming pint of lager in his hand, that he did not expect us to always read absolutely every single page of those big Victorian novels. I did, and the more I read the more unfixed and provisional not only the texts but everything else seemed, a landscape of moving parts. I worried about not having strong opinions. The truth was, I did not care much for opinions. I wanted instead to be in the silent activity of a good book, to observe and feel. I did not have to worry, though. I sailed through, and was treated with regard by my professors and fellow students. I began to enjoy myself.

I made some friends, casual friends. They gave me, to use my father's criteria, pleasure, but I was never certain to what extent I could trust them. I often sensed that gap in our dealings. And, even though I knew it was my doing, I could do very little to change it. But that little I tried.

I had some lovers. Nothing ever lasted long. When we were finally in bed and before the clothes came off, I made sure the lamp was out. If her hand lingered on the scar, or the indentation in my back, and the questions came, I reached for the lie Rana suggested when we were in the sea together: "A car accident when I was a child."

Once I decided to tell the truth. It was less out of a sense of closeness, I told myself, and more as a kind of experiment. But that was untrue. Her name was Hannah. We met in a poetry class. I remember how she altered the air a little. She spoke softly, with a sweet tone, her s's ever so slightly splintered. And when she looked at me, I felt stilled and did not then want for much. She came over for dinner and brought a gift, *Praise,* a thin volume of poems by Robert Hass, an American poet I had not heard of. The book had a slate-green cover with an etched illustration of berries in black. She read a poem from it that she particularly liked. I still remember her face, the equanimity in her voice, when she came to the lines:

> There was a woman
> I made love to and I remembered how, holding
> her small shoulders in my hands sometimes
> I felt a violent wonder at her presence
> like a thirst for salt, for my childhood river.

She wanted to know about my childhood. I said there was no river but there was the sea. Then in bed she wanted to know about the scar. She rolled over me, turned on the light, her eyes squinting into the brightness, and studied my chest as though it were a document that contained important information. Her soft and warm hair, the color of autumn leaves, spread wide over my skin. With every slight movement she made, it moved. I tried to answer her questions. I wanted to answer them. I told her what I had never told anyone. She turned silent and sad. Her eyes were now a sore red, as though walking through smoke from a fire. She suddenly left the room and my heart beat wildly. She will collect her things and leave, I thought. But then I heard her pouring drinks. By the time she came back I decided that the best way to conclude the conversation was to say that it was good to finally talk about it. She kissed me passionately.

"I'm so sorry," she said. "I'm sorry for all that has happened to you."

There was no doubt in my mind that she meant it and, having not heard it from anyone else, I found it bewildering how wanted it was, how parched the earth had been, and before I knew it my tears fell. We made love again and remained there in each other's arms a long while after. What was meant to happen then was that we would both have slept, entered the night as equals, but I remained awake and the tears fell again but hotly, with a frightening abandon. I locked myself in the bathroom and hoped she would not hear. I returned exhausted and lay beside her, watching her as she slept in the weak early light, hearing her name, Hannah, repeat softly in my mind, and then imagined its variations: Anna, Annabelle, Annie—the Arabic Noona. It was then that I glimpsed it, the possibility of being free, the work it would take, the turns and conversations and confessions and time. I saw it all.

46

I TURNED DEEPER INTO reading and I became acquainted with progress, or what I saw as progress. For example, I saw, or believed I saw, why Woolf believed that Richardson had made things possible for Henry James. I saw that, although Gustave Flaubert was half a century younger than Walter Scott, the Frenchman was the more mature of the two. I saw why some thought Naguib Mahfouz owed a debt to Stendhal or how Tayeb Salih was touched by Joseph Conrad and Ernest Hemingway. And when I read Laurence Sterne, I was convinced that Ahmed Faris al Shidyaq had read him too. I believed I knew something of what was meant by the spirit of Goethe and Hölderlin, or how *The Thousand and One Nights* was among the texts that had influenced both Goethe and Cervantes. I was very excited to discover that Robert Louis Stevenson too had been inspired by my childhood tales. I could detect in Jorge Luis Borges both Stevenson and *The Nights*. I saw these cross correspondences and exchanges as threads weaving together the whole of literature, that nothing here was disparate. I began to see novels and poetry—indeed, the entire human event—not as a field of demarcations, made up of languages and periods and styles and schools and civilizations, but rather as a great river with its own internal ancestry, that no matter the surface changes, from T. S. Eliot to Badr Shakir al Sayyab, from Chaucer to Derek Walcott, there was a unity in the depths that stood ready and available for the next writer. I had a hope, and it grew bolder the further I progressed down this road of learning, that Hosam Zowa, the author whose short story had affected me so deeply when I was fourteen and stood behind all my reading since, would participate in this great march, that, although he had fallen completely silent since his collection of stories appeared in the month I was shot, April 1984, he might sing again and do so with greater power.

47

A YEAR AND A half later, midway through my degree, I told my family that I had graduated from UCL and was now starting a master's at Birkbeck.

My mother was surprised. "What does this mean in terms of when you'll be coming home?" she asked. "And how could you graduate without telling us?" she said.

"I would really love to go on and do a doctorate," I said.

"Was there no celebration?" she said.

"The British are a hardworking people," Father told her.

"Fine," she told him, "but not to celebrate?"

By the next time I telephoned, Father had done some research. "Did you know," he said, "that T. S. Eliot taught at Birkbeck? Bear that in mind the next time you enter the university."

Shortly after I graduated, I got a position as a teaching assistant at a state school in Battersea. Autumn that year was exceptionally long and colorful: the turning leaves lingered on the trees, and the warmth of summer remained perceptible in the air. I was on the bus to work one morning and, just as the driver turned on to the western end of Kensington High Street, I saw emerging from the concrete hotel on the corner my uncle Osama, my mother's younger brother. He was dressed in a suit that was a little small for him, carrying a briefcase. I was gripped by panic. I rushed to get off the bus but froze at the threshold, annoying the conductor. "Make up your mind, then?" he said, and snapped the bell. The bus moved and I watched, through the open rear, with nothing between us, my uncle, the youngest member of my mother's family. He had lived with us for a time when he was at university and was useless in the kitchen except, everyone agreed, he made an outstanding omelette, and whenever he did you had to go in after him to clean up the mess and check that he had switched off the burner. And it all came to me: his absentmindedness, the delicious buttery smell of those omelettes, his quick and sometimes lurid sense of humor, his love of the music of Ahmed Fakroun and Nasser el Mizdawi, the way he used to tease me, twist my name, "Khaloodee," inflicting it with endearment and mockery. He now had an administrative job at the Ministry of Agriculture. It was in that capacity that he had come to London. He was receding into the distance. It will pass, I told myself. A week or so from now and you will hardly think of it. The bus stopped in traffic and I jumped off. He was stunned to see me, seemed genuinely moved, embraced me several times, releasing me to look once more at my face. And all along there was that mild critical bafflement. I imagined him talking to my mother about me, about her son who, notwithstanding how closely knit a family we were, found it easy to drift away. Looking at his happy face, with its resemblance to Mother's, made something inside me dissolve.

"I told them to put me in touch with you," he said, "but they said they didn't have a number for you. Only a PO box address. What bloody good is that?"

"I have to run," I said, "or I'll be late for work."

"And you are working already," he said. "How wonderful. Tell me everything."

"What are you doing tonight for supper?" I asked. "But I insist. I won't take no for an answer. I'll pick you up from your hotel—that's where you are staying, isn't it? 7 P.M.?"

I ran for the bus and he did not move, stood with his open palm stretched high above him, a beacon in the dark, his face smiling with the unrestrained joy of a happy child.

"7 P.M.," I called out again as the bus moved.

48

THAT WHOLE DAY, WHILE I worked in the classroom and chatted amiably in the staffroom, I felt impatient, as though I were about to embark on a journey. I finished work and went shopping, buying expensive face creams for Mother, books for Father, a trendy leather purse for Souad. In less than two hours, I had spent the equivalent of a month's rent. I also decided to pay for dinner, to show Uncle Osama how happy I was to host him in what was now my town. I found him waiting in the hotel lobby. I took him to one of the nearby Iranian restaurants on the Hammersmith Road. He said he did not know anything about Iranian food and wanted me to order. I ordered too many dishes. We laughed when the waiter tried to fit them all on our table. We were moved to a larger one. Uncle Osama got out his camera and asked the man to take a picture.

"Documentary evidence," he said. "Or else my sister won't forgive me."

This will be the first time, I calculated, that they've seen me in five years. Straighten your collar, smile, look settled.

"How is she?" I asked.

"A little older but just as beautiful. Proud of her son. We all are.

But," he then said and stopped. "Not that she said anything, but I know my sister. She doesn't understand. She knows how much you love home and so she suspects the worst. We all do."

"I can't be sure I would be let out again—or allowed much else," I said.

He clenched his jaws. "We feared as much," he said.

I watched his face working. If he guesses right, I thought, I might not be able to resist telling him everything.

"Did you blab at university?"

"Something like that."

"Got yourself in bad books?"

"I fear so," I said.

"How do you know? You could be imagining," he said.

"I'm definitely not imagining."

"In any case," he said, suddenly whispering, "probably wise. Things are very bad right now. Thousands in prison. I know people who have been arrested for only voicing a reluctance. And the bastards have ears everywhere."

For a moment he did not speak, but kept his eyes on me.

"Tell them I have a good job and that I'm about to start a PhD. Make sure you tell them that. Particularly Father."

"I will," he said. "What's the subject?"

"A comparative study of *The Epistle of Forgiveness* and *The Divine Comedy*; al Ma'arri and Dante. Please don't forget to tell him that too."

"I certainly won't," he said.

After a brief silence I said, "And tell them that I'm happy."

"Listen," he said, leaning forward, "I know the minister. He's a good man. I can ask him to inquire."

"No point," I said. "I wrote a condemnation of the dictatorship and published it in the local paper in Edinburgh. The wires picked it up and sent it to Tripoli. They pulled my scholarship, asking me to go back to Tripoli to account for myself."

"Oh my God," he said. "That's worse than I thought. Much worse.

But, Khaled, why go and ruin your future like that?" And then he said, speaking more to himself, "I always had you as a smart boy."

I dropped him off at his hotel. He was to catch the morning flight. I gave him the gifts and he said they would take up no room at all. "I'd pack you too if I could," he said, and teared up.

I had never seen Uncle Osama cry before.

I do not know what came over me then. I felt I was not there at all. That it was all happening to someone else and I was merely a spectator. We embraced and I said, in the way an adult might tell a child who has yet to fully understand that time passes, that the present is impermanent, "Nothing lasts forever."

49

MUSTAFA'S FRIENDS NOW CAME from a different circle entirely, a world of political Libyans living in exile. He joined one of the opposition groups that had its headquarters in Cairo but with several members in London. He had given an oath of loyalty in a special ceremony, witnessed by the leaders of the group. A lunch followed.

"It was a celebration," he told me proudly.

"Did you have to prove you've been circumcised?"

"Go on," he said, "mock away. Live your reluctant life. One day you will see."

"See what?"

"See that you have to commit to something."

"But I have."

"I mean something beyond yourself."

"I have," I said again, and was thankful when he did not persist.

He must have sensed my relief, because I then saw pass over him a shadow of that magnanimity that the merciful experience when they are reminded of their power over others, and reminded too of the pleasure that they take in their ability to restrain and moderate it.

We sat in that silence before he asked, "Why not come to one of the dinners, see with your own eyes?"

I refused, and in the weeks that followed each time he asked again it weighed heavily on me how best to refuse. Then, one of the leading members of the group passed away. There was good reason to suspect that he was poisoned. Mustafa had liked and admired the man very much, which, given his general reluctance toward praise of any kind, made me take note. A wake was being held at the dead man's house in Willesden Green in northwest London. Mustafa was unusually nervous and did not want to go alone. We took the tube there. When we emerged from the station, the sky was thick with clouds. The sun was entirely shut away. I could tell Mustafa appreciated my being there and, even though I silently regretted having come, as we walked down the unfamiliar suburban streets, I was consoled by the fact that I was pleasing my friend.

The house was huge, occupying an entire block, and had a fleet of black BMWs and Mercedes-Benzes parked outside. Mustafa had that same air of pride as he had when he first brought me to the brothers' house in Kensington. The wealth of his friends fortified him and, although the confidence it brought never lasted long, or perhaps exactly because it did not, he sought to regain it.

He pressed the doorbell and we waited. There was something outrageous about the familiar scents of orange blossom and Libyan cooking: lamb and cinnamon and steaming couscous and the sharp edge of freshly made harissa. I said I could not go in and turned to leave when Mustafa grabbed me by the arm.

"If you leave now," he whispered, "I'll never forgive you." The true volume of his words was in the eyes.

We were welcomed in by a servant. Judging by his manner and features, I asked if he was from the Philippines.

"No, sir," he said, smiling. "Malaysia."

"What is it to you?" Mustafa asked me in Arabic.

The man asked us to take off our shoes. As it was a Libyan house, this should not have come as a surprise, and yet having the privacy of my socks on display served only to accentuate my anxiety. The scale was all off. The ceiling was low and yet the staircase at the end of the entrance hall was wide and attempted to sweep up as though we were in a Baroque mansion. Ornately framed reproductions of English landscape paintings hung unevenly along it. Beneath each, the name of the artist, JOHN SINGER SARGENT, was stamped on a brass plate. I had no idea who he was then nor had I seen his delicate studies of clouds, but the doubling beat of "Singer Sargent" sounded like a military joke. We were led into a large hall, with men sitting all around the perimeter. The center of the room was empty. It felt as if we were stepping on to a stage. Everyone stood up and we went around shaking hands, offering one of the standard commiserations used on such occasions. I had my favorite and kept to it: "Our grief is one," which I repeated to each man. I knew no one here and yet I knew them all. I knew this tentative silence, these faces and their cautious withholding. I could sit without saying a word, enduring that discreet anonymity of Libyan male society, with its careful social architecture that allows each one to keep to himself all that matters, that one could come to know an individual intimately and yet have no idea of an essential fact about him. I suddenly felt neither a supporter nor a critic of this, and, enjoying my indifference, wondered if perhaps one needed to know something very well before being able to be ambivalent about it; and I realized then that this was why it had become impossible for me to feel ambivalence toward much at all. I suffered an opinion about nearly every detail of my new life.

Such composure disappeared when I saw him, the man who had visited us at the hospital and sent us those packages containing money and clothes. I remembered the trust that I had initially felt toward him and the deep suspicion that later rose in me. Maybe he was so good that he had managed to infiltrate these exiles. To my eyes then, he appeared far more intelligent than anyone else in the room. I could not help but feel a little flattered when he greeted me warmly, kissing me on both cheeks.

"I'm absolutely delighted to see you looking so well," he said, and seemed to mean it.

Several in the room took note. I was afraid he would expose me and yet wished he would. The man next to him asked how we knew one another. He smiled and said nothing. I moved on before the question could be repeated.

Mustafa was three or four men ahead now. He too came upon someone he knew. They embraced and then I saw that it was Saad. It surprised me how happy I was to see him. We embraced. It became clear to me as the evening went on that Saad too had joined the opposition. I could not understand this and wondered what changed the man who, as he told me when we first met in Edinburgh, had liberated himself from any interests. I remembered his words: "I have resigned myself to the fact that I live in a world of unreasonable men . . ." I remembered how happy they had made me then and how they were later echoed by my father, when we spoke after the shooting, and he said, "The question is, my boy—and it has always been the most important question—how to escape the demands of unreasonable men." The unlikely symmetry of those two statements struck me very powerfully.

Mustafa and I took our seats. We knew what to do. When a new arrival entered the room, we stood up and exchanged the reliable platitudes. We drank the tea when it was served and I enjoyed its bitter sweetness more than ever. Occasionally, when one lone voice broke through and told an anecdote about the deceased, often with heated enthusiasm, we listened with careful attention, as if we were being handed a delicate object. Then the poetry came. One man leaned forward, placed a hand over his eyes, and the room fell silent.

Camaraderie,
To guard
I would have laid my life
If I had known

How temporary
If I had known how temporary
I would have laid down my life to guard our camaraderie

The cadence and repetition, starting from the last word and working backward, until the puzzle settles. The familiar national elegiac
form, seeking to mend the severance. Another was encouraged and
yet another, and with each poem I found myself more and more
moved and delighted.

I could not help, from time to time, looking toward the man who
had visited us in the hospital. I was struck by the way he sat, leg over
leg, and the fact that he was the only one who had not taken off his
shoes. They were highly polished soft leather ankle-boots, quite elegant. He was not arrogant, or at least I did not think so, but I suspected that people thought he was. He seemed to think as much but
did not mind or did not mind enough to make him change his manner. It was this that I found attractive, attractive and suspicious, because it gave the impression that he was invulnerable and, therefore,
perhaps supported by powerful people.

We said goodbye to everyone and left. I could not quite believe
how much I had enjoyed myself.

"Thank you for bringing me," I told Mustafa.

He did not respond.

"Such nice people," I said. "I now see what you mean."

Even that drew nothing from him. If he were to ask me now, I
thought, I might say yes.

We turned a corner and suddenly Mustafa was not there. He had
fallen behind. He had his back to me. When I put my hand on his
shoulder, he covered his face and began weeping. I tried to hold him.
Not knowing what to say, I told him that what he needed now was a
drink. I talked on and on, not about the Libyan gathering but about
anything and everything else, as we walked back to the tube station
and during the half hour or so it took the train to travel from Willes-

den Green to Oxford Circus, and again as I led the way, walking quickly as though we were late for an appointment, to the Dog and Duck in Soho. Standing at the bar, waiting to order, I told him how much I loved this place, and as I did I heard a genuine passion in my voice. He looked about, nodded, but remained silent. I had brought him here before. Even though I had up to then distrusted the pub's claim, advertised on a sign placed right outside the gents' toilet, that "It has been well documented that the world-famous English novelist George Orwell drank in the Dog and Duck," I found myself saying things like "Isn't it amazing to think of him walking in here and ordering a drink?" Mustafa did not appear impressed. I mentioned that I had recently read *Homage to Catalonia*—when the truth was that I had read it a while before—Orwell's memoir of the Spanish Civil War. I urged Mustafa to read it. I told him how those young men Orwell joined to fight Franco's troops reminded me of us, and of those valiant streetwise boys in Benghazi, who you knew would give up everything they owned to get a friend out of trouble. Here Mustafa's eyes glittered. He smiled. He finally smiled. We remained in the pub for well over three hours. At one point, he wrapped his hand around the back of my neck and squeezed hard.

"You have no idea how much I love you," he said. "I would do anything for you."

"And I for you," I said.

And, even though we were both drunk, we both meant it.

Then he said something about a girl he knew back home and stopped, refusing to tell me any more about her. "Because," he said, "all I really want is to tell you about her hair." Then he looked at me and said, "Isn't it just terrible how life keeps on? It just keeps on and on and on, without a pause."

"Terrible and beautiful," I said.

"Beautiful only sometimes," he said, and began talking about the dead man, how brave and kind and honest he was. "I could imagine one day loving him the way you love your father."

I listened, but wished I could talk to him instead about the other man, the one who had given us the money. I was particularly thinking of the expression that came over his face that day as he left the hospital, the look of profound sadness. I wondered if Mustafa had noticed it too.

50

IT TURNED OUT THAT I had been both right and wrong about our benefactor, the man who claimed to have known my father before I was born. I was wrong to suspect him of being a member of the regime. But, given what befell him, I was right in noticing in him a sense of impending calamity. In 1990, two years after I saw him in Willesden Green, when I had all but forgotten about him, it was reported that he had disappeared from his home in Cairo. It later emerged that he had been kidnapped by Qaddafi agents, bundled into an airplane, and flown back to Libya, where he was tortured and eventually killed.

We did not know it then, but such kidnappings and assassinations were the beginning of the end of the Libyan opposition. Mustafa did not see it that way. If anything, the suspicious death of his mentor deepened his political commitment. He handed in his notice at his day job and joined the military wing of the organization as a full-time, salaried member of the group. He went on several training missions. Would disappear for weeks. Stopped drinking and began to look fit and muscular. He was terribly secretive about it. But the last time he went on such a mission, he called me from abroad and told me where he was: Cairo. He sounded anxious. A week or so later he telephoned again, and this time his voice was close and easy. It turned out he had come back and was calling me from his flat in London.

"It's obvious our group had been infiltrated," he said. "Would chop my right arm off if some of those arseholes in Cairo aren't working for Qaddafi. You could smell it. Woke up one night and followed my heart. Left without anyone noticing. Bought a one-way ticket home."

After this, Mustafa got a job at a big estate agency and worked with such hungry focus that he quickly rose up the ranks. As well as his salary, he was now on a handsome commission. He got a mortgage, bought his own place, and tried to convince me to do the same—kept going on about the importance of getting on the "property ladder." He took out another loan and got a brand-new red Alfa Romeo. His English accent started to change a little, turning posh. At first, I would tease him about it, but then I began to hear my own alter slightly to meet his. Now he wore a freshly ironed shirt even on weekends and saw all that had come before as wasted time. His friends were mostly British and European. His time with them often felt like a perfor-mance. He would make stuff up, rarely tell them the truth, and I mostly enjoyed the conspiratorial confederacy that lying created be-tween us. He would start with a made-up fact and, as though we were playing tennis in front of a small circle of spectators, toss it over to me and I would try to advance it a little.

By now Mustafa was as far away from literature as he could get. Whereas back in Edinburgh it was the passion that had united us and formed the main subject of conversation, now the mere mention of a book or a writer made him a little uneasy, I suspected, because it is difficult to be indifferent about a subject one had once felt passionate about. I would wait for him at a café or a restaurant, then we would embrace and I would catch him casting a quick look of disapproval at the book I was reading.

V. S. Naipaul was speaking at the Royal Geographical Society. When Mustafa and I first met in Edinburgh, one of the novels we endlessly discussed was *A House for Mr. Biswas*. I got tickets and we went together, saw the great man arrive wearing a hat that did not fit him. It was an outdated English idea of what an author was, we agreed. The place was filling up. We found two seats not far from the front. I laid my scarf on them and we went to get a drink. When we returned, we found a couple had taken our seats. Even as the woman leaned forward to release my scarf, I could tell that she was pretending, that she had known all along that the seats were taken. I did not mind. There were a couple of free seats further back and anyway I preferred not to sit so close to the stage. But Mustafa was furious, convinced that it was the arabesque pattern of my scarf that had made the couple feel they had the license to steal our places. I told him he was being ridiculous, but this became harder to refute the more Naipaul went on about the evils of Muslims. We left accompanied by a heavy silence, feeling that our former selves, those two young and unscathed teenagers back in Edinburgh, had been betrayed.

"Why is it that all the writers we admire let us down?" Mustafa said as we walked. "Hosam Zowa and now Naipaul. It's all so fucking dismal."

51

FOR THOSE FIRST TEN years in London, Mustafa was my closest friend. There were moments when, sitting together in silence, I believed I knew exactly how he felt; I do not mean only his opinions, but his innermost temperament, what it would feel like to be in his skin. I trusted if not his judgment then his independence. He was incorruptible, or that was how I thought of it back then. But perhaps to be incorruptible is to also be unchangeable. There was a rage within him, which cost him great effort to keep at bay. He would get into arguments with waiters over nothing. He kept switching jobs, claiming that people were not nice to him. Women liked him, though. For a stretch he was in love. Her name was Charlotte. She came from an aristocratic family. Her father was a member of the House of Lords. I still remember how she would look at him sometimes with an amused and tender enthusiasm, as if taking in a delightful gift that she had never expected to possess. Two years into their relationship, she took him to her old family home, the country house where she grew up, to meet her parents and two brothers. Mustafa grew somber and silent in the days leading up to this. The father welcomed him warmly, but then, when Charlotte was out of the room and the two men were alone, he turned to Mustafa and in a calm but determined voice said, "You'll soon be out of the picture. It is only a matter of time, boy."

"See; I was right," Mustafa told me. "I shouldn't have gone."

"I still think you should marry her," I said. "I mean, what could possibly go wrong with a woman like that?"

I still remember the look of fear and offense in his eyes. "It'll never work," he said.

He stopped seeing Charlotte and she never knew why. Now he preferred European women studying or working in London. Italian and Spanish and Portuguese. He introduced me to their friends and together we shared some fun evenings.

They come to me now, those days lived waiting, paused at the isthmus between this and the next life, considering our options, whether to remain in London until we could return to Libya or go on somewhere new, somewhere, we imagined, more accommodating to our natures: Italy or Spain or Greece or Brazil.

"For, let's face it," Mustafa liked to say during those days, "there is something perverse about two Mediterranean Arabs making a life in England."

We searched for places to rent abroad, possible jobs we could do. All the while the hourglass emptied. And with each day we became a little less Arab and a little more Anglo, like a wall gradually losing its color to the weather.

Maybe this is why I have succumbed to these thoughts, walking home to Shepherd's Bush, to the same flat I have rented for the past thirty-two years, letting my mind reach back. Perhaps there I might come upon myself, or come upon a crucial detail that I have overlooked, and that may help me with the present. For, even though I remain standing in St. James's Square, thinking about all that has happened since the day I was last here, my devotion is not to the past but to the present.

52

A FEW DAYS AFTER Uncle Osama left, I called home. Mother and Father held the receiver between them and took turns speaking, sometimes saying the same thing at the same time. Their voices were imperceptibly different, as though a mist had fallen over them. They thanked me for the gifts.

"Best of all," Mother said, "was to see you."

"And to think they met in the middle of the street," Father told her.

"A blessed fate," she said.

"Meant to be," he said. "High Street Kensington."

"We're getting the photograph framed," Mother said.

"We made sure Osama told us everything," Father went on, "including the name of the street where he found you."

"It's such a good photograph," Mother told him. "And to see his face."

"You look good, son," Father said.

"Khaled," my mother said, "don't worry, my love; time passes."

Here none of us spoke.

"Yes," Father said into the silence. "So grateful that most of the news is good. Teaching and about to embark on a PhD. Excellent."

"Yes, we are proud of you," Mother said with a hint of insistence. "Don't worry; time . . ." and she stopped.

"Come, come," Father whispered to her.

Four years later, in 1992, the Libyan regime began to ease travel restrictions. And by now the UK government, which, following the shooting, had stopped giving Libyans entry visas, was offering them again. My parents and Souad were finally able to visit. I had not seen them for almost nine years, not since I was seventeen. Now I was twenty-six, had a beard, and wore glasses. I bought two single futon mattresses from Shepherd's Bush Market, carried them home on my back, tidied the place up, scrubbed the bathroom, cleaned the windows. Waiting at Arrivals in Heathrow Airport, watching passengers appear through the sliding doors, I felt light-headed. I kept believing I saw them. And suddenly there they were, unquestionably real, filling the air they occupied. We embraced and held on to one another. People were looking at our little group, curious and pleased. My father ruffled my hair and laughed, pinched my beard.

"You haven't changed," Souad said, slapping her palms together and repeating, "He hasn't changed."

My mother called me "Khalood," and hearing it in the open was a tug across time.

When we got off at Shepherd's Bush Station, I was proud to show them where I lived. Walking into my flat, my mother turned around and hugged me strongly and for a long time.

I apologized for how small my place was. My parents slept on the bed and Souad and I rolled out the futons at night and in the morning folded them up. I stopped feeling bad about it when Father said, sounding like he truly meant it, "This to me is the ideal arrangement. My whole family sleeping in one room. Why we haven't thought of it in all these years is a mystery."

We told stories into the night and, whenever we fell silent, Souad or my mother would say, "Khalood, what else?" and I would tell some story from the years we had been apart. When I could not think of anything, I would make things up or recount a borrowed tale, claiming it had happened to me. We got on so naturally, with such effortless ease. There were moments in the night when I would stir awake and listen to their easy breaths and feel such aching tenderness for them.

Souad loved to walk unnoticed, without being looked at, not needing to worry about whether others thought she was dressed appropriately or not. I took her marching across town, our arms locked together, and she would often compliment me on my knowledge of the city. I had never felt closer to anyone in my life.

"I've missed you so much," she would say into the silences and pull me closer. I always replied that I had too. She would then rest her head on my shoulder and leave it there for a moment. When I asked her why she and her fiancé had not got married yet she said, "We are waiting for somebody very special to return home."

"Promise me you won't do that," I said.

"Uncle Osama told us," she said, "but don't worry, things change. Several people in your situation, who criticized the regime, were later forgiven."

"Don't wait," I said, my hands wrapped too tightly around her arms.

53

I CHANGED INTO MY pajamas in the bathroom. I never took off my clothes in front of them. Every time we embraced, I hoped that their hands could not read the scar. One evening, I decided to tell them. Mother cooked. We ate around the small table in the kitchen and then lounged in the main room. My heart raced. Why tell them; what good would it do? Then Saturday came, and Mother and Souad wanted to go shopping. My father and I decided to stay behind and meet them later in town for supper.

"I have something to tell you," I suddenly heard myself say. "Something important."

He looked up at me and I thought this was how he looked when he was young, when he was my age.

"I attended the demonstration in April 1984, the year I left home. This is why I haven't been able to return."

So far, he seemed fine.

"I was among those wounded," I said.

He shot up on his feet, his face dark and anxious. "Where?" he said.

"In St. James's Square, in front of the embassy."

"What do you mean, wounded? Wounded where?"

"Only lightly," I said.

"Where?" he repeated, and the word now was a command. "Where?"

"Here," I said and pointed to my chest.

His manic fingers were all over me, trying to unbutton my shirt and pull it off at the same time. I gave him my back and did it myself. He took hold of my vest, and the child I once had been surrendered his arms. What happened next broke a crack through me. My father, the tallest man I know, bowed and began to trace his fingers along my scar, reading it, turning around me as he followed its line, tears streaming down his face.

"My boy, my boy," he whispered to himself.

I told him that it was really not that bad, that I had healed quickly, that there were no aftereffects. None. "Honest, I'm fine," I kept repeating.

He slapped my cheek. Not hard. Not hard at all. More play than punishment. He struck me again, but it was as ineffective as the first time. He then apologized, kissed the same cheek.

"You shouldn't have," he said, his face wrinkled by pain. "You shouldn't have, you shouldn't have."

To this day I do not know what he meant exactly by those words, whether that I should not have gone to the demonstration, got shot, or kept it from him. Maybe it was all three. Or perhaps he was not talking to me at all, but to the man who had shot me, or to the entire political reality that had made such an act possible. Or maybe he was neither speaking to me nor to the perpetrator, but to no one other than himself, that he should not have ever let me leave home.

"Father, please, I'm fine." I put on my shirt. He looked startled. "Please go wash your face," I said. "I'll make coffee."

I had never been so overcome with regret. It snaked up from my ankles to my neck. We sat around the small table by the window. I poured the coffee.

He was determined to know all the details: who I went with, what convinced me, and so on. It was the first time that I had shared the details in full, holding nothing back. I told him that I had had no intention of taking part, that I went to accompany a friend and to see London. A hint of relief passed across his face.

"You know me," I said.

"I do," he said. "This is why I never expected this from you. Osama told us you wrote an article. That's bad enough, but this? And who was the friend who took you there?"

"He didn't take me there. I went of my own free will. Anyway, it doesn't matter now," I said.

He wanted to see the doctor's report. I brought it to him and he read it all the way through. Then I watched him follow the same train of thought I had had in those early days. Had I tried to have the report changed?

"Did you ask them properly? Did you insist?"

Then he wanted to know what happened afterward. I told him everything: the hospital, staying at Rana's, going to Spain, the help and guidance of Professor Walbrook, all the way to the present.

"I'm sorry," I said, and kissed his hand.

"Poor child," he said, "and having to keep it from me all those years."

"I had no choice," I said.

"To think of you alone . . ." he said, and his voice broke.

My father needs me, I thought. I held his hand. "I'm fine now," I said again.

It was so easy to lie to him and I lied with a passion in my voice, told him that I believed I was a better man for it, that God had willed this to happen so as to spare me a worse fate, that the day would soon come when I would be able to return home again. "Nothing lasts forever," I said, words that he had told me many times when I was a boy and scraped my knee or was in bed with a tummy ache or had to study endlessly for an exam. I returned them to him now and it meant he had no option but to agree with me. Then I quoted the famous line, "The strike that doesn't break your back strengthens it," attributed to Omar al Mukhtar, although it was my father who had always maintained that, apart from the film *Lion of the Desert*, directed by Moustapha Akkad, in which Anthony Quinn plays the great man, there is no historical record of al Mukhtar ever having spoken those words. I deployed this old artillery, while all along a fury was burning inside me, unable to rid myself of the image of my father's face, broken and tearful, lost, bowed in front of me, as he traced my scar, as though hoping to find his way back to the boy he knew.

"I want to go to St. James's Square, to see the place for myself."

"I can take you there," I said, and then said, "No, let's not do that, please."

"Why?" he asked, and then, when I could not explain myself, he said, "But you are right."

From then on, he was tender and quiet. We went to Piccadilly Circus, where we had planned to meet Mother and Souad. Against the busy activity and the lights, he looked small and hesitant, a figure full of doubt.

"Don't ever tell your mother," he said.

But the moment she sees you she will know, I thought. And just then they appeared and he put his old face on, smiling.

"We have decided," he told them, "on a change of plan. Instead of going to a restaurant, we will get sandwiches and go to the cinema instead." Then he looked at me and asked, "Isn't that right, Khalood?"

Inside the cinema, he told Souad, "Go on, sit beside your mother."

When the lights came down, I could feel him thinking. He brought his mouth close to my ear and whispered, "Your breathing, is it back to full capacity now?"

"Absolutely," I whispered.

"No shortness of breath?"

"Nothing," I said.

"Not even when you run?"

"Not even then. The only thing that is holding me back now is my laziness," I said, and when I looked at his face there was no smile on it.

"They're in love," Mother said, leaning over Souad.

"Only in the first few months," I said a little while later. "But not now."

"Good," he said.

I have no recollection of what we watched. My thoughts were totally focused on him. Midway through the film, just at the point when I hoped Father was being carried away by the story, he said, his breath warm against my ear, "Every tyrant has his end."

He was looking at me for a reaction. I was sure that my face, like his, was lit up by the screen.

"Soon," he said, "you will come home."

We remained in silence, under the obscured light of the cinema, till the film ended.

On the bus home, Mother and Souad teased us about our romance.

"You leave them for an afternoon and all they want now is to be whispering together," Mother said. "What's up with you two? What are you plotting?"

That night I woke up a few times and each time I did not move. I was captured by childish fears. I held myself in place and could hear from the silence that my father too was awake. When the delirium passed and I was spent, I thought, there is nothing else I can do here. Nothing I can say, nothing I can give, and nothing I can retrieve.

In their remaining days in London, Father continued to be affectionate and close. On the way to the airport, his hand was always reaching for me, holding me by the arm, squeezing my shoulder. When we finally embraced, he held me so tightly I could hardly breathe.

"Never forget what I told you," he said.

"And what's that?" Mother told him.

"It's none of your business," he told her. "It's between me and my son."

I went to see Hannah that evening. My family's spirits were all over me—in my clothes and in my hair—and I wanted to be with her before that vanished. I told her about their visit, the things we did together, the dishes they cooked for me, our nocturnal chats in the dark.

The fact that we had all slept in the same room amused her the most. I told her that during these past few days my jaws had ached from smiling.

"I wish I'd got to meet them," she said.

"You will. Next time," I said.

54

THE FOLLOWING CHRISTMAS, HANNAH invited me to her parents' in Ealing. It was a large family gathering that included a couple of her aunts and uncles and several cousins. She had one elder brother and he too was there. His name was Henry. Her parents were David and Stephanie, but everyone called them Dave and Steph. Something about their manner suggested that Hannah had told them about the shooting. I did not mind. Henry was in the army and had taken part in the Falklands War. The knowledge that we both had faced bullets established a silent affinity between us. Several of the younger members of the family spilled out into the garden, chatting and smoking in the dark. When I approached, they fell quiet in the way people do when they are keen to hear from you. Hannah and I stayed until everyone had left. We helped with the tidying up. Her father and I took turns at the kitchen sink. Every time I handed him a clean plate, he dried it promptly and was ready for the next one. John Coltrane played on, warm and steady in the background.

When everything was put away, Dave insisted we stay on for one last drink. Steph put on the kettle and asked if anyone wanted chamomile tea with her. Dave turned Coltrane down to a whisper and poured three small glasses of whiskey. He asked about my parents. I answered but briefly, because I did not want to speak about them just then. Hannah told them about our house in Benghazi, describing it with surprising accuracy.

"Would love to visit one day," she said, and her mother and father looked on. Then she told them that when my parents and sister had visited, we all slept in the same room.

"Adorable," Steph said and Dave smiled.

Hannah slept at my place that night. We had been talking and laughing the whole way home. But in bed, after I put out the light, the air changed. She was silent, but I knew she was not asleep. Then I heard her breathing break. I turned on the light and kept asking what was the matter. She shook her head and said nothing, her tears passing. When I tried to embrace her, she did not yield. A few minutes later we were sitting at the kitchen table, with glasses of water. I waited and my heart raced in my chest. I had no idea what was the matter and yet I suspected what it was, because, when she finally said, "It's like you are constantly at the threshold," I said, "I'm sorry." My reply had come too quickly and had the opposite effect. She looked at me daringly, doubtful of who I really was. "I don't wish to live like this," she said. Then she surprised me, stretched her hand over mine, her face yielding. "I want you to be with me, but I want you to really be with me."

A few weeks later, on a cloudy February afternoon, I was on a bus going along Regent Street when I spotted Hannah and her mother walking on the busy pavement. Hannah seemed under strain but patient. Her mother, walking half a step behind her, looked a little vulnerable, as though all this might be too much without her daughter beside her. Something about the scene affected me very deeply and I still do not know why.

55

RANA JOINED HER FATHER'S architectural practice in Amman, and a few years later he retired and left her in charge of the company. She opened an office in Beirut and moved there. She seemed both burdened and energized by the responsibility. She would pass through town every year or so and tell me all sorts of intricate details about the various conflicts and problems she faced: an irksome male colleague who continually challenged her authority; the unadventurous taste of a client; a corrupt official's financial demands in return for granting the required permits and planning permissions. She also spoke of her Beirut friends: how, with everyone being so busy, there was no time any longer for hanging out.

"Remember when you and I would spend hours in your flat doing absolutely nothing?"

Perhaps, like all meetings of friends who live apart, these encounters took the form of reports, whereby each one of us attempted to list the things that had happened since we were last together. When we bid farewell, I reentered my solitude with a sense of regret. Her life was so much more active and populated than mine. A life in which, I was certain, it would be easy to lose oneself to the needs of others.

And there were other things that I gleaned from these reunions. The way she had changed, as though reverting back to an expected life. And how this appeared to harden in her the native confidence of one who knows where she belongs. She would get a hotel room by Hyde Park Corner and spend two or three days shopping for clothes and visiting museums. She was always so happy that it made me wonder whether this was what London was made for. Although living here often felt like hard labor, visiting must have seemed like life itself.

She got engaged to a Jordanian graphic designer. His name was Hyder and he came with her to London on one of these trips. He was a little nervous at first, which made me nervous too, but eventually we eased into the encounter and I came away thinking he was a decent and reliable fellow. When she looked at him, she seemed both embarrassed and proud. And when she was in the middle of telling a story the lines in his face eased and gave way. I remember thinking, this must be what it is like to be in love. Love as a place of rest. They had set the wedding date and insisted I come to Beirut for it.

"We won't take no for an answer," Hyder said.

"You are going to be my best man," Rana said.

I said I would be there and tried to ignore the doubt in her eyes. When I did not go, she was terribly cross.

They got married in 1993. A year later, she visited London alone. She wanted to meet for supper at the restaurant in her hotel. She looked preoccupied, was called to the reception twice to answer calls.

"Problems with work," she said. "I'm not supposed to be away."

When I asked after Hyder she said he was well and smiled. I walked her to the lift, and it was after she called it that she said, "I'm getting some medical checkups." Just before the doors closed, she added, "Nothing serious."

The following year, 1995, eleven years after I was shot, Rana telephoned and asked me to meet her in Paris. She was going there for medical treatment. She did not want to say more. But then she said, "It's brain surgery. I've no option. Treatment here failed. I've made up my mind. And," she said, "you have no excuse, it's summer, school is out, and now London and Paris have a train between them. Besides, I don't want you to come, I need you."

"I'll be there," I said. "When do you and Hyder arrive?"

"Hyder," she said, "won't be coming. No one knows. I just couldn't bear it. My doctor helped to convince Hyder and my parents that I was making a good recovery. I'm telling them I'm going to Paris to meet a client."

"You should tell them," I said.

"It's another thing to have to deal with other people's fears. I thought you especially would understand that."

56

THAT WAS THE TRIP that brought me face-to-face with Hosam Zowa, the author who had cast such a long shadow on my life.

I chose the hotel mainly because of its proximity to the hospital—not so close that I could pop back and forth endlessly, but not more than half an hour's walk away—and its modest price, as I feared I might have to remain in Paris a while. I boarded the train, the same train Hosam took a little while ago. The whole way I was thinking about Rana, who was herself setting off from Beirut that day after depositing her little lies into the ears of those she loved the most. Thinking about her put me in a gray mood and, together with my anxiety about travel, about moving beyond the borders of my daily life, held me at the window. I watched as we threaded out of London and into Surrey and then Kent. I left my seat and stood between the carriages, where I could just about catch the occasional fragment of birdsong. Then we plunged into the tunnel under the sea. Minutes passed before the engine began to strain uphill. When we emerged, the light was massive and soft and brilliant. It filled the entire gap between the earth and the sky. The landscape looked like England, but that light told you it was a different country. Then, as a key might glide into a lock, the train entered Paris.

Rana's flight was expected to land in about two hours. I pictured her in her seat, her perfect head with its thick black hair leading her to the Frenchman's knife, the famous surgeon who had come highly recommended by her discreet Lebanese doctor, who, apart from me, was the only other person who knew the truth.

At the Gare du Nord, I did not want to take the steps down to the Métro. I walked instead, and the people, the color and way of things, that peculiar signature that each city creates for itself and somehow maintains, all made it seem as though I were entering a performance.

When I walked into the hotel, the man sitting behind the reception seemed familiar. But how could he be? How could I have recognized this man based only on a book of short stories read more than a decade before, and hearing his voice utter no more than a single word, "Yes," on that BBC radio interview? I remember Henry once telling me that in a writer's prose, in the sounds and rhythms of his sentences, "there lies the inner logic of the person." Whatever it was, what I sensed on entering the hotel lobby, and it hit me with profound certainty, was that this stranger sitting behind the reception desk was somehow known to me.

"Welcome, Mr. . . ." he said in English, leafing through my British passport, "Mr. Khaled Abd al Hady."

He pronounced the name perfectly. His accent had, ever so slightly, the refined edges of an educated North African. And, given that this was Paris, I assumed that he was from one of the former French colonies: Algeria, Tunisia, or Morocco. I knew this game: he would not ask where I was from and I would keep to the same policy. Whoever blinks first loses. An immigrant's test of discipline, most probably ancient, for this instinct to pass unnoticed, to veil oneself, must surely be as old as time, as old as exile, as old as when Adam and Eve, cast out of Eden and sent down to earth, were made to live on opposite sides of the empty planet. I judged myself good at this—very good, in fact—but he was older and not only appeared to have more experience, but looked like a man who had, in the time allotted to him so far, lived more than most. I was twenty-nine and guessed he was about ten or fifteen years older, when, in actual fact, he was only six years my senior. His lips ran in a straight line, hinting neither at a smile nor a frown. The skin on either side was slightly discolored. Perhaps long ago he survived a fire. It stretched like a drum across each cheek. It conveyed power and control and something else just beyond reach: the determination of a person in hiding. His entire face was fastened in place by his eyes, which held you with force. Two deep wells. It was as if a trace of everything they had ever witnessed was retained within them.

"I hope you enjoy your stay," he said, handing me my room key.

His English had a hint of an Irish accent.

"Thank you," I said. "And what is your name?"

"Sam," he said, and tried to smile.

I know this too, I thought: the shame felt in concealing one's identity and the shamelessness that comes to our defense. I thanked him and felt tempted to say more, to reveal something of my plans. And so, even though I had already checked the route on my map, I asked him for directions to the hospital.

"Oh, no," I said, "I have no intention of taking the Métro."

"In that case, *c'est une belle promenade*," he said.

The French here seemed deliberate, a placeholder for the phantom language we both knew we shared.

"I don't speak French," I said.

"I beg your pardon," he said. "Walking, sir, is an excellent idea. Forty minutes at most. A couple of good cafés on the way, if you fancy."

Yes, the accent was definitely Irish. I thanked him and climbed the stairs to my room. I felt a thrill at the prospect of sleeping in an unknown bed, a bed that, no matter how many nights I would stay, would never be mine. Sam, I thought, what a name to hide behind. But then the shallow judgment faded and, in its wake, arose that magical quietude that only occasionally opens up within us when the absent-minded wanderings of our thoughts play on as though we had become, accidentally and by the most unexpected of turns, free from our mind's habit. I found myself enjoying the impenetrable surface of the man. Why this suspicion of what is concealed, I thought, when there is pleasure in opacity? Is it not more revealing to observe a person clothed than naked?

The room was small and plain, with a large window that looked out on to the opposite building. Some of the windows across the way were curtained, some were bare, and others were, like mine, open. Through them I could see a kitchen, a bedroom, a table with one empty plate. Perhaps if I'm lucky, I thought, I might spot someone unawares, sleeping or reading a book, or a couple embracing or sitting quietly, possibly with music playing just out of earshot. I showered, shaved, and put on fresh clothes. "Wishing you a very pleasant walk, Mr. Khaled," Sam said, as I handed him the key.

57

AT THE HOSPITAL I was informed that Rana was expected to arrive any minute and that I could wait in her assigned room. I was led there by a nurse who had a slight sideways gait, which made her progress both courteous and hesitant. A little while later the famous surgeon walked in and introduced himself. With his eyes on the empty bed, he asked what my relationship was to the patient.

"She's my friend," I said.

He smiled weakly. "Madam Lamesse has arrived," he said. "She's just finishing registration."

He left the room. I stood by the window. A view of the side street. You could pretend you were in a hotel. A few minutes later I heard the nurse's voice coming from the corridor. The door opened and Rana appeared. She smiled as soon as she saw me. We embraced.

"Thank you," she said right beside my ear.

The nurse instructed Rana to change and then quietly closed the door behind her.

"It's better than I thought," Rana said, looking around the room.

"And you've got a view of a beautiful quiet street," I said.

"Who needs the Ritz?" she said.

I left so that she could change and settle in. I walked slowly down the stairs. What if she doesn't make it, I thought, or emerges impaired, unable to walk or talk or see? Such fears remained with me throughout all the days that she was in hospital. I found a corner shop and bought crisps, biscuits, bottled water. When I returned, she was dressed in a baby-blue hospital gown and tucked beneath the sheets. She looked smaller. She asked how I was.

"Very glad to be with you," I said.

We talked about Paris, the weather, some new restaurant she had read about in the inflight magazine.

"Let's go when all this is over," she said.

"Absolutely," I said.

After a moment's silence, I asked, "Are you sure you don't want to tell your family?"

"Hundred percent," she said. "It'll all be over soon. Couple of weeks at most."

"Won't they suspect?"

"I'll say work is taking longer. Anyway, it's not a bad idea for Hyder and me to be apart for a bit. He knows I'm hiding something. It's hard work hiding things. Have to watch yourself, the way you walk even, how you eat and sleep. And I'm terrible—you know this—a terrible liar. Back then I was bad at lying because I didn't know how to do it; now I'm bad at it because I know how to do it. I married out of love, but even that has its limits. All marriages do. The secret is to know where those limits are. It's not so much that I don't want to worry him, worry my parents and everyone else; it's just that I wouldn't be able to bear it."

She stopped and waited until her face was calm again.

"On the plane, as we were over the sea, I remembered when I was a child and they used to tell us those slogans at school that you are part of a body, the body of your family, your society, the Arab World, the human race. Remember?"

"Yes, I do," I said.

"If you are healthy, they told us, the rest of the body is healthy. Back then I thought how silly, but that's exactly how it feels."

Tears gathered in her eyes. I said nothing. You must help her, I told myself. This is why she chose you. Don't let her down.

"Whatever you do," she said, her face looking very earnest now, "don't bring flowers."

I laughed and she did too.

"Of course I'll bring flowers. You love flowers."

"Not in hospital I don't."

"I'll bring flowers."

58

THERE WERE A NUMBER of tests that needed to be done before the operation could take place. These took several days. I visited Rana every day in the early afternoon and stayed till evening. I saw Sam whenever I left or returned to the hotel. He was always there. We continued to greet one another briefly and in English. "Back to hospital," I sometimes said, hoping to provoke an inquiry or a platitude. He never budged. But with every passing day the air around him seemed to grow more fraught. Instead of looking across the small lobby, which, initially, when I first arrived, seemed to be his private domain, now I often found him facing downward, forehead cradled on his hands, engrossed, I assumed, in a book. But when I approached, I would find him staring into absolutely nothing, facing the wood grain of the desk, taken aback by my sudden appearance.

Whether it was the adventure of being in a new city, or the good purpose of caring for Rana, or the ambiguous sense of victory, of gaining the upper hand in the immigrant's game I was playing with the stranger behind the reception desk, my mood brightened. One afternoon, on arriving at the hospital, I began to exchange the usual greetings with the nurses and then took to teasing them.

"I mean, the decor here is truly dreary. And look, ladies, at your clothes. You really need to widen the color palette. My suggestion is to revolt."

They laughed.

"And the rooms!" I went on. "Any chance of a minibar? For goodness' sake, roll in a grand piano. Failing that, a television and video player at least."

A couple of hours later a knock came at the door, and a table was wheeled in by a couple of rosy-cheeked nurses. It had a television and a video player. Rana teared up with joy, which surprised me. The nurses rushed over and wrapped their arms around her.

I went to Fnac, a shop recommended by one of the nurses, and spent the afternoon buying films. Initially, I thought to get new releases, but then remembered our days in Edinburgh and got some of the old classics we had watched there together. *Cairo Station, L'éclisse, Pickpocket,* and, miraculously, Rana's favorite, *Journey to Italy,* which back then she believed was the most perfect film ever made.

"If it were a building," I remembered her saying, "it would be a modest but glorious thing, hardly noticeable by those who never truly look."

I remembered the scene when the married couple, played by Ingrid Bergman and George Sanders, who on arriving in Naples realize that their life together has turned into a loveless one, are taken to a dig in Pompeii and witness the unearthing of the ghostly shape of another couple buried in ash nearly two thousand years before when Mount Vesuvius erupted, embracing one another for eternity. Nothing is the same after that.

Waiting in line to pay, I wondered if Rana still felt the same way about *Journey to Italy,* whether she had seen it in the eleven years since. I then tried to imagine where these videotapes in the basket would end up, in whose house? They were too cumbersome to carry back to Beirut or London. Most likely, I thought, they would end up in a Paris secondhand shop, to be bought by individuals who will

never know the circumstances under which they were originally purchased. I paid and, as soon as I was out on the street, clutching the
bagful of videotapes, I felt a childlike rush of excitement. I could not
stop smiling at everyone I passed. I felt such love for her, and such
desire that she and Hyder should be happy. She was wrong, I thought,
about the limits of a marriage. And, even if she is right and there are
limits, they ought never to be accepted. I stopped at a bakery and got
a large box of gateaux for the nurses.

59

WE SPENT THE NEXT few afternoons stretched side by side on the
hospital bed, watching films. She would often fall asleep and wake up
asking me to fill her in on what she had missed. It became our joke.
"What happened, what happened?" she would say, and I would tell
her, only for the whole thing to reoccur a few moments later. Sometimes I turned down the volume and listened to her long breathing.
She was growing weak. We were alone and away, as if in hiding, in a
hospital in a foreign country where we knew no one and had only a
partial command of the language.

"This is what it must be like," she told the doctor later that evening,
"to be awaiting the day of your duel."

"But, madame," he said, "we won't be fighting."

"You won't be, Doctor," she told him.

The day came. Rana, without providing any instructions concerning what to say, handed me Hyder's telephone number. The doctor
then took me to one side and warned me that the surgery would take
hours. "Five minimum," he said, sounding both anxious and excited.
I tried to leave, but could not. In fact, I hardly moved from the seat in
the empty waiting room. My own days in hospital returned to me.

One detail in particular. I had all but forgotten it till then. It concerned a dream I kept having immediately after the operation. I am about to cross a road and nearly get run over. I am violently startled awake and tell myself I must look both ways next time. But each time the same thing happens. It got so bad I could hardly sleep. I told Nurse Clement that I kept having the same nightmare.

"Are you about to cross a road?" she said. "You step off the pavement and nearly get run over, right?"

"Exactly," I said. "How do you know?"

She enjoyed my astonishment. "It's the painkillers, love. A common side effect. We'll change them and you'll be right as rain."

Seven hours later, Rana's doctor emerged.

"It went very well. As well as we could have hoped," he said. "Now the critical stage begins. She'll be in intensive care for a few days. You won't be able to see her, but don't worry, I'm pleased with how it has gone."

I thanked him and could not help but embrace the man.

60

ONLY WHEN I WAS out on the street did I notice that I was trembling all over. The city was shrouded in night. The soft amber lights emerging from inside cafés and restaurants looked warm and inviting. A sensuous hunger swirled in my veins. I wanted to drink and eat and lie naked with someone, to burn or break something inside me.

Several hours later I was walking back to the hotel with the world swimming a little, the pavement as soft as a trampoline. I was tired and ashamed and could not imagine going to sleep. I kept breathing in deeply, wanting to clean out my nostrils. The prostitute I had been with was Moroccan. She pronounced my name perfectly and then said, "I know that isn't your real name." She did not think it was strange, she said, that I wanted to lie beside her and do nothing else. "You're sweet," she said, and it made me sad being next to her, breathing in her sweat and the sweat of others. I guessed that she too was in her late twenties. I held her from behind, her head and agitated hair resting on my arm. I watched the back of her neck, the dim pulse tapping there.

"Think what you will," I said, "but Khaled is my real name."

A few minutes later—it could have been an hour—she nudged me awake, her eyes on my scar. Had she not noticed it till now? I put on my clothes, paid her, and left. Now I was thinking, I should have fucked her. That would have been less horrible.

When I entered the lobby and saw Sam lost as usual in his downward gaze, I burst out laughing.

"So," I said, speaking much louder than I had intended, "you say . . . No, you, in fact, don't say; you don't say at all; you insist that your name is Sam."

There was fear but also vague relief in his eyes, as though he were thinking, finally, here it comes.

"Well," I yelled out even louder now, "if you are Sam, then I'm Kafka."

The night porter appeared, looking ready to act. Sam waved him aside and rushed toward me with his hand outstretched. I was certain he was about to strike, to slap or punch me. I tightened my fists, panic already in the knees. Instead, he took hold of my arm and did so with a peculiar confidence. He calmly told the porter to keep an eye on things. The man acknowledged the instruction gratefully, which made me think Sam was known among his colleagues for being good in emergencies. He led me out, pulling me beside him all the way to the corner of the street.

"You know what I feel like?" he suddenly said, speaking softly but with a tremor in his voice. *"Un bon chocolat chaud."* He looked at me, and when I did not reply he said, "Fancy a hot chocolate, Monsieur Kafka?" And before I could answer he looked left, right, and pulled me across the street. "There's an excellent place nearby. It might even still be open."

I moved helplessly beside him. The ground now was as hard as a solid fact. The air was crisp. I had not noticed that it had rained. The tarmac was glazed. Shards of light bounced off it like broken glass. I touched the top of my head with my one free hand and found my hair damp.

"I'm sorry," I said, but he was already talking, saying, "When all is said and done—"

"I mean, if I caused any trouble," I interrupted.

He paused and, without acknowledging what I said, continued, "French cuisine, despite what people say, is somewhat average." Then, lowering his voice as if we were in danger of being overheard, he added, "Mind you, there is nothing, absolutely nothing, you can say here that would be more offensive. Sheer blasphemy. I mean, the food is good, but it would be even better if they weren't so adamant about it. To my taste at least, give me Derna any time."

Hearing the name of that dear and familiar city where my mother was born, the place where my parents took us in summer, and hearing it pronounced so perfectly, brought me to a standstill.

"Come," he said, looking at me directly.

Like a child, I obeyed and continued moving beside him.

He switched to Arabic, speaking it in a perfect Benghazi accent, which, out of all the dialects of the world, is the closest to my heart. Things said in it are not mere ephemeral utterances, but structures that are as known and reliable as the house I was born in. I cannot be objective about it. I cannot judge if it is beautiful or ugly. His superiors, those who selected him for this task, must have known this about me. How stupid to have thought that my British passport would conceal my origins when it clearly states that "Benghazi" is my birthplace, the head's landing place, as the expression goes in Arabic. I longed with such violent force for that city now, the warm shelter of my family, and saw, in my mind's eye, as vividly as though it were right in front of me, my mother's neck, the strong and gentle and hospitable curve of it. I remembered, as though I were a boy again, the curious urge to forever lay myself entirely there. Panic ran through me. Is this the moment I am going to be forcibly returned, I wondered, to be paraded on television, where, like so many before me, I will be asked to admit guilt for my actions and then praise the regime or else be made an example of? Run. This is the moment to run. But I felt the weariness of one who had been running for so long.

"What I would do," he then said, "for Derna's tomatoes, those from the high plains. You know the ones I mean"—it was not a question—

"shaped like dates but taste even sweeter. Or the olive oil when first pressed and is peppery, burns down your throat. The festivities of those days in the swani, the pastures cloistered between houses. Did you know that this unique planning feature of Derna, which we attribute to the ancient Greeks, had been set in place a few centuries before by the Phoenicians, who were, by some accounts, a little more sentimental, with that note of nostalgia in their art—that same nostalgia I feel now as I remember our olive oil, the mountain rosemary and mint, the wild thyme and the sage that we call apple because it has in it the aroma of apples? But enough. Mustn't allow ourselves to become too sentimental. Or, you know what, to hell with it," he said, raising his voice a little. "Doesn't our country deserve our sentiments?"

He faced me, as if the question was not rhetorical at all. Is this meant to be a test, I wondered, or admonishment for my previous actions? His learning, or his desire to give the impression that he was learned, knew his Phoenicians, was also, I suspected, very much like his accent, there to win my confidence.

"Of course it does," he said, answering his own question, and continued walking. "Some even believe it deserves our blood. But let's not speak of blood. Not tonight. Let's speak instead of Derna, that 'Pearl of Cyrenaica.'"

Here he laughed a strange laugh—somewhere between a bark and a cackle—that was, I thought, either the expression of a furious soul or else the anxious utterance of a man who was as frightened as I was.

"'Pearl of Cyrenaica,'" he said again. The bitter irony in his voice echoed against the buildings. "Lady Hay Drummond-Hay. We have her to thank for that. And she should know, I suppose—the first woman to fly around the globe in a zeppelin, would you believe."

"What do you want from me?" I asked.

"What do I want from you?" he said, surprised, as though I were the one who had come to him with questions. "Nothing at all. Was just telling you about Lady Hay Drummond-Hay."

He looked up at some window in the opposite direction and then continued walking. What was he thinking?

"A great-uncle of mine knew her, you see," he continued. "I hope I'm not boring you? Well, that's a relief. She visited Derna in the 1920s, waxed lyrical, describing it as 'A town of palm groves and gardens, abundant sweet water, flowers, grapevine pergolas, and peaches. A veritable modern Eden.' My great-uncle called her by her first name, Grace. They were close enough that she confided in him how, after a brief marriage to a man fifty years her senior, she escaped to travel the world. 'A veritable modern Eden,'" he said again and stopped.

In the silence that followed, I heard his breathing and it sounded tired. We walked at a slower pace.

"But do you see what just happened?" he then said contemplatively, all the irony now drained out of his voice. "Our country does this. A broken vase on the shores of the southern Mediterranean. The moment the light hits it, it bounces elsewhere. We started with Derna and ended up with a flying Englishwoman in a zeppelin."

"Yes," I said, and did not know why I said that except perhaps to encourage his change of tone.

"Better be thankful," he said. "'God veil our faults,' as the old folks say. A simple, much overused prayer. But what little wisdom it contains. A philosophy of sorts. I love how modest it is. I mean, they could have said, 'God erase our faults.' Now that would've been ambitious. But 'veil' is better. It presupposes that to live a life is to have faults, that no one is perfect and certainly no one is innocent. Not even you and I."

He fell silent and I listened to the sound of his heels strike the ground. Mine were less audible and out of step.

"Lethbridge," he suddenly said. "That was it. Grace's maiden name." He looked satisfied. He turned us down a silent side street that ended at a small square with nothing on it but one café. "And look," he said. "It's open."

61

COUNTLESS TABLES, ALL EMPTY, spilled out of the small café. The
square too was deserted and looked as temporary as a stage set. It was
nearly midnight. Sam chose a table at the outer periphery, obliging
the waiter, who just spotted us, to travel the longest distance. Sam
ordered hot chocolate and water for both of us, and, just as the waiter
was leaving, he asked for a box of matches. From these brief exchanges, it was clear that the two men knew each other and yet were
careful not to reveal their acquaintance. Sam was silent. Now that we
were sitting face-to-face, his enthusiasm, or whatever it was that had
caused him to speak continuously, left him.

"You are Libyan," I said, but it did not come out right. Somewhere
between a question and an answer.

"Please," he said wearily, "let's not play games." Then, adjusting his
posture, he glanced back at the windows of the building behind him.
Nothing stirred there.

What drives the crows, I wondered, those nameless men we call
the implementers. I remembered my teacher's face when I was nine.
The hard heels coming up the corridor. Two men burst into the class-

room. They slapped and kicked him. It was not till they took him away, his back whitened by the chalk on the blackboard, that some of us began to cry. What struck me most, what kept me awake that night, was the men's impatient boredom as they went about their business. Ever since, I have associated political violence with boredom and impatience. I recognized it in the three men in the embassy window, those who had diverted my life.

And now, sitting in the empty square facing Sam, who might or might not be my adversary, and who seemed to have the same question about me, I too was becoming vulnerable to that sense of impatience. I now thought, as frightening as the prospect of abduction is, it is the only rational conclusion to everything that has happened since the shooting. And I felt myself to have been waiting all this time—more than a decade—for the circle to close.

I remembered the man who, under interrogation, had peed himself on television. Sam put out his cigarette and immediately lit another, his leg constantly rocking. The waiter brought our order, shook a small box of matches beside his ear, and placed it in front of Sam.

"Try it," Sam said, grabbing hold of his cup.

I took a sip.

"Not too bitter?" he said.

I shook my head.

"How did you find me?" he said, and quickly corrected himself. "I mean, the hotel?"

"Through a travel agent," I said. "I chose it because it's cheap and not too far from the hospital. My friend is ill. Brain tumor. They opened her head today," I said, and then heard my voice grow louder. "I'm not sure who you think I am, or who you think I think you are, but I have nothing to explain or apologize for. You saw my passport and know my name. Khaled Abd al Hady, the son of Ustath Kamal Abd al Hady."

Hearing my father's name in the open both confused and steadied me.

"Kamal Abd al Hady," he said to himself, not using the formal pre-fix, as though he and my father were very well acquainted. "Isn't that the school principal?"

Here the very air changed. Benghazi is a small city, and therefore it would not have been unusual for someone from there to have heard of my father, but the confidence with which he asked the question made it seem as if he already knew the answer. At the same time his doubts or excitement or whatever it was that made him talk nervously on the way here did not vanish.

"Your family are from the old downtown, aren't they?" he said. "Never met your father. Has a good reputation. A golden name, as the old folks used to say."

"He's the finest man I know," I said. "My faults are mine and mine alone."

His eyes grew sharp and the silence stretched.

"You didn't ask but I'll tell you. I'm also from Benghazi. From the very heart of it too. The same neighborhood. We might've been neighbors. I go by Sam. Easier that way," he said, looking very uneasy. "My real name, however, is Hosam, Hosam Rajab Zowa. I tell you only because I suspect you already knew that."

The square turned. The distances between us—my hand resting on the table, the table, the wet cobblestones, the surrounding build-ings, the black sky above—all became uncertain. I had not touched a cigarette in eleven years, not since my lung was damaged, but now every cell in my body was thirsting for one. I laughed. He was taken aback by this.

"I'm sorry," I said. "I just never expected . . . Not in a million years."

This put him at ease a little, and it was only then that I realized how worried he had been.

"May I have a cigarette?" I asked, and before he could respond I reached for the packet.

He struck a match and the flame stood perfectly still but we both felt the need to cup our hands around it. His knuckles were cold.

They trembled as though there were an engine running inside him. And I saw that his eyes were on my hands too.

"Not in a million years," I said again, exhaling a large cloud of smoke. I coughed, I coughed again before my chest steadied. "I thought you were someone else," I said, and heard myself laugh once more. "I mistook you for . . . What I'm trying to say is . . . I thought I was being followed."

"Me too," he said.

Now we both laughed, but he sounded uneasy, a little forced, perhaps because the admission had left him a little ashamed, as if a trace of his suspicion persisted. Only today, walking home after bidding him farewell at the station, can I see how our friendship had been marked by that moment and remained never entirely free of distrust, as though the loyalty and affection we shared were in part stimulated by that doubt.

"Your extraordinary book. It came at such a crucial moment in my life. Defined my reading since."

Here a reconsideration flitted across his eyes. He seemed to be involved in an ongoing reassessment. And, beneath the surprise, he glowed with what could only be satisfaction. Even in a situation as strange as this, I thought, a writer cannot help but be vulnerable to flattery.

"It was because of your story 'The Given and the Taken' that I ended up studying literature."

I went on and told him about my early days in Edinburgh, Professor Henry Walbrook and his essay "The Consequences of Meaning in the Infidelities of Translation." I heard genuine enthusiasm in my voice as I described how that essay taught me that interpretation is the most exciting thing in existence, "because it means nothing is fixed."

I continued and told him, to my astonishment and confusion, that I had taken part in the 1984 embassy demonstration. His face changed ever so subtly here, and then it settled and he continued to gaze blankly at me. He did not ask if I were among the injured. He did not ask anything at all.

"I regret attending," I said, and meant it, but was also wishing to absolve myself. "It's not true what some say, that dying, when it comes, brings with it its own acceptance. The opposite, if you ask me. It brings rebellion. Because you realize then that you've spent every day of your life learning how to live. That you don't know how to do anything else. Certainly not death. And I could see it, the blackness. And could see also how endless it was. But even that wasn't the worst of it. What horrified me was I knew then that part of me, a spot of consciousness, would survive and continue even after death, trapped within nothing and silence for eternity."

I had never told anyone this before and, as I spoke, I felt I had come upon something I was saying for the very first time, certain that he understood me perfectly. I told him about Nurse Clement, the way she used to tuck the sheets beneath me with the outside edge of her palm, and how I never forgot it, that it was one of the greatest acts of kindness I had ever experienced. But then something about him, a vague indifference, stopped me.

Is he doubting me? Should I stand up, unbutton my shirt, show him my wound?

But the telling was as much for me as it was for him.

I quickly continued and told him about the trip to the Costa Brava, momentarily falling in love with my friend's friend and how something, I still did not know what, prevented me from acting on it.

"Perhaps it was a weakness," I said, "or, as Leo Tolstoy says somewhere, the lack of a necessary weakness."

I stopped and, without asking him, lit another cigarette. The fog filled my lungs.

"The impediment continues," I said, and described the days after the demonstration, getting my own place, studying at Birkbeck, becoming a school teaching assistant before gaining a full teaching qualification.

"Following in your father's steps," he said, and I honestly had not made the connection up to then. "Did you ever see your family again?"

I told him about their visit, my father's face when he saw my chest, and how that frightened me.

A silence fell. If his intentions are peaceful, I calculated, then everything I have just said would stand to make us better acquainted. If, on the other hand, he intends to betray me, my testimony might dissuade him, because it is much harder to destroy someone you know.

But there was nothing now in his face that was reserved. It was an open field. Believing I had achieved my aim, I felt naked.

He reached for the cigarettes and lit one. He gazed away with a look of placid concern, perhaps thinking about what I had told him. Not so much, I got the impression, assessing it but imagining it. I thought, to hell with him if he still doubts me.

"I would be lying," I went on, referring to my father, "if there isn't a small part of me that doesn't welcome the gap. It's as though the moment the bullets entered me they drove away everyone else. What is there to do with a wounded man? One of the things that has always puzzled me about Joseph Conrad," I said, and saw how his eyes grew a little wider, more alert, at the mention of the Pole's name, "what I could never understand about him is that when he got to England, he burned his father's papers. Did you know this?" I asked, as if we had talked about Conrad before.

He shook his head.

"I mean, haven't you noticed how we Libyans never leave home? We go far, and might stay decades, but remain strapped to the old country. It's an accomplishment, I think, a genuine achievement, to forget one's father. I would like to do that. To wake up one morning and commence life without giving him a thought."

"Yes," he said. I did not expect that. I expected him to disagree.

"I mean," I continued, "if suddenly you are confronted with death, with the irrevocable probability of life ending, everything that has come before—the power of your motivations, the reasons behind your convictions, your entire mental and spiritual motor, everything you know and even the things you don't know—is never the same again. The world is a different country."

All this business of forgetting one's father, I thought, and that a brush with mortality could offer insights, could be misconstrued by him for a version of that toxic cocktail for which Qaddafi's secret services were notorious: made up of one part rebuke, that his father was part of the ancien régime and therefore on the wrong side of history; one part threat, that the danger he is facing is serious but, if he so wishes, could be turned into an opportunity; and one part advocacy, that it is never too late to change and denounce your old ways. In other words, whereas I was beginning to feel secure, he was perhaps still suffering the possibility that I had come here to trap him, that the crows who were about to emerge from the shadows would be mine. I thought again of standing up, stripping to the waist, to show him what, at public swimming baths, in bed with lovers, I always wished I could conceal. The temptation passed and right behind it came a wave of raw emotion. Tears fell and I was not ashamed. I felt I was crying to him, to the writer who had moved me and was now, because of a most unlikely coincidence, my evening companion.

62

HOSAM EXCUSED HIMSELF, WALKED away, and disappeared inside the café. The waiter remained by the door, gazing abstractly toward me. When Hosam reappeared, the two men exchanged some words, then Hosam followed him back inside and they were there for a few minutes before he returned.

"Apologies," he said, as he sat down.

He lit another cigarette and exhaled slowly, the smoke hovering over us in the still night air.

"Do you enjoy working in a school?"

"Very much."

"What's the name of the school?"

I hesitated and saw, in my mind's eye, a needle being forced through fabric. This would be the first piece of information that would allow him to find me, I thought.

"Battersea Park School. There is no reason on earth why you should know of it."

His lips curved into a smile. "Battersea," he said. "And what subjects do you teach?"

"English," I said.

"Is that so," he said with a hint of sarcasm. He caught it too and sought to erase it. "And what are the students like? Are they clever?"

"Not particularly, but I like them. Sixth formers; so, they are sixteen to eighteen."

He shut his eyes to say he knew what sixth form meant, that he was familiar with the English school system.

I told him how my family and I had listened to his story on the radio, how proud it made us feel, but also how stunned I personally was by it, how it infiltrated my dreams. This made him uneasy, yet it was also clear, from the invisible weight on his shoulders, that he was taking pleasure in it too.

"And then later," I continued, "just as we were gunned down in broad daylight, your book, this spark, this package of eloquence, emerges. We waited so long for it and yet, when it arrived, its timing was perfect. It felt like a personal vindication. Nurse Clement got us not one but two copies. This way Mustafa, my friend, who was also injured that day, could read aloud while I followed."

"Tell me about Mustafa," he said.

I did, but only giving him the bare facts.

We walked back to the hotel. Now the silence that accompanied us was tentative and awkward. He spoke softly and slowly into it.

"I have always tried to be honest," he said. "With myself, if with no one else. Believing that there's nothing more dangerous than a man who doesn't know what he's doing, a man who doesn't know his own mind."

Until today I am not entirely sure what he had meant by that. We shook hands and I climbed the stairs to my room wondering if he still doubted me.

63

I DID NOT FALL asleep until the early hours of the morning. In contrast to the anxious thoughts that had kept me awake, I had a wonderfully gentle dream. I was walking together with a friend. That was it. There was no story or event. Nothing was said and nothing happened. Just being completely at ease. It could not have been more vivid. Thinking of it today, from this great distance, I am able to recall it perfectly, and can summon too the bright wake it left behind, the reassuring feeling of having been found just when I wanted to be.

I did not leave the hotel room till early afternoon. Hosam was not at reception. In his place there was a woman. She had a healthy, suntanned face and wore a freshly ironed shirt that was the pale blue of a clear morning sky. She stood leafing through paperwork. I handed her my key, but then returned again to ask if she knew when Sam would be back.

"My colleague," she said, "is now on holiday."

"But he was here yesterday," I said. "I mean, do you know when he will be back?"

"In a few days, I suspect," she said. "Is there anything I can help you with?"

I thanked her and left. He has run away, I thought, and pictured him gathering his belongings, which I imagined to be very few. I tried to retrace my steps back to the café. I walked right through the square without recognizing it and went in circles before I found it again. It appeared larger and the café too looked different, a much brighter affair, with most of the outside tables taken for lunch. The waiter recognized me and smiled discreetly as he listened to my order. I had an appetite. I ordered a glass of wine, a salad to start, followed by steak and fries. Then I had coffee and dessert. Several of the windows of the surrounding buildings now stood wide open. Barely perceptible sounds emerged from them: snippets of conversation, cutlery on plates, a chair being moved, a child laughing. I looked up every time someone entered the square.

As I was paying the bill, I asked the waiter, "My companion from last night, will you be expecting him later today?"

He looked at me for a second and said, "I don't know, monsieur."

I walked to the hospital. The nurses were cheerful. Rana was making remarkable progress. They expected her out of intensive care in less than a week.

"Isn't that longer than the doctor predicted?" I asked.

"Yes, but it was a grave operation," one of them said, probably making a literal translation from the French word.

I left and wandered aimlessly, propelled by a new lightness. What would it be like, I thought, to proceed from here on the assumption that the best will happen, to live undistracted by fear? I thought of Hannah. I stopped at a telephone box and dialed her number, which never left me. She answered and my heart raced.

"It's me," I said.

We had not spoken in a few weeks and yet her voice, like a bird alighting on a branch, turned vivid.

"I'm in Paris. Calling from a public phone. Line will probably cut soon. Just thought of you, is all."

"Good," she said, upset and hoping a little sarcasm might hide it. "You ought to do that more often."

64

BACK AT THE HOTEL, there was a small white envelope on the floor as I entered my room. There was nothing written on the outside of it.

Dear Khaled,

Thank you for your company last night. If you are free this evening, I would be delighted to see you again. You will find me at the same café from 6 P.M.

Yours,

Hosam

The handwriting curved on to itself, one line involved in a continuous elaboration, not lifting even in the spaces. He had not run away. But what I did not know then, and would only learn years later, is that when Hosam got home the night before, he telephoned Benghazi and asked his elder brother, Waleed, to investigate. Then, in the morning, he called my school to confirm that they did have a teacher by my name. Next, he contacted the Literature Department at the University of Edinburgh and managed to get them to confirm that a professor of postcolonial literature by the name of Henry Walbrook did work there and at the time I had attended. Then he called Benghazi again. His brother had asked around and found out that ours was one of the oldest families in the neighborhood, that we lived a quiet life, "interested in neither money nor influence," and that the father was proud of his son's academic achievements and for winning a scholarship to an esteemed university in Britain. Later still, for he confessed these details to me over a number of years—the closer we grew the more access I felt I had to his mind—I learned that Hosam then did something that I could never have expected and, although I understand perfectly why he did it, I am still unable to entirely forgive him for it. He had a friend from university who was now a doctor working for the NHS look into whether a nurse by the name of Rachel Clement had worked at Westminster Hospital in the mid-1980s. This could not have been straightforward, for the hospital had closed a couple of years before Hosam and I met, its resources moved from Pimlico to the new Chelsea and Westminster Hospital on the Fulham Road. So I imagine his friend the doctor would have had to do quite a bit of digging around. I saw, in my mind's eye, Hosam and his friend pursuing Nurse Clement. Out of all that I learned about the investigations that he had conducted on me, this detail was the one that upset me the most. And, judging from the color that entered his face as he told me this, he could see my displeasure. And in this way, by around lunchtime the day after we met, Hosam had gathered all his answers, and was as satisfied as one in his situation could ever be that I was not his enemy.

In the early evening, I set off to the café. A church bell struck six as I entered the square. The majority of the tables outside the café were taken. It was the easy hour at the end of a working day and just before supper. Hosam was at a table in the shade, close to the entrance, reading a newspaper. Even from this distance, it was evident that his entire demeanor had changed. When he saw me, he smiled in an open and unaffected way.

Out of the nervous habit established the night before, I attempted to resume recounting details of my life, ones selected to impress and reassure my companion, but the moment I started to tell him something or other about the Edinburgh days, he looked disinterested and, with an air of apology, as though partly holding himself responsible for inspiring such a need to exonerate myself, he glanced across the square, toward the small and diminishing patches of evening sunlight. He asked me about London.

"Are you happy there? Do you like it?"

The question betrayed his affection for it. In fact, the mere mention of London seemed to please him. He began to tell me how, although he had written the short story I had heard on the radio when he was twenty and still at university in Dublin, it was later, when he had graduated and moved to London, that he wrote the rest of his book. Therefore, the two things for him were linked.

"In London, I'm writing or not writing. Everywhere else, I just live."

"Is it true that you and Mohammed Mustafa Ramadan were friends?"

"I knew him a little from Benghazi. He was really my elder brother's friend. But then I would see him whenever I went to London in the holidays. I would often spend the summers there. And we grew close then. He was encouraging and kind to me."

After a little silence, he said, "Friend. What a word. Most use it about those they hardly know. When it is a wondrous thing."

65

WE SPENT MOST OF the following days together. The tables turned
and he did most of the talking. I recall how I then, and for a while
after too, wanted, with the shame that such wishes carry, to be him.
Not that Hosam was ever my role model. He was a fantasy, and fanta-
sies can build lives but also bring them crashing down. The way he
dressed, carefully but in a small selection of beautifully made items:
no more than three or four pairs of trousers and jackets, about the
same number of shirts, one pair of shoes, and one pair of boots, all
looking old and well used, giving the impression that they were not
only made for him but by him too. There was often a telling detail, a
perfectly stitched shirtsleeve, a jacket lapel that was neither too narrow nor too wide.

When I asked about his writing, he became less animated. He preferred to tell personal stories taken from his childhood in Libya,
boarding school in England, university in Dublin, the years in London, and the various European cities where he had attempted to live.
He seemed to be remembering each detail as he told it, retrieving
fragments and holding them to the light. Time passed quickly and
strangely, in that I often felt at once mesmerized and detained by his

company, wanting him never to stop and yet wanting to flee, to run and stand in front of a painting, watch a film, meet someone new. This state of contradiction made it hard at the end of each day to account for where the time went.

I did not expect the way he talked to mirror the way he wrote, but I was nonetheless struck by the distance between the two. There was his interest in people behaving in ways that are both compelling and mystifying, but his oration was given to humor and moved, very much as those afternoons and evenings moved, in a leisurely and tangential manner. Whereas his prose on the page was, as Mustafa had put it, "gaunt," written in short and clipped sentences, here the language was languid and the stories followed an elaborate route, taking several digressions. He loved the performance itself, a chance to display his authority over the Arabic language, wielding its majestic formalism and irreverence in ways that excited my longing and regret at having allowed it to wither in me. Perhaps this was part of his purpose: to help reawaken my passion for the mother tongue. And sometimes I wondered whether he was telling me these stories and recollections because he wanted me to locate him within some wider geography.

66

Rana was out of intensive care and back in her room. The television and video player, the small library of films I bought, were all still there. When I walked in, she was in bed with her head shaven entirely and the crown of it bandaged in white, her face red and a little swollen. She was speaking on the telephone, the receiver pressed tightly, whitening her ear. She was crying. She shielded her face from me. I stood at the window, looking out.

"I know," she kept saying in Arabic. "I'm sorry. I love you too, darling. Yes, I will tell him. He's here if you want to speak to him. Okay." She handed me the phone. "It's Hyder." When I hesitated, she said, "Please."

"Hyder," I said, trying to sound cheerful. "Congratulations on Rana's good health. She's looking great."

"I hate secrets," he said, sounding raw and solemn. He must blame me, I thought. "All I want to know now is if she's well. Please tell me the truth."

"I spoke to the doctor and he assured me that the operation was a success. The nurses are very pleased too. 'Couldn't have gone better,' was what they said."

"Really?" he said.

"I swear it on my grandfather's grave," I said.

"Thank you," he said. "Thank you."

"She's tremendously brave," I said.

"I know," he said in a tearful, barely audible voice. After a few seconds he said, "I'll be there tomorrow."

"That's excellent news," I made sure to tell him.

"Would come today but couldn't find a flight. I can't believe she didn't tell me." There was something about the way he said that that made it seem like a question.

"I look forward to seeing you," I said, because I did not know what else to say. And then I wondered if that came across as admonishment.

"How do I reach you?" he asked.

I gave him the hotel telephone number.

When I hung up, Rana covered her face. I placed my hands round her ankles. She looked at me.

"I tried to pretend," she said.

"I know you did," I said. "I'm glad you told him. Glad he's coming."

"Me too," she said.

67

EARLY THE FOLLOWING MORNING, the telephone in my room, which had never sounded before, began ringing. It was Hyder, calling from Beirut Airport. His flight was expected to land around lunchtime. After a little silence, he said, "Will we see you, maybe tomorrow?"

This was why he was calling, I thought. He wanted time alone with his wife. He wanted to arrive and not have a third person there.

"Of course," I said.

"Tomorrow, then," he said.

I went the day after, so as to give them more time together and also because I was nervous to see Hyder. I was right to be. He was awkward, squeezed my hand tightly, a raw pride in his throat. He also looked exhausted, with dark bags beneath his eyes. The nurses told me that he had not left the hospital since he arrived, sleeping in the armchair beside his wife. I helped him to check into a nearby hotel. Told him to get some rest and that I would be back in the afternoon. I walked off feeling disassociated from my surroundings. Why I was in Paris no longer made sense. When I returned to pick him up, I found Hyder looking better. He asked if I fancied a walk.

"I still can't believe she did not tell me," he said again.

I said nothing, tried to change the subject, but after a little silence he said, more to himself, "Why would she do that?"

"Something terrible happened to me," I said. "I'm sure Rana told you. And I too didn't want the people I loved the most to know."

"You're a good friend," he said.

"I love her as much as I love my own sister," I told him and hoped he did not doubt me. "We should celebrate," I said. "Rana has made it through and that's all that matters."

I pulled him into a fancy bakery and we bought a large box of delicious things. He insisted on paying. Back at the hospital the nurses said something in French and Hyder replied easily. He then explained that they were teasing me about having a sweet tooth.

We found Rana sitting up in bed. A big smile on her face when she saw us enter together.

68

WHEN MY LAST DAY in Paris came, Hosam gave me a piece of information I had never expected.

It was a sunny day. He suggested we walk to the Jardin sauvage Saint-Vincent, a small park behind the Sacré-Cœur in Montmartre.

"A wild garden," he said. "Almost always closed, but shall we try?"

I do not know why, but I have since suspected that he had made a secret pact with himself: if the garden was open, he would tell me; if not, we would turn back and I would never know.

Our conversation meandered as we climbed north. Every now and again he would point to where a writer or a painter had once lived. I would come to remember this when he eventually moved to London and would do the same here, only with more confidence. In Paris he was unmoored.

"Do you ever think of going back to London?" I asked, as we crossed the Seine.

"Funny you should say that," he said, pointing to a handsome building on the north bank of the river. "See that top floor? The whole thing," he said, with a little vain amusement in his voice. "My father bought properties as he traveled, and then one by one they were all gone. This was the last—not counting something in far-off California—and, until recently, I believed there was a chance of retrieving it. A month ago, I lost all hope of that. Foolish business to run after things."

Once we were folded back inside the streets, he said, "So many so-called noble families are only noble because they were, for centuries, good at being on the winning side."

I did not tell him what my father had told us or anything about those afternoons my family spent, after hearing his short story on the radio, discussing the history of the Zowas. Instead, I said, and only to please him, "I'm not sure about that. There are things to be proud of there."

He blushed and said, "I doubt it very much."

I thought, probably unfairly, that he must have learned this trait at English boarding school, to claim an honor while seeming to denounce it.

We reached the Jardin sauvage Saint-Vincent and found it open.

"I didn't tell you, only out of fear you might lose interest, but this place is always closed. In all the years I've lived here, this is the first time I've entered it." He proceeded to tell me about the garden, how it was part of an old piece of fallow land, that the trees, plants, and flowers were all self-sown. "A little wild meadow locked inside the city."

We walked through the pathways and, although the park was small, the air in it felt heavy. We leaned on the fence by a pond that was entirely covered in an unbroken sheet of bright green algae. I wondered what was in the dark water beneath and how deep it ran. I felt the temptation to throw a pebble, tear the surface open.

"I too was there," he said, his voice careful and low. "It is even possible," he went on, gazing at the fluorescent green, "that at one point you and I stood like this, side by side." He turned to me, unsure if I understood.

I was determined to give nothing away, to hold fast to some semblance of equilibrium. I thought I knew all I needed to know about the events of that day. And yet I had imagined the others, the many more who attended the demonstration and then resumed their lives, able to walk away on their own two feet. I feel underwater when I think of them, because to think of them is to imagine that other, unharmed version of myself, who got back on the bus to Edinburgh, and could fly home for the summer, to sleep in his own house and swim in his childhood sea. The line that now separates me from my former self is the chasm that I remain unable to bridge. You cannot be two people at once. Hosam continued looking at me for a reaction. And, just as we were enjoying this newly discovered common ground, I thought that whereas on the day of the shooting my covenant with fate was shattered, his was strengthened.

"I too turned up late. And, like you, ended up there through an impulsive decision made at the last minute. But, unlike you and your friend Mustafa, I didn't bring a balaclava. I tied my handkerchief around my face instead. You are right: one could sense immediately that something terrible was about to happen," he said, with a crease of regret in his voice. "Where were you standing?" he then asked, and, before I could answer, he said, "I was right in the middle."

Even as he said this, my mind pictured him not inside the crowd but to one side of it, standing on the pavement, observing the scene from a distance, and then, when the mayhem set in, walking away as if nothing had happened. A long time ago I was sitting with my father at a café in Benghazi. He was talking to someone he knew and I was daydreaming out the window. I was suddenly gripped by a dark premonition. Just then my eyes fell on a woman crossing the street. I saw her thrown up in the air, her clothes fluttering, then landing on the tarmac, where she lay completely still. The car that struck her came to a screaming halt a few feet further on. I could never explain how I sensed it before it happened.

"When those men opened the window," Hosam said, "I moved to

the rear lines. The moment the firing started, I must have run, because I suddenly found myself gasping for air around the corner, on the little street that leads to Regent Street Saint James's."

"Charles II," I heard myself say.

"Yes, maybe that's the one," he said. "I was drenched. My entire body. I turned left, going up toward Regent Street, but then, thinking I was being followed, I stood at the bus stop. I hovered there for a moment before continuing on, turning left again, going down Jermyn Street. I was, in effect, circling back. I knew it but couldn't help it. I reached that little street—what is it called?"

I kept my eyes on the sealed surface of the water. The green algae now appeared as a metal sheet, hard and unyielding, stealing the light. "Think you are a man?" I heard those words I had expected the eavesdropper to say, just after he cleared his throat into the silence, when my father had gone to fetch my mother and Souad. I heard them, with uncanny accuracy, spoken lazily and in the same ambiguous tone, as though the intelligence officer were lying on his back.

"What was that street?" he said again. "You know the one that leads back into the square, where the wounded sheltered till the ambulances arrived?"

Duke of York Street, I thought to myself, and remembered how, when I first told him of my experience of that day, I had deliberately left out any mention of Duke of York, because the moment I saw myself sitting there on the pavement, bleeding beside the drain, my mind coiled away from it. St. James's Square appeared to me now as the kernel at the center of my life, the place from which everything unraveled. As the sun is to the solar system, my life has revolved around it. And not since that day have I been able to approach it. Not until tonight, the same night that I said goodbye to Hosam for what feels like the very last time.

A violent rebellion churned within me as we left the garden and reentered the cobbled streets, walking back south through Paris.

Freedom, I told myself, is also the freedom not to be suspicious, not to fear, and not to envy.

"Did you see me?" I asked, long after he had moved away from the conversation and was instead telling me about what Julio Cortázar had apparently said somewhere about the city plan of Paris, which, the late Argentine author believed, resembles the ideal sentence, one concluding, like a Parisian crossroads, in three or more propositions from which to advance. "I mean, as you stood at the top of Duke of York Street—did you see me? I was the first there. I sat on the pavement. It would have been on the left of where you were. A policeman propped me up from the back, kept me from falling over. It must have made an unusual sight. He had a strange, generic face too, the policeman. Like a joker in a deck. Could have passed for anyone. Does any of this ring a bell?"

He watched me openly, with a look of genuine sympathy. "I saw a few people on the ground," he said, "but the place was cordoned off. It was chaos. I left when I heard the ambulances."

And where did you go, I wanted to ask, but stopped myself. I stopped myself because I believed his story was less important than mine, and that this needed to be expressed somehow, even if in silence. But I later learned that by the time I reached Westminster Hospital, and that young panicked doctor was screaming, "Here," Hosam was well into Hyde Park, "Walking home," as he had put it, "accompanied by the sense that I had been extracted from the beast's mouth. Like Jonah and the whale." He told me this not in Paris, but fifteen years later, in Café Cyrano, the place we used to go to on Holland Park Avenue. It was a warm autumnal evening in November of 2010. We had met to celebrate his fiftieth birthday. He had been drinking before, and quickly, after the first round, became tipsy and nostalgic. When he said, "extracted from the beast's mouth," there was a hint of self-congratulation to it. I could not understand it and wondered whether Hosam, contrary to everything he had told me, did believe in a divine will that oversaw human affairs, that decided, according to its own mysterious reasoning, to spare one person while casting another to the wind—for what else could explain, I thought to myself, the hard edge of moral pleasure that I heard in his voice then? I kept my eyes on the colorful cocktails between us, which suddenly seemed hideously bright and cheerful. I was disquieted by his insensitivity, his taking comfort in his good fortune, knowing full well what had happened to me. It was outrageous how similar and yet profoundly different our experiences of that day were. And perhaps it was my presence, sitting opposite him, that reminded him of his good luck, or even consoled him on the occasion of his fiftieth birthday by making the past, everything that had happened up to that moment, seem ordained by a gentle God, exonerating mistakes, placing him very much at the center of his life, for he suddenly seemed to be beaming with happiness. Just as I thought this, he said, "Isn't it magical to be alive?"

I tried to smile. I raised my glass. "Happy birthday," I said.

And, although I was looking at him and speaking, my mind was already back at St. James's Square or, more precisely, Duke of York Street, by the same drain where I had sat, seeing, in my mind's eye, the house opposite with the monochrome man who stood expressionless at the window, watching me bleed, with a face that has since revisited me in dreams, and which seems to me still to be the face of life's indifference. As I sat with Hosam in Café Cyrano, thinking back on that moment on Duke of York Street, I remembered Aristotle's words, which were read to me by my father, and therefore in Ibn Rushd's Arabic, that "Not pleasure, but freedom from pain, is what the wise man will aim at." And now I have returned to Duke of York Street, almost free of pain. I walk to the corner where Hosam stood unmasked, observing the scene with other bystanders. He then continued down Jermyn Street, walking quickly, almost running, as he told me on his first mention of it, on that day we walked back from the Jardin sauvage Saint-Vincent. "Stopping every twenty feet or so, to contemplate going back. To do what, I didn't know," he said. "But it was so mad to keep on going as if nothing had happened. And everything around me insisted that nothing had happened. The shops were open, people utterly oblivious, as though what I just witnessed was an event that occurred only in my mind. Yes," he said, "that's why I wanted to return. It was the opposite of madness."

69

RANA CONTINUED TO IMPROVE. She was released from hospital and moved with Hyder to a much nicer hotel near the Jardin du Luxembourg. When I visited, we would have tea in the lobby. The only sign that persisted was an impression in the eyes, a look of quiet bewilderment.

On my last night in Paris, she was well enough to come out for a celebratory dinner. We did not go to the restaurant she had read about in the inflight magazine, but one Hyder picked, a fancy place with high ceilings and chandeliers. I spotted two men at a table for four on the opposite side of the room. They sat not facing one another but side by side, with their backs against a long wall covered in large mirrors. They hardly looked at each other. Instead, they followed with dispassionate interest the various goings-on around them: the patrons who came and went, the few but efficient waiters who moved between the tables with artistic economy. Both men looked in their seventies and were dressed in elegant but understated clothes that looked comfortable and well used. But, no, they were not brothers, for, although they looked alike, their resemblance was more in manner than in features. Nor did they appear to be lovers. Their confederacy was not that of a couple but of autonomous individuals. They were, I decided, old friends who knew one another intimately, had seen much together and arrived at this old age with very little drama, and were now enjoying the easy confidence that must come with such an attainment. I continued to covertly observe them, all the while feeling grateful that Rana was well, dressed as she was in the beautiful new maroon suit that Hyder had bought. He managed to judge her size perfectly, a fact that surprised and delighted her. "As if made for me," she kept saying. The soft fabric curved comfortably around her shoulders. The tenderness between him and her. All this inspired a happy optimism in me. The three of us promised to return to Paris again. Just then the two friends sitting at the opposite side of the room let their eyes alight on us for a couple of seconds. Hyder teased me about my fear of flying and then said, "I so wish you would visit us in Beirut." When the bill came, he insisted on paying and I did not put up a fight.

We stood outside the restaurant waiting for a taxi. When one arrived, I said I was going to walk. Rana looked concerned. I said goodbye first to Hyder. When I went to embrace her, Rana's eyes turned red. Hyder held back, careful not to rush the moment. I was grateful to him for that. Right beside her ear I whispered, "Thank you for asking me to come. It's the greatest compliment anyone has ever paid me."

She could not speak. We held on to each other. Hyder waited. The taxi driver waited. My eyes fell on the two old friends who were still inside the restaurant, sitting in the golden light. They looked different from out here. A little bored or at a loss somehow. I opened the car door and Rana and Hyder entered the cab. Rana looked back as the car sped off.

The videotapes ended up in her house in Beirut. Sometimes she still sends a photograph of her television, burning blue in the dark, with a still of one of our films. Apart from this, we never speak of Paris. She hardly ever comes to London now. Children, aging parents, no time.

70

IT WAS LATE WHEN I arrived at the hotel. Hosam was back behind the reception desk, looking more confident than ever. Said he had been waiting for me and insisted that we go out for a brandy before I went up to bed. He called the night porter and asked him to take his place. The man smiled, seemed amused that Hosam and I were now friends. We returned to the café on the square. It was close to midnight and, as on the first time we came here, we found it open and entirely empty. Hosam was in a jolly mood. Now that I was leaving, he wanted to celebrate our unlikely meeting and, I could not help but feel, the ease and anonymity that would come with my departure. He talked about London, asking about the current political mood, rent prices, etc. I did my best to answer, hearing an eager enthusiasm in my voice, and sensing that old animalistic instinct of the salesman, learned back when, before and while studying at Birkbeck, I worked at a high-end clothing shop on the King's Road and came to know when to approach and when to hold back. A silence followed. I assumed he was considering what I had told him. He gazed up at the buildings surrounding the square.

"I knew a girl who lived here. Algerian. Had a bicycle with a rack over the back wheel, sturdy enough to sit on. One day she took me around. Had to lift my legs up out of the way. Held on to the underside of her saddle with my fingertips. Occasionally, I had to place a hand on her waist to steady myself. She pedaled, rising and sitting, the wind rushing through her dress, through her hair. I caught her perfume, hints of soap and shampoo, and that other thing that was hers alone: her body and days and nights. She wanted to take me to the 9th arrondissement. I had just moved here. Hardly knew my way around. I remember we stopped and ate salt-beef sandwiches standing on the pavement, then raced across to a library she wanted me to see. I don't know what it was called and have since failed to find it. The windows stood high and turned in half-moons at the top. Too many books, too few people bent over them. We went on. She stopped in the middle of an unremarkable street, looked up toward one of the windows, and said, 'My grandmother lived here, during those nervous early years before she got papers.' She mounted the right pedal and pushed forward. I held on to her with both hands. The wheels turned and the wind was a lovely thing."

The waiter collected our empty glasses and asked if we would like another round.

"Why on earth not," Hosam told him, and the man smiled back.

"Najma, that was her name. And I have a sister named Najma. The youngest in the family. Hardly know her by now. We went back to her place," he said, pointing to a building opposite. I turned to look. "The apartment on the corner, right on the top floor. It was a hot day. She opened all the windows and a breeze blew softly across the room. We sat cross-legged on the cool wooden floor. I remember so much her knees, how strong and delicate they were."

As I listened to Hosam, I saw Hannah's knees: at first seeming one color, but then a vapor of pink beneath the almond skin, a deep green vein passing, the distant faint blue of flesh.

"Her bare feet were slightly stained from the leather sandals. The straps left halos around her ankles. Her toes were open and free. She made Japanese tea. 'Everything has to be precise,' she said. 'You need to be patient.' She smiled. I remember wanting so much then for her to tell me something she had never told anyone. The tea was ready. She poured it and we drank it in silence. I wonder whatever became of her."

"Are you no longer in touch?" I asked.

"I think she's still in Paris but not sure. In any case, the trouble with me," he said, and stopped. "Well, it has only one name: Claire. Although it's been ages since we were together, she still manages to appear between me and every other woman, even that heavenly Najma. It's not love exactly."

Up to then, Hosam had only told me a little about Claire. I knew she was from Dublin, that they had met at university there, went out on and off for years. But it was not so much what he said about her but how the mention of her name softened his voice.

"Just learned she bought a house in north London," he then said. "Got a job at a legal charity assisting asylum seekers."

71

MUSTAFA WAS EXCITED AND intrigued that I had met Hosam
Zowa. Could not believe it at first. With flushed cheeks, he wanted to
know how it happened, what we spoke about, what he was like.

"I want all the details," he said.

I gave him a faithful account and was glad to relive the experience.
But soon the novelty wore off and skepticism, like a stain spreading,
entered his voice. He began to make pronouncements that were all
the more upsetting because they corresponded with the ones I was
secretly resisting.

"He's scared. Has exaggerated the importance of his stories and
allowed himself to wither away in a pointless job," Mustafa said.
"Proof that talent alone isn't enough. Courage is also required. Courage that he obviously doesn't have. I knew it from that interview."

His verdict had the violent vitality of a door slamming shut. Although I knew Mustafa well, and believed I knew how his mind
worked, that it was often powered not by reflection but a hot momentum that took him to places he neither expected nor necessarily desired, his judgment remained compelling.

"Be careful," he said. "Don't surrender your trust completely.

There is nothing more dangerous than a writer who has given up on writing. Remember what happened to Sadeq al Naihoum."

That was an old argument. I still found al Naihoum's essays interesting, whereas Mustafa had written him off entirely, because, after leaving the country and facing the difficulties of exile, the Libyan author accepted money from the dictatorship.

"Al Naihoum never returned," I said.

"It would have been more honorable if he had," Mustafa said. "The moment you accept Qaddafi's money, you are finished. And you saw what happened to his writing, how it became esoteric and abstract. A pothead's ramblings."

"Hosam is different," I said. "For a start, he stopped writing all together."

"Exactly," Mustafa said.

The last thing I wish to be doing, I thought to myself, is arguing about Sadeq al Naihoum. I asked for the bill. I was glad not to have told Mustafa the most important detail of all: that Hosam was at the demonstration. That he had been there and still refused to speak on the radio, I was sure, would have further provoked Mustafa's disapproval.

We embraced on the pavement outside the café and I walked home alone, very much as I am doing now. I thought, how did we become so unmoored? I tried to imagine the people Mustafa and I would have become if we had never left and were meeting at a café in Benghazi instead. Those two, I imagined, embedded in the society that formed them, would have had less time to listen to the past. We need our families and the obligations of others to silence the unsaid and the unsayable. I imagined children. I imagined a variety of voices. I imagined rituals and routines. I imagined cooking not for myself alone and I imagined being cooked for. I wanted, more than anything else, the wants and demands of others. Those are versions of myself that continue in the dark.

I called Hannah and it was like opening a window and breathing in the air.

72

A COUPLE OF MONTHS later, Hosam telephoned. He was in London.

"Thought of spending a few days here," he said. "To see Claire and you, my new friend. I've missed this old town."

I imagined him looking out of a window as he said this. He was staying at a hotel in Paddington, owned by a cousin. I met him there and we set off. We walked the city, which he knew better than me, but his knowledge was a little out of date. He kept returning to places that were no longer there. And, apart from Claire, he did not seem to have any friends here, or none that he was keen on maintaining.

Once we bumped into someone he knew, an Englishman with a gentle and open face. He was clearly pleased to see Hosam, and kept looking at me, expecting to be introduced. We never were, and when we walked on Hosam did not say a word. He did, though, introduce me to Claire.

I do not know what I expected, but whatever it was it bore no relation to the woman I met. Hosam invited me to her place, said Claire was looking forward to meeting me and that she was making dinner. I stopped to buy a bottle of wine and took a long time choosing it.

Hosam met me at the door. He was more animated than usual. I could smell cooking, and, when we passed through the kitchen, I heard a pot simmering quietly. Claire was nowhere to be seen. Hosam thanked me for the wine, asked what I would like to drink, then led me into the lounge. We turned the corner and I saw her sitting on the sofa, with her legs folded beside her, a shaded lamp burning on the side table by her elbow. Her dress was plain and was almost the exact color of her skin. Her chestnut hair was tied back, leaving her face naked and elegant. A practical face, I thought, one well acquainted with human affairs. Each earlobe was punctuated by a small pearl. She rose to her feet.

Throughout the evening, an unequivocal sympathy passed between them. When she talked, an expression of gentle curiosity came over Hosam, which surprised me a little, as I did not think then that old friends or lovers could continue to be so enthralled by one another. His interest made her all the more beautiful and made her independence appear as a precious object. It quieted him but also left him searching. He got up several times, went to the kitchen, and returned with nothing. At one point after the meal, just as he was pouring the coffee, her left hand fell on his right. A faint green vein ran above her poised fingers and vanished up her arm. One evening in Paris, Hosam told me that he believed that the most important human dramas take place not on battlefields but in the quiet hours. His phrase, the quiet hours, came to me then.

She talked about her work, complained about the unjust way in which immigrants were often treated, the complexities of what was needed, and how difficult it was to arrive at any easy solutions. She asked if I had ever been to Ireland, then wanted me to tell her about Benghazi.

"He doesn't like to speak about it," she told me.

Hosam's face gave nothing away.

73

A COUPLE OF MONTHS later, Hosam resigned from his job at the hotel and surrendered the flat where he had lived for the past four years in Paris. He arrived at his cousin's hotel in Paddington with two small suitcases. He was excited and nervous. Weeks passed without him finding a flat. Being unemployed and living in temporary accommodation made it difficult, but this was only part of the problem. He did not put enough energy into it. Preferred instead to roam the city.

"I worried about coming back, but I'm really finding myself here again," he told me one afternoon.

The couple in the flat below me had vacated weeks ago and the place was still empty. I telephoned the landlord and he said he had been meaning to have it redecorated and never got around to it, but he would be glad to show it in its present condition to my friend. I left it a couple of days and then mentioned it to Hosam.

"Sure," he said, but with none of the enthusiasm I had hoped for.

I brought him to it. The place was tired, a little dark, but big and had access to a private garden. I remember him pausing for a moment in the empty living room, gazing down toward his feet. I somehow knew what he was thinking. To live so close to someone he knew.

After all, to go home is to disappear. I too feared being witnessed. The landlord and I wandered off to the next room. We spoke about changes taking place in the neighborhood, the new shopping center, planned to be the largest in Europe, and the negative effects we feared it might have on local businesses; and then, without giving any reasons why, we both agreed that on balance it would probably be good for the area. Hosam caught up with us, inquired about the rent. The landlord said he saw no reason to raise it from what the previous tenants paid. He looked at me and repeated what I had heard him say before, that he was not one of those who took pleasure in raising rents. I attested to the fact that he was a decent fellow and that I had always appreciated this about him. This pleased them both. They shook hands.

I still remember the day Hosam moved in, how happy and excited I felt, and how the happiness and excitement belonged to childhood, from when my favorite cousins came to stay, or when we headed east out of Benghazi and into the mountains, to my mother's country. Packing the car and leaving the city. That was the best part. I had not felt like this since. It amazed me how none of the features of my life changed and yet everything was made different by Hosam becoming my neighbor. I was put back together, accompanied, and my life in London, which I cherished with a quiet pride, now had the feel of being part of a family, where a drink, a meal, a coffee, a walk could be shared spontaneously, without the tiresome need to plan and arrange.

It all happened so quickly that I did not have time to tell Mustafa. When I did, he was careful not to express surprise. But I knew this about him: the more surprised or impressed he was, the less he wanted to show it.

"Now that explains it," was all he said.

"Explains what?" I asked, with a little challenge in my voice.

"Nothing," he said, satisfied at his ability to provoke. "Just that you've disappeared, is all. Haven't heard from you for days. So when will you introduce me to your new famous friend?"

I left it for as long as I could, and when I arranged for us all to meet, walking to the café my heart beat wildly in my chest. It did not go badly, but it did not go that well either. Mustafa talked endlessly, was loud and brash, and everything he said sounded as though he were boasting. At one point in the conversation he kept repeating to Hosam that he could not believe that he had never read Milan Kundera.

Hosam sat back and waited it out. When we left, he said, with a tone of genuine sympathy, "A little nervous, your friend."

"He admires you," I said, which was both true and a lie.

74

WHEN HOSAM ARRIVED FROM Paris with only two small suitcases, I assumed the rest of his belongings were in storage and would follow once he was settled. But there was nothing else. The contents of those bags were all that he owned. One held books and the other clothes. His policy was that it was better to own few well-made garments than be continually obliged to replace them. I was by now familiar with his wardrobe. And there was no point, he maintained, in owning a book unless one intended to reread it multiple times.

"In which case, a handsome edition," he said. "But to have an endless number of books sit on the shelf just because one has read them or might one day read them is absurd. Besides, is there anything more depressing than a wall of books? But you, my dear, disagree. Like Montaigne, you believe that the very presence of books in your room cultivates you, that books are not only to be read but to be lived with."

When he would visit me upstairs and his eyes would fall on my wall of books, something resembling delight and regret would pass across his face, as though what he secretly found troubling was not the sight of a large number of books but the stability that such an acquisition assumes. Reading requires one to be still. So does writing.

He borrowed books from me, from the public library, and some-times clandestinely from bookshops, stealing them, carefully reading them, making sure not to crease the spine or leave any marks, and then returning them without anyone noticing.

"I like the idea," he said, when he first confessed this to me, "of a new book read without its future owner ever knowing it. A secret just between me and the pages."

Outside of this, he hardly ever ventured beyond the thirty or so volumes he owned. I got the impression that this was not only out of the desire to be frugal, to remain light, to be able at any moment to move, but also to be, if not rooted in a physical location, habitually residing in the same literary terrain, with its familiar quarters, loved lines half forgotten, and to know, over a lifetime, as much as possible about a few books, until they came to seem like native land.

Behind our conversations about literature lay always my wish that he would write again. I suggested he write a book about his reread-ings.

"A sort of diary of your impressions, and how they have changed over time," I said. "A record of a writer's close reading."

There was little I could do about it. I could not help believing him to be, at his most essential self, a writer. I often heard encouragement and admonishment braided into my voice. He heard it too. The closer we grew, the harder it was to hide such yearnings.

75

THE NIGHT HAS GROWN all around me. I am finally leaving St. James's Square. Neither bless nor curse. Let all your elsewheres go. London is where you are.

I reach Hyde Park. It is nine in the evening. The twilight is gone. The moonless night is black. It is disturbed only by a reflected glow, making it possible to make out the skeletal shapes of the large leafless trees. I have never stopped being frightened of the dark. I have only got better at tolerating it. The deeper I go into the park, the less discernible the city becomes. Its sounds are stretched and mute in the distance. The air here is moist and still and as dark as an inkwell.

Hosam moved to London and we became neighbors in 1996. By then I had been in the same flat for twelve years, whereas he, since leaving Benghazi, had moved between some half a dozen cities. On graduating from Trinity College Dublin, he went to London and wrote the collection of short stories, making frequent trips back to Ireland to see Claire. Then, shortly after his book was published, and just as I was starting my new and uncertain life in London, he embarked on several attempts at making a life elsewhere and always with, as he put it, "the honest intention of settling down forever." He tried Barcelona, learned Spanish and Catalan, then, having Italian already, on account of learning it as a child in Libya, he moved to Naples. After a year or two, he went north to Milan, only to return back to Naples. He then went to live with Claire in Dublin before eventually moving to London again. A little while later, he went to Paris. This was his most successful attempt, he said, because he managed to remain there for four years, until he and I met. For each of these relocations, the motive remained unclear.

All this made his life here seem a temporary pause. We often went to his favorite bar in Soho, the French House. One night we drank and ate and drank again. Hosam got talking to the table next to us and told a story. I do not remember much of it, but I remember the faces of those strangers, their surrendered attention and delight. And I remember Hosam's face too, enjoying the power of his storytelling. And I remember thinking, this is what happens when a writer stops writing. I tried to smile the thought away, but I think he read it on my face. He paused for a fraction of a second before continuing, but doing so with less vigor.

We ended up going home through Hyde Park, along the same path I am walking now, which follows the Serpentine. That night was bitterly cold, and, as we became ever more enveloped in it, he began to speak. His voice sounded different, and the dark made it impossible to read his face. He began to speak of a discrepancy that existed, a growing and unbridgeable gulf, between the fact that he was no longer a writer and the ideas he continued to get for new works.

"They come and hover like bats," he said.

"I think if you look closer, you'll find they are robins," I said.

"Maybe," he said, and sounded a little proud.

And so, I decided to continue. "It's dangerous to ignore such gifts."

"Maybe," he said again. "But I was only once a writer. That ended long ago. Must accept fate."

"But those ideas are also your fate," I said. "We call talent a gift for a reason. You are merely a custodian."

"I refuse it," he said, and did not speak after that.

We listened instead to the night's silence thickening all around us.

Now that he was living in the flat below, he began to do what I suspected he had done in those other cities where he had lived, going from one half-hearted employment to the next. He would get a job at a bookshop or waiting tables at a restaurant only to walk out a few months later, often without offering his employer any explanation. On more than one occasion, he spoke of moving back to Paris or Naples. He considered new places too, where it was cheaper to live: Lisbon, Trieste, Palermo, Valletta. When I asked, he said, no, he did not know anyone in those places. As he moved in his mind from one place to another, borrowing books on each, life to him seemed more an idea than a reality.

I was a little reassured when I visited him and found a new map of west London pinned to his kitchen wall. It stretched from Shepherd's Bush to the Royal Albert Hall. He had marked several locations on it with a black X and, using a red marker, he had written initials beside each: VW, FMF, JC, EP, TSE, RLS, and so on. Seeing me studying it, he said, "Because those who are lost at sea must gaze up at the stars." I was amazed by how many of the authors we read and admired had at one time lived in such close proximity to where we were. The fact cheered Hosam up too.

"Let's visit them all," he said.

VW was Virginia Woolf. We agreed we should go to her house first.

"It is," he estimated, "just over two miles from our front door." We stood in front of the white building on Hyde Park Gate. This was where Woolf was born and spent the first two decades of her life, which were, Hosam was keen to point out, "One third of the time she spent on this earth." We loitered on its steps, as though we were expected, then walked the few feet to Hyde Park and tried to guess which gate she would have entered through.

Pilgrimages have never interested me, but it was impossible not to be fascinated by the practical fact that Woolf had once lived here, walked into the world out of this exact door, and retreated away behind it. It made her books even more miraculous, that they managed to exist in a world of so much variance, where with one wrong step everything can change. I began to find it fortifying too to trace the paths of these long-dead women and men, whom I felt intimate with in ways I rarely do with living persons. On Campden Hill Road, a mile and a half away, once lived Ford Madox Ford. We stood outside on the opposite pavement and pictured D. H. Lawrence turning up unannounced, as the story goes, and somehow managing to enter like a thief.

For a year or two, Joseph Conrad lived nearby. This was not a coincidence, as he and Ford were intimate friends. We walked between the two houses, imagining them visiting one another.

Ezra Pound had lived at 10 Kensington Church Walk, about 1.7 miles from us, in a small cottage down the quiet dead-end road. We both mimed unzipping our trousers and pissing right outside his front door. A few days later, we returned to Pound and walked the third of a mile or so eastward, to 3 Kensington Court Gardens, where T. S. Eliot had lived. The two were also friends. We tried to imagine them walking back and forth, but it was less fun, given that we both could not forgive Pound's admiration for Mussolini.

Henry James lived at 34 De Vere Gardens, two miles away, a stone's throw from Woolf and Eliot, for some twelve years. But, most exciting of all, and right beside us in Shepherd's Bush—"So close that," Hosam said, "if we called his name from your kitchen window he would have heard"—was none other than Robert Louis Stevenson, the writer Hosam and I loved the most. We stood in front of what Hosam believed was his door. There was no plaque, but he insisted this was the one.

"We should visit the living," I said.

Hosam looked perplexed. "Who?" he said.

"I don't know. The lady that runs the bakery down the road. Anyone, anyone alive. Writers too. Tayeb Salih, for example. He lives in London. Why don't we visit him, take flowers and bread?"

I realized as I spoke that this was again me trying to tell him that he ought to write, stop this historical romanticism, and get down to business. The world was burning.

"Did you know, for example," I said, "that Borges disliked pilgrimages, thought them sterile, believed that they achieve the exact opposite of their intention?"

He looked heavy again. "Anyway," he said, "we are almost done."

There was something in the way he said that that worried me. That was when he came up with the last author. He had organized our visits from the furthest to the nearest, like a net or a noose tightening. The nearest and the last was our fellow African, Dambudzo Marechera, the author whose book I came upon at the library during my early days here, and was both drawn to and unsettled by the expression on his young face in the black-and-white photograph. Hosam learned through his research that, after growing up in the slums of Harare, miraculously winning a scholarship to Oxford, only to revolt against the university and wander the streets, Marechera had ended up sleeping rough in Shepherd's Bush. Hosam was pretty certain of the exact spot on the pavement where the author had made his temporary home. It was right outside our local tube station, the old entrance. He insisted we go there now. He paused across the street from it for a bit. Then we crossed at the wrong moment and had to run for it.

"We should sit down where he did," he said.

I tried to laugh, but he was serious, more serious than I had ever seen him before. I was struck by the temperature of the pavement, as though everything hard and cold in the world had seeped in there. I turned to sit more on my hip. Rows and rows of legs hammered the ground in front of us. I tried to look amused. But the next time I turned to Hosam I found his eyes filled with tears.

76

Instead of being a galaxy with which to orientate himself, Hosam's authors' map turned into a survey of London's inherent instability. Lawrence died in New Mexico. Conrad remained rootless till the end, even regretting having had a child in England, where he had no relations. Eliot's face said it all, "a sensibility that was free only in the interior; all outward forms had to be controlled severely." Even Ford, "with his confident English metropolitanism, had to get the hell out eventually." Hosam was convinced that even that last afternoon, when Woolf stuffed her coat pockets with stones and walked into the River Ouse, was evidence of London's failure to be a gentle shelter to anyone who was not part of what he called "the orthodoxy." To tell me what he meant, he said, he would need to borrow my Jean Rhys novels. He returned a couple of days later and could not have looked more excited. With *After Leaving Mr. Mackenzie* in hand, he read the lines when Julia Martin, desperate to make a life in London, thinks, "'This place tells you all the time, "Get money, get money, get money, or be forever damned." Just as Paris tells you to forget, forget, let yourself go.'"

I suppose when I look back, the signs were all there; that the best

I could have hoped for was that my friend would live near me for as long as it was possible for him to remain in one place, that I could never take his companionship for granted. Besides, where an exile chooses to live is inevitably arbitrary.

He began to see more and more of Claire. She was good for him, softened the precariousness he felt. Refurbishment works needed to be carried out on her house in north London. She moved in with him downstairs while that took place. At night, their light came through the gaps in the floorboards, and I often went to sleep to their voices murmuring softly. My feeling of being complemented by Hosam living below doubled now that Claire too was there. All the while, though, I had the sense that the ground was shifting. A few months later, when Claire's house was ready, Hosam told me what I had suspected, that he would be moving in with her. He had already handed in his notice to the landlord. I was hurt and angry and embarrassed that I was hurt and angry and so hid it, tried to explain my unhappiness in the light of the abruptness of the news.

"You could have told me earlier," I said.

He embraced me, said, "You are always good and I love you for it. No matter where I am, you'll always be my neighbor."

As the date approached, he grew nervous. He measured the distance from Shepherd's Bush to Kentish Town in tube stops, then the number of minutes it would take by bus and, because I had started cycling to work, he also figured out the nicest cycling route to cross the six-mile distance.

The day he and Claire moved out, the house and the very street changed. Indeed, the whole of Shepherd's Bush and London too. Standing at my kitchen window, I tried not to look down at what used to be their garden.

Claire's place was beautiful, the floor made of newly cut planks of wood that met perfectly. She owned the house, with no one above or below. She wanted kids, Hosam told me.

Now he and I met in town at the French House. Sometimes I took him to a play. Mustafa lived up north too, and so we occasionally met at his place, but those evenings I did not enjoy as much. I was convinced that my two friends represented two separate and irreconcilable parts of my life that I had somehow to keep in balance, and that if it were not for me, they would never see each other. But time would prove me wrong. When they met on the battlefield in Libya, they became closer than I could ever be to either one of them.

77

THE YEARS PASSED AND each of us settled more deeply into his life. The image that often came to mind was of outdoor furniture sinking into the earth. It was clear by now that the Libyan regime had won. There was no serious opposition to speak of, and the dictatorship had never been more secure. It no longer needed to assassinate or abduct its critics because, from its point of view, such tactics had already served their purpose. Mustafa became manager of a local estate agency, and Hosam found employment as a literary reviewer for a London-based Arab newspaper—publishing under his real name. For the first time since working at the hotel in Paris he was getting an annual salary with paid holidays and a pension. The work was light and he could do it from home. Although he and Claire never did have children, their life together, at least judging by outward appearances, for he almost never now disclosed any private details, seemed good and loving. They often went to Devon, where they knew no one but liked to walk the hills and, even in the depths of winter, swim naked in the River Dart. We teased them about it, that Claire's north European temperament had won over his Mediterranean soul.

"I'd take the Mediterranean, thank you very much," Claire said. "It's your friend who always insists on those ice-cold plunges."

One Saturday, I invited them all for dinner. I wanted to finally introduce them to Hannah. I decided to make couscous and Hannah came early to help. The dish became horribly complicated and I made several mistakes. Seeing how flustered I was becoming, Hannah suggested we order Indian instead and said she knew just the place. We tidied up the kitchen and, when the food arrived, dished it out and placed it in the oven to keep warm. Only then did she become a little nervous. She sat down and looked at me. I poured us drinks and a few minutes later the doorbell rang: Mustafa, Hosam, and Claire, all arriving together. Mustafa had bought Hannah a gift. I was surprised by this; surprised too by the thoughtfulness of his choice. A book of essays by Robert Hass.

"I remember Khaled saying you like this writer," he said.

"That was years ago," I said.

He smiled at me with gentle eyes. "I remember," he said, and then to Hannah, "I hope you don't have it already."

Hannah was visibly touched. She leaned over and kissed him on both cheeks.

At one point in the evening, Mustafa and Hosam sat on either side of Hannah and began to quiz her:

"Tell us the truth about our friend?"

"Why has he kept you from us all this time?"

"If he gives you any trouble, come to us immediately."

Claire told her not to mind them, that each one of us three was equally crazy.

The food was so delicious and so spicy that we all could not stop eating and sweating. Afterward the conversation turned to literature and even Mustafa seemed to enjoy it. It was clear that Hannah had fun. After they left, she kept saying how nice they were. She was energized, did not wish to leave. Holding her in bed, I felt grateful for her and grateful for my friends.

78

HOSAM, MUSTAFA, AND I fell into the easy habit of meeting at Café Cyrano, the French bistro on Holland Park Avenue, on the first Friday evening of each month. On warm summer evenings we sat around one of the small tables on the pavement and tried to make ourselves heard above the rush-hour traffic. The rest of the year we would share one of the booths and spend an hour or two before Hosam would stand up and announce, always in English, "Must be off," the tone not permitting resistance. Sometimes Claire joined us, and occasionally Hannah too, but usually it was just the three of us, which allowed us to speak in Arabic. It was April 2010.

"This Sunday," Hosam said, "is the thirtieth anniversary of the assassination of Mohammed Mustafa Ramadan."

"Is it true that you were friends?" Mustafa asked.

"Thirty years already?" I said.

"The 11th of April," Hosam said, and looked at me as if I were forgetting or neglecting something.

"Is it true you knew each other?" Mustafa asked again.

The next time we met, in May, Hosam was animated.

"As you were not interested, I decided to mark it alone," he said, and when he could tell that we had no idea what he meant, he explained, with an enthusiasm that I found upsetting, that two days after we had met last, on the very day and around the same hour that Mohammed Mustafa Ramadan was shot, Hosam went to the Regent's Park Mosque and stood in the courtyard, at the scene of the crime.

"And what did you do?" Mustafa asked.

"Nothing," Hosam said. "I brought some press cuttings and determined the exact spot where he had fallen."

"Maybe you will write a book," Mustafa said.

Hosam did not reply, but he had none of the discomfort that usually came over him when the subject of his writing came up.

In the days that followed I tried several times to reach Hosam. When he eventually picked up, he sounded distracted, said he was tied up but looking forward to our next rendezvous. I waited for that first Friday of June. All the while a shadow of foreboding grew in my heart. I had somehow sensed that something was going on with him. When the day came, I arrived early at Café Cyrano. Mustafa turned up on time. But Hosam, always the punctual one, was nearly an hour late. I do not know what made me do it, but, while we waited, I found myself telling Mustafa something I had never disclosed to him before and that I had kept back out of fear that it might prejudice him against Hosam. I told him that Hosam too was there at the demonstration. How long had I known this, he asked?

"Since Paris," I said.

"This makes that interview with the BBC all the more lamentable," he said.

I agreed, even though I did not agree. I knew I was betraying Hosam and could not understand why.

When Hosam walked in, he was distracted, standing for a couple of seconds beside us to read a text on his phone. Only then did he look up and apologize for being late. He was again in that same excited state.

"I have so much to tell you," he said, waving to the waiter. "Got hold of the police report," he said, and, again seeing that we were at a loss as to what he was on about, he said, "Concerning the murder. Of Mohammed. It's amazing what you can find these days on the internet."

"You should write a book about it," Mustafa suggested again.

This hardly caused Hosam to pause. He pulled out a small notebook and, with that same enthusiasm I had seen in him before, he said, "The two men who shot Mohammed were Najib Jasmi, twenty-six, and Bin Hasan el Masri, twenty-eight. I imagine the older one led the planning. Not to raise suspicion, the two men arrived on separate flights from Tripoli. Najib Jasmi rented a flat in Princess Court in Queensway. I went there, looked up at the window."

"Why would you do that?" Mustafa asked with genuine bafflement.

"Why not?" Hosam said, and smiled tolerantly, like a connoisseur enduring the disinterest of a layman.

"I also found out," he continued, "the type of gun Najib Jasmi carried to the mosque. A .38 Charter Arms special revolver. The number refers to the size of the bullets: 38mm in length. The size of your thumb's first knuckle. An American gun, small enough to hide in a jeans pocket. I imagine Najib Jasmi that morning taking a handful of extra bullets and stuffing them in the other pocket, rattling there with coins from the day before."

The beers arrived, and he took two rapid sips. He had the legitimate excitement, I remember thinking, of one involved in a creative act, as though the picture he were drawing presented the possibility of exceeding reality itself.

"Bin Hasan el Masri," he went on, "the twenty-eight-year-old, lived in Cornwall Gardens in South Kensington. A beautiful square with a handsome green right in the middle."

"You should come work for us," Mustafa said.

This made me laugh, which in turn made Mustafa laugh even more.

"We could use a writer at the agency," he said.

Hosam looked a little surprised, which showed itself in a shade of embarrassment on his face. Don't wake him up, I remember thinking, let him keep on going.

"All the surrounding flats," he continued, "have a key to the green. Children play there in the afternoon."

"You don't mean you went there also," Mustafa said.

"I did," Hosam said, and looked at me with genuine innocence.

What I remember next was the silence that fell on us and stretched as Hosam consulted his notebook again. Even Mustafa looked a little concerned. Hosam had replaced visiting the homes of writers he admired with sites of political violence. It'll pass, I thought, and felt deeply nostalgic for those times, our rereading Conrad and Woolf and Eliot together, or in parallel, which is as close as two people could ever get. I regretted not paying attention when he first mentioned the Mohammed Mustafa Ramadan anniversary. I should have gone with him to the mosque. That, I sometimes still believe, might have changed the course of things.

"Bin Hasan el Masri had a different gun," he continued, consulting his notebook. "A German Reck pistol, which is also conveniently small in size. Its bullets are even shorter in length, 22mm, about the size of a Polo mint."

Mustafa placed his elbows on the table and leaned forward toward Hosam.

"There is no evidence," Hosam said, speaking more to Mustafa now, "that either Najib or Bin Hasan had ever done anything like this before."

He then looked at the time, made some excuse about why he had to dash off, placed some money on the table, and was gone. I remember what unsettled me most was not only hearing him refer to the two assassins by their first names, but also in a tone that made it sound as if they were friends of ours.

79

THE FOLLOWING MONTH, CLAIRE came to the restaurant with Hosam. The conversation flowed easily, even though Hosam hardly spoke.

Then, when a silence came, he said, "Do you guys know of a Libyan journalist named Mahmoud Abu Nafa?"

Neither of us did.

"He lived here," Hosam said. "He wrote anonymously under several fictitious names. Was a real job to locate his articles," he said, and turned to Claire, who smiled at him softly. "Exactly two weeks after Mohammed was murdered in the mosque," he told her, "Mahmoud Abu Nafa was gunned down too, in the doorway of his London office."

"Did you go there as well?" Mustafa said with a vague smirk.

Hosam, with Claire's eyes still on him, shook his head unconvincingly.

"What were the articles like?" I asked.

"Oh," he said, glad for the question, "terrible. You know, the usual stuff, calling for liberty, against Qaddafi, but very badly written."

"Well, that's okay, then," Mustafa said and laughed. He told Claire,

"I wouldn't be surprised if these two, with their lofty ideas of literary aesthetics, would think a man deserves to die for a bad sentence."

She pretended to share his humor, took hold of Hosam's hand, and said, with genuine joy in her eyes, "We're off to Devon next week."

"Are we?" Hosam asked.

"Yes," she told him, surprised that he had forgotten.

After we parted ways that evening, I sent Hosam a text asking if I could see him alone before they left town. He responded immediately, said he would like that, and we set a time for him to visit me one evening. I cooked dinner and, when he walked in, he said how much he missed Shepherd's Bush, that he felt terribly sentimental walking here from the station. I poured him a glass of wine and asked what he had been up to.

"Nothing," he said.

"Have you located any more murders?" I said, half expecting him to laugh, but instead he looked pleased to be invited to speak on the subject.

"Indeed, indeed," he said. "It's an endless quest and London is a bottomless well. A city of blood and fire."

I was right, thinking he trusted me; that in the absence of Mustafa's sarcasm, he could freely be himself.

"I must tell you," I said, with my heart in my mouth, "I told Mustafa that you were at the demonstration. I feel terrible about it."

"Don't be silly," he said. "Why not tell him? He's our friend."

I filled our glasses, sat opposite him, and asked him to tell me everything he had discovered.

"Well," he said, "in January 1980—"

"That's what?" I said interrupting. "Three months before Mohammed Mustafa Ramadan—"

"Exactly," he said.

"And two months," I went on, "before I heard him read your story on radio."

"Yes," he said. "In that month, a twenty-three-year-old Lebanese student named Hassan Elias Badir checked into the Mount Royal

Hotel on Marble Arch, and, while assembling a homemade bomb, blew himself up. No one knows why he checked into that hotel or who the bomb was intended for. But I found a photo. An uneasy and shy face with a little warmth in the eyes. I keep seeing him going down for a little walk, grabbing something to eat on the Edgware Road. I then see him sitting cross-legged on the freshly made hotel bed, with the pillows piled up behind him, working quietly. Sometimes I can even hear his thoughts. Then everything goes white."

He looked both moved and enthusiastic, how I imagine an artist might feel when his work is finished. I remembered then what Mustafa had said, that there is nothing more dangerous than a writer who does not write. He took out his notebook, I suspected as much to hide his face as to read out his findings.

"On the 28th of July 1978, a couple of years before Hassan Elias Badir killed himself, a bomb was placed under the Iraqi Ambassador's car in London. He wasn't in it, but the two other diplomats who were sustained serious injuries.

"In 1972, three young men entered the London home of General Abdul Razzak al Naif, an Iraqi former Prime Minister, spraying bullets as they moved from room to room. Amazingly, the General survived. Six years later, in July 1978, he was getting into a taxi in front of the Intercontinental Hotel by Hyde Park Corner when a man approached him from behind and fired several shots. The General was rushed to Westminster Hospital, the same place where you were taken, but died the next day."

He leafed through his notebook, which was covered in curling and continuous handwriting that went from edge to edge.

"Before that," he said, reading from his notes, "in January 1978, Said Hammami, the London representative of the Palestine Liberation Organization, was murdered in his Mayfair office. A few days before, on New Year's Eve, a car carrying two employees of the Syrian Embassy exploded in Mayfair."

He looked up and his faced was pleased.

"So you see what I mean about London? And it has been the case for a very long time. For example, on the 1st of July 1909, Madan Lal Dhingra, a young Indian student, the sixth of seven children of Dr. Sahib Ditta Mal Dhingra, a wealthy and pro-British Hindu civil surgeon, left his flat on Ledbury Road in Bayswater and went to a National Indian Association meeting at the Imperial Institute in South Kensington, where he managed to assassinate Lieutenant Colonel Sir Curzon Wyllie, an official of the British Indian government. Dhingra was hanged the following month. On sentence of death, he thanked the judge, saying: 'I am proud to have the honor of laying down my life for the cause of my motherland.' His last wish was for a bath and a shave. He was executed at Pentonville Prison on the 17th of August 1909. On the following day his statement was printed in the *Daily News*. In it Dhingra described himself as a patriot working to emancipate his motherland. He ended: 'The only lesson required in India today is to learn how to die and the only way to teach it is by dying ourselves, and so I die and glory in my Martyrdom. Bande Mataram,' which apparently means 'Hail the motherland.'"

He went on and relayed several such stories of political assassinations that had taken place here, and that involved individuals of all types. I felt my kitchen grow smaller. When he left, I washed the dishes and tried to convince myself that all this might lead to him writing again. I could not rid myself of the image of his filled notebook, with its manic and relentless activity, like a man scratching a wound. I went to bed that night with a deep sense of disquiet, convinced that I had overlooked an important detail.

80

THAT NIGHT I HAD a dream that I have not been able to forget. In it, the world, everything and everyone I knew, nature and my sentimental life—the entirety of my emotions and ideas and opinions and hopes and dreams and my grief—all of that which is in me and outside of me appeared as a single piece of fabric, large enough to cover a child's bed. The sheet was suspended in midair, worn thin and billowing weakly, its edges fraying.

The following month, Claire telephoned. She and Hosam had got back from Devon several weeks before.

"I need to speak to you," she said, and suggested we meet a couple of days later at the National Gallery.

I found her waiting on the steps. I remember thinking she looked shy, that waiting was an awkward activity for her. We wandered through the galleries. She seemed nervous, kept speaking about a picture she had been looking at and could not make head nor tail of.

"Would you like to see it?" she said, and stopped to ask a museum guard for directions to the "Hans Memling paintings." The man did not seem to understand. "Never mind," she told him and kept on walking. "Hans Memling," she said, "was born in the mid-1400s. He died in his late twenties. This particular picture was painted when he was in his midteens. A child, really," she said. "It depicts a young man lost in a daydream. Or so I thought before I read the title."

Suddenly we were right in front of it. It was called *A Young Man at Prayer*.

"I can't work it out," she said.

I looked at the deep green background, made lush and more verdant by the boy's pale face, his open and blatant expression, as if no one, truly no one, could see him. We took a bench in the middle of the room and looked at him from there. I thought of telling Claire about my dream. I wanted to share with her my bewilderment about why I no longer pray. I had stopped years ago and still did not know why. And, as I thought this, I saw the unattended room inside of me where prayer used to happen gathering dust. Did she pray?

"Just imagine," she then said, "regardless of how strong one's faith might be, that you would actually know what to ask for."

I wondered what happened in Devon?

"But isn't it wonderful?" she said. "The whole picture is so available that you're at a loss as to what to do with it. And isn't his face sweet?"

"A little confused," I said.

"Yes," she said, and smiled. "Not sure whether God exists but thought, what the hell, might as well, just in case."

I enjoyed the easy and warm sound of her laughter. How could anything be the matter, I thought?

I went to stand in front of the painting again. The boy's hair, eyebrows, and eyelashes were all made of delicate and determined lines cast this way and that, like wind-combed fields.

"I'll tell you how I see it," Claire then said softly. She was now standing right behind me. "It's a performance. Both the painting and what it depicts."

I nodded without understanding what she meant. I began to see something else in the picture. I felt certain, too certain to have to say it, that what the boy was involved in was a reckoning with the possibility of prayer, that at that moment he was not praying so much as coming to terms with how he might, and to what end, which surely must be a sort of prayer in itself.

Then, long after we moved on, and after standing in front of a handful of other paintings, I thought, no, that was not it either. The boy was not coming to terms with how to pray, but rather making space, and in so doing he had inadvertently arrived at the furthest reaches of himself. This would explain, I thought, why his face appears to be that of one standing on a summit, looking out on to a vast landscape, and, also, the opposite, that of one who has arrived at the limit of himself and, with cautious hope, decided to look inward.

We went to the café next door, in the basement of the National Portrait Gallery. We sat beside the curving wall, with people's feet walking above us on the glass ceiling. Here it comes, I thought, what she has come to tell me.

"How was Devon?" I said.

She looked at me wondering if I knew more than I was letting on.

"Well, that's it," she said. "I mean, we had a good time. Everything was as always. Hosam is a dear heart," she said, and her voice cracked. "Never complains. Have you noticed?"

"Yes," I said. "What happened?"

"He was fine. A little somber, but that happens sometimes," she said, nodding to herself. "We had a good day walking. He was quiet, hardly said a word, but that too happens. Except," she said, and stopped, looking at me with open, doubting eyes. "There are times, it has always been the case, when I sense an abyss opening within him. I don't know. I've always felt it and it frightens me. But this too passes. That day it remained, and at night, leaving the hotel for supper, he suddenly unhooked the fire extinguisher in the corridor and aimed it . . . well, at nothing, absolutely nothing, there was nothing there. He emptied the entire cylinder, yelling out something I couldn't understand, something in Arabic. Everything was covered in white powder. It went up his arms, and on our shoes and trousers. I laughed, or attempted to anyway, but he wasn't fooling around, he was dead serious, had a face, his face . . . I'd never seen it like that. As though something broke in him, and it broke my heart to see it."

"What do you mean 'something broke'?" I said.

"He said the same thing he had yelled but in a quiet voice, hardly audible. Repeating it over and over. I cried out for him to stop. The manager of the hotel came running through the doors."

"And what did Hosam do?"

"Nothing. He turned to the man and slowly told him, 'The fire, the fire.'"

The worst of it, the detail that accompanied me all the way home after Claire and I said goodbye, with me trying to comfort her with generic words about how everything will be fine, and so on, and her nodding into the distance, was what she said happened after Hosam spoke those words. She led him slowly back to their room. He sat on the edge of the bed, unable to speak or move or look into her eyes. She lifted his chin but his gaze remained downturned. There was only a moment when, whether meant to comfort or as a plea for help, he placed a hand on her thigh. Eventually, Claire told me, he managed to change out of his clothes and lay curled in bed all night with a face, as she described it, "stripped of all effort."

81

THE NEXT TIME WE met at Café Cyrano, Hosam was nearly his usual self. His eyes seemed a bit slow, so that when he held me in them time seemed to stop for a fraction of a second. He sat next to Mustafa, facing me. His shoulders were a little hunched. At one point, when he went to the toilet, I watched him, overwhelmed by the urge to embrace him. His face, which was expressionless, stirred with emotion when Claire walked into the café.

"I love how predictable you three are," she said.

She smiled knowingly at me as she took the seat beside me, facing Hosam. Hosam registered this. Perhaps he suspected that Claire had confided in me or perhaps he was suspecting something else altogether. I became nervous, told some humorous story concerning the school where I worked, and then, because outrage is a great camouflage, I hotly complained about budget cuts and expressed with passion my love and concern for my students. Mustafa said something about how bad David Cameron's government promised to be. We ordered drinks and, without waiting for a silence, Hosam interrupted to recount a dream he had had the night before. He looked at Claire when he spoke, and only when Mustafa or I said something did he turn to us, which gave the impression that we were eavesdropping on a private conversation between him and Claire, who listened attentively and with a hint of anguish, devoted but not unquestioning, an independent woman in love. All I cared about was that Hosam was telling us a story again, even if it was a dream.

"I was here, in this café," Hosam said. "But Cyrano had become a secondhand furniture shop. Mostly Chinese, some Arabic pieces, Islamic carvings. An old man sits outside by the entrance. I wander in and find the waiter, but he doesn't recognize me. In fact, everybody working here is suddenly Arab, definitely North African, perhaps even Libyan. They hardly notice me. They are busy discussing the arrangement of the furniture. I feel myself in the way. I leave, walk aimlessly around, and when I return, they have laid out the place but are still debating. I am looking for a coffee table for the house. The old man sitting outside on the pavement begins to sing softly to himself. I recognize the tune, but can't place it. Then I realize the old man is me, years from now, and, just as I do, I spot a desk. I think, finally, I found it. I search for the price tag, but there isn't one. The old man is now being teased by the others. 'What a voice, old man,' one says. But he, toward whom I dare not look, continues singing to himself. Now I know the tune. A lullaby my grandmother used to sing to me." Hosam hums it, and both Mustafa and I recognize it immediately. "He sings it with feeling," Hosam said, speaking more to us now, his fellow Libyans, who have had that same lullaby sung to them as young children. "But singing requires a dire effort from him. The young men notice this too and stop teasing him. They too seem moved. I continue to examine the writing table. I am no longer sure about it. It has a thick wooden frame. The top is padded in green velvet. I place a hand on a patch of the worn velvet. Too heavy to carry home, I decide."

"What happened next?" Mustafa asked.

"Nothing," Hosam said.

"What do you mean, nothing?"

"I woke up."

"Don't worry," Claire said, "episode two will follow."

This made Hosam laugh. But then he continued laughing more than seemed necessary, until his eyes teared up.

We then tried to interpret the dream. The familiar café that had become a furniture shop was an allusion to the fear of the world changing, Mustafa suggested. I proposed that the dream had to do with writing because of the desk. Mustafa insisted that the old man was an expression of Hosam's anxiety about growing old away from home. This, to my surprise, solicited a sympathetic response from Hosam.

"Perhaps," he said, "perhaps."

"After all," Mustafa went on, "you're this peculiar creature: an Arab writer living in England."

"Just as peculiar as an Irishwoman living in England," Claire said, and I was the only one who agreed with her.

Hosam looked at Mustafa not harshly but with a sort of reflective bleakness, like a still sea under an overcast sky. Mostly, however, Hosam and Claire listened to our interpretations with an expression that was at once amused and consolatory, as though they already knew the meaning of the dream but had decided, silently, in the way couples do, to keep it to themselves.

As the evening went on, color entered Hosam's face, and there were moments when he was almost his old self again. I could tell that Claire was delighted, with a quiet but profound sense of gratitude directed at Mustafa and me. When she laughed, the vein on the side of her neck bulged. The couple stayed beyond the usual time. Every extra minute felt like a conquest. When they stood up to leave, Mustafa insisted we all have another round of drinks. He went as far as swearing on the lives of his own parents. Hosam said nothing. He simply smiled and walked away; Claire was behind him, looking back at me in such a way that made me believe that for that instant I perceived her hopes and fears as she did mine.

82

MUSTAFA SAW ALL THIS differently. It always took him a few minutes to settle down once Hosam had left the café. He was always
ruffled by him, but much more so on that occasion.

"Well, this confirms it," he said. "He must've seen the video."

"What video?" I asked.

"First, did he tell you anything? He seemed strange, like a zombie.
Came to life only a little at the end. And she, obviously preoccupied.
Did they tell you anything?"

"What's the video?" I said.

He came and sat beside me. "Do you remember," he said, taking
out his phone, "the rumor we heard around the time of the shooting,
that Hosam's father, Sidi Rajab Zowa, went on television and praised
Qaddafi?"

"Yes, but there was never any proof of that."

"Now there is," he said. "And it's worse than anything we could
have imagined. Hold your horses." He was busy with his phone.
"Someone," he said and stopped. "Someone recently . . . posted it on
YouTube. In a matter of days . . . three exactly, it had over five thou-

sand views. Quicker than a pop single," he said, and laughed a horrible laugh. "Here it is."

I felt captured by his terrible certainty. He was busy digging in his pockets, bringing out the earphones, unknotting the cable.

"He had a nervous breakdown. In Devon. That's what it was," I heard myself say, and, to myself, I thought, if he had, I could too—we all could. "We must keep an eye on him."

"Here," Mustafa said, handing me one of the earphones.

How could he have not heard what I had just told him, I thought, and, at the same time, I was relieved he did not hear. There was hot enthusiasm in his progress. He took the earphone from my fingers and plugged it into my ear.

"Life is a traitor," he said, "always waiting to stab you in the back. Watch, watch." He pressed "play," then paused the video immediately. "Note the date," he said, pointing to the tiny print on the bottom of the screen.

"This broadcast," it read, "was originally aired live on the 24th of April 1984."

"Isn't that amazing?" Mustafa said, excitement and outrage having found a perfect union in his voice. "Seven days exactly after we were shot. Seven days. Isn't that amazing?" he asked again.

Whenever Mustafa spoke like this, a will inside me, wanting to resist, accused him of exaggeration. "Play it," I said, and we came closer together in the booth, instinctively pulling into the corner, so that no one could see what we were watching.

The setting was identical to those interrogations that I had secretly watched as a child on our television at home. The old 1980s film was grainy, and its mustard and pink and bluish-greens bloodshot and vivid, as if colored in by hand. It was obvious what he was going to say: denounce the old order to which he had once belonged and praise the young Colonel. But I was wrong. The statement Sidi Rajab Zowa read, unable to stop the sheet of paper from trembling in his hands, concerned neither the past nor the present, neither the deposed monarch nor Qaddafi, but the future, his heir, his luminous son, the writer Hosam Zowa, whom, at one point, looking up toward the camera, the old man called "a stray dog," that poisonous phrase the dictatorship enjoyed using to describe anyone who did not agree with it, anyone who had left the pack.

Although Mustafa had seen the clip several times already, he appeared riveted. We watched our friend's father, the elderly grandee, sitting in the corner of a windowless concrete room. At one point, he is interrupted by an impatient young voice from behind the camera.

"Old man."

Sidi Rajab Zowa looks up toward the camera.

"What kind of cap is that?"

"Excuse me, my son?" he asks, his eyes widening innocently.

"The cap. And I'm not your son."

The old man apologizes.

Another voice says, "The thing on your head?"

There is some laughter in the background.

"Oh," he says, and, as though the wind has just picked up, places his hand on top of his head.

"We know exactly what it is," the first voice says, who sounds much closer to the camera and therefore could not be more intimate to us.

"He thinks we are stupid," the other one tells him.

"Oh, but absolutely not," Hosam's father says, his eyes widening again.

"Old style," another voice says. "With a tassel, a dog's tail. Isn't that the old al Senussi cap?"

"This?" Sidi Rajab Zowa asks and slowly pulls off the hat. He folds it tightly into his right hand and says, "No, this has nothing to do with all of that."

"Haven't you heard?" the first voice says, but now in a pragmatic, almost kindly instructive tone. "There has been a revolution, old man."

Hosam's father says nothing.

"Continue," the voice instructs. "And hurry up. We don't have all day."

Now the strangest thing happens. Sidi Rajab Zowa's manner is completely altered, and it suddenly becomes clear that all his quiet staring was evidence of a furious labor aimed at quickly discerning how he might escape. He goes from a softly spoken and dignified intonation to loud and thunderous assertions that in places thin his voice, making a screeching wire of it.

"My son is a traitor. I forbid him," he says and pauses. "I forbid. I forbid him. I forbid Hosam. Hosam Rajab Zowa. My own son," he shouts and his voice breaks. "From ever." He stops again, and then in a strong and capable voice, free of hesitation, he says, "From ever entering my house, or carrying my name, to the end of time."

He then folds forward and shakes from weeping. The camera zooms in. A voice behind it whispers, "Keep it there."

83

IN THE DAYS AND nights that followed, I watched the video several times, all the while trying to imagine Hosam seeing it. I wished he would say something about it. But, in the few calls we had, he sounded distant and weak. The day before we were next to meet at Café Cyrano, he texted to say he would not be able to make it. Nothing more. No explanation was offered. I wrote back saying, "If you change your mind we'll be there." He did not change his mind, and Mustafa and I spent the evening alone.

"Did you know that Edward Said was married before?" Mustafa said, sitting down, waving to get the waiter's attention. "Years before he married Mariam Said. Did you know this? To an Estonian-German university professor." He took out a piece of paper. "Listen to this," he said, and began to read words attributed to the Palestinian author, stopping dramatically at every full stop and comma: "'There's a symbolic dimension to it. I married a European. We had nothing in common. She was very beautiful and incredibly brilliant, studied at Vassar, Harvard, Cambridge. It was a great ordeal.'" Mustafa repeated the last sentence.

"It's not fucking poetry," I told him.

"What's ruffled your feathers?" he said. "Might not be poetry, but it's the truth. Mariam, I tell you it was Mariam—you have to acknowledge this—who took Edward Said to the next level, made of him the man he was to become."

I said a run of things that, if I am to be honest, were motivated less by the intention of persuading my friend than distracting him. I told him that Edward Said was a cultural critic, a polymath, whereas Hosam was an artist. "That's a very different thing. I don't think it matters who he loves."

"Listen, if a writer is to achieve his full potential, he needs to be connected to the source. 'From the root the sap flows to the artist,' as Paul Klee put it."

"Fuck Paul Klee," I said.

"What's the matter with you? You're sounding more like me. And it was you who introduced me to that line in the first place."

"What about *The Given and the Taken*?" I said with anger folding my voice, making it smaller and quieter, as though I were hearing myself from a distance. "Or have you forgotten how it spoke to us, to everything that we were, all that we had lost, and everything we felt we were becoming, lying there in that miserable hospital?"

"Yes, yes," he said gently. And then, after a perfect silence, he added, somewhat rhetorically, "But there is one piece of evidence that no one can refute: Hosam Zowa has not written a word since."

"That has nothing to do with it."

"You cannot remain connected to the motherland if you share your bed with a foreigner," Mustafa said, slowly and calmly.

84

ON THE 24TH OF November that year—I know the date because I still have the tickets—three months before the February 2011 revolution, when none of us could have predicted what was about to happen, I got three cheap seats in the rear rows to a concert at the Royal Festival Hall. It was a Russian program: Stravinsky's *Scherzo fantastique,* Prokofiev's Piano Concerto No. 3 in C, and Shostakovich's Symphony No. 11 in G minor. I knew that Hosam admired Prokofiev's music. And I remembered Claire speaking about Shostakovich. I waited for them at the bar. I saw them before they saw me. They were laughing as they entered. I was overcome with joy to see them and to see Hosam looking so well. When we took our seats, I apologized for how far back we were. We could hardly make out the stage.

"Music is to be heard, not seen," Hosam said.

"Besides," Claire said, "everything sounds better from back here."

The music was wonderful, and, when we emerged in the interval, we were all excited. The second half was even more thrilling. We decided that we could not part ways just then, that we needed to sit and talk about what we heard. I asked if they had had supper and they said no and that they were famished. We went to a nearby pizzeria and were seated at a round table. Our excitement about the concert pro-pelled us forward until the food came and then the mood shifted.

"I have felt for a long time that something terrible is going to hap-pen," Hosam said, and fell silent.

Claire took hold of his hand. I waited and, for reasons I cannot fathom, was as certain then as I have ever been about anything that those words he spoke in Devon, "The fire, the fire," were somehow connected to this premonition.

"I do still," he continued, saying this more to Claire.

She nodded consolingly.

"But," he said, letting go of her hand and facing me, "life, detect-able in the common structure of days, one rolling after the next, must go on. And, once all is said and done, things, most of our affairs, work out in the end, don't they?"

Claire and I quickly agreed.

"It is perceptible, isn't it," he went on, "for example, in the confi-dence of doctors, in the will of trees, in the sunlight, in the river? To live a life is not, as I have sometimes thought, to be condemned to witness the slow death of things. Or it's not that alone, but, chiefly and above all else, certainly above country and religion and our various affiliations, life is for the living."

I cannot say I was convinced. Life is for the living was hardly a philosophy one could rely on. Nonetheless, I was so moved I had to hold back tears. Claire's fell and she laughed. I laughed too.

"The Irish cry at everything," Hosam said.

She threw her napkin at him.

"They cry and throw things."

Walking across Hungerford Bridge, the cold November air was crisp and quick, and the night lights carried on shattering into a thou-sand pieces against the uneven Thames. Hosam, walking in the mid-dle, threaded one arm through Claire's and the other through mine.

"My dad isn't well," he said, and told me, in Arabic, that his old man had had a stroke, had come out of it diminished, unable to walk, spoke with a slow tongue.

"I'm so sorry," I said. "If he needs anything I can get my father to visit."

"I must go myself or else I might never see him again," he said, speaking in English now.

Claire kept quiet.

"Not sure," I said.

"It is so obviously a bad idea," she said.

85

APART FROM OUR MONTHLY meetings, which continued without Hosam, who always had an excuse, Mustafa and I led independent lives. We were connected by the fondness we had for each other and the complicated intimacy of two who had shared and survived a terrible fate. We never spoke of it, and had not done so for years. As our ways diverged and distances grew between us, and regardless of how undesired or natural those gaps were, we each secretly accused the other. One of us was always to blame. What I did not realize was that all the while the silences were doing their work on us, gradually driving us apart, until the places where we connected became few and slender. If friendship is, as it often seems, a space to inhabit, ours became small and not terribly hospitable. This was wordlessly acknowledged and lamented by both of us.

That was the equilibrium we shared. But by January of 2011, my old friend began to undergo a transformation, one as radical as it was imperceptible. When we were together, I would sense his disquiet. I felt partly to blame, because, whenever Mustafa was agitated or unhappy, I could not help but feel responsible. It was the same for him. Perhaps it was an echo of the guilt we both felt toward one another for what happened in St. James's Square, as though from that day on we had become the fathers of one another's fate. Or maybe it was not that at all, but that we each resembled a reflection of the other and therefore any dark mood was instantly mirrored and doubled. On the day we were due to meet next at Café Cyrano, I texted to say I was under the weather, and then, overcome with regret, spent the rest of the afternoon thinking of a way back.

Everyone was focused on reports coming from North Africa. The region was stirring with hope for change. Pro-democracy advocates spoke on radio and television with unprecedented confidence. And then news began to emerge of large-scale street demonstrations in Tunisia. They looked irreversible. More than one news reporter used the expression "The genie is out of the bottle."

On the 14th of January, Zine el Abidine Ben Ali, who had ruled the country for twenty-four years, fled abroad. I stayed up all night, looking at clips on my phone in bed. One in particular, I watched several times. It showed a middle-aged man alone on a main avenue in the capital, Tunis, in the dead of night. He wore glasses, paced back and forth with a determined rhythm, like one trying to remember something. No one else was around except the man or woman behind the camera filming, following the lonesome pedestrian with, it seemed, a deep feeling. The man screamed with a desperate but controlled fervor, repeating "Ben Ali h'rub," Ben Ali has fled, over and over, his voice hoarse and strong and empty, seemingly not only echoing against the silent buildings under the streetlamps, with their electric-blue light, but also emanating from within a private desolation. It moved me to tears, as it sounded like hope, that if hope itself had a voice it would sound like this. I wondered what Mustafa and Hosam made of it. I was sure they were up too.

The following morning, I went to work feeling exhausted. My classes were more demanding than usual, and that whole morning perennial questions, which I thought I had survived or discarded long ago, returned with a vengeance. My students are not interested in literature; they are not convinced by it. They are perpetually at risk of falling off the edge, and therefore one's task is less to teach them and more to serve as a barrier, in the hope that one day, by sheer will of practice, they will no longer require us. My colleagues felt this too. We were all so overstretched that, paradoxically, we often felt superfluous. This was accentuated in my case by the fact that I had no bond with the kids; or the sort of bond I imagined I would have if they were Libyan or if I were English. Instead, I felt I could be easily replaced, and that where I was truly needed was elsewhere.

At lunch break, a couple of my colleagues asked me about events in North Africa. I said I had only read the headlines. My phone buzzed in my pocket, and I saw that there were three missed calls from Mustafa. He had not left a message. I rang him back and he answered immediately.

"Where the fuck are you?" he said.

"At work. Why?"

"Have you not heard the news?"

"What news?"

"About Tunisia."

"Oh, that, yes."

"Fine," he said, evidently disappointed. After a pause, he added with intolerant certainty, "Cairo will follow. And then the country."

The country always meant Libya.

"Maybe," I said.

"Hundred percent," he said. "They are even speaking of a date: the 17th of February."

I did not ask who "they" were, partly because it was pointless—as I would have got a vague answer—and partly out of the weariness I felt, which lack of sleep alone could not have explained.

Hosam, on the other hand, was peculiarly unconcerned, focused much more on his father's health. That was the chief topic when we spoke. When I would bring up events in Tunisia and Egypt, the possibility of their spreading to Libya, he looked sad and weary.

"Let's see what will come of it," he said.

"I mean, think about it," I told him. "Tunisia, our neighbor to the west, and now Egypt, our neighbor to the east, have both risen. It surely must be only a matter of time."

He went quiet, then said, "Let's see."

Each of my two closest and only Libyan friends stood at one extremity of my will. I could not help being Mustafa with Hosam and Hosam with Mustafa, as though condemned to maintain their voices in some kind of balance.

Over the next few days, I held on silently to my hopes, observing every turn in events. Cairo's Tahrir Square was packed with protesters, and it looked like there was no way now that the tide could be turned. Once, in between classes, I locked myself in one of the school toilet cubicles and cried into my hands, praying no one could hear, praying, suddenly I was now praying, for the end of tyranny, a word that was no longer abstract, no longer for slogans alone, but an intimate offense. I burned with hope; hope and fear and a violent impatience. I tried to keep it all at bay during the day but gave in to it entirely at night. And it had a name, the Arab Spring, a temporary state but one that knew no bounds or borders, a condition as much for the heart as it was for parliament, and one belonging to nature, to the eternal cycle of the seasons, confirming what I have always secretly believed: that as sure as blossom, freedom would come, and, even though winter is just as certain, it can never last.

I continued to sleep little, staring at my phone in the dark. Everyone was active: my sister and mother, friends and cousins. I bounced between the various social media apps for hours. My longing now for my sister and parents, for our house and my childhood sea, a longing long managed and kept in place, rose up wild and unhindered, its ardor causing me at times to tremble.

Souad was now relentless, sending me messages, snippets of news from Cairo and Tunis, personal testimonies of men and women running against their frightened hearts. I did not know how to respond. There I was, in my forty-fifth year, held in place, in my bed, in my room, in my small rented flat in Shepherd's Bush where I could be evicted with a month's notice, inside the fragile life I had made for myself these past twenty-seven years, ever since I was eighteen. I knew that, given the indiscretion of these apps, my sister could see that I received and read her messages.

My colleagues at work wanted to know what I thought of the Arab Spring, if my family back home were safe. The head teacher called me in to kindly inquire if I were all right.

"I have just noticed," she said, "that you have been looking tired." When I did not say anything, she said, "I appreciate you must be pre-occupied, what with the news."

"I'm fine, really," I said.

86

I BEGAN TAKING SLEEPING pills and tried to limit how much news I was consuming. I did not return Mustafa's or Souad's messages. Then, in early February, I called Mustafa and we met under Hammersmith Bridge. We walked beside the river. He looked restless.

"I'm worried about Ali," he said, and then started talking about something else, his flat and how he was thinking of moving.

Ali was Mustafa's younger brother. He had had to grow up fast and assume more responsibilities when Mustafa could no longer return home, responsibilities that had only been increasing over these past twenty-seven years.

"Why are you worried?" I asked.

"I don't know. Been hearing rumors," he said. "About a genuine movement, an uprising. They say the 17th is the date. A parallel demonstration is planned in front of the embassy," he said, and stopped, looking back at the high bending river. The surface of the water was calm but moved at a quick pace. It was while facing in that direction that he then said, "I'm going to go."

"Twenty-seven years later," I said.

He looked trapped, in a corner. "Totally different," he said. "We have a real chance now."

Love for my friend, opening now like a hunger in the chest. I was cleaving inside. With worry in the blood, I thought of how to restrain him, interrupt his momentum, give him a chance to reconsider. But reconsider what? All things, most of our affairs, as Hosam had put it not long ago, work out in the end. Besides, you are probably worried less about him and more about yourself, about what will become of you. I put my arm around his shoulders. He did not yield, but I was sure that he knew what I was thinking.

What I did not know was that he had already spoken to his employer about an unpaid leave, accepted without hesitation the consequences of being demoted from branch manager. He was, in effect, footloose. The following day, he called me during my lunch hour, voices around him, the sound of traffic. After the shooting and the siege, the Libyan Embassy, when it eventually reopened, took on new premises in Knightsbridge, facing Hyde Park. The location was chosen because, like the Iranian Embassy further down the street, the pavement there is too narrow to host a demonstration. Anyone wishing to voice an objection would have to stand on the opposite side of the street and scream their displeasure from there.

It was not the 17th of February yet, but a small cluster of Libyans was gathered there, Mustafa among them. I could hear chants: "Down with the Dictator," "Free Libya," and so on. He enjoyed my perplexed questions, and it was then, at that moment, that the new tone emerged in his voice: a little formal, pronouncing my name, which he knew so well, as though it were an object outside him, one to navigate around. His wish that I be beside him made him behave as though we were strangers.

He was there every day for the three or four weeks that followed, standing in the cold, becoming more connected to the Libyan community, the very people we tried to avoid. In the evenings they dined together at one of their houses. His speech pattern began to change, becoming more colloquially Libyan. He almost never now spoke to me in English.

87

I STOPPED TAKING SLEEPING pills and was soon back to staying up most of the night. I looked for tickets to Benghazi. On more than one occasion, I felt tears rolling down my cheeks in the dark and heard them tap on my pillow.

On the 17th of February, after a few days' silence, Souad sent several texts, one after another, at around 2 A.M. her time, 1 A.M. mine.

> We are on the steps of the courthouse.
> Hundreds, maybe even thousands.
> Many women.
> Mama and Baba are here too.
> Baba says to tell you that the time you have been waiting for has come.
> We've been here since midnight.
> The sea behind us.
> Black because it's night.
> But you can hear it.

I wish you were here, I wish you were here, and I wish you were here.

The whole country is holding hands, stepping over an invisible line
together.

Mama says it's now or never.

Pray for us.

88

MEMBERS OF THE LIBYAN Army stationed in Benghazi joined the revolution, and soon the city was liberated. There were celebrations on the streets. The courthouse became the center of the festivities. People singing and dancing, locked in a mass embrace that curled and straightened their lines very much like the waves of the witnessing sea behind them. Young faces unable to keep from smiling, all quickly united by the song that became the rallying cry of the 17 February Revolution:

We will live here
Till the pain is gone
We will thrive here
Till the melody turns a sweeter tune

All restrictions on internet calls were now lifted. My family and I spoke or messaged one another every day. There was no fear in our voices any longer.

"Soon you will be home," Mother would say. She said it nearly every time we spoke, and each time I said yes I believed I meant it—

and not just because I did not know how else to answer or how to account for the fact that, though Benghazi was the one place I longed for the most, it was also the place I most feared to return to. The life I have made for myself here is held together by a delicate balance. I must hold on to it with both hands. It is the only life I have now. I would have to abandon it to go back, and, although I wish to abandon it, I fear I might not be able to reconstitute a new life, even if that would be in the folds of the old one. It is a myth that you can return, and a myth also that being uprooted once makes you better at doing it again.

"Soon you will be home."

And then my father rang one Sunday morning, pretending to ask how my week went. I complained about the long hours, exaggerated the hardship, stressing how understaffed we were. But he knew what I was really saying and decided to tell me about the old fig tree in the courtyard instead, the one that had been skirting death for years now.

"It's suddenly blooming. Leaves as wide as dinner plates. Packed with fruit. I'm going to have to make jam."

When I did not say anything, he spoke again.

"You grow and live and you come to know how things are likely to be. A certain feature, the way someone holds their head. And you, my dearest child, have always been a careful angel, even as a baby, born with your own basket of worries."

"I'm hopeful, Father," I said, because I did not know what else to say. I was sure he had not told my mother of the shooting, but nonetheless I said, "No matter what comes out of these events, please don't mention what happened to me. Not to anyone, particularly not to Mother or Souad."

"I won't," he said.

"I don't think I could bear it," I said, and wondered if he thought I was chiding him for his reaction when he saw my scar.

"I promise," he said. "As long as you promise me that you wear it like a badge of honor. Events today are vindicating you."

They were talking about me, my parents, and at night in bed I imagined their words about the son who could not come home and now would not come home and who, at forty-five, remained unmarried and childless. His life had come to a standstill. I felt ashamed and yet there were moments during those early days after the fall of the regime when I had never felt more settled. I would stand at the corner of my street outside the local pizzeria, waiting for the takeaway I ordered, and catch myself delighted by the familiar light, sensing the thread of a routine—I could anticipate the rest of the day, the way the light would change and the hours after.

Then my mother called and this time asked the question directly. "Why have you not come home? I understood before. Your father told me." My heart sank, but then she said, "You wrote an article in a university paper and it got you in trouble. So what? That's long ago now. What's keeping you?"

My mouth was full and empty all at once. Empty because everything in it had no shape or sound or form. And full of everything that I felt then and feel now. That what I want to return to I cannot return to because the place and I have changed and what I have built here might be feeble and meek, but it took everything I had and I fear if I leave I will not have the will to return and then I will be lost again and I have been lost before and will do everything not to be that again and that I do not know if it is cowardly or courageous and I do not care and I have decided without deciding, because it is my only option, to keep to the days, to sleep when it is good for me to sleep and wake in good time to attend to my work and the people who depend on me. I wanted to tell her that I like being dependable. I like the fact that my colleagues rely on me and my students and their parents and my landlord. That I wish to be better to Hannah, that out of everyone I know here there is no one else that I would rather depend on or have depend on me and that I hope one day she will meet her and know what I mean. That, although all these people would be fine without me, I am held together by their demands and that I am very sorry not to be beside her, to be the son I had always imagined I would be and desired to be. And that my train can only continue or else I fear I will fall off a cliff. And I wanted to tell her that flying, being divorced from the earth, was like being separated from her and, now that I am on land, I never ever want to be unearthed again and that I am ashamed of it and was ashamed of it for a long time but I am no longer. And that I know Father is growing old and needs me and Souad now has three children for whom I have been an absent uncle and I have not given my father an heir and I know how important that is to him and that it all left me with the conviction that no one should ever leave their home. That no matter what happens to you when you are at home happens to you at home. My friends never stopped wanting a different life, I wanted to tell her. But I have managed, Mother, not to want a different life most of the time and that is some achievement.

89

I FOLLOWED THE NEWS obsessively. The revolution was now edging westward toward the capital, Tripoli. But victory was far from certain.

I came out of class one afternoon and found three missed calls from Hosam. I tried calling him back, but the line went straight to voicemail. I listened to the message he left.

"Khaled, my dear," he said, with genuine warmth and not a hint of hesitation in his voice. "I'm at the airport, going to see my father. I know things are unstable, but late last night I decided. It might be my last chance to see him. And now that I'm going, my longing for them all is endless. I'm sorry it wasn't possible to see you before. But, who knows, maybe we'll meet up there. Goodbye, my friend."

I tried him again and then called Claire. When she did not answer, I rang Mustafa.

"Well done to him," he said. "We should follow."

In the evening, Claire returned my call. She began to relay to me— in the way people do when recounting a series of events that had led from the calm predictability of life to a calamity, attempting to locate the sudden turn from which nothing was ever the same again—how terribly indecisive Hosam had become in the days leading up to his departure, unable to sleep, constantly on the phone with his family, or else quiet and distracted. Then into the brief silence that followed she said, "Maybe it's for the best."

"You speak as though he's never coming back," I said.

"He took his books with him," she said.

"But he always takes his books wherever he goes."

"Precisely," she said, and then I heard her say, "Sorry," through tears before hanging up.

90

EARLY THAT SUNDAY MORNING the doorbell rang. It was Mustafa.

"Still in bed?" he said.

I buzzed him in and went into the bathroom. I came out and found him smoking in the kitchen. I made coffee, toasted some bread and buttered it. I sat opposite him beside the drafty window, looking out at the empty and unloved back gardens of the neighboring houses, lined up like a row of nervous and unkempt children. The sky, sealed behind folded clouds, filled the upper half. I should move to a better neighborhood, I thought. Live among the well-to-do, people with well-kept gardens.

"It's fucking cold in here," he said.

"The boiler packed up," I said. "Landlord promised to fix it."

He wrapped his hands around the coffee cup, feathery steam rising and vanishing before his face.

"Ali joined the front," he said. "They're already at Ras Lanuf. I'm leaving the day after tomorrow." Then, before a silence could stretch, he said, "I don't understand you. You just carry on as though nothing has happened."

I waited for the panic to subside.

"Your country needs you," he then said and said it sympathetically, with neither doubt nor irony.

"What will happen will happen, with me or without me."

"It's narcissism," he said, his tone hardening, "to hide one's intentions behind theories of the inevitable."

The silence that followed was as veiled and vast as the cloudy sky above.

"I'll drive you to the airport," I said, and he did not disagree.

I called in sick and rented a car. He hardly said a word the whole way to Heathrow. But then, when we entered a tunnel approaching the terminal, he began talking.

"Scientists have gathered some of the most compelling evidence yet of the existence of water on the moon. It had been assumed that the moon's surface was dry, but in the 1990s some indications of ice were found. Now NASA scientists have detected water and that in turn has implications for lunar missions, because apparently it could be treated and used for drinking. However, that would mean harvesting it from dark, steep-walled craters where the temperature apparently barely gets above −230 degrees Celsius." A little while later, as we were turning up the looping ramp of the car park, the tires screaming quietly, he said, "Doesn't it make you shudder to think that the heart of the universe is so cold? It's only because of the accident of the sun that all this . . ." he said, gesturing with his hand.

I remained with him till he checked in. He was flying to Alexandria and from there would take a car to the border. I was surprised by the strength of his embrace. He held on to me for longer than I expected and I believed I could sense his fear. I thought, all that business of wanting me to come with him had nothing to do with politics. When we pulled apart, his eyes were red and his hands remained on my shoulders.

"You lucky bastard," I told him, and tried to laugh.

He gave a weak and complicated smile, one intended more for himself than for me.

91

WITH MY TWO COMPANIONS gone, I was now standing at the edge
of a precipice. That night, after I made supper and ate it in the same
place in the kitchen, with Mustafa's half-drunk cup of coffee still on
the table and my neighbors, if they cared to, able to see me eating on
my own, my phone began flashing, showing a Libyan number. It was
Mustafa. A whole fleet of first and second cousins had gone to collect
him at the Egyptian border. He sounded jubilant, as though he had
finally arrived at the center of things, where there was no fear of interruption and he could simply rely on the attention of others.

"Ali," he called out, "where's the car, man?"

"Is that your brother?" I asked.

But Ali was telling him something.

"Fine," Mustafa replied at the same high volume, "but then go
fetch it, man."

Ali says something else.

"Okay," Mustafa tells him, "I'll wait here, then. God be with you."

He returned to me, his voice changing a little, asking that superfluous question, "How are you?"

"Is that your brother?" I asked again.

"Yes," he said. "He returned from the front when he heard I was coming."

"Please say hello."

"The boy has put on muscle," he said. "Will do."

"What is it like being back?" I asked.

"What is it like? It's beautiful. Fucking beautiful. Like being brought back from the dead. Air filling your lungs."

And there it was again, the other new quality in his voice, the tone beside the admonishing one, that I could not immediately discern. He sounded strong, accompanied; that was the word: accompanied.

92

SHORTLY AFTER HOSAM ARRIVED in Benghazi, he began sending me emails. They had a nocturnal quality, as though written deep into the night, after everyone had fallen asleep and the day's events were subsiding. His father was home but lay in a hospital bed in the middle of what used to be the dining room on the ground floor of the family house. This was the same house I once stood outside of, a short walk from ours, in the old downtown, the Benghazi district where, three years later, and a good while after the fall of the regime, warring factions would force residents to evacuate, obliging my parents to move into rented accommodation. But well before this, when our house and Hosam's stood undamaged by bombs and bullets, Hosam's father, his mind diminished, lay mostly alone, convalescing. The main activity of the house was in the less formal rooms on the upper floor. Sidi Rajab Zowa—who, as my father pointed out, used to be known by the nickname "The Radar" because of his intuitive ability to guess King Idris's secret inclinations, so perfectly attuned was he to what my father described as the monarch's "political reluctance and self-effacing manner, his preference for quiet resolutions"—now could hardly detect the identity of those around him, members of his own family.

"Every evening," Hosam wrote in one of his early emails,

my father forgets who I am and we have to meet for the first time all over again. He prefers to speak in English. Doctor says this is normal, to be expected. It is impossible then not to forgive him. I sit beside him and we talk like fellow passengers on a train while the room darkens around us. I have learned a great many things about my father and his younger days. We have, with no redress or explanation required, forgiven one another. At one point, he offered me a job. "I'll put in a good word for you at the ministry," he said, his eyes eagerly widening. Mostly, I remain beside him till midnight. Some mornings he recognizes me and it's like the sun shining. I check my posture, rise up, kiss him on both cheeks. The first time this happened, something about his face—its gentle confidence and bewilderment—set me off. He patted my head and said, "You've always been like this." And no sooner did he say this than he disappeared into the mist again, his eyes changing and my heart too, taking me further back, to half-forgotten recollections.

For some reason, he always refused to teach me how to swim. Whenever my mother asked him, he simply didn't respond. Not a word. And if I were there, he'd turn to me and sustain that infinite expression of his: solemn, blank, vacuous. A bit like now. But she had a way with him, my mother, and she knew that this, like other questions, is what drops of water are to earth. Repeated enough times, a path eventually opens. When I was seven or eight, she brought me along to the boat my family kept in a small forested cove near our farm in the Green Mountain. My parents used it to sneak around the bay, searching for well-sheltered places that could not be accessed by road. This way my mother and three sisters, Hania, Siham, and Najma, could take off their dull dresses and be in the bright bathing suits they got on trips to London, Paris, or Milan. They dived into the water, unashamed, screaming and laughing, and with each dive the small boat rocked from side to side. Father, smiling through it all, put his arm on my shoulders and we watched my mother and her daughters swim in the deep blue water, the sunlight bouncing off the pale sand beneath and dancing up around them. They climbed back into the boat and my sisters sat nestled in their towels, their hair dripping. Father asked a couple of times if anyone had seen the knife and then began tearing the bread with his hands, prying it open with his fingers. He spooned in the tuna and harissa and then, using his thumb, pressed in the black and green olives. We ate with great relish. My mother or father, I do not remember who, said again what I had heard them say many times before, about how the sea makes the simplest food taste delicious. My mouth burned but I could not stop eating. Then we lay beside one another and breathed easily as the boat rocked. On such outings, my parents never took servants or friends. This was their secret. There was a silent recognition of this, which excited my sisters, but also made it impossible for them to be entirely at ease. They sunbathed and pretended to be relaxed, but the slightest sound or movement on land—a wandering goat clambering up the cliff or a bill-clattering stork or some other large bird alighting on a rock—would startle them, make their hands reach for the towel, bring panic into their faces.

My mother sat with her feet dangling in the water, facing the land. She saw me watching her. "Come sit beside me," she said, then walked over to me, causing the boat to totter. She picked me up, her fingers strong around my rib cage, and deposited me on the edge of the boat beside her. "It is hard to sink," she said, her toes dabbling the water. "The sea pushes you up. Don't be frightened."

I looked back and saw my father watching me. He looked a little sleepy.

"But people drown all the time," I told her. "Entire ships."

"The sea is your friend," my father declared.

I was trapped. There was nowhere to run. I looked at my sisters and they had their eyes closed at the sun. If my brother Waleed had been here, I thought, he would have taken the attention off me. Now my parents' silence was expectant, interrupted only by the soft lapping water against the boat. In those seconds my fear turned into defiance. I could see no reason why I was being subjected to such a demand. I pressed my palms down and tossed myself overboard. The water slapped my chest and the side of my neck, salt burned up my nostrils. I beat the calm water white. I could hear shouting and my mother saying, "Not like this." The water was much harder and heavier than I had imagined. My father was suddenly beside me, the white fabric of his shirt ballooning all around him. I remember his firm and gentle arms propping me up from behind. His love and fear. My sisters were already laughing. Even after I climbed aboard, dried off, and all that was to be said on the matter had been said, Mother continued, less frequently now, to report to my father, who was driving the boat back, and sometimes so softly and abstractly that it seemed as if her words were intended for no one else except herself: "I didn't think he would actually do it." I faced in the opposite direction, looking backward at the snaking wake, the wind pushing my hair forward, and wondered if perhaps her intention was not for me to act but rather to remind my father to teach me how to swim, and therefore her words, what she was telling me about the sea as I sat beside her on the edge of the boat, was intended as much for him, and that when he said, "The sea is your friend," he was edging closer to accepting his duty, and perhaps I somehow knew that and jumped to refuse it.

93

AFTER FALLING SILENT FOR a couple of weeks, Mustafa sent me several texts, one after the other, in quick succession:

It's impossible to bridge the gap.
Our country is too distant in the past for our British experience to be of any use here.
We are shadows.
Here and there.
Shadows.
Unless we go back.
I mean really go back.

"And what of progress?" I wrote. I had meant the question ironically.

"Sometimes to move forward you have to move back," he replied.

I received several more such cryptic texts from him, and, whenever I tried to find out more about his meaning, he would change the subject, or say, "You have to be here to understand." And so his communications came to resemble proclamations, as though I were the announcement board upon which he was projecting his insights. I stopped replying immediately, and sometimes not at all.

After another few weeks' silence, I got these messages:

I don't have long to tell you this.

I've joined the fighting.

Too much at stake.

I'm leaving everything behind.

Facing forward. I will only tell you this once.

Join us.

My family will know where I am.

Wish your old friend luck. Forgive his mistakes.

I tried to call, but he did not answer. I did not try again. What was the point? What could I have said? I did not have enough conviction to convince him not to fight. And I vowed long ago never to try to convince anyone of anything I was uncertain of. Perhaps fighting is the right thing to do.

I spent that whole day on fire. Several times I checked for trains and ferries. I even asked the head teacher, making sure I assumed a hypothetical tone, about the possibility of taking unpaid leave. When she did not seem to understand the question, I said, "I mean, has anyone ever done this? I suppose what I'm asking is: what is the school's policy with regard to unpaid leave?"

"Our policy?" she asked with a chuckle. "Our policy is teacher takes unpaid leave and ship sinks."

At the end of the day, I went home and looked for trains and ferries again. I called Hosam for guidance. He said I was mad to consider it, that I was already too old and that anyway my wounds had been far more serious than Mustafa's and had, in his opinion, rendered me unfit for the demands of war.

"How reckless of Mustafa even to suggest it," he said.

"He didn't," I said, lying. "I mean, not really."

"If you want to come," Hosam said, "come to see your parents and your beautiful country. Come to see me. You would make us all so very happy."

I did not hear from Mustafa for another month. I called his family. His mother told me he was well.

"Comes home every couple of weeks for a change of clothes, proper food, and a couple of days' rest. His spirit is high," she said. "His faith in God is strong. We will be victorious."

I was certain that the bit about his faith in God was wishful thinking on her part. I had never known Mustafa to pray. We fasted Ramadan but more out of habit and the joy of the festivities associated with the holy month. His opinions about observant Muslims were often critical, even derogatory.

"I have both of my boys in the war, thanks be to God," Mustafa's mother said.

I asked her if there was anything she needed.

"God looks after us. Thank you for the call, my son. Take care of yourself and do let us know if you need anything from here."

94

IN THE SPRING OF that year, when it was still unclear whether the revolution would succeed, Hosam's father died in his sleep. The instant I got his text I rang.

"Yes," he answered and went all quiet and I knew he was crying.

He gave the phone to his brother, Waleed, who thanked me for calling, said this was the way of the world and wanted to know how I was.

"Aren't you going to come see us?" he said. "Freedom is at the door. Or so everyone keeps saying."

In the days after the burial and the wake, Hosam returned to writing me emails. These in particular transported me home. I had never since leaving felt more vividly connected to my country. I realized then that I had always somehow anticipated this, perhaps even from as far back as when I was fourteen and first heard his story read on the radio, that he would be a medium, that we ask of writers what we ask of our closest friends: to help us mediate and interpret the world.

"Across the course of the afternoon," Hosam wrote,

the house usually fills up with my sisters and their children, cousins and so forth. Then the women in the kitchen start planning the meal, sending the young boys out to get this and that. Yesterday, the wave of such demands reached us. Waleed was first naked, then quickly began to put on his armor. He was cajoled, teased, pleaded with to go find olive oil, because, with the current chronic shortages, he was the only one who knew where to find some. "In this area," Mother said from the kitchen, loudly, so everyone could hear, "he's the maestro." One of her contingent compliments. Waleed saw through it, but the spell was already cast. I offered to accompany him. He did what he used to do when we were young, appeared tired and said, "No need." But, instead of remaining there, I got up and insisted. It is better to be a man than a child. The strange thing, though, was that, as soon as we were out, approaching his car, parked in the noonday sun, he turned lively, delighted we were going together. The car was burning. I could hardly touch the door handle. We opened all the windows and set off quickly and the wind did its work. Now there was something pleasurable about the heat, the way it forced itself through your clothes and deeper into your flesh. At a traffic light he reached over and began rummaging in the glove box. The lights turned and the driver behind us pressed his horn and would not stop till we moved.

"Look in there," Waleed said. "Your old favorite."

I found the white cassette, covered in fine, clean desert dust, capable of clinging to the smoothest surface.

"*Astral Weeks*," I said, and he laughed that old familiar laugh, like cracks running along a solid wall.

"That's what we listened to the morning I drove you to the airport," he said. "You were fifteen; I nineteen. Kids. How sweet were those days?"

I put in the tape. He took it out, flipped it to the other side, and began rewinding and stopping, rewinding some more. I remembered walking away from the car and into the Departures lounge, the pain in my chest and the thrill too of leaving. He found the track. We listened and when Van Morrison sang "And jump the hedges first," the first line to "Sweet Thing," we were both with him. By the time the line, "And I will never grow so old again" came, we were singing strongly in perfect unison, repeating, "sweet thing, sweet thing."

We were now driving by the corniche. To one side, the glittering sea, with its own blue history, its pale and dark regions, and the surface marked by current lines. The mocking cries of the seagulls. And, on the other side, the town. The cross-less and deserted old Italian cathedral, the weary old Ottoman domes, and, vying in between, the three- and four- and five-floor-high blocks of flats, with life and laundry and satellite dishes. Whenever we stopped at a traffic light, we greeted those beside us. I can live here forever, I thought.

We went deeper into the city, and Waleed pulled up by a small shop on a residential street. Asked me to wait in the car. I watched him speak to a young muscular man wearing a tight white T-shirt with the sleeves cut at the shoulders and the word HERO printed in gray bold caps across the chest. He pointed to a building across the way, and Waleed sprinted there and disappeared inside. Five minutes later he returned struggling with a heavy box. I opened the boot. The rear of the car sank a little. With a satisfied grin he said, "You realize what your brother just did?" He punched me in the arm. "A whole box of extra-virgin olive oil from the Green Mountain, when the shops in the entire city are clean out of it. No one," he said loudly and defiantly as we drove off, "no one in the whole of Benghazi could do this."

"Well done," I said.

"I thank God," he said, his voice turning mellow, "but, in all honesty, your brother has his place here."

"You do," I said.

"It pays to be in your hometown," he said, and we both kept the silence.

I pretended to be listening to Van Morrison, who was now singing, "Saw you walking down by the Ladbroke Grove this morning . . ." You know the tune, "Slim Slow Sliding," set in your neck of the woods. Made me nostalgic for west London.

"Our mother will be happy," Waleed said, and two seconds later, "I like to make her happy."

I tried to remain with the song, but my mind was already telling me that something breaks when you're away so long: ties and modes of being and days—the days themselves, they shatter in halves—and so much else I can't describe. And other things are born too, but those become unkind to share, because they help only to remind us and those we have left of what has been erased in their place. And so you keep your mouth shut because you don't want to admit how different you have become. This is why it is perfectly reasonable never to come back (don't let anyone tell you otherwise), although I wish you would.

We got home and I started to carry in the oil, but Waleed said to leave it there, smiling mischievously. Inside the house he resumed a bored and lethargic voice. "We failed," he said, loud enough so that Mother and everyone with her in the kitchen would hear. Mother came out with her apron in hand, little pearls of sweat on her upper lip, her aged face rosy.

"Don't say that," she said, her eyes genuinely worried.

"I'm afraid so," he told her.

"What are we going to do?" she said.

"Use steam," he said, and just then she saw his face frowning to hide his smile.

She swung her apron at him, whipping him quite hard. He laughed. We were all laughing now.

"You donkey," she told him.

"A whole box, Queen," he said, wrapping his arms around her and kissing her on the head.

Mother's eyes were happy and the way she smiled was beautiful, so full of all she was and is: the child, the adult, and the aging woman, her born and dying selves. I could see what Waleed meant.

95

Several accounts began to emerge on social media, telling of how Mustafa was distinguishing himself on the battlefield.

"Certain men are made for this," one anonymous contributor wrote. "Guys, you know what I mean. You've seen them at family gatherings, at weddings, at funerals, on school trips when the bus suddenly has a flat tire. They always know what to do. Mustafa al Touny is one such man. God bless him. Left a life of easy luxury in London, where he was the manager of a big international property firm, to fight for his country."

Another man who claimed to have fought beside him wrote, "He has the heart of a general, brave but not careless, capable of taking great risks, but also intelligently strategic. I would follow him into hell."

His mother posted pictures of him in various postures, decked with weapons, wrapped in bullet belts, and not in one was he smiling. Instead, his face showed an ageless and weary sadness, that this was the destiny he had secretly feared. The slight paunch had vanished entirely. His arms looked sculpted, his beard thick and long. There were pictures of him praying in the open, his men beside him, rifles by their feet. He appeared earnest and his humility privately and genuinely felt, which made it hard to accept that he was praying only out of obligation, to help keep morale or evade criticism.

He soon became, among the diverse group of individuals who joined the fighting—students and professors, shopkeepers and lawyers, judges and mechanics, all untrained and new to war—a leader, one who was never hesitant to hand out orders or slap anyone who was out of line. "Because discipline," the anonymous author of one post declared, "is essential." I suspected Mustafa did this with great difficulty at first, but I was somehow certain that such assertions of his authority became easier, and arrived with the irrefutable quickness of a whiplash, making good use of that mysterious impatience that had always accompanied him. And so these snippets of news about Mustafa, coming from individuals who knew him or claimed to know people who were fighting with him, did not surprise me. Instead, as I studied the photos of my friend and read what others were saying about him, I felt I was observing a parallel self, the self I was not, the self I had failed to be. I spent those days with the sense of being twinned, taken out of my life. I often was not the one on the bus to work, but an external being, observing the counterfeit version of myself and doing so from an intimate distance.

My nights were not safe either. I began to dream of Mustafa. He often came with words, speaking them softly to me, as if we were inseparable, walking side by side as we used to do. In one such dream, I go to meet him in some hiding place where he is resting for the night. I offer to cook for him, but he shakes his head and smiles.

"The stink of your own unwashed body," he tells me, "even that becomes normal, becomes, at times, as you are rushing, pleasantly familiar." And then he says, "Tired days when the flesh continues," a sentence that, when I woke up, seemed the anchor of that dream.

In another, he says, "The joy of praying together," and says it with a keen longing, as though I had refused a previous invitation to pray with him. "The unexplainable sudden fits of nausea," he goes on, not wanting to press the point.

"A window left open and I glimpsed through it the normal happenings of life. A woman mopping. I shall never forget that woman mopping," he says, and comes close to tears. I come close to tears too in the dream.

In another dream he comes toward me and whispers, "Life and everything in it is here contained in each ray of light. The boys with me. The responsibility I feel for them. The diminishing glory of war. The way patience is consigned to another self. The sea when spotted. The food and how you cannot help either overeating or not eating at all. Nothing in between. Nothing here is in between." And his face then, regretful, wishing he never had to tell me this, wishing I knew it for myself.

96

I WROTE TO HOSAM about the dreams and told him that I was seriously considering visiting. I was fishing for encouragement. I think—no, I am certain—that if he had been in London during those feverish days and said, "Come, let's go home," I would have done it. But Hosam wanted to write about something else. He wanted to tell me about Malak, who, as he would much later say, "appeared as my destiny."

"She's my mother's cousin's daughter, the youngest of seven," he wrote in an email.

She was born the year I left home. A year later, her mother died and she moved in with my parents. They put her up in my old room. She is now thirty-six, the exact number of years that I have been away. A life lived in the life I have lived elsewhere.

A few days ago, I was walking in the garden and heard the water running in the bathroom, the window left ajar. No one did this except me. I liked seeing the trees and the weathered wall from under the water. I caught a glimpse of Malak's body glistening bronze in the hazy green light. I looked away and don't think she saw me. But maybe she did, because ever since a cautious silence has lain between us. About ten years ago I heard that she got married to a man she liked, one no one chose for her, one she actually picked for herself. But, as often happens here, such marriages rarely work. Up against the generational knowledge of families, a couple with little or no freedom to spend time together before wedlock will always have a thin chance. In their case, they separated just three days after the wedding. No one knew why, and neither she nor the fellow ever said a word about it. Rather admirable, I thought. But, as I found out today, people won't let it go and, even a decade later, she continues to face questions about her brief marriage.

Her face is captivating. Stone-cut features and a silent life thriving passionately. The nose, like those few statues of Cyrene that have managed to remain intact, stops just before it is due, with a slight flatness, making her seem as if she is constantly coming up against the obstacle of the world. "There are faces that call your attention by a curious want of definiteness in their whole aspect, as, walking in a mist, you peer attentively at a vague shape which, after all, may be nothing more curious or strange than a signpost." Do you remember this line from the Conrad story we love so much, "Amy Foster," about the exile who loses his language and loses with it his way? Found it online and reread it. Broke my heart even more this time. And before Malak and I spoke, before much happened between us, before any of that, her face did seem a sign, one that has been slowly coming toward me from a great distance all my life. It is now in full view. And I recognize her. I hope you won't laugh at me, but I know now that my entire life has been an arrival, a coming to this point. That even my years with Claire were slowly leading me here. For how else to explain that from the moment I saw Malak, before we exchanged any words, I was moved by her presence and felt grateful to my old lover for showing me how to be moved by another's presence. Love is as much a miracle as it is an education.

Today we all ate lunch sitting upstairs in a large circle on the floor of the living room. More people than usual. The French doors were open, and the high sun made of the tiled floor of the terrace a shimmering blade of steel. The mature potted plants there helped tender the light. And beyond them the tops of the lemon and peach and plum trees swayed ever so gently in the garden. The breeze entered and passed across the room at a corresponding pace. In the evening, the scents of the fruit trees will fill the air, but now, underneath the early-afternoon sun, they held all that within their veins.

Waleed continuing to insist on treating me as a guest, loading my plate every time it was half empty, swearing on Father's grave that I eat and that sort of nonsense. Mother took note with a tired acceptance in her eyes before she told him, "Enough, you'll put him off doing that." Then the plates were cleared away and Waleed spread his legs over the tablecloth and lit a cigarette. "Tea," he called out abstractly toward the kitchen. When he saw that I was watching him, he said, "How are you, Hosam Tasha?" Then, a little while later, "We are happy to have our great writer home."

Malak carried in the large silver tray, sat cross-legged, and began to mix the tea.

Waleed, no doubt detecting my interest in her, said, "Your cousin Malak is a great lover of poetry. And now that she is free and single," he continued, "she has nothing better to do than read and memorize pages and pages of it."

"Grow up," Malak told him.

"But it's true," he said. "You practically have an entire library in your head."

"True," Mother, who sat right beside Malak, said admiringly, taking personal pride in the matter.

Malak's face eased a little. "Yes," she said to Mother, "but since when is Waleed interested in poetry?" Then to me she added, "Do you know, Hosam, that your brother has never read a book in his life? I'm not sure how he got through school, let alone university."

"That's true," Maha, Waleed's wife, said, her face red with laughter.

"Perhaps," Waleed said to the gathering, as everyone was listening now, amused by the familiar conflict. "But what we all want to know," Waleed continued, "and have been waiting all these years to learn— and, who knows, perhaps the happy occasion of Hosam's return will help us here and we will finally succeed in uncovering the mystery—is what did our dear and beloved cousin do to her groom that he should run away after only three days?"

Malak focused on her task. She held the large teapot as high as her arm would reach and filled each of the battalion of small glasses, fringed at the rim with gold latticework, and did not move on till the froth reached the top. The perfume of mint and wild sage roamed the air. Her face gave little away.

"Behave yourself," Mother told Waleed.

"It's a great mystery," Waleed went on, directing his words to me now. "I mean, after all, our dear and beloved cousin is smart, clever, well-born, and not at all unpleasant to look at."

Before he could finish, a cushion came flying and hit him right in the face. Several laughed, including Mother.

"And," Waleed said, adjusting his glasses, and doing so slowly, theatrically, "a crack shot too."

Several joined him and laughed. Malak gave a faint and careful smile. She knew she was still in danger, that the merciless wolf was not done yet. It was also the smile of one who has been here before.

"Very well," Waleed said, "have it your way. But if you won't tell us about your brief marriage, at least enlighten us about your ideal partner, so as we can keep a lookout."

"Stop being foolish," Mother told him. "You're embarrassing the girl and embarrassing yourself."

"But it's an interesting question," he said. "Remember, Mother, how you used to want to inspire in us an adventurous taste for conversation?"

"That was long ago," Mother said, flashing her eyes toward me.

"Well, listen, as it is all my fault," Waleed said affectionately to the gathering, "I'll begin, shall I?"

Several said, "Yes!"

"Oh dear," his wife, Maha, said, and several laughed. "Okay, brave one," she told him, "begin."

"My ideal woman, apart from you, my love, who represents," he said, his hand taking to the air in mock loftiness, "the model of femininity itself."

"Shut up," Maha told him.

"For this, I take my cue from the great Gibran Khalil Gibran," Waleed said and, turning to me, added, "See? Your cousin Malak was unjust in accusing me of ignorance."

"Gibran and the Quran," Malak said. "That's pretty much the extent of it."

Several laughed, but Maha in particular enjoyed this joke. She laughed so hard that Malak began affectionately inquiring, "But, Maha, what is it? You liked that one?"

Waleed's wife, still unable to speak, nodded, her face darkening further. Several pointed at her with delight and laughed to see her so.

"It's just—" she finally said, and stopped.

Waleed looked at her both cautiously and amusedly.

"It's just that he hasn't even read those."

Everyone laughed now, including Waleed.

"Cruel woman," he said.

"If he gets stuck," Maha continued, barely able to speak, "and he must lead prayer . . . he can recite only two suras."

"Don't believe such lies," Waleed said. "I can recite three," and laughed louder than anyone else.

"Anyway, allow me to finish, heartless woman, and stop your disgraceful conduct. No more interruptions, please."

"Only if you behave yourself," Maha told him.

"I will," he said, and smiled at her. She smiled back. To me he said, but loud enough for everyone else to hear, "I love my wife, but she torments me. This is nothing. You should see what she does at home. The whip comes out. Tortures me. I'm relieved you've returned. Finally, a shoulder to cry on."

"He's a crazy boy," my mother said to Malak, her eyes watering.

"Okay, let's get serious now," Waleed said. "When asked who was the most beautiful woman, Gibran the great Lebanese author and renowned womanizer—"

"You cannot be a renowned womanizer," Maha told him. "A renowned scientist, scholar, artist, yes. But womanizer, no."

"When asked who was the most beautiful woman, Gibran the great Lebanese author and not-renowned-at-all womanizer, responded, 'My mother.' The European interviewer, who must have thought, here is another crazy Arab going on about his mother, asked, 'Who else, Monsieur Gibran, besides your mother?' And Gibran replied, 'My mother's reflection in the mirror.' The interviewer persisted. 'We understand,' he said, 'that you love your mother very much, but who else beside her, and her reflection in the mirror, represents to you the feminine ideal?' And Gibran replied, 'My mother's shadow as she passes by.' "

I laughed, taking it for what it was, Gibran avoiding the question so as not to upset his girlfriends, but the gathering heard it differently and were now passionately voicing their praise and appreciation and, to my surprise, Mother was moved, had tears in her eyes. Waleed rushed over and embraced her.

"You're a silly boy," she told him, her voice muffled against his shoulder.

Waleed kissed her head and returned to his place, sitting beside me, smiling victoriously.

"He's a silly boy," Mother said again, more to Malak this time.

Malak let her hand rest lightly on my mother's arm. Then she said, "Well, that's easy. Waleed loves his wife and his mother. Hardly radical stuff."

"I'm sorry if my heart, when I open it, does not reveal any scandals."

"In love there's no shame," she told him. Someone clapped.

Only then did I realize that, in the course of these few minutes, Malak had been preparing herself, for now instead of dread she was alive with anticipation, shrugging coquettishly, facing my mother for permission. Outside, the sun had dropped a little, casting some of its reflected glow across the wall. And with that the breeze came in more abundantly.

"She's going to do it," someone said.

Waleed tapped my thigh with the back of his hand. He had the expression of one who had just hit an unlikely target. And he was not alone. The very air in the room changed. Everyone seemed to know this about her, that she was capable of such turns, and for a moment even I believed myself to belong to an elect band of elevated souls gifted by being beside her.

"My ideal man," Malak said ponderingly. "I'm not sure what that means. I don't want the ideal. I want complexity. I want passion. I want imperfection. My ideal man is not ideal. But," she said, leaning forward, "I'll tell you about him."

Mother was smiling. The entire room was held in attentive silence.

"I want him to have lunch at home. I want him to help me with my own mind. I want him to be bookish, wise, cunning, and exemplary. I want him to be a good storyteller, and always on my side."

She paused, blushed a little, enjoying the room's attention, but also receding inwardly, aware of her own vigor, perhaps surprised too, discovering as she spoke what she actually desired. And then, as if responding to a silent accuser within her, she said, "Yes, I suppose I am greedy," she said, her eyes taking us all in. At that moment, hers was the face of one engaged in the noblest of battles, when we reach for what we dream of, throwing caution to the wind.

"Yes, I want him to be near me. A good conversationalist, proud, not afraid of the lofty heights."

"Beautiful," Mother said, and said it more to herself.

"I want him to be a singer, one who knows and loves a good song, can play an instrument, the oud or the ney, and preferably both. I want him to be a good mourner, know how to attend to the pain of others, a consoler who could assuage the grief I have for all those I loved and befriended and who are no longer here. I want him to be a healer, an expert in all that troubles me. I want him to be a fire that annihilates all danger that lies ahead and behind me and that which I have, somehow, without his help, found a way to avoid. I want him to be faithful—"

"Faithful," my mother echoed.

"Incapable of deception. I want him to be constant—"

"Constant," several now echoed, as if in agreement that Malak's words had launched themselves into poetry. "Constant in his love and in his prayers and, when those prayers are not answered, I want him to change reality with his own hands. I want him to be my lord—"

"My lord."

"For all the world to see. I want him to make me proud, to make vanish old and fresh longings, new and unremembered regrets. I want him to be vigilant—"

"Vigilant."

"To protect me from sorrows even once their great heights have passed. I want him to know how to deal with the past. I want him to be occasionally gripped by fear—"

"Fear."

"The fear of losing me. I want him to be patient, to help me to endure the injustices visited upon the houses of those I love. But I also want him to be impatient—"

"Impatient."

"To lose all reason and hurry off, forgetting his shoes and hat, and ride—"

"Ride."

"His horse flanked by wings of angry dust, galloping, if need be, all night to find the traitorous, to change my fortunes and avenge me."

Only then I realized I was alone again, the only one who did not remember the famous poem she had been quoting from, or the one she had merged her words with, one familiar to the gathering, for now they too began to murmur along with her the lines. And because I, the one who had been away, was the only one who could not join in, I blushed a little, and therefore came to seem as though I were the subject of Malak's words.

And then I want him to return to me,

to prosper by my side. I want to take him

to the clearest stream, one only I know the way to,

and there quench his thirst.

I want him to look at me sometimes

as if he does not know who I am.

But I want to be forever recognized by him,

come what may, to point me out in a crowd when,

after the passage, we are reunited.

I want him to see me when I cannot see myself.

All exploded with cheers. Several clapped. Mother pulled Malak to her and kissed her, tears now streaming from Mother's eyes. "Gorgeous," she said, and repeated the word three times.

"But Aunty," Malak told her, "please don't cry."

Mother waved her hand and said, "I'm not crying," which made everyone laugh.

"And you call that not ideal?" Waleed said. To which Malak could not help but look flattered.

A little while after everyone settled down, Waleed leaned over to me and right beside my ear said, "Isn't she brilliant?" And just then Malak's big and clever eyes fell on me.

97

THERE WAS STILL NO word from Mustafa. I followed what news I could gather from social media and the various independent Libyan podcasts and radio stations that had sprung up around that time. I furiously tried to get hold of him, hoping that hearing his voice might resolve the discordance I felt between the man I once knew and the one I was reading about. None of the numbers I had for him answered. I called his mother again and she said she would let him know that I called.

"Is it urgent?" she asked.

I hesitated, and then said, "Yes, it is."

A few days later, I had a missed call from a Libyan number. I dialed it and Mustafa picked up immediately.

"Been hearing great things about you," I said.

"We are making progress," he said, his voice tired and housed deep inside himself. I wanted to know more, but he said, "Can't speak long. These lines are vulnerable. I heard it was urgent."

I did not know what to say. I felt ashamed and in the way.

"The other day," I said, "I remembered what you once told me long ago, that when we are old and everything is done we ought to speak only about ideas, food, and dreams." I paused and, when he did not say anything, I continued, "Your three favorite subjects, remember?"

"I said that?"

"Yes," I replied enthusiastically. I saw the small space between us opening, sunlit and warm, and it made me hopeful and it made me sad, because I could see how much effort it would take to broaden it, to make it hospitable again.

"I don't remember ever saying that," he said. "In any case, I'm not old and everything is certainly not done yet."

The silence now was impatient.

"I was just wondering if there is anything I can do, anything at all?"

"Well, like I said, the lines are compromised. Compromised and erratic. Satellite phones would be useful. As many as possible. Call this number when ready," he said, and hung up without saying good-bye.

I spent a couple of days searching. I bought two for a total of three thousand pounds. That was pretty much my entire savings. I considered applying for an overdraft and buying more but decided against it. I called him and my heart raced in my mouth. But someone else answered, someone curt and formal, said Mustafa was unable to speak.

"Tell him I'm ready," I said.

The man asked me my name again, and then told me to hold. I could hear him relay the message and then I could hear Mustafa beside him say, "Tell him we'll send someone."

A week or so later, I got a call at work. I rang the number back and a man, with a Tripoli accent, answered. He asked how I was and then asked after my family. I was then surprised, given the leisurely pace of the conversation, to learn that he was waiting in a café a few doors down from Shepherd's Bush tube station.

"Mustafa said you live nearby."

"Yes, but I'm at work now."

"No problem," the man said.

"I'm afraid I can't leave."

"No problem."

"And I won't be able to for at least another three hours."

He paused, then said again, "No problem."

It was already dark when I got home. I fetched the phones and hurried to the café. The place was full, but when I walked in he put his hand up, and to this day I do not know how he recognized me. I joined him at a small table. He looked nervous, was rocking his leg the whole time. I handed him the package and he left it on the table.

"How will you get them to him?" I asked.

"We have our ways," he said. "Many good people are helping." And with a broad smile he said, "Please forgive me, but I have to leave now."

We walked out together and I watched him head off toward the station, carrying the package beside him as easily as if it were a stack of borrowed books he intended to return to the library.

98

In another email, Hosam wrote:

Mother never really forgave me for leaving. I often catch her witnessing my reactions. Her maid knows more about her than I could ever know. The woman had been raped, disowned by her family, and found refuge here with my mother. The sadness of the world is in her face. You think people don't notice but then everything is seen. And I know that Mother has the intelligence of a blade. She doesn't like my aloofness. Her silence is the silence of outrage whenever I make a mention of my plans to return to England. She thinks the revolution is the most golden moment of her life.

Today it all came to a head. She and her maid were sitting stoning olives, their backs hunched, their faces downturned, the black flesh staining their fingertips. I merely passed by, but something about the scene struck me as tragic. It is a mistake to think this, I know. Love and pity are not the same. Sometimes the love we feel seems much more easily endured if converted to pity, when that just kills it.

A little while later Mother called me into her room.

"Sit down," she said, brushing her long white hair in the mirror. "Don't look at me like that again," she said. "You have no cause. If there's anyone worthy of pity, it is not me, not even my wretched maid with all her troubles and misfortunes, troubles and misfortunes she has yet to find words for. No, it is not us but you, living outside your country and doing so for such a length of time that a sad distance, which you with your high ideals call objectivity, stretched and extended between you and your land, your people and your family—that you could dare to look at your mother like that."

I was caught and felt it and looked it.

"No man should seek to see his family objectively," she said. "Not only because of the sheer impossibility of the task, but because such an ambition alone breaks the covenant between kin. The whole point, silly child, is to love unfathomably. Where hate and affection, bewilderment and clarity, are braided so tightly that they form an unbreakable cord, a rope fit to lift a nation. That's what your forebears did. And you—it's not your games with the truth, your disregard for God and tradition, but this, this above all else lights the fire in my veins: you sit, as a stranger would, as a member of the audience, observing, affording yourself the space created by that objectivity of yours, which is nothing but a cold and empty schoolyard at night, a sad and abandoned place, in order to watch from a distance. Watch, then, as we lift our loads, as if you were the master and we the slaves. For the point about this life, my boy, is not to be good or wise but to be human, not to show the rest of us up."

She turned and faced me. Asked me what I thought of Malak, and, when she saw my face, she smiled. There is a joy to be taken in one's aging mother. A joy in seeing her. A joy in seeing her power. That that is possible with time. Frail as we get. And her smile then, Khaled, after everything that she said, broke me. Made my heart give way. She could see it too and laughed. We both laughed.

"You're my eyes," she said. "It's wonderful to have children."

"Frightening," I told her.

To my surprise she did not dispute that. Instead, she said, "At first I thought, to be a parent you have to be an idealist. Then I learned that to be a parent is to be continually coming up against everything that is not ideal about you."

99

A FEW DAYS LATER, I received this from Hosam:

Soon after that, everyone began to retreat. Malak and I suddenly found plenty of opportunities to be alone, forgotten in the kitchen or the living room or under the vine in the garden. One of the frequent topics was words. Me searching on my phone for translations of those that occur to me only in English, and she asking me to transform a dear old Arabic word into English. And so it went, each peeling a word into the other tongue, and every time it was like a distance was being bridged, a fracture mended. Her enthusiasm when she asked me about a certain word, her eyes as she did so. How strange, she thought, that there is no word in English for "injustice," for example, that a state of injustice is, to that language, merely the opposite or absence of justice. Whereas the Arabic thulm, which shares its root with thalam, or "darkness," is far more profound. I agreed. And, she went on, there is no word for fu'aad either. The dictionary has it as "heart." But fu'aad is not heart, but an in-between space, the correspondence or communication between the heart, the spirit, and the mind, and therefore it relates not to human anatomy but rather to metaphysics. How the English language can do without such a word, she said, is unfathomable. She also found that the genderless nature of English renders the nouns "antiseptic," that was the word she used, dispossessing inanimate objects of character. When I disagreed, she said, "I would be lost if the moon and sun had no gender."

"An English poet once said that arguments convince no one," I told her. "And about that I believe there should be no arguing."

She laughed wonderfully, and I enjoyed making her laugh. She was competitive about our language, whereas, I told her, I found it interesting to introduce words to one another, to bring the Arabic and English of a word side by side, make them meet, touching stones. And the words did feel like that: impervious. Then she looked at me and asked why I no longer wrote. I told her a very good friend of mine asks the same question and she wanted to know all about you. I told her how we met. She could hardly believe it. Said our friendship was meant to be, that it was God's will, and that one should always guard such gifts. I told her that one of my favorite things in the world is talking with you. And that's when she asked me to stop, "Or else I might get jealous," she said.

I must sound like a boy in love. I am. And the man in me knows I am, and knows that the fervor will pass and I will see her faults and will then believe that I'm seeing clearly. But today I am brave. My heart has never been stronger.

Yesterday, Waleed and I planted a tree in the garden. Neither of us actually said it, but we were both thinking of Father as we did it. Forty days since his passing. Today my mother and sisters dressed in color. Afterward I sat in the shade under the vine and Maha, Waleed's wife, joined me, her eyes on her husband.

"I don't know why your brother insists on carrying the spade like that," she said, her eyes following Waleed.

He had the handle under his arm, the long stick protruding out, with the blade, covered in earth, pointing forward.

"Charging ahead in battle," she said, and laughed. "Waleed," she called out with a smile in her voice, and ran to him, helped him to wash the blade clean.

Maha and I sitting in the shade, under the coolness of the vine, she saying her words, particularly the phrase, "charging ahead," which struck me with mysterious power, changed the air in me. My chest was the host of an invisible atmosphere that now stirred. Waleed dried his hands and walked toward me. He reached into his shirt pocket and pulled out two cigarettes. We lit up and even then, and from within my torment, the thought struck me, as agile as reflected light, that it is a mercy to be caught in the schemes of others. But it was too late. I had already surrendered to what seemed, with a force unknown to me, absolutely inevitable. I must leave and join the front. That word, "front," had filled up with its own intent, as though up to then it had merely stood in place of a meaning, waiting to be deployed. All words are like this, I thought, soldiers waiting to be marshaled, and the purpose of living is to enliven the words we have been taught, and people die or take their own lives when words fail them. And I wanted to tell my brother then what I couldn't, but what I can now tell you, that it was my encounter with Malak, what she had awakened in me, that brought me to this decision. That she made all my suspicions about action disappear. Leaving only this will, which, I somehow know, will sustain me.

I know these words will make you anxious. Perhaps you are even surprised or disappointed. Maybe you disapprove. But it is what I must do.

100

I RANG HOSAM AND he did not answer. I telephoned again and he picked up. I knew from his voice that he was with others. He pretended he did not know what I was talking about, that he did not write the email sent just the day before. He walked away, entered a quiet room, and shut the door behind him.

"Haven't told anyone," he said, whispering.

"You are not seriously considering this madness," I said. "I mean, for a start, you are too old."

"Well," he said, "Mustafa joined, didn't he?"

"Yes, but you are six years older," I said.

"You're right," he said. "A foolish plan. Just a wild thought. This place inspires them." He tried to laugh.

"You are neither the right age nor have you the temperament for war."

Even as he agreed I knew I had lost the argument, said too much, that had I held my tongue he might have been persuaded. And the next few nights I would wake up in the dark and find, suspended above my head, that word, "tem-perament," spoken as though a series of stepping stones: temper-a-ment. Then I would hear him say what he had said in reply, "I know."

He fell silent after that. I attempted, with all the will I had, to focus on my work. I began to take pleasure again in teaching. My faith in literature too returned. Books, particularly great novels, never before seemed more practical to the business of living. Any doubts about that vanished.

Hannah, after waiting for me, married someone else. An Englishman named Matthew. She invited me to the wedding. Her father greeted me formally, and seemed a little surprised that I was there. Her brother, Henry, shook hands with me as though congratulating me for being a good sport. Her mother was rushed off her feet and I do not think she noticed my presence. Several of the old faces from Birkbeck were there, and it was good to be reunited with them. When the bride and groom kissed, I felt some of their eyes on me. I hardly saw Hannah after that.

She and Matthew had two children, a girl and a boy, Jack and Layla, one after the other. A couple of years after Layla was born, they separated and Matthew moved out. The first few months were difficult. Hannah was angry, and did not seem angry just at Matthew. But soon that passed and even the sadness did too. She came to seem unmoored more than anything, as though in danger of losing her balance. She continued to live alone with Jack and Layla in the house that she and Matthew had bought in Camden, slowly adjusting to the new arrangement. When the events in Libya erupted, she called with happy tears in her voice.

In the early days of the revolution, I did not go to Camden. We would speak on the phone every few days. She would tell me what was going on with her and I would tell her the latest from home. We eventually returned to seeing each other, taking small steps. I kept hearing a voice tell me, "Get it right this time." She remained full of tender and careful questions about what was going on in Libya. She was older and all the more beautiful, had the weary tiredness of one who, in surrendering to her fate, was ennobled by it. And, although the demands of this new life left her with very little time for herself, it seemed to also, strangely, help bring that self into sharp focus, dignify it, and make its needs apparent. She looked at me with all of that and I loved her for it.

I liked her kids too. I liked how she was with them and how much she enjoyed my being with them. She was careful that they did not see us kiss or hold hands, that they continued to believe that we were only friends. There was a magnetic force between Jack and Layla and me, as though they were mine but in translation. I was embarrassed by the thought, because they were not mine, and the fact of their not being mine was so bloody obvious and clear, and yet I could not help but feel that they stood in place of the children Hannah and I could have had together. I was convinced that she gave the girl an Arabic name because of me. And, as all children seem to belong to the same universe of unmade innocence, their existence, their mouths and fingers and hair, their smell and voices, painfully wove together what is with what could have been.

101

IT HAD BEEN TWO weeks and I wanted to know if the satellite phones had reached Mustafa. I had made a note of their numbers. I dialed one and it was engaged. The other one had hardly rung when Mustafa picked up.

"Brother," he said, and resumed in a formal, platitudinous way. It was obvious that he was surrounded by others.

"So the phones reached you," I said.

"They did," he said. "How many did you send?"

"Two."

"Then they all arrived."

He did not thank me, did not say they were enough, did not say they were not enough. I am not sure why, but I asked him if he had heard from Hosam.

"Hosam," he said affectionately, and as if it were a name written in bright colors.

I misread him, thought he was pleased to be reminded of Hosam, longed to hear his latest news, and that the mention of our friend had evoked happy memories of the lives the three of us had shared in London. I told him that Sidi Rajab Zowa had passed away.

"I know," he said. "I know. May God have mercy on his soul." Then his voice brightened up again and he said, "But, listen, you won't believe it. Guess where our old friend is right now?"

The question hit me with a mysterious terror. "What do you mean?" I said.

"Hosam Zowa, the great writer and man of principle"—it was clear Mustafa's words were not intended for me alone—"is proving himself bravely on the field. This is the stage upon which the drama of our history must be enacted. We didn't choose it, but the battlefield is the arena, and Hosam is an eagle."

I was sitting at the kitchen table and felt the room turn around me.

Mustafa was now laughing and speaking to those beside him. "He's gone all quiet; doesn't believe me. Can someone get Hosam, please?" he said. "Anybody seen him? Tell him I have a surprise for him." Then he returned to me. "He was here just a moment ago." Then to the others he said, "What did you say? Do I trust him? Shut your mouth. We stood together and fell together at the London demonstration. You are too young and stupid to remember. Khaled," he said, "I'm sorry but Hosam seems to have gone off somewhere."

"Hosam is there with you?" I asked, sounding terribly incredulous, naive.

Mustafa laughed. A grown man's laugh. The laugh of a man who had witnessed death and decided that, in the light of that truth, one must laugh watchfully.

When the call ended, I was delirious with confusion and jealousy, wishing I were there, wishing they were still here. I paced around my flat, which had never felt smaller. I went walking and had no idea how long I had been gone when suddenly I realized I was passing Regent's Park, heading north toward Camden. I wanted to be with someone who remembered me.

I was dumbfounded. Hosam and Mustafa, my two closest friends, with their divergent temperaments, had been reunited by the war, fighting side by side, no doubt feeling closer than ever before, closer to one another than to any of the other men, closer to one another than to anyone else on earth, because their lives and deaths were in one another's hands. And yet some secret part of me was not surprised, had somehow foreseen it, and that made the feeling of being forsaken, left behind, even worse.

I decided the word Mustafa used to describe Hosam, "eagle," was partly intended as a criticism of me, and so I ridiculed it, macho hyperbole, I judged. But the ridicule was silent and internal and, therefore, had no effect and signified nothing. I also knew that Mustafa meant it genuinely, and that it was proof that he had cured himself of his age-old dislike of Hosam, or dislike of the need to admire him, and that alone must have been a relief to him. There was a depth of feeling in his voice when he said it, and an ease. The ease of one who can finally let go of a cumbersome object he has been carrying for a long time. It's London, I told myself. The place is infected with irony. Cynicism here is not only tolerated but essential to one's survival. I accused London of this and other ills and the accusations hardened my anger. So much so that by the time I reached Hannah's house, I was ready for a fight.

I rang the doorbell, lifted and smacked the metal letter flap twice, making a sound much louder than I anticipated. She opened the door, surprised to see me, but then clearly pleased too—although, I thought to myself, it is impossible to know and it will remain forever impossible to know how anyone feels about anyone.

"Come in," she said softly, and then, recognizing a new feeling in my face, asked, "Won't you come in?"

I did, walking behind her.

"Perfect timing," she whispered. "I've just put them to bed."

I followed her quietly into the kitchen. She asked if I would like some tea. The place felt warm and smelled of grilled cheese and potatoes and children. How glad she was to see me, she kept saying. I wondered if I was making her nervous. Perhaps I have frightened her, turning up like this. I should come with them one day to the Hampstead Ponds, she was now saying, join her for a swim.

"It's lovely to see the trees from the water," she said.

I said something about not liking cold water. Then a weariness came over me and I knew that everything I had been thinking on the way here had nothing to do with it, nothing to do with the real malady, and that the real malady was nameless and incurable, and this made me feel winded. My tears fell. "What is the matter?" she said. I said that I was worried about my friends, that Hosam and Mustafa were both in the war now. She was amazed, her eyes affectionate and curious and intrigued. I thought of that word again, "eagle," and found it changed and rehabilitated, and I knew that being with Hannah had done that. I was certain, as she kept looking at me, that, in some contexts, "eagle" would be the right word.

She brought the tea and sat opposite me. Her cheeks were flushed from the labor of keeping house. Looking at her, I thought, I do like the English. I love them. I detest their unreconstructed imperialism and prejudices, but, apart from that . . . And I immediately heard the rebuke, "apart from that," spoken mockingly inside my head. It's true, I thought, I do not love the English. You cannot love an abstraction. But I do love Hannah. Each one of her fingertips resting on my palm.

"Can we go to bed?" I said.

She was taken aback, laughed, and, realizing I was not joking, took my hand and we tiptoed upstairs. We made love silently. Then I held on to her and buried my face in her hair. Let's speak of nothing about tomorrow or yesterday, I wanted to say. But I was choking up and thought better to remain quiet and pretend I was falling asleep. I want you to depend on me, I wanted to say. But then she moved.

"I'm sorry, darling," she said. "Layla keeps having bad dreams. Crawls into bed with me at all hours."

102

EVERY DAY I SIFTED through pages and pages of social media posts. Facebook in particular had become the place where Libyans went to share, read, or comment on bits of news. There were countless images of dead and mutilated bodies, people burned and left charred by the roadside. The first time I stumbled on a mention of Mustafa and Hosam, I could not believe my eyes. I then found several accounts of their bravery and how inseparable they had become. "They," as one person put it, "best exemplified the noble spirit of revolutionary brotherhood." Another, agreeing, added in a comment below that: "Where you find one, you know the other is nearby."

Then a photograph emerged, showing them at one end of a long and bare room. Light rushing in from a window or a door behind the photographer. An early-morning light, a sea light. Perhaps the room was in an abandoned chalet that had once been filled with summer children. It floods and changes the walls, which were once painted pink on the bottom half and yellow on the top. All fading now and the sun summoning up the white background, making it seem as if the paint were vanishing right in front of your eyes. Although the room is empty, Hosam and Mustafa are sitting close together, side by side, on a thin mattress laid on the floor. Their skin tanned and their beards thick and unkempt, speckled with gray, and their bodies are fit. Mustafa's eyes are shut and he appears to be fast asleep, his lower lip giving way. Hosam, on the other hand, is busy writing in a notebook that is small enough to fit in the palm of his hand. I zoom in and can see the pencil between his fingers. It has been sharpened with a knife, the tip long and slender, and stands shorter than his thumb.

I was due to meet Claire that evening. It had been postponed long enough. We tried making plans before, but for some reason it was always difficult to find a time that suited us both. But now we did and, more out of habit than reminiscence, I suggested the same place we used to gather before, Café Cyrano on Holland Park Avenue. She did not sound enthusiastic. I said I was happy to meet anywhere else. But then she said, Cyrano was fine. The conversation was awkward. We had little to talk about. It was clear that Hosam had fallen out of touch with her too. And it was clear that she had moved on, or at least begun to consider how she might. I pulled out my phone and showed her the photograph of Hosam and Mustafa. She looked at it for a few seconds, using the tips of her fingers to zoom in.

"He looks well," she finally said, handing me back the phone.

It struck me as a very odd thing to say, because he was evidently not well at all. He was tired and fighting a dangerous war.

Then her eyes changed and rested on my left shoulder. She said, "I'm moving back to Dublin. I decided. Got a job. My parents are aging. And I miss my friends."

I thought of how I might dissuade her, then the energy left me when I realized that I would be doing it for my own sake, and mostly because it would comfort me to know that there was still someone here who knew me from the time when Mustafa and Hosam had lived here, seen me with them.

"I really thought," she said, and stopped when the tears hovered in her eyes. "That this was . . . Only to be left behind."

She paused for a bit and then added, "No one should be treated like this."

I felt responsible, not only for my friend's conduct but also for my country. "The place can really swallow you up," I said.

"No one should be treated like this," she said again.

Just before we parted ways, she asked me about my plans. The question surprised me. "Are you thinking of going back?" she said.

"I don't know," I said. "I doubt it."

She asked after Hannah, and then said, "Let's please see each other again. It'll be at least another three months before I move."

I promised that we would find a date.

We embraced, and, just before she left, she said, "If you hear from Hosam." The way she pronounced his name—unchanged, intimate, and expectant, as though he might appear at any moment—struck me. "Please don't tell him my news. Just ask him to take care of himself." Her voice cracked.

We embraced again and I heard myself say, "I'm so sorry."

103

A FEW DAYS LATER, a couple of short video clips, filmed on a mobile phone, were posted and shared by several individuals on Facebook and Twitter. In the first one, Mustafa is momentarily facing the camera, his face vague but recognizable. He turns quickly and moves forward with relentless determination. The camera is trying to keep up, shaking, about three feet or so behind. Mustafa is holding a rifle in his left hand. His back is a landscape of activity; the hollow between the shoulder blades is calling for a hand or else vulnerable to a strike: a bullet, the blow of an axe. It reminds me of how, twenty-seven years before at the St. James's Square protest, when we were only eighteen, he placed his hand on that very same spot on my back just moments before we were shot and just as I was thinking of leaving, of giving my back to the demonstration and walking into London, a city I hardly knew, where it was easy to lose oneself and to forget, and where I am moving now, edging ever closer to the flat in Shepherd's Bush that has become my only home, and where I am unable to forget.

To the left of Mustafa, half cropped out of the frame, moving in unison with him, there is another man, slightly taller. Just when I think I recognize the lilt in the gait, the man turns to Mustafa and I am certain that it is Hosam. He is holding in his right hand, in that familiar hand, a hand I had shaken countless times, struck in enthusiastic agreement, a thick black pistol, his fingers wrapped tightly around it, the finger ready at any moment. The person filming falls back a step. The camera swings from side to side. The wind is whistling. For a second we see the sky, that vacuous blue of my childhood, open and without end. There are distant sounds of gunfire. Chestnuts cracking open. Then the camera steadies and we see a house. Mustafa and Hosam approach it cautiously. Mustafa looks back, ordering his men to lower their heads. For an instant, his eyes fall on the camera and therefore on me. There is hesitant approval in them, directed at the person filming, and from this I assume that he means this film to act as a document of some sort. The camera is now close to the ground. The short shadow of garden trees. The sun is nearly vertical.

They are edging closer to the house. They huddle beneath a window. Hosam rises slowly.

"Be careful," I can hear Mustafa whisper.

Hosam cups his hands over the window to peer inside and says, "It's empty."

The camera rises, comes up against the dusty windowpane, and settles there. We see what Hosam is seeing. Sheer curtains, the ghostly shape of a room, furniture, and the light emerging from the background. Maybe all the windows in that far end of the house are open, life there is taking place, lunch, perhaps, is being prepared.

Comfort is far, and houses have become magical, I thought as I watched.

They move carefully, ducking beneath each window, but everyone stands up straight when they see the back of the house. They are no longer whispering either.

I hear Hosam say, "As though ravaged by a virus."

"The fuckers," Mustafa tells him.

The man filming comes right beside Hosam, and for a moment I see my friend's face, the side of it, sunburned, the long hair and beard making his ear appear larger and more wanting somehow, a firework of wrinkles by the corner of his eye. He softens and I somehow know then that he is fond of the man doing the filming.

"Let the world see," Mustafa says, and the camera points down at a crater in the ground, then lifts to show the rear façade of the house, eaten away by the explosion. "This," Mustafa says and the camera lifts up to his face again. Apart from the beard, it is remarkably unchanged, except guarded. A veil has fallen over it. "This," he says again, pointing to the wall-less house, "is what they do to the families of those who refuse to bow."

Then, whether overcome with emotion or turning to other business, he looks away.

"This is a blessed house," he says, his voice barely audible. The camera shakes again, there is a flicker of sky, and then the film ends abruptly.

The whole thing is exactly 26.6 seconds long. I watch it over and over, studying each frame.

A couple of days later, another clip emerges, continuing where the first left off. The light has changed; the shadows are now long and low. The movement of the camera is less erratic. Slowly, we are shown the damage caused. The bomb has sliced the kitchen cleanly, leaving the breakfast table undamaged, with one of the four legs cantilevering in midair, like an animal readying itself to leap and surprise its prey. The pendant light above is intact. Our cameraman wants us to see all this. He moves with quiet care. He turns to the wall cabinets, which have lost their sides, revealing their confused contents: tins of tuna, spice jars, a bottle of the same brand of orange blossom that I grew up with. In the bottom cabinet, a large bag of rice. It is torn and its burden spreads white and gleaming where the floor once used to be. The person filming comes close and the grains of rice turn silver in the evening light.

The filming stops and starts again at an even later moment. Everyone is gathered in the dusk around the kitchen table, several empty tins of tuna in front of them.

Someone suggests lighting a fire.

Mustafa tells him, "Don't be an idiot."

Hosam explains, "It would give our location away. And, lads, please, no cigarettes either."

The film stops and starts again. The camera wanders outside and moves around the crater. To the side, the shape of a man sitting on the ground with his back against the wall, probably keeping watch, because he is facing down the garden path that they had arrived by. The camera points up and we quickly see that the sun has gone. The sound of gunshots in the distance again, a little closer now. The camera turns around and we see Mustafa walking out, carrying a large mirror, frameless but with beveled edges. The man filming rushes over to help, but Mustafa shakes his head. He seems tired, exhausted. The man with the camera steps back and admiringly waits. The mirror, held in the sling of Mustafa's arm, cuts out his midriff, replaces it with the darkening sky, glowing purple now, and below it I see the man filming. Mustafa calls to him and I make out the name: "Ali." And I think to myself, Mustafa did it; he went back and was keeping an eye on his younger brother, standing, as much as he can, between him and the world. Ali turns and points the camera at the man keeping watch, the one looking down the garden path, and even in the twilight I recognize him: Hosam, half reclining on the floor, leaning with his elbow on a rock by the wall. He turns to Mustafa and Ali with a look that has no questions in it, and that is how I guess that he was the one who came up with the idea in the first place: to put the mirror where he is, lean it against the wall, and in this way they can monitor the only entrance from the safety of the kitchen table.

104

A FEW WEEKS LATER, on the morning of the 21st of October 2011, on my way to work, I caught, from the corner of my eye, as I walked to the bus station, the front page of *The Guardian* newspaper. It showed a large out-of-focus photograph of a man surrounded by figures, their hands lifting him by the back of his blood-soaked shirt. His face, painted in lighter shades of pink and purple, is tired, resting against someone's lap, his left eye looking straight at us, his mouth dark and open as though in mid-utterance. The headline—but before I read it, in the fraction of the second before, I thought I recognized the man in the photograph, was sure I knew him, that he was not only known but familiar, perhaps a friend or even a member of my family— was made up of four words only: DEATH OF A DICTATOR.

The day was a fog. Claire called a couple of times. There was one call from Hannah too. Three from Souad. One from my father. The head teacher called me into her office and asked if I would be prepared to give a presentation to the students during the next school assembly on the Arab Spring. I declined, telling her that I knew very little about politics. She was disappointed but did not persist.

That night, after not hearing from him for nearly six months, I got an email from Hosam. It was sent at 2 A.M. my time, 3 A.M. his.

Dear Khaled,

You've been with me all these past months, days fused together, made of a single instant. I sometimes believed that you could hear me, could imagine where I was even better than those beside me. I have carried you everywhere, wishing I could tell you the things I can tell only you, you who have always understood me. But perhaps today you will judge me.

I'm typing on my phone in the dark, in a borrowed room in a house belonging to people I've never met before. I'm in the same clothes and boots. But there is nowhere else to run to now. We have reached the end. We are in Misrata. Arrived yesterday. You've no doubt read the news, seen the pictures.

I joined the armed resistance five and a half months ago. Was sent to a makeshift training camp. Chaos, no one knew what they were doing, but then your old friend turned up. Mustafa had by then already gained some valuable experience and managed to impose some order. But when he first saw me, he broke down, covered his face, and wept. I couldn't understand it then, but now I do. In war you are nowhere, neither part of the past nor the future, and it opens up a hunger in you that widens with each day. Until that is all you are. You could easily get swallowed up by it. I've seen it happen. At times I believed I saw life as it truly is, naked, and it shook my soul. It is a terrible thing to see.

Mustafa and I have not parted ways since. He and his younger brother, Ali, are fast asleep on the floor beside me. There have been days with these men when, no matter the desperate fatigue and the danger, the endless stress that sharpens your mind, makes a blade of it, I thought I would happily do away with a lifetime of days of rest, dismantle the house I carry on my back, the house each one of us carries, even people like me who have never been all that good at living.

And yet in dreams, the dreams that I have been having these past few months, that emerge with such power in my brief sleep, I'm always traveling alone, obliged to rely on strangers, people who don't speak my language and have no particular connection to me. I try, in these dreams, to be funny, agreeable, all the while aware of the poverty and desolation of my life. I don't understand this. How, from within such camaraderie and the fervor of our cause, which I feel has enduringly connected me to the passions of my country and people, could my dreams be so desolate?

And yet the morning washes everything away. Even the relentless sound of bullets dies out momentarily, and I think, where would humanity be without morning? Even the most violent need is calmed by dawn, and you can almost catch the fresh scent of hope. The day is a child before it ages and it ages very quickly here, making those early hours all the more miraculous.

For Mustafa, the past and all the years spent abroad have receded into a fog. He tells me the revolution has washed him clean of exile. Several here feel that way, that their past lives are no longer theirs. It isn't so for me. There is no salvation in war. If anything, it's the opposite. Everything that happened is always with me and right there on the surface, unbearably so. All the places and times, the details, the numerous and vivid details, you, Claire, Malak.

Malak's face has kept me steadfast. Whenever my will waned and I was tempted to surrender—death has been all around me and the more familiar it has become the more it's wanted—the memory of her came to my rescue, rising bright as a beacon. Khaled, I think I want to have children with her, live and write books beside her, have hers be the first face and the last that my eyes see. To know her better than I have ever known anyone and be known by her in the same way. I want to lose all demarcations, not know where I end and she starts. I felt this most strongly in battle. It was one of the reasons, perhaps the most compelling reason, that I did not want to die.

The last two days have been relentless. We were exhausted but had to continue. There was a rumor that Qaddafi had retreated to his birthplace, Sirte. War makes of time a material, tightens it, and, if you learn how to read it, to sense where it is taut and where it slackens, it can help you discern danger and opportunity. Or anyhow you fool yourself that you can. Yesterday, as we approached the outskirts of Sirte, I could see the eagle that had been following us all morning fly ahead and hover in the mid-distance.

There was someone there and they fired repeatedly at us. And then they stopped. Were they drawing us in or did they run out of ammunition? We edged closer. There was a concrete pipe, brand-new, never before used, half buried in the sand. The round shape of a howling mouth, I remember thinking as we approached. Definitely large enough for someone to hide in. Here things became very strange. I was convinced I was about to get killed. In a fit of madness, I rushed forward and plunged inside the pipe. And there he was. His face lost. I believed my eyes and couldn't believe my eyes. I had all of him, from the young idealist to the corrupt megalomaniac, and all the stages in between. The child in him has been all the while falling toward this moment, into this pipe and into my hands.

Coming out, I tried to shield him, to break the news softly. I waved to Mustafa and Ali. I led him out by the elbow and was surprised by how willingly he moved beside me. Mustafa and Ali took hold of him, and, when the rest saw who it was that we had captured, some began to howl and cry. The numbers quickly grew. Other units descended on us and it became very difficult to manage the situation. Rounds were fired in the air in jubilation. Many started to scream and the screams were dreadful. They couldn't believe their eyes. None of us could. Every so often someone would break through the throng and strike him. Mustafa and I did all we could to hold them off. We wanted a trial. We weren't alone. We placed him on the bonnet of the truck and gathered around to protect him. At one point, he looked straight at me, with his left eye already closed and bleeding, and asked, "But what did I ever do to them?" I wanted to answer. But there was no time to answer.

Few were immune from the madness. There he was, after all, the kernel of our grief, the one above whom there was no one, the person from whom everything emanated. We had caught the spirit of things, the very essence of our lives, the source, the maker of our reality, the one who parted and gathered us, who took and gave, who punished and forgave. He was, whether we liked it or not, our father. Even people like me and Mustafa, who were trying to restrain the others, could not resist occasionally reaching for him, huddled at our center, to pick him up and rearrange him on the bonnet of the truck, not so much as punishment but to reassure ourselves that it really was him and that he truly did exist.

Even though we shouted among ourselves, and there was constant conflict between those who wanted to protect him, to put him on trial and get all the answers we could, and those who wanted to eat him alive, in all our different colors and backgrounds we became at that moment one creature, a tearing and gnawing beast whose hunger was insatiable and whose prey had only one sure fate. This is why we could not have done it with a clean bullet in the head. I need you to know this. In case the images gave you the wrong impression. You and I have always detested violence. But what tore Qaddafi apart was what tore us apart. Our anger as well as our disagreements. Those who sought justice in the law and those who sought it in retribution.

By the time we entered Misrata, it was over. The oddity of revenge is that it leaves you defeated. All we had now was a corpse, unable to confess, unable to repent. People wanted to see with their own eyes, to believe, to have it affirmed. When they took him, my hands and clothes were covered in his blood. I collapsed on the ground. They picked me up and carried me into someone's front room. All the people gathered mistook my tears as tears of joy.

The body was laid on an old dirty mattress on the floor of a large disused warehouse. A long line formed. Men and boys shuffled in and out, turning around him. Perhaps they believed it was really him and perhaps they didn't. My trousers are still stained with his blood, dry and waxy now, and, as our skin, like the clothes we wear, is porous, it has entered me.

So much has been taken out of me. I am not the same and yet I am the same and I am not sure which is worse. Wherever I go from here, I must carry with me everything I have seen. I know I'm victorious. I feel it and believe it. And victory is an honor. But my heart is full of dread. A revolution requires a great deal of imagination, which is why it often confounds the imagination of those involved in it, leads them down dead ends. And perhaps that is part of the purpose of every revolution: to drive its protagonists to the barricade, to compel them to break through to the other side. And, believe me, Khaled, I hammered away at that obstacle with a terrible faith. Terrible because beautiful, beautiful because, like the most essential expressions of the imagination, it paid not the slightest attention to personal gain. And we did it, we broke through. But it is not enough to vanquish your enemy. I know this now and I fear for tomorrow. But I also know that now the work begins.

Yours eternally,

Hosam

105

FROM THAT POINT ON, Hosam was sucked into the whirlwind of establishing a new parliament, elections. For a brief period, he served as Minister of Culture. I began to see emerge in him, in the speeches he gave, several of which were shared enthusiastically online, the prospects of a statesman, a civil servant who carried out his work with great commitment and pride, often shadowed by an entourage of young men and women who clearly looked up to him. Eventually, as the coups and countercoups mounted and the country descended into chaos and confusion, he retreated from public life.

Even today, whenever new footage emerges of the capture and murder of Qaddafi, I study it carefully, hoping to make out Hosam or Mustafa among the masses.

Last year I finally completed a translation of his book of short stories. With his permission, I found a publisher for it. He came for the launch. There was an event, part of a postcolonial literary conference at SOAS. I had never heard him read before. He read, from the original Arabic text, "The Given and the Taken," the story that had first brought him into my life. He read his short, clipped sentences, which often end where you least expect them to, at a peculiar pace, moving rapidly but pausing at each full stop for a second longer than necessary, then attacking the line solidly before his voice would taper away again. It gave you the impression that he was reading against a persistent obstacle. Afterward he was asked a question about the meaning behind the man's actions or inactions in the story.

He responded: "I have always been aware of death and see it as a figure who, when he arrives, will come at me from the side, at a 90-degree angle, appear in the corner of my vision only when it's too late. Part of me has never stopped waiting for him and, as futile as it is, being on guard. But that was back then. Now I think differently."

That was the only literary question, if one could call it that. The rest were all about the current situation in Libya, about which he spoke very well but in a voice that was less reflective and more impatient.

We decided to slip away and go to have dinner alone in Soho. Now, instead of the excitement he felt when he first returned from Paris or the weariness that slowly set in later, he looked at London with the amused indifference of a visitor. He told me that, after Misrata, he and Mustafa hardly saw one another. Whereas Hosam moved to Tripoli to pursue a role in the new parliament, Mustafa believed the war needed to continue, that there were still some anti-revolutionary elements that must be rooted out. He went back east to Benghazi, becoming the leader of one of the militias fighting a general wanting to reimpose a one-man rule. The nation was tired of fighting and disorder. Many longed for the days of the dictatorship. The general garnered support and eventually won Benghazi.

"But not before flattening the entire downtown," Hosam said. "Our old neighborhood is gone. Mustafa's militia counted its losses and retreated deep into the mountains near Derna. Then all news from him stopped. I even wondered if he was still alive. Then I heard a rumor that he had got married," Hosam said, and fell silent.

Perhaps he too was thinking the same thing, or not thinking but seeing, and not even that but feeling, what those words "flattening the entire downtown" actually meant. Our houses destroyed. My parents, refusing to live under the general's rule, moved to Tripoli.

"Your mum and dad are in good form," he said suddenly. "As soon as I knew I was coming here I visited them."

"They said they were renting a house in the suburbs," I told him.

"Yes, a nice district. Tall trees and not far from the sea. They rented it furnished," he said.

"That's a strange thought," I said.

"Yes, but they are better off than others."

"Was my father's library lost?" I asked. That was the question I did not dare ask my family.

"I'm afraid so. Most of it. The one at the school too. He managed to rescue a few books. His old students have been bringing him books. I have been buying him some too. Every time I pass by. Before you know it, it'll be an even bigger library." After a silence he said, "They were very happy to know I was going to be seeing you. Your mum wants you to come home. Your dad said, 'I don't blame him for never wanting to set foot here again.'"

"But it's not like that," I said.

"Go see them," he said. "It's safe. It would do them a lot of good. You too probably."

For some reason, as he said this, I thought of Walbrook. A year ago, he retired and bought a cottage in Cornwall, had been wanting me to visit ever since. Perhaps I will go see him now, spend a couple of days, and then pay a similar visit to my parents, I thought. Pack a weekend bag and go in that light spirit, stay a few days and then return. Return. That word had always been reserved for going to them.

106

ON THAT TRIP TO give the reading, Hosam stayed for only two days. A couple of years later, he and Malak made up their minds to emigrate to America. And, just before he left the country, he went east and managed to meet with Mustafa. Last night, when he arrived and we had supper at my place, he told me about that visit.

"The thing about war is that if you are in it long enough, it hardens your heart," he said. "Mustafa was formal, short. Turns out he's not only married but has three children: two girls and a boy. Gave them old-fashioned names: Khadija, Jaafr, and Aisha. But didn't want to say much more about them except the usual platitudes: 'Thanks be to God,' and, about his wife, 'She's a good and God-fearing woman,' and so forth. But this was in front of others. I recognized none of his men. They were all new and not like those we fought with. For these guys war was a vocation rather than an unfortunate means to an end. But, at last, he and I slipped away, with a couple of his men guarding us from a distance. They were often so near that we had to whisper. We were high up in the mountains and the valley opened in front of us. I had brought my binoculars. The beauty was as accessible to the eye as it was inaccessible on foot, with terraces hugging the curves, rising and falling. The green gave way in places to caves, rock-lipped open mouths, good places to hide. We continued, talking about the current troubles. He blamed the parliament and I blamed the militias. I asked him about his family again. He said it was very hard to live like this. We looked out. Nothing moved and all was stillness. His eyes fixed on something far off in the distance. He extended an open hand to me and, like the days when we fought side by side, I knew exactly what he wanted. I handed him the binoculars. A donkey or a mule was moving slowly along a narrow ledge by a steep drop.

"'It's going to fall,' Mustafa said softly, more to himself. 'It's carrying something. Look,' he said, and handed me the binoculars.

"It was a mule. I watched it move precariously. It kept stopping and trying to move back. But it was trapped, unable to turn or proceed in any other direction except forward. Mustafa was right: it was carrying a load. A sack of flour or rice. Where was its owner? Then the sack shifted a little. It was in danger of falling off. The mule paused. The burden moved again and I could see that it was a waking child. 'A girl,' I said, and Mustafa grabbed the binoculars from me. We waved and called out, shouting at the very top of our voices. But our words ricocheted and rebounded across the valley. The child, startled and confused, kept turning this way and that, trying to see where she was and from where the desperate and unintelligible voices were coming from. The ridge went up and turned around a high point and the child and the mule slowly vanished around the corner."

107

I AM ALMOST HOME and remember a dream that I had last night, in the brief hours that I managed to sleep. I am walking with my mother. An Italian woman, dressed in black, is following us. Mother believes that the woman is someone I know. Now the Italian is right beside me and, with passionate and sad eyes, says, "Your friend needs you." I know whom she is referring to. And only then do I recognize her. A girlfriend Mustafa had for a brief period shortly after he and Charlotte broke up. Her name was Sabina or Sabrina. She had a vague disappointment about her, as though a part of her always worried that things might not turn out well. I was then in Mustafa's house. A small cottage in the Green Mountain. Two rooms. One where he and his wife ate and the other where they slept, with a kitchen tucked away in the corner. But their bed is occupied by a dead man. There is no other place to house the corpse. But, although he was dead, the man could speak. Mustafa is busy with chores, dashing into the kitchen and so forth. It is not clear what he is up to exactly. He is nervous and his tasks seem more than anything else a remedy for that. His wife is nowhere to be seen, but I can sense her presence and a hint of her old-fashioned perfume of musk and oud and frankincense. The corpse does not have much to say and seems to speak only out of politeness so as to keep me entertained. The room is excessively warm. A heater in the corner is on at full blast. I tell Mustafa he should turn it off and instead get an air conditioner or else he will only speed up the corpse's decomposition. I whisper this out of consideration for the corpse. Mustafa disagrees. Says his wife told him this would help keep the dead man's organs working. The way he mentions his wife suggests that now she was the voice he trusted the most. I choose not to argue and tell myself, well, it is his house.

When I woke up I missed him terribly and felt as though I had actually seen him.

108

I WILL VISIT MY parents. Visit them in their rented home. Kiss their hands and foreheads. Embrace Souad and her husband. Take their children to the sea, and if any of them has yet to learn how to swim I will teach them. And I will bring with me the book my father gave me, *The Epistle of Forgiveness* by Abu al Ala al Ma'arri, the most valuable object I own, to return it to him. He will resist and I will insist and he will win and I will let him win. But in the morning before I depart I will leave it in his study, or wherever he sits now to read the few books that have survived the war, with a note telling him that I will return to collect it.

I reach Shepherd's Bush Green. My phone makes a sound. A message from Hosam. A photograph of the inside of the Gare du Nord train station: fuzzy, taken quickly, flushed with green and blue light. One word attached: "Arrived." I take a similar one of the green, and the sky above is filled with the night's sulfur light, the trees naked against it. But I do not send it. I keep walking home. I am suddenly overcome with the desire to be home, to walk into my flat, take off my coat, and sit in the warm familiar atmosphere. And I know, even before getting there, that it will be like a book closing, an undramatic end, and that I will sleep tonight and wake up and take my Sunday, my day of rest, like the gift that it is. I slide the key into my door. The place is unchanged. We left in a hurry. I collect the cups of coffee Hosam and I drank and place them in the kitchen sink. I fold away his blanket. And before I take off my coat I make my bed.

Acknowledgments

THIS IS A BOOK that I have been thinking about ever since the Arab Spring of 2011. Or so I thought, until I recently discovered a note, written on the back of an envelope from 2003, where I had scribbled an idea for a novel about friends in exile and the emotional country that certain deep friendships can come to resemble. I am indebted to all my friendships, the abiding ones and those which, for whatever reason, ran their course. If friendship is an education, it is, at least in this one regard, similar to literature.

Thank you to Gini Alhadeff, David Austen, Devorah Baum, Rachel Eisendrath, Keren James, Patrick Morris, Kevin Conroy Scott, Mungo Soggot, Juan Gabriel Vásquez, and Paul van Zyl. Thank you to Bashir Abu Manneh, Ibrahim Al Moallem, Ibrahim Al Sharief, Josh Appignanesi, Chloe Aridjis, Roser Ballesteros, John Banerjee, Linda Bell, Andrea Canobbio, Peter Connor, Sonali Deraniyagala, Jacobo, Diego, Carla, and Sofia Gil De Biedma, Mary Doyle, Mohamed Elewa, Lara Farah, Grazia Giua, David Gothard, Johanna Hamilton, Rebecca and Alistair Hicks, Hazem Khater, Nathalie Latham, Jaballa, Tarik, Mariam, and Mohamed Matar, Andrea Milanese, Mariana Montoya, Anna Nadotti, Kate Norbury, Sondra Phifer, Adam Phillips, Judith

Ravenscroft, Steven Rhodes, Philippe Sands, Natalia Schiffrin, Robyn and Linda Scott, Kamila Shamsie, Fiona Shaw, David, Mary, and Kathleen Smith, Jabu, Teddy, and Louis Soggot Scott, Emile Sun, Rupert Thomson, Carlota and Martina Vásquez, Layla, Theo, and Max van Zyl, and Gregory Warren Wilson.

I am hugely grateful to Hakim Naas and Jalal Shammam for all that they shared with me. Thanks also to Leslie Pariseau and Felix Bazalgette for their good hunting and help with research.

I am eternally grateful to my late friend and publisher, Susan Kamil. My thanks to my excellent editors, Andy Ward, Mary Mount, and Isabel Wall, for their intelligence, generosity, and good humor. Thanks to the whole team at Penguin Random House, in London and New York, for their commitment and passion. And thanks to the exceptional close eye of my copy editor, Donna Poppy.

Heartfelt gratitude to my agents, Georgia Garrett and Zoë Pagnamenta, and their teams, for always being there for me.

And, although it is perhaps odd to thank a city, this book owes much to London, as do I.

Immeasurable thanks to Moza for what can never be counted, and Ziad for being my first and oldest friend.

This book, as everything I have written and will ever write, owes so much to my heart's companion, my most intimate friend, Diana.

ABOUT THE AUTHOR

Born in New York City to Libyan parents, Hisham Matar spent his childhood in Tripoli and Cairo and has lived most of his adult life in London. His debut novel, *In the Country of Men,* was shortlisted for the Man Booker Prize and the National Book Critics Circle Award, and won numerous international prizes, including the Royal Society of Literature Ondaatje Prize, a Commonwealth First Book Award, the Premio Flaiano, and the Premio Gregor von Rezzori. His second novel, *Anatomy of a Disappearance,* published in 2011, was named one of the best books of the year by *The Guardian* and the *Chicago Tribune.* His work has been translated into more than thirty languages. He lives in London and New York.

To inquire about booking Hisham Matar for a speaking engagement, please contact the Penguin Random House Speakers Bureau at speakers@penguinrandom house.com.

ABOUT THE TYPE

This book was set in Caledonia, a typeface designed in 1939 by W. A. Dwiggins (1880–1956) for the Merganthaler Linotype Company. Its name is the ancient Roman term for Scotland, because the face was intended to have a Scottish-Roman flavor. Caledonia is considered to be a well-proportioned, businesslike face with little contrast between its thick and thin lines.